THE DARKEST REDEMPTION

THE DARKEST REDEMPTION

BRITNEY JULY

THE DARKEST REDEMPTION

Editor: Erica Russikoff

Cover Design: Cass at Opulent Designs

Character Art: Yenthe Joline (@yenthejolineart)

ALSO BY BRITNEY JULY

for survivors

Playlist

◄ ► ►|

Teen Spirit • **SZA**
Seen it All • **Jeezy feat. Jay-Z**
Poledancer • **Wale feat. Megan Thee Stallion**
Partition • **Beyoncé**
Roc Boys (And the Winner is)... • **Jay-Z**
The Devil is a Lie • **Rick Ross feat. Jay-Z**
Feels like Vegas • **Tinashe**
Cabaret • **Justin Timberlake feat. Drake**
How to Love • **Lil' Wayne**
Just So You Remember • **Pusha T**
Off to the Races • **Lana Del Rey**
Is It a Crime? • **Mariah the Scientist feat. Kali Uchis**
Loyalty • **Kendrick Lamar feat. Rihanna**
'03 Bonnie & Clyde • **Jay-Z feat. Beyoncé**
I Care 4 U • **Aaliyah**
peace • **Taylor Swift**
Stickwitu • **The Pussycat Dolls**

Prisoner • **The Weeknd feat. Lana Del Rey**
It's Okay • **Tommy Genesis**

Why crawl out of hell when the devil is such a heavenly lover?

— JESSICA KATOFF

I

Eden

FLASHING LIGHTS, A SMOKY ROOM, A THICK HAZE OF desire, and a crowd of eager men. Crazy Legs was alive with high spirits that Saturday night. I could feel the drum of anticipation all the way in the dressing room.

It was almost time for me to go on. I stole one last glance in the bulbed mirror at my vanity station, catching my stoic reflection looking back at me. A mere glimpse at my true self before I put on my mask when I hit the stage and became the ideal male fantasy.

I had been dancing since I was fifteen, and I liked to think that after four years I was numb to it all. But sometimes, I'd get this feeling. Butterflies in my belly. Nerves, I guessed.

Due to my position as one of the top dancers at the club, I always made sure I was on my A game. Being one of the best made me a target. Not many of the other women at Crazy Legs liked me from the beginning. I was younger, smaller, private, and kept an air of mystery about myself that made some think I was stuck-up. Really, I was doing my best to conceal my age and homelessness.

I didn't mind not making any friends, even if it made work lonely. Dancing was a competitive job, the money was unpredictable, and everyone was hungry.

Bedford Heights, where I lived and worked, wasn't an upscale city by any means, but we weren't too far from LA. That and the local hustlers were generous whenever they came through the building.

It was Saturday night, the weekend. There was no telling who would be waiting for me when I went up to the main floor to dance.

Easing out a final breath, I did a last-minute adjustment of my cleavage, made sure every strand of my dyed red hair was in order, and smacked my glossed lips.

A piercing whistle shot through the air and I turned in time to catch the club owner, David, gesturing for me to get a move on as he came and stood in the doorway.

"Let's go! It's time for my best girl to get up there and earn us some money," he said, rushing me through my process of finding my Zen before I went on.

Around me, other girls kept on doing what they were doing at their stations, some chatting, others applying makeup or removing it.

I stole one last look at my reflection before rising to stand on my six-inch heels. At fifteen, I could barely walk without nearly biting it. Now at nineteen, I was a pro. They gave a healthy boost to my otherwise petite height of five-three.

Smoothing my hands down the sheer material of my pale pink negligee, I made my way over to David.

He appraised me as he always did. Long and slow. A wolf marveling at an ensnared lamb. "Lookin' good, kid. Knock 'em dead."

I went on by him to get to the stairs. I took them two at a time to get to the main floor and backstage area where another dancer, Amber, was just coming off the stage. She had her top in one hand and a bag of money in the other. Body glitter glistened off her perky breasts making her sparkle.

"They're all yours, Bri," Amber said to me as she passed by.

Just behind the curtain, I braced myself to go on, closing my eyes and breathing in a deep breath.

"All right, all right, all right!" Our DJ, Shae, could be heard throughout the speaker system as he shouted into his mic at the DJ booth. "Coming to the stage is the always sexy. Always elusive. Our very own baby girl, Sabrina!"

I exhaled and emerged onto the stage as Shae put on my chosen record for my set. Janet Jackson's "Would You Mind" wafted through the airwaves as I fell into the scene. The room was dimly lit in dark purple lighting, I couldn't see many faces, but I used that to my advantage as I slipped into my own world and sauntered over to the pole. Leaning against it, I rolled my body in tune with the song.

Against Janet's soft vocals, hooting and hollering could be heard from the men crowded around the stage and out beyond on the main floor.

Crazy Legs was a topless strip club, unless you paid the price for a private room where anything went.

I never offered private dances in the back rooms, much to the chagrin of many.

There was only so long before David stopped letting me keep rejecting offers. Once, a man had waved a wad of hundred-dollar bills and David had seethed when I shot him down.

I raised my arms above my head and wrapped my hands around the pole as I continued to move. Even without looking, I could feel all eyes on me as I abruptly dropped down into a split. Money began flying to the stage. When the chorus hit, I untied my negligee and tore it off, exposing my pasty-covered breasts. On my knees, I pretended to sensually ride the stage like a cowgirl as I twirled my negligee in the air.

"YEAH!" men echoed loudly wanting more.

Nights where the men stayed in line I felt like a temptress. Something like a goddess. Hypnotizing them with every wind of my hips.

Some nights, I'd take my top off, bare my pasty-covered nips, and soak in all the men salivating over the sight of me. Other nights, I kept it all on and stuck to my dance.

I thought that was part of my appeal. The fact that I wouldn't bare all. I was a tease. And they loved the hunt. The chase. The enigma and allure. The idea of what lay beneath my thong and pasties. The reality that even within inches from them, I was still untouchable.

Truth was, that was what empowered me the most. Making them wait. Making them squirm a little. Making them *ache* for me.

Yeah, I felt like a goddess.

"I just wanna take you home, baby," a man leaned over and shouted at me as my set came to a close and I began collecting my earnings.

Abandoning my money, I leaned close to the man, invading his space, teasing, taunting, nearly lining my lips with his. He came closer and I pulled back, grinning playfully.

"You have to love me first," I told him as I winked and blew him a kiss.

He slipped a twenty-dollar bill into my thong and was bold enough to pat my ass. "I do love you, Bri."

As earnest as the young man in the black graphic tee and black baseball cap looked, I knew better.

I let him fall back down to his table to be clowned by his friends while I collected the rest of my money.

At Crazy Legs I was nothing more than a great pretender. An actress who slipped into a role the moment the lights dimmed and I heard the DJ call my name.

None of this was real, and for that, there was no way any of these men could ever love me. And that was what I wanted most. True love.

I guessed I was naïve to believe I'd ever really have it. It wasn't like I'd ever been lucky in the relationship department.

The worst thing about being a romantic was living in a cold-hearted world. You fell in love with too many possibilities, just to get gutted in the end.

But I was also hopeful, clinging to my optimism to see me through.

With all my money stuffed in a bag, I took my cue and left the stage. David was there to massage my shoulders as soon as I disappeared behind the curtains.

"You're so fuckin' majestic on that pole," he mused into my ear, his heavy cologne and cognac smell filling my senses.

The pole. Through tears, sweat, and a lot of pain, I found my calling when I mastered the art of pole dancing. It was why I was able to make so much money *with* my clothes on. Coming into this, I wasn't athletic by any means, but I learned my way around the pole with late night practicing and studying videos online. Over time, I became one with it. In seconds, I could wrap my body around the pole, glide down it with my legs spread-eagled, and mesmerize the men without even breaking a sweat.

I made my way back to the dressing room to get cleaned up so I could work the floor. The night wasn't over just yet. Sometimes I gave lap dances, but most times the men wanted to chat with me. When I was younger, my mother told me I talked too much. A reprimand that haunted me all throughout my years at home. Here at Crazy Legs, some men didn't mind a simple conversation. I once made five hundred dollars talking to some customer about vaccinations and government conspiracies.

Back in the dressing room I toweled off at my station, cooling down with what little air the AC provided.

DJ Shae put on a song by Tyga and the few girls in the room began moving to the beat. I nodded along to the rap as I sifted through the bills in my bag, prepared to organize and count.

"What the fuck is goin' on in here?" David's loud voice boomed through the room, startling us. Behind him, the closest thing I had to a friend at this job, was Mercedes. David eyed the other girls, Starr, Cali, and Tip. "Are you tryin' to make money or not? Y'all need to be socializin' out on the floor."

The girls clicked their tongues and scrambled to get out of the dressing room to hit the floor.

David zeroed in on me next, a mischievous look in his eye. "You did great out there. You're a star."

"Thank you," I said, not liking the way he was looking at me.

Mercedes folded her arms and made an impatient face.

David clasped his hands together, swinging his gaze from Mercedes to me. "I have a proposition for you."

I didn't like the sound of that. "I'm not doing a private dance."

He rolled his eyes, scowling at my intrusion. "Shut up and let me talk."

Mercedes tossed me a look that said to do just that, and I quieted down.

"I got a cousin over in Hampton Hills and he's got this gig coming up where he needs some pretty girls," David began. He held his hands out in a placating motion. "Nothin' shady or anything. You don't even have to show your tits." His corny chuckle made me squirm. "Basically, some big shot is hosting a high-end ultra-private casino night at this hotel, and he needs models to help with catering. A thousand dollars to hold trays and smile for a few hours." David backhanded Mercedes's shoulder and gestured to me. "You two are my best girls. This'll be easy money."

It wasn't dancing, just modeling. Still, though, I wasn't sure about it. David wasn't the nicest. Greed was his biggest sin. Against regulations he let some customers smoke in the building and he let anything go down in the private rooms as long as he got a fee out of it.

As shady as David was, I didn't trust that his cousin was any better.

"So...?" he pressed, looking at me for a hint of excitement.

"I don't know," I admitted.

David let out an exhausted breath as his shoulders visibly

drooped. "What's to think about? You're just serving drinks and appetizers to a bunch of bougie motherfuckers."

"Scared money don't make money, girl," Mercedes said with a judging look.

I wrung my hands together in my lap, uncertain as I faced David. "It's just a private event?"

"Yes," he insisted as he crossed over to me. "A casino night. Bunch of gamblin', drinkin', and schmoozin' among the elite."

The job didn't sound so bad, even if it was coming from David. I'd never been out of Bedford Heights before. Taking a trip to Hampton Hills, a city often dubbed "the Black Beverly Hills," did sound a little appealing.

"When is it?" I wondered.

Sensing that I was coming around, David lit up. "Tomorrow night."

Blinking, I eyed Mercedes. "Tomorrow night?"

"Ain't like you doin' anything important, Bri," she pointed out. "Shit, girl, let's go make this money from these rich mothafuckas and enjoy a night off from all *this*."

It was short notice...but it wasn't dancing.

Who knew, maybe it'd be more fun.

"Okay," I agreed.

"Who knows, maybe if you're lucky, someone will offer you somethin' worth your wild," David said as he caressed and tapped my chin. Soon, he was snatching a few bills from my hand. "Finder's fee."

I had just begun to frown when Mercedes did the same thing, issuing out, "Driver's fee."

Though I didn't have my license, I didn't mind. I liked riding the bus or walking if I had to. If I really needed to get around, Mercedes was good for a ride.

With the job settled, David took off for the door. "Get back on the floor. Time is money."

Mercedes was right behind him. In her tiny black bikini that clung to her curves and figure, fishnets and heels, she was about to make bank. Mercedes was beautiful, and with her sex appeal came an attitude that told the men not to test her. They loved stirring her up just to see her pop off. In the end they always tipped her well and came back for more.

I faced the mirror once again, thinking over the decision I'd made. It was new scenery, probably an adventure even.

As I went back to counting my money, I decided to be positive. Hampton Hills would be fun. Tomorrow night would be easy money. Everything would be all right.

2

Eden

My roommate said I had a death wish, and I supposed he was right.

I had a habit of sleeping with my window open, craving the night air and sounds of life below.

In our tiny fourth-floor apartment, my bedroom faced the street. Directly outside of my window was a fire escape. Some nights when I was free, I'd sit out there and take it in.

The quiet drove me crazy sometimes. It was a very loud reminder that I was often alone. And what a terrible feeling that was.

Sunday was alive and well when I woke up that morning. To my surprise, sitting on the windowsill was a familiar face. A cat who would show up every other day was perched there in my window as if he were waiting for me to wake up. Because of its curled ears, gray fur with darker gray stripes, I thought his breed was called American Curls.

I sat up and smiled at my friend. "Hey, American Joe."

He perked up, angling his head a little and offering a soft *meewr*.

I got out of bed and collected the bag of cat food I'd started buying for him. We strays had to stick together after all.

I poured some food into a little bowl and set it out on the fire escape for Joe to eat peacefully. He let me pet him and I closed the window.

It was a little after ten, so I padded over to the bathroom and washed up before heading to the kitchen. On the refrigerator door on our dry-erase board I found a note from Duane.

Doll, I got a shift at the grille until five. I got some errands after. See you later, D.

So much for making us breakfast. I loved cooking. It was one of my favorite hobbies next to reading. But I hated cooking just to be the only one to eat.

I grabbed a couple slices of bread and placed them in the toaster before taking out the Cinnamon Toast Crunch spread from the pantry. While the bread toasted, I poured myself a glass of milk and sat down at the island when it was ready.

As delicious as the toast was, there was no stopping the inevitable as I looked around my surroundings and came up empty. An ache settled in my chest, and no amount of anxiety over the evening's plans would take away from it.

It was a dreadful feeling, to be so lonely.

Sometimes, the walls would shake before metaphorically closing in on me. Outside of Duane, I was otherwise a bad judge of character. Everyone I flocked to turned out to be the worst thing for me. It took a couple of bad boyfriends to realize this.

After everything, I always strived to believe the best in people. To live with an open mind. A little hope never hurt anyone.

A part of me wanted to take a walk to the nearby park just to get some fresh air. But then I decided against going through the process of getting dressed. Perhaps a movie instead?

Growing up, we only had one TV and it held two channels, one for cooking and one strictly for classic movies. As a result, I loved both. *Sabrina* was my favorite, hence my dancing name. I must've watched it every week when I was eight. I'd go through the motions with Audrey Hepburn's character as she lamented over David, until she matured and fell for the more serious Linus.

Sabrina did more than entertained me; it awakened my love for romance, my love for love. My desire to *be* loved.

Just thinking about my favorite movie lifted my mood and gave me purpose.

A series of rapid knocks sounded at the door before I could get up and grab my Blu-ray.

It was Mercedes, or *Jenesis*. She filled the doorway with her hands planted on either side of the frame as an impatient look hung on her face. Dark shades covered her eyes, but there was no hiding her irritation. She was ready for the day as she wore a long-sleeved beige crop top with *Prada* embellished across the front, black biker shorts, and designer platform tennis shoes.

"Morning," she chirped as she blazed in past me.

I shut the door behind her and soon followed her to the kitchen where she made herself comfortable. She set her Burberry purse down and removed her sunglasses.

I remained standing, bracing myself for whatever it was she had to say.

"Duane here?" Jenesis asked as she glanced around the apartment.

"He's at the grille," I informed her.

Most days, Duane worked at a bistro in town, while every other night he bartended. With his warm personality, and quick sense of humor, he often raked in tips from either establishment.

Still, though, he was only pleasant with Jenesis because of me. Duane liked to tell it how he saw it, and he didn't like Jenesis for me.

Duane was just about the only one who Jenesis kept it together with, because he was the only one who wasn't afraid to call her out.

Jenesis smirked, running her hand through her long ponytail as she lounged back in her seat. "So, ready for tonight?"

I'd never been out of Bedford Heights, so in some ways, I was excited, but then I was nervous, too. Hampton Hills was full of the sophisticated and uber rich. What if we didn't fit in?

"Kinda," I admitted. "What time do we have to be there?"

"The red carpet is at seven, and the whole event starts at eight and ends at, like, eleven." Jenesis gazed at her long stiletto nails and shrugged. "*We* have to be there by six for the rundown and to get dressed up. This shit is a big deal to these people. It's invite-only, and even then, they have to purchase tickets."

"*Tickets*?" I repeated, intrigued enough to come over and sit with her at the island.

Jenesis went on, her eyes lighting up. "It's a themed night. Monte Carlo. The hotel's owner is throwin' it to showcase some project he's workin' on and to donate proceeds to some fundraiser for the Gulf."

It sounded legit. Rich people loved to throw parties to raise money for things.

"And this isn't your everyday gamblin'," Jenesis went on. "It's big boy money. High rollers only. David said it's private because a lot of millionaire *and* billionaires will be in attendance."

It sounded so lavish and important. Again, I was nervous about making a fool of myself.

"You think we can handle it?" I wondered.

Jenesis shrugged. "They're goin' to brief us and probably have us sign NDAs or some shit." She waved me off at the thought. "It's no big deal, E. It's just like at the club, except we get to keep our clothes on and make some money.

"Which reminds me, don't be afraid to put a price on it. We ain't dealin' with no average prospects in the Hills, so you might as well get your money's worth."

I swallowed, not liking what she was getting at. "Price on it?"

Jenesis clicked her tongue. "See, I don't know why David chose yo' scary ass."

Her harsh words were nothing new, so I didn't even flinch. Our "friendship" wasn't the best. There had been a few times when she'd left me hanging. Deep down, I knew I should've left her alone, but I was a sucker for any nicety issued my way, and I took her back every time.

It sucked being the forgiving type.

I could never forgive my mother, though. When I was hungry, lost, and alone, she never took me in, never rescued me, never wrapped me in a warm embrace and kept me sheltered. She left me in the gutter, and I had to save myself. At least, I'd tried, until Duane came along and helped me.

Jenesis leaned into my space, as if she was about to give me the lowdown on what we were going to embark on in Hampton Hills. "We about to be around *millionaires*. This could be our way out of the Heights. Anyone tries it, put a price on it, is all I'm sayin'."

At my lowest, when I'd been out on the street, I'd considered selling myself for money, and the thought of doing that in Hampton Hills triggered something vicious in me that had me looking away from Jenesis.

"Think I'll just stick to the job," I said in the end.

"Suit yourself," Jenesis gave up. "Your pretty ass could probably rope you a sucker without givin' it up anyway. Bottom line, tonight is goin' to be big."

Her excitement for the evening was contagious and I found myself lightening up and becoming hopeful.

So, I grabbed my glass of milk and raise it in the air. "To tonight."

"Ayy!" Jenesis cheered. "To tonight."

Private affairs, high-stakes gambling, fancy dresses—it sounded like something out of a fairy tale, and I'd always been a fan of *Cinderella*. Reading too many books and watching too many classics made me a hopeless romantic. My heart swelled at the possibility of meeting my own Prince Charming. For just a sliver of a second as I toasted with Jenesis, I couldn't help but cross my fingers and pray to a fairy godmother that it all could come true.

3

Eden

THE RIDE IN TO HAMPTON HILLS WAS A WONDER. Jenesis was in her own world, rapping along to the Lil' Wayne song that was playing on her Spotify account, while I sat up and took in all the shops, luxury vehicles, landscaping, extravagant homes, and overall opulent vibe Hampton Hills offered as we passed through.

It was nothing like Bedford Heights. So gated and exclusive, it was mesmerizing.

But we weren't here to gawk and sightsee. The Monte Carlo night was being held at The Residence Hotel. All models were supposed to report to the hotel by six, but Jenesis and I showed up early to have time to get ready. David's cousin, the concierge, Winston, greeted us before handing us over to the event planner, Ana.

Ana pulled us all together in a large backroom off the hotel's ballroom where racks upon racks of dresses were held. All alike in that they were long black velvet gowns with a slit up their thigh, and had a built-in corset bodice that would require me to be braless. According to David and Winston, Jenesis and I were last-minute replacements, so we had to make do with the dresses on hand and the provided pairs of black stiletto ankle-strapped sandals. Thank God they were in our size.

Chairs were lined up toward the back of the room where Ana had us sit so we could be briefed. She herself was in a black sweater with black pinstripe slacks, looking all things professional as she clutched an iPad to her chest. Her inky black hair was tousled casually as it fell down past her shoulders, almost to her waist line.

"You're to be friendly, polite, and personable," she said as she stood in front of the group of models who'd shown up. "We will pass out a pamphlet of faces of who will be in attendance. You're not expected to, but knowing their names will be a real plus. These people are of importance, and everyone likes to have their egos stroked."

From there, she broke down the rules and expectations of the models.

"You're going to be walking around all night holding trays of appetizers and drinks. Make sure your trays are never empty. You're welcome to try a sample of what you're serving, just make sure it looks pretty. That's what you're here for, to look pretty and to make our guests comfortable.

"Don't be afraid to network, either, ladies. A lot of big deal clientele are in attendance and you just may have the look for their various brands. Not only are you selling hospitality, you're selling *yourselves* as well. Be poised, be bright, be brilliant."

Beyond the nice paycheck we'd be collecting, tonight's gig could open doors for more opportunities. Jenesis and I were just a couple of girls from around the way in the Heights; I wasn't sure if either of us had what it took to stand out among these models.

While I chewed my lip with unease, Jenesis sat up straight with her head held high. Confident. Fearless. And ready.

I tried to mirror her attitude, to fake it until I made it.

Jenesis hadn't lied; before we were allowed to even get ready, we had to sign our names on an NDA, swearing to secrecy over any and everything we'd see during the night. Our cell phones were stored away with our personal items, as we were strictly prohibited to record or snap pictures.

Given the space we were provided, every model made do with securing areas for themselves to change. Jenesis and I brought our own hair and makeup kits, as the event didn't have anyone on hand to do it for us.

I helped Jen with her lashes and makeup and she helped me style my hair in an updo.

When every model was dressed and ready, leaving all ten of us looking like identical clones fresh off an assembly line, Ana guided us over to the ballroom. Directly outside the double doors was a sign illustrating the night's event and info. One single line stuck out, echoing our signed NDA.

THE ONLY RULE IS DISCRETION.

As Ana opened the doors up ahead of me, I paused and took a deep breath.

This is it.

The room was abuzz with chatter. Everywhere I looked packs of bodies could be found.

It wasn't as hard as I'd thought. It was just like at the club. I thrived as I went around the room, talking and dazzling the guests with my personality as I offered up gourmet hors d'oeuvres. When we'd been preparing for the night, I hadn't had time to browse the folder with all the guests in attendance, so I didn't know names, or recognize faces, but I played it off well.

Jazz was playing. Sinatra or Dean Martin. I couldn't tell. Guests were too busy talking, gambling, or eating to notice.

"Sushi cup?" I swung by a woman standing near the exit by herself. By now the auction was over, and the rich had already donated generously for the items up for sale. All that was left was the endless amount of gambling going on in the room. Slot machines had been wheeled in, roulette and crap tables aligned in neat rows adjacent from each other, and a cash-out table was set up by the front of the room.

In a dramatic theme of red and black, Sin City had come all the way to Hampton Hills.

The woman eyed the tray I balanced in front of her. "*Sushi*?"

I'd only ever had premade sushi from a supermarket—with imitation crab, but I did like it.

The vegetarian sushi cups on my tray were amazing. By far one of my favorites of the appetizers they were serving. The blend of the rice muffin, avocado, cream cheese, cucumbers, sesame seeds and green onions were to die for. It was easier to sell food when you really liked it. The way I saw it, I got to make a thousand bucks *and* eat on their dime.

"They're *so* good," I swore as I waved a hand toward them. "I could eat these all night."

The woman chuckled, going and helping herself to two of them. She plopped one into her mouth just in time as another woman came striding over.

This woman was beautiful. Tall. Gorgeous dark brown complexion. A diamond stud in her exposed ear as her hair was swooped to one side. And a flawless cream-colored gown that made her look like royalty.

She was oblivious to my staring as she ran into who was clearly a friend.

"I know you're not leaving early, are you?" the woman I'd served asked as she chanced a look at the nearby clock on the wall. A glass clock that was in analog, the hard kind that was only the big numbers in Roman numerals.

The beauty made a face. "I hate these things, but Daddy insisted his 'children' show up, so I did my part." She glanced over her shoulder at no one in particular. "*He* can handle this on his own."

The other woman playfully slapped Beauty's arm. "Oh, please, we all know why you're rushing off. And honestly? If I had someone as handsome as you do waiting on me, I'd be on a timer, too."

Beauty blushed. And then I spotted the rock on her hand. Of course this princess had a prince. I didn't even know her, and the thought made me smile and be happy for her. The way she was glowing, smiling at the simple mention of her guy.

Beauty suddenly noticed me and offered a kind smile as she and the other woman continued on through the exit.

I turned, ready to get back to—

"Oop," I let out. I'd whirled around and almost dropped my tray. Almost walked into another figure.

Out of a cloud of cigar smoke, *he* appeared. It was as if he materialized out of thin air, the way he emerged in front of me almost making me crash. He was tall, causing me to gaze up at him as he peered down at me. In doing this, I sucked in a breath.

Dressed in a fine royal blue suit with a white dress shirt, he was sharp. He didn't just dress well; *he* was also good-looking— really good-looking. Smooth honey-brown skin, dark thick eyebrows, and a groomed goatee, it was a wonder no one else was stopping to stare at him. He was so effortlessly handsome.

A twinkle met his dark eyes as he lowered the thick roll of tobacco to his side and took me in, making sure I wasn't harmed in our near collision.

"Apologies, I really should be watching my surroundings," he spoke in a rich tone, direct and confident. Evidence from being raised among the crème de la crème.

"It's okay," I told him. And then, to segue back to my purpose, I lifted my tray. "Sushi cup?"

His gaze slid from mine to the sushi. "No, thank you."

The way he appraised them, I could tell they weren't up to his standards. And I didn't want to be seen upsetting a guest. "Well, if there's anything I can get you, sir, just let me know."

He tilted his head slightly. "*Sir?*"

I paused, gulping internally. I really should've put names to faces. "Y-Yes?"

"I must say, I'm a little disappointed you don't seem to know who I am..." His eyes bore into mine, stilling me in place. "But I can't quite place who you are either. Perhaps we're even."

This man was young, older than my nineteen for sure, but definitely young enough to where I wondered how he'd already acquired millionaire status so early in life to be invited here.

"Maybe," I said.

Curious, the man took a pull from his cigar and examined me, blowing out smoke. "What's your name?"

"You first."

He grinned, the action causing a crinkle in his eyes. "Sinclair."

Sinclair. Somehow, he managed to *look* like a Sinclair.

We weren't required to wear name tags, and I usually fibbed about my name when meeting strangers, but for some reason, I gave Sinclair the truth. "Eden."

"Eden." My name sounded decadent in his mouth. He stole another drag from his cigar and was bold enough to ash it onto my tray, directly into a sushi cup. Looking around, no other man in the room was smoking—I wasn't even sure whether it was allowed.

Sinclair showed no sign of fear or care as he continued to smoke. "You're not from around here, are you?"

"That obvious?" I wondered.

He looked around the room and came back to me, quirking a brow. "I mean, from what I know of Hampton Hills, everyone's a little...*conservative.*" His eyes roamed to my hair, glowing in an apparent approval. "I like the red, it's different."

Something about this man said you *wanted* to have his blessing, as if he were picky and held things to a high regard.

I touched a lock of my hair. "Thank you."

His gaze traveled to mine. "You're very welcome, Eden."

I went to pitch the now ruined tray of sushi cups. As I headed toward the nearest wastebasket, I noted Sinclair was following me. He smoked his cigar leisurely, boredom teeming from his person.

"You here all night?" he asked lazily.

While we weren't expected to clean, we were supposed to stay readily available until the last guest left.

"Yeah," I said.

"Bummer," Sinclair responded. "I barely have an hour in me."

There was something friendly about Sinclair, friendly and honest.

"Truth? I'd rather be at home watching a movie," I admitted with a helpless shrug. "Pop some buttery popcorn and just curl up and soak it in."

My words caused a corner of his lips to tilt up. "Boring's the new cool."

Sinclair snuffed the flame of his cigar, grabbed a napkin from a tray a model was carrying as she passed by, and wrapped his remains in it before tucking it into his suit.

"So, Eden," he began as he peered around the floor. "Feeling lucky?"

"*Lucky?*"

Ten minutes later Sinclair was in front of a craps table with me by his side, prepared to take a risk.

Around the table people gathered to watch Sinclair take his chances, waiting on bated breath.

It was all new to me. I was excited just to have a front-row seat.

Sinclair was a big spender, not at all afraid to play with the big bucks. After an hour at the Monte Carlo night, I knew the color-coded chips by heart. White chips meant a hundred-thousand dollars. Red meant twenty. Blue meant ten. And green meant five. Most games were high-end, meaning players had to pay a lot to get in. I thought I heard Ana briefly mention a private room in the hotel, which was so exclusive, the *minimum* entry was a million dollars.

"This is partly for charity, and partly to showcase the new hotel and casino the owner is opening next year," Ana had said as she led us into the room.

As I stood at the craps table with Sinclair, who was starting off with a hundred-thousand-dollar bet, I felt a rush of adrenaline in my veins.

He gathered the dice from the dealer and shook them in his hand, and then, in the next moment, he faced me. Palm up with the dice in view, he said, "Blow."

I'd only seen this done in movies. It was meant to be for good luck. I wasn't the luckiest girl on the planet, but I was feeling the moment, feeling the table's energy, so I threw caution to the wind as I leaned close and blew on the clear blue dice.

With his eyes on me, Sinclair smirked and tossed the dice across the table.

"Eleven!" the dealer called out.

The table roared with applause and cheer. The celebration was infectious as I jumped for joy.

Carefree, Sinclair gathered his dice for his second throw and presented them to my lips once more. "It appears you're my good luck charm."

His words were seductive and hypnotic. He didn't even have to ask, I just blew on the dice and watched as he tossed them again.

"Ten!" the dealer called out, soon moving a puck onto the section of the table that was marked *ten*.

The dealer slid the dice back to Sinclair and I blew on them before he tossed them again.

"Ten!" the dealer shouted of the outcome.

"Yesss!" the table cheered at Sinclair's streak.

It went on like that. Sinclair would offer me the dice and I would blow on them, and then he would secure a winning roll.

Everyone was having a good time. No one noticed I wasn't doing my job. That I was too busy dancing and celebrating Sinclair's stroke of luck. He was up half a million dollars and wasn't fazed a bit.

I envied the carefree nature in which he played. The way it wasn't about winning, or losing, just doing something to be active. A dangerous glow would light Sinclair's eyes before each throw, almost as if he was betting against himself internally.

Hushed murmurs spread like wildfire across the room, pulling us from the game. Everyone was looking toward the entrance. Even in my heels I couldn't see what had everyone in a stir.

"Right on time," Sinclair mused as he pulled his cigar from his pocket and unwrapped it. He soon lit it with a Zippo lighter and focused on the entrance at something I couldn't see.

"I better get back to work," I decided since I wasn't able to get in on the commotion happening across the room.

Sinclair came back to me. He reached out, taking my hand and sliding a chip onto my palm. "For keeping me company, Red." With a wink, he was gone.

Red. The chip in my hand was red. Red equated to twenty thousand dollars.

My eyes grew like saucers and my mouth fell open. *Holy crap.*

Very quickly, as if he would come to his senses and come back to retrieve it, I tucked the chip into the bra of my dress and got a move on.

Twenty thousand dollars. That was enough to not have to worry about rent. To maybe take a week off from dancing at the club and just relax. And the books. The books I could buy with twenty grand.

I was smiling like a fool as I went over to the bar and gathered a tray of champagne to offer guests next. Ana wanted us to be a revolving door of appetizers and drinks. To never have an empty tray. The half hour I spent with Sinclair hadn't drawn attention to myself, fortunately. At the most, we were supposed to be providing the guests with a pleasant time, and Sinclair had seemed happy, even if he hadn't wanted my sushi cups.

Back on the job, I went around the room, shelling out champagne and smiles. Earning myself an extra five-thousand-dollar chip or two from a couple of men along the way.

And then I saw him.

As I stopped by the buffet table along the left side of the room, I finally set eyes on *who* was causing a frenzy as I'd positioned myself to a better view. He was still in the entranceway, with an entourage of two men in tow. The epitome of tall, dark, and handsome as I stopped to take him in and the scene he was causing. Tall, because he easily eclipsed my five-three. Dark, because that was the only way to describe his deep dark brown skin. And handsome—there was no other word for this man's impeccable looks.

Just by looking at him I knew I was watching someone of importance. Someone *powerful*. He moved like the president, shaking hands, giving nods, and offering formal smiles—polite. Staring harder, I saw that none of this met his eyes.

A dark prince in a fine bespoke suit, tailored to his body in such a way I wanted to run my finger across his broad shoulder blades.

Something about his energy said he was older than me, but his features were young, fresh, boyish. His only facial hair was the hair on his chin.

I couldn't take my eyes off him. Even from across the room. There was something...*classic* about him. Movie star enigmatic and majestic. And at the same time, formidable, too.

Jazz was still playing. A woman was singing about putting a spell on someone, much like this man had done by showing up to the Monte Carlo night.

"Get real." A woman materialized beside me, going and swiping up a flute of champagne. Her eyes were glued in on the movie star. A covetous look in her gaze. "That man is untouchable."

"Who is he?" I dared to ask.

The woman considered me and soon shrugged, bringing her attention back to the man. "The only CC the girls want more than Chanel is Mr. Cain Carter himself." She eyed him like he was the golden ticket and a full-course meal all in one. "Hampton

Hills's own little eligible bachelor. Then again, he never settles. We're not good enough for his likes."

Cain Carter. He certainly was a hot item. Almost everyone in the room was tracking him.

I went back to the appetizers.

"*That's* the dream right there," the woman continued on a heavy sigh. "A man with fuck-you money? Ugh, I'd do anything he told me to."

She placed her empty flute on my tray but before walking off, she stole another look in Cain's direction hopefully.

All around the vicinity, I noticed matching looks of want and desire. Men and women alike looked on at Cain with dollar-signs in their eyes. Some for business ties, and some for their own personal gain, I was sure.

It was time for a break, so I got rid of my tray and camped out by the buffet, allowing myself to partake of the different hors d'oeuvres.

"E!" I'd bumped into Jenesis. She was yielding a tray of smoked salmon crostini with herb aioli. I stole one and sampled it. "I don't know about you, but I'm makin' bank!"

She fished out some chips from her bra, some green and a couple blue, and one red.

I wasn't too much of a fan of the smoked flavoring the salmon held, but the crostini was otherwise not bad.

"How did you get all that?" I wanted to know at the amount Jenesis had acquired in the almost two hours we'd been here.

Jenesis gave me an impish grin as she shrugged. She leaned close to my ear, her voice shaking in disbelief herself. "Some, I got from guests, and some, I stole." She reeled back, popping a daring brow. "They're so drunk or zooted up, they don't even notice." She nudged me. "You should try it."

It was one thing whenever she'd get me to steal from the local gas station or corner store, but to steal on the job? The idea made me uneasy, even if these were million- and billionaires we were talking about.

Sensing my hesitation, Jenesis rolled her eyes and took off.

I was having too much fun to take such a risk. I didn't want my first time in Hampton Hills to be soiled in any way.

I got back to the food. No one else was around and I had the whole spread to myself as I scooped up a cucumber canape. It was topped with spicy crab salad, leaving me instantly moaning as I tasted the dish. *Mmm.*

"I could make this," I said to myself as I made a mental note to play around in the kitchen the next time I was off. One of the reasons Duane and I worked so well together was because I loved to cook and he loved to eat. He was a stickler for green foods, and I just knew he'd love these canapes.

As I reached for an Italian clam stuffed mushroom, a hand beat me to the punch. A dark hand with a single stem rose tattoo along the side.

A look over had me taking a step back.

Cain.

He picked up a mushroom and helped himself, taking his time to chew and swallow. He was an appreciative eater, I could tell, by the way he bobbed his head and licked his lips. He set a small drawstring pouch on the table, the sound of chips colliding with one another echoed briefly as he helped himself to another mushroom. "The only reason I come to these things."

His voice. Smooth like silk, yet warm and deep. It matched his package perfectly. Everything about this man was dazzling.

His words caught up to me and I focused on what he'd said. The food. He didn't mind enduring these events because of the catering.

I couldn't blame him.

"At least it's good food," I quipped as I grabbed a tzatziki shrimp cucumber round.

Cain paused in his hunt for food to regard me. He started at my hair and slowly worked his way down, so thoroughly it left me nervous.

A spark lit his gaze. "Caviar?"

It took me a second to register what he'd asked.

Caviar. He was showing a hand toward a plate of orange caviar. The tiny place card said the dish was *Blini with Caviar*.

I wasn't experienced with it, but I knew caviar was fish eggs.

The mere recollection caused me to frown and shake my head. "No, thanks."

Cain blinked, and I thought this man had never heard the word *no* in his life. "It's a delicacy."

I wrinkled my nose. "It's fish eggs."

Quizzical, Cain asked, "What do you eat for breakfast?"

I didn't get the topic switch, but I obliged him with an answer. "Eggs, bacon, toast...?"

"So, you can eat *chicken* eggs, but not fish?" he seemed to challenge me in a playful manner.

He had a point, I hated to admit.

A shyness took over under his scrutiny. Goose bumps prickled my skin as I neared closer to where Cain was standing in front of the plate. He took a step back to watch me try it, and that made me blush. His eyes were on me as I picked up a blini and sniffed it. Closing my eyes, I stuffed it into my mouth and hoped for the best.

Oh.

The caviar was salty, yet buttery and smooth. Mixed with the sweetness of the pancake-like bread, it worked.

My eyes popped open as I found myself nodding at the delicious taste. "Mmm."

Beside me, Cain broke into a grin and it was a total distraction. "Try the tuna tartare."

My attention shifted to the plate with the place card in front of it. Little pucks of red tuna and what looked like avocados sat under a garnish of chives and green onions, and some type of white sauce. At least it looked pretty.

I helped myself to a puck and once more closed my eyes to taste it. *Oh God.*

It was nothing like the stuff in the can. All of the flavors mixed together so well I greedily ate my sample and had no shame in licking the sauce off my thumb. I *had* to make this at home.

Cain watched with intrigue as I finished off my tartare, smiling at the sight of my admiration, once more making me freeze.

There was something about Cain's smile that took my breath away. It was lazy. Crooked. Charming. It all met his eyes and caused my heart to skip a beat. No wonder he was a highly sought-after bachelor here in Hampton Hills.

My belly was too full to eat just then.

I bit my lip and took a step back. "I better get back to work."

Cain peered around us before coming back to me. "If you're hungry, you should eat."

I wanted to stay and try more foods, but it wasn't my job to do that. "It's...it's okay. Thanks for talking me into the caviar and tuna tartare. Maybe in another life, I'll get to have some again."

Curiosity masked Cain's face and he opened his mouth to say something, but he never got the chance.

"Cain!" Another man across the room standing among a pack was flagging him down.

"Excuse me," Cain issued out before walking away.

The moment he stepped away I found myself taking a big breath and letting my shoulders sag. *Whew.*

From afar he was gorgeous, but up close he was a god. Heat radiated off his body, his expensive cologne almost pulled me under, and his attention could set my soul on fire if I'd stood with him any longer.

Cain Carter.

He was definitely worth the hype.

I was about to leave the table when I saw it. Sitting where he'd left it, was the tiny black pouch Cain had had.

Across the room, he was caught up in conversation with a group of older men, making them laugh as he spoke to them. His hands were in his pockets, his postured relaxed, showing no sign of intimidation.

Something told me he was probably the richest man in the room, if not, one of the top.

Fingering the pouch, I felt chips inside of it.

I wrestled with myself on what to do. Walking away and leaving the pouch was the most sensible. But then Jenesis's advice came back to me. It would be so easy to take the pouch. Cain wasn't looking, and it was a crowded event. He'd never know it was me if he even remembered where he set it down.

In his three-piece dark gray suit, it was even a wonder if he'd *miss* the money.

It was a bad idea, I knew, but before I could second-guess myself, I swiped up the pouch and hid it behind my back.

Pivoting around, I made an attempt to get far from the area.

Only, I didn't make it an inch before walking into another person.

A man had planted himself directly behind me. He was looming over me, shaking his head, disappointment clouding his olive-brown features.

A second passed before I recognized him from entering the room with Cain.

He nodded toward what was behind my back. "That doesn't belong to you."

Gulping, I backed up, instantly feeling another person behind me.

Another man from Cain's entourage was standing there. This one was heavier than Cain and the other man, and a little less threatening as well. Boredom coated his dark eyes as he peered down at me. "We'll take that."

The man in front of me seized my arm so quickly I hadn't had time to panic or make a move. The man behind me snatched the pouch from my grip and pocketed it for himself.

They didn't let me go.

As busy as the room was, no one seemed to notice what was going on. No one paid attention as the two men ushered me toward the exit. A scream bubbled up from my belly, but got lost in my throat as I threw my head back and found a warning in the heavier man's eyes.

If I screamed, they'd *hurt* me.

Still, I prepared to take that chance. I opened my mouth—

"Make a scene and you'll die right here," the heavier man said flatly.

Horror drenched my body as I allowed myself to be dragged out of the ballroom out into the hall. The door shut behind us and the party went on without a clue.

The other man, muscular and cold, shook his head as he typed something onto his cell phone. "Wrong move, girly."

I wasn't too proud to beg. "Please—"

Jazz filtered out into the hallway as the door from the ballroom opened once again.

Cain stepped out into the hall. He took in his men and examined me. "What's the problem?"

The heavier man lifted his hand and dangled the pouch I'd stolen. "She tried to run off with this."

Cain's gaze went from the pouch to me. A blank mask encompassed his face, and his next few words sealed my fate. "Grab her, and let's go."

4

Eden

I was about to be kidnapped. The realization paralyzed me as I stood in place, hearing it all over again.

"Grab her, and let's go."

The words echoed in my ears, sending dread throughout my body. The thought of being dragged away and leaving the safety of the public caused me to panic.

Just then, I seriously doubted I could make it far running in these heels. Still, my gaze slid around our surroundings, looking for an opening to at least try.

The heavier man stepped into my line of vision, shaking his head.

I wasn't above pleading for my life. "I'm sorry! Please, don't do this."

One of the men, the lighter one with fine hair and cold eyes, blatantly chuckled at my expense. "Don't start coppin' pleas now."

Cain was unimpressed as he merely looked at me. He held his hand out, and I realized he wanted his money back.

The heavier man reached past me and handed over the stolen pouch. Cain opened his jacket and a gasp escaped my lips. Underneath his jacket he was wearing a holster with a gun tucked away. He made no move to pull it out. He simply placed his pouch into his pocket and closed his jacket once more.

Something told me *all* these men were packing.

I was gonna die.

"Please," I begged. "I...I have my things in the back. They're going to come looking for me."

The men snickered at my desperation, but not Cain.

For a moment, Cain was quiet as he took a second to think. Time ticked by as my life was on the line and I could barely breathe. Cain was so eerily calm, and that's what scared me the most. There was no rage, or emotion, just a blank slate as he pondered over what to do with me.

Cain suddenly lifted his head, peering past us up at something in the distance, before coming back to his lighter complexioned associate. "Vino," he started rationally. "Get rid of the camera footage." He went to the heavier man beside me. "Beans, take her to get her things. Don't lose her."

Vino took off down the corridor, and before Beans could lead me to the back room to collect my belongings, Cain stepped closer and stood in front of me.

The lack of anger did nothing but give me false hope. That he'd simply lecture me on my foolishness, and eventually let me go.

Up close, in the light, I could see a small imperfection on Cain's otherwise flawless face. On his bottom lip was a small jagged scar. It did nothing to take away from his image, but I wondered how he got it. Who had dared to hurt this man whose presence was so much.

"You understand you fucked up, right?" Cain began nodding, guiding me to do the same gesture.

"Y-Yes," I stuttered, doing my best not to break down.

He accepted my compliance and went on. "What you do next will determine the outcome in this. Go get your things with Beans, and don't make a scene. Asking for help will make this go from bad to worse, understand?"

His voice was soothing, contradicting the very threat spilling out of his mouth.

"Yes," I agreed.

Cain took a step back, showing a hand to allow me to go.

Beans didn't grab me. He let me take the lead over to the back room where he waited outside while I slipped in to grab my stuff.

"Oh, hey." Ana was in the room, lounging back in a chair, stealing a moment to vape and scour her phone. She was only the event planner. She'd probably been to one too many parties, where the idea of staying long among the atmosphere bored her.

Either way, she wasn't supposed to be back here.

She sat up in her chair, peering me at curiously. "Everything all right?"

My body was shaking and my breathing was heightening.

Oh God. Oh God. Oh God.

All it would take would be for me to open my mouth, to say that there were men intent on taking me away from the hotel.

But then I thought of Cain's gun, the fact that Vino was erasing camera footage, and how much power he really had.

"I-I was just coming to get my things. I'm not...feeling well," I spoke up.

Ana studied me, giving me a once-over. "What's wrong, do you need some aspirin? I always keep an emergency medical case on me for *any* situation."

I opened my mouth, trying to conjure up another lie.

Behind me, I heard the door open. His aura met my back and I bowed my head at the sight of Ana scrambling to stand to her feet and look presentable.

"Mr. Carter, sir, anything I can get for you?" she asked chipperly.

"I was just coming to check on her, actually," Cain spoke up. "She wasn't feeling well and was too afraid to let anyone know."

A flush spread across Ana's tan cheeks at the mere interaction with Cain. Like a lot of other women at the event, she was a goner for Cain.

He wasn't even fazed.

"Oh, honey, it's all right. These things happen." Ana waved me off. "Actually, since we didn't get your bank info in time, we have your check right here." She went over to her bag and riffled inside of it before pulling out a manila folder. She procured a slip of paper and soon walked it over to me.

Had I kept to myself, I would've been walking out of here with thirty-one thousand dollars.

"Please, feel better," Ana issued out with a sympathetic look. She glanced at Cain and then stepped out of the room, leaving me to my doom.

On all of the chairs in the room where we'd sat for briefing, were little gift bags, or goody bags, courtesy of Ana no less.

Stiffly, I went and grabbed my backpack and my purse, not even bothering to change given my lack of privacy.

Cain was waiting by the door, watching me.

"I'm so sorry." My voice trembled, giving away all the fear in my body at the thought of leaving with him.

Cain shook his head and took a step closer to me. "I never say I'm sorry. The world is an ignominious unforgiving place, so fuck it." Before I could blink, he'd snatched my things and nodded toward the door. "After you."

There was no escaping this.

With my head down, I stepped back out into the hall. Vino was back and waiting on us with Beans.

"All done," he said to Cain.

"What's the move?" Beans asked next.

Behind me, Cain sighed. "Something told me I should book a suite tonight. It's a good thing I did. We'll go to my room and I'll deal with her there."

I didn't like the sound of that.

Nudging in my back sent me forward. Beans took the lead to the nearest elevator, and along the way, we passed hotel staff. As much as I wanted to speak up, to make eye contact, I knew better. If they could get rid of camera footage, I was sure it would be nothing to make a person disappear—just like they were about to do with *me*.

We boarded a private elevator and goose bumps pebbled along my skin as Cain hung back against the railing, and Beans and Vino stood in front of the door. As we rose higher in the air, the reality of this being very real took over me and I became hyperalert of everything.

"Goody bag?" Cain offered as he held out my gift.

Vino turned and smirked, wasting no time in grabbing the bag and rummaging inside. "Ooh, chocolate." He lifted his head and eyed me. "Didn't think they'd give models such rich foods." His dark eyes measured me out boldly. "I bet everything you eat goes straight to that ass."

I took a step back, not liking the way he was looking at me.

"Vino." Cain's tone read of a warning and authority.

Vino turned around and shrugged, going and helping himself to the chocolate.

There were *three* of them and one of me, and we were heading to a private room.

Bile rose up my throat as my mind mentally pictured the scenario and what it could ultimately lead to.

Cain leaned against the wall, nonchalantly scrolling through his phone. "Xenophobia: it is the fear of the unknown. Your imagination right now is far more terrifying than what I have planned for you."

What he had "planned" for me.

Oh God.

The car came to a stop and I didn't want to move. Didn't want to step off the elevator.

But I had no choice as I felt Cain behind me, ready to get off, and as if he pushed me forward, I followed behind Vino and Beans. We were on a private floor; directly across from the elevator was a set of double doors leading into what was surely a luxury suite. A small standing sign by the right door illustrated that this was the PRESIDENTIAL SUITE.

Of course Cain only slept in the best.

He came past me, swiped a card near the reader, and pushed open one of the doors, allowing us to enter.

Vino took off toward the bar that was right off the living room in the center of the room, and Beans headed toward the kitchen area.

I had just taken in the gorgeous white piano far off in the next room when snapping drew my attention over to where Cain was standing.

To his associates, he said, "Order some food from the restaurant downstairs. I'm fucking starving." His eyes settled on me, impassive. "Come with me. Let's sort this out."

Reluctantly, I followed Cain through the suite until we were in the master space. He shut and locked the door behind us.

The entire suite seemed to be awash in cool colors of blue and gray. The theme bled into the master suite; in a room off the bedroom reserved for a lounge area, there was a navy-blue sofa with gray accent pillows along one wall in front of a coffee table, matching gray chairs sat in front of a floor-to-ceiling window, and the carpet was marble-like with blue lines throughout the light gray design.

Cain paid none of this any attention as he shimmied out of his jacket and laid it gently on a chair. The sight of him in his vest and dress pants did nothing to take away from the fact he had *two* guns tucked away underneath his jacket.

"You hungry?" He looked back at me. "Because I barely got to eat, and I love to eat."

Quietly, I shook my head, too terrified to stomach the thought of food.

Cain appeared quizzical at my hesitation, and then he looked down at himself. "Is it the guns? They scare you?"

I didn't have to answer. He simply walked over to the safe that was nestled in another corner of the room and punched in the combo before storing his guns inside.

At least he was considerate and wouldn't shoot me.

"Apologies," Cain started again. "Where I'm from, you can never be too safe." He suddenly chuckled, the sight admittedly heart-stopping. He was so handsome when he lit up. He pressed a hand to his chest. "My mistake, I'm Cain, and you are...?"

When I didn't speak up, Cain shrugged and grabbed my purse. He held up my phone and slid it into his pocket, cutting off my communication to the outside world.

Closing my eyes, I willed myself not to cry. *You are okay. You will be okay. You will make it out of this alive.*

Cain procured my wallet and went through it, and I watched as his brows furrowed at what he found. He peered over at me as he pulled out my four ID cards. "A woman with a backup plan. I respect that."

The first ID I'd ever purchased helped me get my job at Crazy Legs, my second and third were backups in case I ever was in a jam. A rainy-day type of thing.

Cain sifted through the cards in his hands. "What's your name?"

"Audrey," I lied smoothly. *Audrey* was twenty-six.

Cain lifted his eyes to meet mine. In a single flick, he'd tossed a card aside, casting it through the air until it landed on the carpet. "What's your name?"

He didn't believe me.

I swallowed. "Jade." *Jade* was twenty-one.

Flick. Another card went flying and Cain took a step closer until he was right in front of me. "What's. Your. Name?"

"Billy," I let out. *Billy* was twenty-three.

Flick. The last card went and joined the others.

"Hello, Eden," Cain said in the end.

Me. Nineteen.

He saw right through me. Cain wasn't like the others; he was smart, calculated, and something told me *deadly.*

With my name squared away, Cain went and made himself comfortable on the sofa. He nodded toward one of the chairs across from him, but I managed enough strength to shake my head. He shrugged.

"What are we going to do with you, Eden?" he punctuated my name, sounding out each syllable in a way that felt like a stab in my chest.

"I-I'll never do it again," I swore. "It was just a stupid thing."

"Oh, I know that." Cain appeared smug. "In hindsight, I should be thanking you. I didn't really want to be down there, but some things are above my head, and appearances *are* everything in Hampton Hills. So, there I was."

He held out a finger, as if to make a point. "But that doesn't make what you did okay." Cain appeared thoughtful as he rubbed at his jaw. "You know, in Islamic law, the punishment for theft can be amputation of the fingers, *or* the entire hand," he pointed out, sending direct terror down my spine. "Some people find the cutting off of hands morally reprehensible, but when you think about it, most stores only give you a slap on the wrist. By Islamic law, you get two strikes, and you're out. Unless you start stealing with your teeth."

His little joke did nothing to take away from the gruesome idea of losing one of my hands, or fingers.

Unconsciously, I curled and uncurled my hands into fists.

Think, Eden, think, I begged my mind to come up with an escape plan.

Even if Cain's guns were tucked away in his safe, there was no accounting for the guns Vino and Beans probably held. Cain was sitting on the sofa. I was in front of the door. If by chance I could unlock it in time before he got up and around the coffee table, there was no telling if one of his men would shoot me before I made it to the front door.

I had messed up. I had really messed up bad this time.

Cain was watching me from the sofa. He knew that I knew I was stuck. Caught. Back against the wall and nowhere to go.

There was only one card I had to pull, a card I hoped would work.

Cain was a man, and men were easy.

"What do you say...I give you one night and we can forget about this?" My steady voice dripped with suggestion and a seductive haze I didn't feel.

I'd told myself a long time ago I'd never put myself in this position. To sell my body to a man to survive, yet here I was, desperate, with no other way out.

Briefly, Cain smiled as if amused, the expression bringing light to his otherwise dark disposition.

He sat back in his seat. "Your pussy is worth a million dollars? Because that's how much you were about to steal from me."

My heart took a dive toward my stomach, but I kept my face even. Putting on an air of false confidence to see my way through this.

"It's good," I said with a limp shrug.

The humor dissipated from his face.

Cain regarded me once more. "Come here."

I blew out a breath. *So far, so good.*

Slowly, I went and stood in front of him. "Turn around for me." Suddenly, I felt like an item at an auction block as he ran his dark gaze down my figure.

The sober expression on his face gave no tell on what he was thinking, on whether he was even interested in the proposition.

Cain angled his head to take me in more. "Do you usually resort to selling yourself to get out of jams?"

"No."

His eyes cut to mine. "If there's one thing I hate, it's a liar."

"I've never done this before," I told him honestly. "I figure if it can get me out of being harmed or killed, why not give it a shot?"

Cain hummed, his dark eyes examining me further. If he were intrigued or aroused by the sight of me, he didn't let it show.

"If I fuck you, will you cry?" he probed.

Men.

"No," I shot back.

Smack. He smacked my ass, hard, yet it didn't hurt. Worse, it sent something lurching beneath my belly unbidden.

"This isn't about my ego. It's about your emotions," Cain clarified. "I can't stand tears."

"I won't cry," I let out. Even if it hurt, I wouldn't allow myself to break. "I'm in your debt."

"What a mighty debt that is," Cain remarked. "Tell me something, got any family? A boyfriend waiting up for you?"

Lonely. It was part of the reason that drove me to even come here tonight. Because I'd been so alone and couldn't stand it.

I shook my head.

Cain whistled. "If you disappear, no one would care or notice."

Despite myself, tears came to my eyes. I held my head high to stop them from falling as I sniffled.

"Ah," Cain said, taunting in his voice. "There's those emotions."

"Sorry." I wiped at my eyes. "I usually tear up when someone threatens my life."

A silence doused the moment, and all I could feel was Cain's eyes on me.

"So, what's it going to be?" I dared to ask.

"I've killed for less."

Oh God. I held my breath, praying and hoping he'd reconsider.

"But look at you." His voice was almost softer now. A timbre I could get addicted to.

"You're not so bad yourself," I mumbled. And he wasn't. Scary as fuck or not, this man was gorgeous. The perfect lure for the innocent.

Something like a chuckle sounded out of him. "I like your confidence." He sat back in his seat once more. "All right, let's see this million-dollar service at work."

I turned around and pushed the coffee table away for room to dance, making sure my ass was in the air as I did so. Glancing over my shoulder, I found Cain staring right at it. "I usually dance to music."

Cain smirked. "Your life is on the line."

Resisting the urge to roll my eyes, I said, "I'm aware."

"The music I like isn't something you really dance to in that way," Cain said.

"What do you like?"

"Jazz."

I blinked. *Jazz*. That was what was playing at the fundraiser. "You own this hotel."

A corner of Cain's lips curled. "Not this one, but I do have a working relationship with the owner and a say in his dealings now."

I should've known. Power seeped through Cain's pores. Of course he had connections since it was so easy for him to destroy the video evidence of him and his men taking me.

"R&B will do," I said in the end.

Cain turned on the TV across from me and set up his phone through the AirPlay capability. In another minute Usher's "Nice & Slow" began playing throughout the room.

Cain came back to me. "That work for you?"

I stood and removed my heels, coming down to my normal height. "Yes."

I took a deep breath and slowly slid into my Sabrina role and pretended this was just another night at the club where I'd given dozens of lap dances.

In front of Cain, I began moving my body sensually, slowly hypnotizing him with the wind of my waist. I fell into the beat as I reached back and unzipped my zipper. As the corset began to loosen its grip on me, I turned my back to Cain, not allowing him to peek just yet.

A rush of air hit my body as my dress pooled at my feet, but I kept moving, kept feeling Usher.

"How long have you been dancing?" Cain asked.

"Four years." I could've lied, but why bother? He could judge me if he wanted. I did what I had to do.

"How far do you go?" There was something in his tone, something dark that almost broke my trance.

"Down to my panties with pasties on my nipples."

"Turn around, Eden."

The command in his voice had me doing just that. With my arms wrapped around my breasts I kept dancing in my little black thong.

Lowering one arm to my side, I captured Cain's direct attention, and when I lowered my other arm, I knew I had him.

Sauntering over to him, I straddled his lap and rocked into him. With my breasts in his face, Cain was quiet. It wasn't until I turned around and rolled my hips into him that I felt it.

He was *hard*. Despite his mask, there was no hiding his arousal as I sat directly on his lap. I sat up and ran my hands down his inner thighs and felt a big bulge down one leg.

My eyes doubled over at the feel of how big he was.

This was the epitome of Big Dick Energy, because Cain sat coolly beneath me, not a hint of arrogance pouring through. He knew his dick was big and didn't have to say much on it.

I leaned back against his chest as I continued to circle my hips on his.

"Can I touch you?" Cain suddenly asked.

Instantly, I paused, caught off guard. No man had ever asked me that before. At the club, they weren't supposed to touch us, but they often did anyway, and David had taught us a long time ago to just shut up and take it as long as they were paying.

Cain asking threw me off.

Something about him told me he wasn't the type of man who asked permission. He just took what he wanted and dared anyone to defy him.

I nodded and kept moving.

"*Oh*," I let out at the feel of his hands on my breasts.

A fire ignited in me at the sensation of his soft hands

massaging my breasts. Cain wasn't grabby, but gentle. Touching me in such a way that we *both* were enjoying it.

I kept winding my hips and the feel of his hardness felt too good. One angle saw a delicious friction brewing between us and I leaned my head back against Cain's chest and chased it as he kept working my breasts. Soon, I was biting my lip, close to something special.

Cain sat up and I felt him so much better now. "Eden."

"Yes." Despite myself, my voice came out breathy.

"You're making a mess on my pants." Cain pressed the words into my ear, liquifying me internally.

I was wet. *So* wet. This wasn't how it was supposed to be. Aroused by the man who'd threatened my life. Yet here I was, aching for him.

The Weeknd was singing about being acquainted as Cain stood and guided me over to the bedroom. In just my thong, I went and got on the bed, propping myself up on my arms. There was now a very obvious tent in Cain's pants and I felt myself smirk at the sight of it.

Cain went over to one of his bags that was sitting on the dresser and grabbed a black foil packet. I was on birth control, but I admired the way he still wanted to use protection. That he wasn't one to try to talk me into going without.

Cain came back over to the bed and when it looked like he was going to join me, I went and planted my feet flat on his chest, something that took great effort on my part seeing how tall he was.

"Uh-uh, don't be weird; take your clothes off," I demanded.

A stinging sensation met my feet as Cain swiftly smacked them off of him. That *hurt*.

"Ow!" I whined. Boldly, I planted my feet back on his chest, even going so far as to raise one foot toward his face. "Kiss it better."

Cain grabbed my foot tightly. I thought he'd shove me away

again, but I pouted, attempting to get my way in some small capacity.

He huffed, throwing my foot to the side and stepping back. He went for his top button on his vest. "Get out of that thong. Now."

I quickly shimmied out of it and tossed it to the side. Cain kept his eyes on mine as he removed his vest and stepped out of his pants. When he went to undo his dress shirt, he paused, catching what lay between my thighs.

A glow of lust colored his eyes and a muscle in his jaw flexed the longer he stared.

Cain shook his head and quietly removed his shirt and undershirt. Leaning up, I took in his body, studying his slim but muscled build. There wasn't a trace of ink on his skin outside of the single stem rose tattoo on his hand. His dark brown torso was blemish-free—no, it wasn't. Looking closer, I spotted a nasty gash on his side that had healed over. Evidence from some type of wound.

I got on my knees and crawled over to him, wanting to help him out of his Tom Ford boxer briefs. Cain watched as I grabbed ahold of his waistband and peered up at him beneath my lashes. Slowly, I tugged his briefs down and lowered my gaze.

Whoa.

He was probably the biggest I'd ever seen and the most tempting. So big. So brown. So beautiful.

I stroked him once before leaning close and running my tongue along his length. Clean skin. Decadent cologne. An energy that pulled you under. I could do this.

Cain reached out, seizing my hair in a vise grip, forcing my head back. "Lie down."

I frowned. "I didn't even get to—"

The words didn't make it out before I went flying back on my back.

All I could hear was the material of Cain's briefs sliding down his legs.

The bed shifted as his weight joined mine.

I spread my legs for him, offering myself up. No matter the earlier tension, I was throbbing with need.

Cain ran his hand across my collarbone, his eyes tracking the movement. He trailed to my right breast and cupped me before tugging on my perky nipple, drawing a moan out of me. His hand traveled to my other breast and mirrored the same motion.

He touched me with curiosity, as if he had all the time in the world. Soft. Gentle. With fascination as if I were a work of art he was marveling. In the wake of his smooth touch, he left behind a trail of goose bumps.

He ran his hand down my belly to my bikini line, tilting his head slightly as he did so.

Sensual. Slow. So unlike the man who was just threatening to end my life.

His approach to my body allowed me to turn off my inhibitions and get into the moment. And see it as a simple hookup. A one-night stand. The sight of his attention and *want* aroused me.

"So perfect," Cain seemed to mumble to himself.

He stroked his thumb from my entrance to my clit. His touch was fire and it felt so good to be burned by him.

I lifted my hips to meet his thumb, needing more. "Please."

He stared into my eyes and pressed down on my clit.

Dots appeared in my eyes and I was close to leaving the planet.

"You can do whatever you want," I let out.

"*Whatever* is a strong word," Cain responded, going back to the torturous flicks of his thumb.

"I'm in your debt," I said as I spread my legs wider. "Just don't hit me."

Cain stopped what he was doing as a scowl covered his face. Soon, he came and planted a hand on either side of me, hovering over me where we were chest to chest. "I'm not a monster."

I almost laughed. "No, you're just a man who threatens to cut off a girl's appendages when she messes up."

A ghost of a smile crossed Cain's face briefly. He caressed my jaw in his hand, running his thumb across my bottom lip. "You're a little mouthy for someone who's in debt to me."

He grabbed the condom and tore it open. I watched as he expertly rolled it on and came back to me.

"I'm going to put it in and start slow to get you adjusted," he said.

I pretended to yawn. "At least I don't have to stroke your ego."

He narrowed his eyes and silently shook his head. And then I felt the tip brushing against my entrance. "Remember that."

Closing the small distance between us, I leaned up to kiss him.

Cain ducked back, as if grossed out by the act.

I rolled my eyes and shoved his chest. "Sex without kissing is lame."

If we were going to do this, I wanted *all* of it. He was too fine not to kiss.

Cain's nostrils flared. Really, it was my first warning of what was coming.

His hand came around my neck, tipping my head back as his mouth soon crushed mine. *Mmm.* His skilled lips and tongue left me clinging to him. Only, his kiss came with a bite, as if he were punishing me for my earlier defiance. As if he were threatening to fuck me into submission.

Without warning he pushed inside of me, causing me to open my mouth to cry out.

Cain swallowed my cries as his lips lingered on mine. One more thrust and more of him was in.

God, he wasn't all the way in yet and already it was so much. I had never felt so stretched. So much pressure. So full.

I dug my fingernails into Cain's back, if only to release the sensation taking over me. It was too much, but not enough. I wrapped my legs around his waist, needing more.

An ugly cry came out of me as he pushed until he was all the way inside me. Chest to chest. Cain stilled and gaped down at me, watching my reaction.

"Look at me," he demanded when I tried to peek between us. I did as told, and found him concerned. "Can you handle it?"

"Pull out!" I begged.

Cain slowly slipped out of me, relieving the pressure, only to enter me again until I was gasping for air.

My body was quaking and one more move felt like I would combust. I wasn't even sure if I could survive his sex, but I was dying to find out.

"Can you take it?" he asked gently with hooded eyes, moving his hips in slow, deliberate strokes.

Hastily I nodded and dove in for another kiss.

Cain started off slow just like he'd said, but when he started going deeper and harder, I felt my vision blur as a wave of pleasure I'd never experienced took over me. Just as I was on the brink of something magical, he pulled out of me and flipped me over.

"Oh God," I whined as he eased into me from behind. One of his hands circled my waist and found my clit, driving me toward the edge. "Yes! Yes! Yes!" I entwined our fingers where his other hand was gripping my hip. Cain squeezed my hand as he began pumping into me over and over.

My eyes crossed. I was close, barely hanging on. But as much as I loved hearing the sound of my own voice, I noticed *he* wasn't saying anything.

I inched away from him, glaring at him over my shoulder. "Act like you like it!"

Smack. His hand came down hard on my ass as he pulled me back and was back inside of me. More, he came down on top of me, resting his body into mine flat on the bed, tangling our legs together. He dug inside me so deep, I knew I'd feel him for days after.

"Mmm." Cain moaned into my ear, rolling his hips into mine. "You feel *so* good. I like the way you take it."

Under his heavenly weight, surrounded by his masculine

scent, hearing those words, and feeling him so deep inside me, as if I had a praise kink, I felt myself release into oblivion.

I opened my eyes sometime later. The sheets smelled like me and a mix of a man. I closed my eyes and engulfed the scent, letting the memories of what had taken place wash over me.

Opening my eyes once more, I realized I wasn't alone. Beside me, Cain was lying on his side, tending to me meticulously as he wiped me down with a warm washcloth.

He was back in his pants, but was otherwise shirtless. Something about the sight made him hot.

"Hey," I said in a shy voice.

Cain looked over and noticed I was awake. He smiled and went back to wiping me up. "There she is."

I watched him clean between my legs with precision and care. No one had ever done that for me before. I couldn't help but smile.

"So, that was intense."

Smug, he asked, "Was it?"

I rolled my eyes. "Yeah."

It was the first time I'd ever gotten to finish like that. Usually, I only got off during oral, or if I played with myself. I never knew it could be like...*that*.

Cain gathered the washcloth and stood from the bed. "Glad you had a good time."

Narrowing my eyes, I watched him go and take the cloth back into the attached bathroom.

"Don't act like it was just me who enjoyed it." The last thing I remembered before blacking out was *him* moaning "fuck" before finding his own release. Feeling him pulsate and come, seemed to make *my* orgasm last longer.

Cain came and stood in the doorway, leaning against the frame as he pocketed his hands. There was a dark spot on his thigh, evidence from my wetness. He noticed it too and suppressed a smile.

"It was...good, Eden," Cain settled on saying.

I sat up and stretched, feeling tender all over. Walking would surely be a feat after taking him. "Just let me get cleaned up and I'll be out of your hair."

Cain made a curious face as he angled his head. "Where you going?"

I chuckled. "Home? We had a deal."

Cain didn't laugh with me. "We did. We *do*."

"Okay, so now that we've had our time, I'll be going," I said as I gathered the sheets around myself to cover up.

Cain pursed his lips as he appeared thoughtful. He soon shook his head. "I don't think so."

"Excuse me?" I asked. There was no way he was going back on his word, not after that.

Cain shrugged. "You equated your sex to a million dollars." He looked around the room as he rocked on the heels of his feet. "But that was more like a quarter of a million dollars. So, by my count, we're not even, not yet."

My mouth fell open and I felt sick.

"I'm going to hop in the shower. Please," Cain seemed to beg. "Do me a favor and don't try to run. It'll only make it worse."

Without another word, he stepped into the bathroom and closed the door.

Immediately, I sprung out of bed and darted out of the room. In the living room section of the master suite, I hopped into my dress and didn't bother to zip it up as I grabbed my bag and purse. Music was still playing, Luke James, but I paid this no mind as I rushed out of the room.

I didn't make it far.

Vino was lounging back in the living room in the main area of the suite, enjoying a drink and something he'd gotten from room service. Standing not too far from the door was Beans, and one look was all it took to send him on alert.

"No!" I roared as I attempted to rush past him for the door.

With my arm around my middle, clutching my dress to my body, I didn't make it.

Beans grabbed ahold of me and lifted me up like I weighed nothing. He turned us around and horror ran through me. In the doorway off the master suite, Cain stood with a towel wrapped around his waist, shaking his head.

He nodded off. "Take her to one of the guest rooms."

"NO!" I screamed at the top of my lungs. "We had a deal!"

Beans wasn't hearing me. He carried me across the suite and tossed me into a small room with a queen-sized bed. I stumbled back and almost fell, nearly dropping hold of my dress.

Cain appeared in the doorway, taking pity on me. "Don't make this hard on yourself."

"We had a deal," I cried.

"And we're going to honor it," Cain responded.

My body began to tremble as I let go of everything I was holding. It all fell to the ground, my bag, my purse, and my dress. Standing there naked, I squeezed my fists shut, ready to let him have me all night if he wanted.

Cain stepped closer, shaking his head. "I'm not in the mood."

"What?" I wanted to know as I looked up at him.

He leaned down to my level, a seriousness on his face. "I'm not going to touch you if I don't want to. And if *you* don't want me to. I'm not going to make you do this, Eden. So, get comfortable and relax. You're not going anywhere until we're done."

"I don't understand," I said as he got ready to walk away.

In the doorway, Cain paused, looking back at me. "You stole from the wrong guy, and now you're going to pay for it."

He didn't say anything else. He just shut and locked the door. But it may as well have been my cell slamming closed.

I was now a prisoner.

5

Cain

I ALWAYS HAD A PROBLEM TAKING WHAT DIDN'T belong to me.

Clack. Clack. Clack.

I rolled my dice around in my palm as I sat back in the suite's dining room musing over my current predicament. The one where I was hoarding a hostage.

After everything I'd been through, I did my best to do things "by the book" whenever I was out as *Cain Carter*. Keeping my nose and name as spotless as possible.

This was too close a call.

Clack. Clack. Clack.

I'd come from the very bottom, and had the scars to prove it. My whole life I struggled under the harshest rejection. Starving for more than just basic necessity. Until the hunger became too much and I started to *take*.

In this life, I learned early on that nothing was given. Not shelter, not food, not happiness, not even love. So, I went after what I wanted. After being thrown into the system where only the strongest survived, I managed to make it out alive. I made a name for myself in the street. I formed a crew, and we established an honor among thieves. I did what I had to do to make it. And when I hit the biggest lick that saw to it that I never had to take again, and I had a seat at the table, I settled down, just a little.

These days, I was good about keeping to myself and staying under the radar, no matter how alluring and mysterious my profile was to the public.

Now, there was just one small problem. A tiny little thing with dark red hair who couldn't have weighed more than a hundred and twenty pounds soaking wet.

Clack. Clack. Clack.

Down in the ballroom I'd begrudgingly entered the Monte Carlo casino night Nichols & Wagner was throwing partly for charity, and partly to give the people a taste of the luxury casino they were building. I hadn't meant to stay long, but thanks to a little thief, I hadn't stayed at all.

I saw her before she saw me.

Hampton Hills was pretty conservative in looks. At most, when it came to the women, you'd see a blonde or two, or someone with highlights. Never red. She stuck out like a sore thumb and I'd tracked her movement from the moment I laid eyes on her.

She was just gliding across the room, this light that was glowing like a beacon in a dark sea, floating on serene energy, earning all the attention around her. Even after I'd made my entrance, she didn't notice me, nor look my way. Everything about her, right away, intrigued me.

The only way I ever made it through these types of events was the catering alone. When I saw an opportunity to feast, I headed straight for the buffet table, and that's when I saw her up close.

Eden.

The distance hadn't prepared me for what she was like head-on. Pretty beyond words, she had a sweet face. Large, dark eyes, and an essence that said she didn't have a mean bone in her body. And what a body she had in that dress. When I'd made my way back up to steal another glance at her face, that's when I noticed it.

It was always in the eyes. The keepers of the human soul. All it took was one glimpse and I knew whether a person was good or bad, or in some cases, *fucked-up*. Looking into Eden's eyes, I saw something that made me flinch.

I saw pain, and a lot of it.

She hid it well behind all her smiles and bubbliness, but right on her, I couldn't miss it.

After a little friendly small talk, I'd left her and the food when I'd been called away by some investors looking to pick my brain on the event. It wasn't too long into our conversation that a text alert from Vino told me there was a problem. I thought he was saving my ass from having to listen to another business proposition, but one step out into the hall saw that wasn't the case.

Here she was once again, darling little red.

She'd stolen from me. I'd forgotten the chips I'd gathered to gamble with, and she'd stolen them from me.

Ordinarily, she would've been let go. Sent off with a strict warning, a heavy scolding that saw her never so much as telling a single lie ever again. But then she offered herself to me. A taste of the ripest fruit. And I had to bite.

Holding her face in the palm of my hand, running my thumb across those glossed big lips, I hadn't cared about her actions or what brought her to me. I *wanted* her.

So, given the chance, I did what I did best: devoured her whole.

Clack. Clack. Clack.

The sound of a loud conversation drew me back to the dining room table, where Beans sat on one end, and Vino far over on the other.

"Pay me my money!" Vino demanded with a huge grin as he looked on at Beans.

Beans made a face. "Even you didn't predict *this*."

"Don't matter, she in that room right now, pay up."

I narrowed my eyes. "You made a bet on me?"

Beans heaved a sigh as he faced me. "I expected more out of you."

"Not everybody is allergic to pussy like you, Beanie Baby," Vino teased with a cackle.

Beans regarded the remark with a simple flip of the bird.

Ignoring Vino's taunting, I kept on with Beans. "How much?"

"Ten grand," Vino cut in, amusement dripping from his tone.

He didn't need the money. I paid them well. This was simply about bragging rights.

I shook my head and snorted as I sank back in my chair. "Jesus."

Beans reached into his suit jacket and pulled out a stack of money and tossed it across the table. Vino made a show to pull it toward himself as if he'd really won big.

The disappointment in Beans's eyes almost made me feel bad.

"It wasn't my idea," I threw out.

Still, he wasn't hearing me as he stared at me knowingly.

Eden's suggestion of us trading sex for her freedom should've gone out the window, but one glimpse at what lay under that dress and there was no going back. She wasn't Hampton Hills. She was *real*. From her breasts that fit my hands just right, to the stretchmarks on her hips, to the bellybutton ring that hung on her navel, and to the couple of tattoos she held.

Aimer et être aimé. Meaning: *To Love and Be Loved*. It was tattooed in red ink behind her right thigh. Behind her left ear was a small Eiffel Tower tattoo.

Eden had an affinity for Paris.

"What, she tried to fuck her way out of this?" Vino asked.

I shrugged. "I told her I've killed for less."

Vino grinned. The sick fuck. There was nobody else I wanted

watching my back but Vino. He got off on the thrill of the game. Despite the fact that he was a skilled shooter, he wasn't afraid to get dirty and fight hand-to-hand. Nobody loved fucking people up more than Vino. And nobody loved goading me into fucking people up more than Vino.

In some ways, Vino was the proverbial devil on my shoulder, and Beans was something like the angel on my other.

"Looked kinda young. How old is she?" Vino pressed, causing Beans to swing his attention back my way curiously.

"Nineteen," I said. "According to *one* of her IDs."

Vino whistled and stroked at his jaw.

The part of me with a conscience winced at the reality of Eden's young age. She'd be twenty in a few months, but still. She wasn't old enough to step inside a casino. She didn't look a day past the barely legal that she was. Not that she hadn't been armed for such an obstacle with her *four* IDs.

At twenty-eight—if I were a better man—I should've just given her that slap on the wrist and let her go.

Clack. Clack. Clack.

"Was it any good?" Vino leaned over to ask, a lascivious look in his eyes.

Quietly, I nodded.

I hadn't had sex in forever, and then to give me *that*? It was like giving an addict the purest strain of heroin, and then trying to wean them off. Not. Fucking. Likely.

Women did what I told them to do whenever I fucked them, and they didn't talk back. That wasn't the case with Eden. Her attitude. Her demand for me to kiss her. Her demand for me to show her *I* liked it. The memory of it all was enough to turn me on.

Curling and uncurling my fingers, I tried to distract myself. I had been close to telling her it was only worth a hundred grand—so I could fuck her nine more times.

Good fuck or not, it was the principle of the matter that had her here. No one stole from me and got away with it.

As if reading my train of thought, Beans stood and collected a briefcase from the living room along with a thick envelope. He set the briefcase on the floor by my side and tossed the envelope on the table.

"While you were *busy*, I went ahead and cashed in your chips. *She...*" Beans said with a look off into the direction where Eden was being held. "...dropped a few chips when she tried to run. Thirty thousand."

I eyed the envelope. *Huh.* I thought about dividing it between Vino and Beans, but then I settled on being nice enough to let Eden keep it whenever I let her go.

In the end, I grabbed the envelope and placed it in my briefcase. "Thanks."

"What are you going to do with her?" Beans wanted to know as he sat back down.

"She said her sex was worth a million dollars." I lifted my gaze to my oldest and closest friend. "I told her that first one was only worth a quarter. So, I'm going to fuck her three more times before I let her go."

Vino laughed and Beans couldn't help but break and smile before joining in.

"She's awfully quiet back there." Vino leaned over and peered toward the back hallway where the smaller rooms were.

"Every room leads out into the balcony on this side of the building," Beans noted. "What if she decides to just jump?"

"Well, that'd be one way to solve this problem," Vino figured.

While I didn't think I could ever get tired of fucking Eden, I wasn't about to keep her. "When she calms down, we can work our way through this. Shouldn't be more than a couple days...a week at the most."

Beans regarded me skeptically at the estimate. "What about Sinclair?"

Immediately my mood dropped and switched over to aggravation. "What about him?"

Beans shrugged and held his hands up. "He's been trying to

talk to you for a minute. Probably the only reason he showed up last night."

Sinclair was nothing more than a thorn in my fucking side. "Maybe he'll finally get the message."

"Can we kill 'im?" Vino asked as he chewed on a toothpick.

Regrettably, I sighed and shook my head as my phone started ringing. Just what I needed. Damon Nichols was calling.

I stood to my feet. "It's Damon."

I saw myself out to the balcony to take the call. A quick sweep around the vicinity showed Eden hadn't ventured out here. Unless she'd already jumped. "Hello?" I answered as I chanced a look over the railing down below. No bloodied and broken bodies were to be found.

"Good morning," Damon greeted me with a little pep in his tone.

At the age of twenty I claimed my birthright and became the CEO of a successful hotel and casino in Las Vegas called Cartier after my biological father, James Carter, met his end. With that inheritance came a new world of wealth and privilege—not to mention, business offers to take the casino off my hands, or venture out and expand.

I'd rejected every offer that came my way, not interested in expanding or selling. One of those people who approached me after feeling me out was Damon Nichols, co-owner of the five-diamond hotel chain The Residence. For years, he and his partner Phil tried and tried to get me to go in on a joint project here in LA, but I hadn't been interested.

What had caught my eye was Damon's daughter, Kennedy. She was by far the most beautiful woman I'd ever seen, and she was kind and poised. She'd rejected me twice already, and when Damon found out he'd developed ALS and once more came knocking on my door, I'd been arrogant enough to offer him a deal: his daughter for my interest in The Residence at Cartier hotel and casino.

Like any father, he'd wanted to wring my neck out and snuff

the life out of me, but like any business tycoon, he relented, especially when I was willing to settle for a thirty/seventy split.

Long story short, Kennedy never cared for the idea of me. She started seeing someone else almost immediately. A man she'd been willing to *die* for when I'd been about to kill him for it.

That was a year ago, and needless to say, it hadn't put a damper in my working relationship with Damon. We'd renegotiated our agreement to fifty/fifty and put the past behind us.

Unlike everyone else who nagged me about business talk, when Damon called, I picked up.

"Good to hear from you, Damon," I responded into the phone.

Damon was a lucky man. Through treatment and support from his family, his condition wasn't worsening, but somewhat stable. According to current research, he'd never *beat* ALS, but at least he was managing.

"Someone told me you and Kennedy couldn't stay last night at the fundraiser," Damon said.

I rolled my eyes. I'd bumped into Kennedy on my way to the ballroom; she'd been in a hurry to get back to Bedford Heights, where *he* lived. "Something came up, for me at least."

Damon chuckled, and it really did feel good to hear him be so spirited. "Well, don't make any plans for *this* weekend, there's another gala. Art or some shit, but it's not about that, it's about investors wanting to talk about The Residence at Cartier. A lot of people loved last night, Cain. They're itching for that Vegas feeling right here in California."

None of this truly interested me. I was just building the casino for the sake of seeing it through. It was a shame Damon wasn't fond of public appearances since the muscles in his legs weakened and he had to use a wheelchair, or else, I'd much prefer being a silent partner than a public figure on this one.

"*Another* gala?" I let my lack of interest show.

This only served to humor him. "That's what you do in this world, network and network."

I paced the length of the balcony, stealing a glance in the room Eden was in. She had the curtains closed. "At what point do you actually get to enjoy getting fat and rich?"

"When you're old and dying like me."

Squeezing my eyes shut, I shook my head. "Shut up, Damon."

His response was a cackle.

He likened himself as a father figure for me, and while I would've loathed being sonned by anyone, I didn't mind. Damon was fair, and was always willing to teach the keys of success.

Rubbing at the back of my neck, I gave in. "When is it?"

"Saturday, and bring a date. That bachelor shit doesn't make you approachable. People like it when you have someone on your arm. Makes you...more humane," Damon said.

I doubted that. "I'll see what I can do."

Finding a date so last minute would take more effort than I cared for.

"So, Sinclair called me this morning," Damon drawled casually.

Fuck, I mouthed to myself as my fist clenched shut. I had to take the phone from my ear to grumble out more expletives at the news. My hand was shaking as I reached up to squeeze the bridge of my nose. *Fuck.*

"I'm sorry about that. He's annoying," I said as I came back to the conversation.

Damon wasn't fazed. "He's a man on a mission. Must be something important he wants to get into with you."

I closed my eyes and gritted my teeth, resenting the fact that Sinclair wasn't a regular person I could kill and go about my day.

The worst thing I could've done was take over James's empire, stepping into the realm of the elite where things had to be handled much differently than in the underworld. Someone annoyed you while making a deal? A bullet to the skull would remedy that easily. Here, in the daylight? Passive-aggressiveness was the norm for exacting revenge. That or hostile takeovers.

I wasn't interested in either.

I didn't make it a habit to kill out of impulse or emotion. Only when I needed to. By no means was I a saint or a morally upstanding individual, but I had a set of principles. And unfortunately for me, killing Sinclair didn't align with them. No matter how tempting it was.

"Cain," Damon said, bringing me back to the moment.

"Yes," I said.

"Talk to your cousin."

It was nothing more than a gentle push, but still, my stomach twisted at the thought. "I'll see what's on my schedule for him."

Damon's laugh filled my ear. "Talk soon."

"Yeah." I hung up and squeezed my phone, doing my best not to chuck it over the railing.

James Carter had no other children outside of me, his bastard lovechild. There was no sibling rivalry to wade through. Instead, I had a nuisance of a cousin I had to deal with at some point or another.

Fuck.

Back inside the suite, Beans and Vino were enjoying room service. A hearty breakfast of eggs, waffles, fruit, bacon, potatoes, and croissants.

Beans lifted his gaze toward me as I came back to the table. "What's up?"

I thumbed at my jaw. "There's another fucking gala this weekend. Damon wants me to bring a date. To be more 'approachable.'"

Vino frowned and kept eating.

Beans tried to throw out a suggestion to resolve the issue. "Alexis?"

My ex. She played her role perfectly. She knew when to talk and when to keep quiet. She thrived at every public appearance I ever had to make.

"There's a thought," Vino agreed at the idea.

I could probably call her up and take her out this weekend. We'd always kept it pretty casual to where I wouldn't have to do much beyond that. Dinner. The gala. End the night with some decent sex, and then send her on her way. It could all be so simple.

My eyes trailed down the hall, at the thought of my hostage. There was just one small problem I'd have to deal with first.

6

Eden

WHEN I FIRST SAW HIM, I THOUGHT HE WAS UNREAL. But I got too close and now I knew better. He was the devil in disguise, and I'd just gotten myself in deep trouble.

Days began to pass and I stayed confined to my room with no means of hope, it seemed. I was let out to use the bathroom and shower, but then I was led back to my cell. There were several attempts by either Beans or Vino to feed me, but I refused to eat, refused to drink, refused to do more than just lay in bed defeated.

Soft knocking sounded at my door. It was always Beans or Vino. Pounding meant it was Vino. His heavy knocks were usually accompanied by a "You decent?" before he came in. I *wasn't* decent as I lay naked under the thick white comforter, but Vino showed no interest once I'd reject the food.

Beans was quieter. He'd say what he was bringing—breakfast, lunch, or dinner—and then he'd leave after a beat once I said nothing.

I thought it was a Wednesday when his soft raps drew my attention from staring ahead at the floor-to-ceiling window. Outside was a balcony I'd discovered when I'd overheard Cain out there talking on the phone days ago.

I watched his shadow stroll back and forth in front of my

window, blocking out the sunlight that had been streaming in that morning. The steady rumble of his voice, the calm in which he paced, and the relaxed expression of his posture—he wasn't worried or thinking about me here in this room. This was probably a normal thing for him.

Definitely the devil.

The *click* of the door opening let me know Beans was entering my room. The familiar aroma of soy sauce, onion, garlic, and ginger of Chinese food wafted in next and I knew it was an attempt to feed me lunch. At least, I thought it was lunchtime.

He came over to my line of vision where I continued to lay staring ahead at the thin curtains of my window. I made no effort to acknowledge Beans, and after standing there for two minutes or so, he turned and left the room, pulling the door shut behind him.

Going without food and water wasn't doing me any good, but I couldn't bring myself to care. To try to preserve—

The door rushed open so fast it smacked against the wall behind it and sent a gust of wind my way. Goose bumps inflamed my flesh at the sudden intrusion. The charge of the air alone let me know it was *him*. His presence washed throughout the room before his scent did and I knew before I even looked over that Cain had finally made an appearance.

From the ground up, he stood menacingly in black. Black dress shoes, black dress pants and vest. His white shirt was the only thing breaking up the dark uniform. But it did nothing to distract from the fact he was back wearing his gun holster, with one visibly tucked away. The sleeves of his shirt were rolled up to his elbows, exposing his vein-littered forearms and large hands.

He stood there, a loud anger radiating from him as he glared directly at me. A sudden clinking of metal caused me to look closer where I discovered he was clutching a belt in one hand.

Eyes enlarging, I burrowed deeper beneath my comforter and backed against the wall. *No.*

With his long legs, Cain crossed over to me in two quick

strides. I was cornered, with nowhere to go but deeper against the wall.

Cain didn't speak. He snatched my wrist and pulled me closer, soon grabbing my other one.

"No!" I screamed as I struggled to get away. It was to no avail. Though he didn't look it, his strength outmatched mine easily.

Cain grabbed my wrists and brought one end of the belt around them securely, so tight, it dug into my skin. "Beans!" he shouted over his shoulder as he began dragging me closer to the headboard to tie the other end of the belt.

No. A chill ran down my spine as vomit lined my throat. I was naked. He was tying me to the bedpost. And he was calling for Beans.

"NO!" I screamed so hard as I tried to fight it.

"Shut up," Cain snapped as he kept on with his task of tying me to the post.

Tears clouded my vision as I began to shake. "You said you wouldn't make me! You promised! You promised!"

Terror ruled my system at the thought of being accosted by not one, but all three of them. Fighting against Cain's hold was a waste. I was weak. With no strength to defend myself against him, I would be nothing for the other two.

Cain finished tying the belt and narrowed his eyes as his gaze settled on mine. Disgust marred his features as he snarled. "I said I wouldn't touch you. I never said anything about not forcing you to eat when you decide to go on a fucking hunger strike."

Hefty footsteps on the carpet alerted me to Beans's arrival.

Cain kept his attention on me a moment longer before going and accepting the brown paper bag of food Beans had brought into the room. Beans didn't stay. Cain shut the door behind him.

A sense of relief quelled my nausea as the reality of the situation came into the light.

With the threat of violence somewhat tamed, Cain came over to my bedside and set the food onto the nightstand beside it. He grabbed the gray suede tufted chair from the corner of the room and brought it over to sit beside me.

His eyes flickered my way, still angry, but less hostile it seemed. "I was in the mood for Chinese."

I couldn't wipe my eyes or face. I sniffled and nodded, speaking up in a small voice, "Okay."

Cain's eyes lingered on me. He soon leaned over and plucked a couple of Kleenex from the dispenser on the nightstand and came and cleaned up my face. The action was so gentle, so mercurial, I was left stunned with my mouth agape.

"Don't cry, Eden. I'm not going to hurt you," Cain spoke softly. "If either of *them*"—he tipped his head toward the door— "ever so much as considered touching you, I wouldn't hesitate to put a bullet in them."

He spoke of murder so casually, as if he were solving a simple math problem.

It was staring at Cain head-on that it hit me. That all the dots lined up and the pieces fell into place. To the public he was some wealthy, enigmatic bachelor. In the dark, he was a criminal. Before me, his hands were clean, but I didn't doubt they had been doused in blood and gunpowder before.

A darkness lingered over Cain like a black cloud. It hung in his eyes, and he embraced it back. It was the way his men moved around him, not like security or bodyguards, but like *bench*men.

I should've put it together before, but there was no denying it now. Cain's aura and manner dripped with the demeanor of a criminal. Not just a criminal. A boss. In Bedford Heights, I saw it all, but this was something more. Something they could never be. *Untouchable. Godly. Lethal.*

Cain's youthful looks did nothing to taint his ambiance. Something about him, right away, said he'd never given off *boy* but was always *man*.

Cain nodded and grabbed the large plain brown paper bag. He unfolded the top and dug inside. "I don't know what you like, but we ordered plenty. I have...shrimp fried rice and chicken lo mein, and some shrimp egg rolls." He regarded me, brows raised eagerly. "Sound good?"

I was tied to the bed. I had no choice. "Yeah. I...I like lo mein."

Cain pulled out a round plastic takeout container. It was still hot and fresh, as condensation had the lid all foggy. Cain dug inside the bag and pulled out a small piece of cardboard that had been inside it and used it as a plate to hold the hot container on. He opened the lid and steam rose from the noodles, the smell tantalizing and arousing my hunger.

Cain held up a slender red package with gold Mandarin script all over it. "Chopsticks?"

I shook my head, feeling like the fraud I was when it came to Asian cuisine. "I don't know how to use them."

Cain flashed me a small smile, appearing bashful almost. "Tell you the truth? Same. I always want to learn, but then again, I'm usually too hungry to."

Same, I mused as I hid my own smile.

Cain grabbed a white plastic fork and dug into the lo mein, swirling his fork around. The squishy wet sound of the food was a reprieve. I hated ordering Chinese and getting dry noodles.

Cain gathered a good amount onto the fork and came closer, holding it out to feed me.

I paused, taking in the position he and I were in. He was really going to feed me over my tantrum to not eat.

He waited expectantly and I hesitated before closing the gap and accepting the food into my mouth.

It was still hot, leaving me to open my mouth to take in air and chew fast so I didn't burn my tongue.

Cain took the fork back and dug into the lo mein again. "Yeah, it's still pretty hot. I didn't want to blow on your food."

I appreciated his effort, but we were a little way past setting up boundaries. "It's okay."

Cain helped himself to a forkful next and then it was my turn.

The slow process wasn't for me, and Cain could see my eagerness to eat as he noticed I'd scooted closer.

"If I untie you, will you behave?" he challenged.

"I'll eat," I promised.

Cain set the food aside, and before he made an attempt to go for the belt, he reached down and pulled out his gun. With his eyes on mine, he set it on the table. The handle in my direction.

He untied me and massaged my wrists, soothing the imprint the belt had made. I wasn't sure I'd ever get used to his soft touch. It was such a contrast to his image. It was almost like...the darkest villain had a white heart.

Cain settled down into his seat and handed over the bowl and the cardboard plate. He reached into the bag and grabbed the white container housing the fried rice. "You like fried rice?"

"Love it," I admitted. "But, not to be gross, I'm almost hesitant to order shrimp anything from places because sometimes they don't use—"

"—deveined shrimp?" Cain finished for me, bobbing his head. "Heard you. I hate that shit too."

He used the second fork he had to dig through the rice. Soon, he seemed satisfied with his findings. "Looks like we lucked up."

Now I wanted that.

It must've registered on my face, because Cain chuckled to himself as he took a quick bite out of the rice and offered to trade meals with me.

I moved my fork through the fried grains of rice and saw that he hadn't lied. Clean shrimp lay inside and I could eat without having to worry.

Cain grabbed an egg roll and bit into it, the crunch making me want a bite as well. He didn't share his, but handed over the wax-paper bag and I grabbed one of the rolls and helped myself.

For a while, we sat like that, in silence, enjoying the food. Or, Cain was.

My mind was too busy to eat. Too hyperaware of Cain's

proximity. I went from sneaking peeks in his direction, to full-on staring.

Watching him eat was so fascinating. The way his jaw worked to chew, the way he concentrated on the food, and the way he seemed to take his time to really sit and enjoy the taste and flavor. He was in no rush.

As if he could feel my gaze, Cain lifted his attention to me. "You're not eating."

I bit my lip and went back to my rice. It really was delicious, but I could only eat so much after the lo mein and some of my egg roll. Cain stepped away for a moment and came back with two bottles of water.

I took a chance and stopped eating. Putting my container on the nightstand, I fiddled with my water bottle.

"Full?" Cain probed as he seemed to be as well.

I nodded.

The quiet was nice, but the fear lingered on.

He said he wouldn't hurt me, but I didn't feel *safe*.

"Are you going to kill me, Cain?" I asked softly, not meeting his gaze. I let the question soak the air before going on, allowing us both to process this whole situation. "Sometimes...people are just meant for sad endings, and that's okay. Just let me know."

That angry energy revved up again, demanding I look over and face Cain.

"No," he said succinctly with finality. "*I'll* die before you ever will."

He was my captor, and somehow I still found a way to dislike the idea of harm being done to him.

The image of his scars came to mind, especially that gash on his side.

"How did you get that scar on your side?" I wondered.

Cain examined himself, imagining the wound beneath the fabric of his clothes. He sat back in his chair and gave a shrug. "Someone who used to work for me decided they didn't like how I ran my ship. They tried to overthrow me and pulled a knife on me." He brushed off this incident as if it were nothing. "Fortunately for me, my men didn't feel the same way, and I managed to survive."

My eyes darted to his side as I frowned. "Where is he?"

A ghost of a smile had Cain's lips twitching. "He's not in the union anymore."

He was dead.

So many questions swarmed in my head and I couldn't stop myself from asking the most prominent one. "What do you do exactly?"

"I run a casino in Vegas," Cain answered. He looked off, appearing thoughtful. "And you might say I'm something like a realtor."

"You sell houses?" I asked.

There was an amused expression on his face. Like he knew something I wasn't privy to. "The *bricks* that build them."

In this light, I knew what he was, and as he looked on at me, watching recollection cross my face, daring me to say something, I kept my mouth closed. I was already in a lot of trouble with this man. Why make it worse?

When I didn't comment on his secular work, he went on. "I'm actually in the middle of opening a casino here in LA with my partners. Part of Sunday was supposed to be a taste for Hampton Hills to see what we were going to be bringing."

Sunday. The day my life turned upside down.

I hung my head, feeling a weight settle on my shoulders. He didn't care about apologies—I'd given him several, but still, I wanted to try for another. "I've never been away from Bedford Heights before. This was my first time ever in Hampton Hills, and I go and do something so stupid and reckless. You could've called the police on me."

Cain ran a thumb across the scar on his bottom lip. "I don't like involving the police."

Obviously.

"I'm still embarrassed, because this isn't me—or, I've done

stupid things because my 'friend' talked me into it before, but I've never been so thoughtless like that. I really am sorry."

Cain propped an elbow onto the arm of his chair, resting his jaw into his hand. "This you pleading for your life?"

He wasn't moved.

I rolled my eyes and decided to never offer up another apology again. *Forget him.*

Cain angled his head, squinting his eyes. "Did you just roll your eyes?"

"What are you going to do about it?" I snapped.

His index finger began tapping his cheek as he sat back watching me. "Easy, you didn't eat for two days. I'm not in the mood to test your strength."

Cain ate up my attitude with amusement. It was a turn-on for him. A turn-on he wasn't interested in *acting* on.

I did the math and tried something else. "So, we have to have sex three more times, right?"

Cain nodded. "Correct."

"Well, do I *have* to stay here? I mean, you could have my number and call me anytime you do want it and I'll come, no matter what."

Amused, Cain swiped at his brow. "Nothing personal, but I have trust issues."

"So, I have to stay with you?"

"You'll be fed, clothed, and comfortable, I promise."

"And all I have to do is have sex with you when you want it?"

"And when *you* want it as well," Cain corrected.

Those stipulations didn't seem so bad.

"I suppose it could be some dank dungeon," I mumbled. "I guess instead of full-blown kidnapping, this is kidnapping-*lite*."

There was a humored glow in his eyes. "More like, kidnapping-*adjacent*."

I struggled to keep my face straight at that one.

Cain smiled, revealing dimples in each cheek. He found me adorable, I could tell.

Despite it all, he was still as handsome as ever himself.

Still, though, being holed up under his watch wasn't going to do me any favors. "I'm going to end up losing my job, you know."

"Ah, yes." Cain clasped his hands together and sat up, leaning over. "Your job as an *exotic* dancer." He stroked at his jaw, appearing thoughtful. "You've been dancing since you were fifteen," he said it more as a fact than a question.

"Yes," I admitted.

"Was your boss aware?"

"We never outright talked about it, but I could tell he knew my ID was crap."

Cain came forward, appearing serious as he rested his elbows on his knees. "Has he ever hit on you?"

"Yes." I bowed my head. "But he hits on all the girls." I wasn't sure why I'd said that last part, as if to protect David. Truth be told, he'd been handsy from the start. Always around to rub my shoulders, touch my hair, and let me know how he was willing to work things out if I wanted extra money or needed anything.

Cain narrowed his eyes, and a muscle in his jaw tensed. "How would you feel if you woke up tomorrow and the club burned down and he was inside of it?"

My stomach filled with nausea. "No!"

Cain arched a brow.

"Outside of me, there are other women who make a living there. Who support their families by doing what they have to do."

Cain sat back in his chair, not enthused by my rejection. "All right then, what about just him? *He* can wake up with a couple of bullets to the head tomorrow."

"No!" The thought of being responsible for someone's life ending made me sick. No matter what they'd done to me. "It's not right. No one deserves that."

Cain lowered his gaze to the floor and slowly shook his head. He glared at me before rising to his feet. "Such a fucking martyr."

He grabbed his gun, tucked it back into his holster, and walked out of the room.

Sometime later, I got the courage to get dressed and venture out of my room. I'd only packed my makeup kit, and outside of the dress, was left to wear my previous street clothes I'd worn here after using the complimentary stick of deodorant the hotel provided. I'd brushed my hair out and thanked God I'd packed a scarf.

It was evening now, and the sun was absent as I took a look at the windows on the right side of the living room.

Vino wasn't around, or Cain, but Beans hung back at the bar that lined the left wall, watching something on the large TV across the room. A basketball game.

"Where's Cain?" I asked.

"Out," Beans said without looking at me.

I guessed I wasn't going to get anywhere with him. I settled down on the sofa and sat cross-legged. There was nothing to do, and I didn't know a thing about sports, just that the men were often fine as hell and huge.

Judah Barrett from the Long Beach Sharks was gorgeous. But Beans was watching basketball, not football. The Cincinnati Chargers were playing against the Sacramento Kings.

Rift Taylor was kinda cute too.

Voices and laughter drew our attention toward the door where it was opening. Cain and Vino were entering the suite, laughing about something.

Cain's gaze came to me and his smile died as his face went sober.

"What's the score?" Vino joined Beans at the bar and watched the game. He scowled as his apparent team wasn't up to par. "Those fuckin' Chargers, man."

For the first time, Beans smiled a little. "Can't beat Taylor."

"Fuck Rift Taylor," Vino grumbled as he kept watching.

Cain paid the game no mind as he walked past the scene and went over to the master suite. I stood and followed him, feeling nervous along the way. I didn't know how to go about this situation, but my latest offer was worth a try.

Cain was in the bedroom of the suite, tugging on his tie and heaving a sigh as I came at a stop in the doorway. "What's up, Eden?"

"I have an idea."

Cain peered my way, taking me in. "Indulge me."

Chewing on my lip, I thought about it for a second before I threw it out there. "Even though I didn't really get away with your money, what if we set up a monetary payment plan? I make good money at the club. I could pay you back in installments."

"That would take years," Cain marveled.

"I know, but I'll keep up with it until you feel I've paid my debt."

Cain hummed to himself as he unbuttoned his vest and pulled it off. The fluid way in which he removed his clothes and moved in general was a distraction.

"No," he said when he finally spoke up, undoing the plackets on his shirtsleeves. "That would be impossible."

"*Impossible*?" I questioned.

A smirk crossed Cain's face and I knew something was up.

"What?" I pressed on.

"We don't hire minors—anyone under the age of twenty-one at my club," Cain drawled.

My club. No. "You...you... What did you do?"

Cain shrugged and opened his arms out, as if it were nothing. "I just bought a strip club."

My lip curled. Had I heard him right? There was no way he'd gone all the way to Crazy Legs and bought it. "No."

Cain stepped out of his shoes. "Yes."

He was a millionaire—probably a *billion*aire. It would be nothing for him to purchase any property or business he chose.

But still, that was insane. "Why would you do that?!"

Annoyed, Cain whirled around and tossed a hand in my direction. "Well, you wouldn't let me kill the guy so what else was I supposed to do?"

Speechless, I could only blink. He'd wanted to really *kill* David, but...he hadn't. "So, you bought Crazy Legs?"

Cain thumbed at his lip and nodded. "Had to get that fucker out of there one way." He glared at me. "And set a better fucking hiring policy."

He'd done that...for *me*.

"Beans cashed in those chips you dropped. It's thirty grand. It's not much, but it's something to get you by until you find a better place of employment when you go back home."

"The hiring age at Crazy Legs *is* eighteen," I pointed out on a whisper.

Cain took in a breath through his nose. "You're not going back there."

"What's it to you when we're done?" I didn't have any real fight in me. I was too caught up on the fact that he'd saved my money, was giving it back to me instead of keeping it, and was intent on saving me somehow from my job.

"Eden." There was a sheer warning in his tone.

I didn't push. "So, you really didn't kill him?"

Cain sighed, shaking his head. "You told me not to."

It was that simple for him.

This was so messed-up.

Worse, I crept closer, going and poking his hand with my finger. Not meeting his eyes, I tried not to let loose and smile. Not to feel too much about it, because there was so much I was having trouble processing. "Thanks."

Before I could do something stupid like hug him, I turned around and went back out to the living room and continued to watch the game I didn't understand.

7

Eden

FIRM KNOCKS MEANT CAIN.

Thursday morning, I was greeted by the sound of knocking. I was still in bed, not ready to get up. The previous evening, we all reheated our leftover Chinese and gathered around the living room area while Vino cursed the Chargers. I didn't comprehend a thing, but I stayed up just to have something to do.

The door opened a smidge and Cain poked his head in. "You good?"

I covered up once more to be modest. "Yeah." I never slept naked at home, but the bed in this hotel was like sleeping on a cloud, a very fluffy and cozy cloud. And I wanted to bask in all of it.

Cain came inside and I spotted the large shopping bag he was carrying immediately. He came and set it on the edge of my bed before shoving his hands in the pockets of his crisp burgundy suit. Unlike me, Cain appeared refreshed and awake, as if he'd been up since the crack of dawn.

I didn't know the time, but it was too early for him to be so ready.

"Morning." Cain took a moment to silently observe me. "Sleep well?"

"Yeah." My eyes drifted to the nondescript shopping bag. "What's with the bag?"

Cain examined the royal green tote bag with the macrame handles and came back to me. "It's time to go." His gaze fell to the pile of my clothing on the floor. There was no hamper in my room to properly store them, so the floor was the only other option. "I figured a fresh change of clothes would be suitable."

I ignored the fact he'd bought me clothes *without* me. I wasn't impossible to style or size, but Cain didn't know me enough to pick something out for me. "So, we're checking out?"

We hadn't had sex last night. Technically, I still "owed" him three more goes at it, but if he was letting me off the hook, I would take it.

Cain nodded. "I don't live here, Eden. I'd feel much more comfortable with our arrangement taking place back at my home."

My spirits took a dive as my shoulders drooped and my stomach knotted up.

Oh.

I thought I knew men, but I was wrong. I couldn't charm my way out of this. Cain wasn't letting me go. He was taking me from the hotel to his private home. From one prison to another.

Slowly, I sat up and reached for the bag. To busy myself to keep from crying. It wouldn't save me anyway.

Inside the bag I found a folded white shirt and upon grabbing it and undoing it, I discovered an extra-*extra*-large I Heart Hampton Hills T-shirt. What more, also in the bag was a pair of gray sweats, and closer inspection found them to be a size too big as well. The only thing that would fit me were the pastel rainbow-colored ankle socks at the bottom of the bag.

"No underwear?" I questioned as I came up empty.

Cain leaned over and stroked my cheek. "I want my captive to have easy access."

His poor attempt at a joke made me scoff. Even more, I shoved him.

The action came naturally, until the shock set in. I leaned away, flinching. Nervous, because I'd just put my hand on him.

Cain had a foot on me. And he was stronger too. I should've chosen my battles wisely.

But Cain was grinning, not at all offended. Until he took in my face, read the fear in my eyes, and I watched as his smile dwindled into nothing as he shook his head.

"Get dressed," he ordered, his tone dry and clipped.

Fingering the material of the cotton tee, I frowned. "You couldn't find anything in a small?"

Cain was at the door, prepared to let me dress in private. He tossed me a smirk over his shoulder, as if he were proud of his selections. "I want you covered."

Narrowing my eyes, I bit my tongue. I'd likely trip and fall if I went through and wore the oversized sweats. Rolling the waist up and cuffing the ends would probably help, but I wasn't feeling it. Instead, I stood, grabbed the fluffy white towel I'd been using for my trips to the bathroom, my bag and the new white T-shirt, and went across the hall over to the bathroom. Upon doing my business and freshening up, I got dressed in the tee only and pulled my hair back into a ponytail.

The shirt fell to my thighs, becoming a dress on me. My lack of a bra caused my nipples to bead through my shirt and the draft from the vent in the wall made me very aware of how bare I was underneath. I padded back to my room and put on my new socks before slipping into my tennis shoes. In reality, I should've taken my time. To prolong the inevitable. I didn't know what this meant. To leave the semi-safety of this public setting to go to Cain's private home.

Come to think of it, the entire four days I'd been holed up in this suite, I hadn't seen a single maid or housekeeper come through to change the sheets or clean.

Cain had probably paid off the hotel staff to keep them away. No wonder he wanted to leave. It *would* be easier to have his way with me where no one could accidentally stumble on what was going on, or question him.

Dread settled into the pit of my stomach at the thought. I couldn't get over how he'd wanted to *kill* David. A thought that some would fume about as a way to blow off steam, an impossible scenario they'd never go through with. But Cain... It was even in his tone when he'd been questioning me the first night during my lap dance. That *darkness*.

He'd mocked me in saying no one would miss me if I disappeared, and outside of Duane, he was right.

My hands shook as I collected my things and prepared to head out to the living room section of the suite. Something told me I was going to die. No matter what Cain had sworn, that this would be my last public appearance ever.

My footsteps were unsteady as I met up with the others. Beans and Vino were lounging at the bar, both dressed in their equally expensive suits and ties. It had been four days, and none of the men had rotated outfits. Somewhere along, they'd all gone to their respective homes and changed.

Vino was browsing the newspaper and Beans was once more scanning the TV. This was just another day at the office for them.

I wondered how many bodies they'd dumped for Cain.

"Ready?" Cain came out of his room with my purse and a duffle bag.

Stiffly, I nodded.

Cain crossed the room, his gaze slowly rising from my feet to mine, disapproval at my naked legs alight in his eyes. He stopped in front of me, silently questioning my disobedience with a raised brow. "We're about to walk out of here in front of a lot of people. Can I trust you won't make a scene?"

Going down to the lobby where security was more than likely around would be my only chance at escape.

As if reading my mind, Vino chuckled. "Don't make this messier than it has to be."

I felt hot and cold all over. A duality that made me sick.

"Eden." Cain's voice was a gentle caress, soothing away the ache building inside of me. "Tell me I can trust you to walk out of here without making a scene."

I didn't want to get hurt, but I also didn't want other people to get hurt at *my* expense. "O-Okay."

Beans turned off the TV and was the first to make his way toward the door to leave.

This was it.

Clenching my fists shut, I tried one last stab at gaining my freedom. "Wait."

Vino didn't listen as he joined Beans at the door, but Cain hung back, his eyes on me.

"I need to stop by my apartment. In...in Bedford Heights to get some things. I have virtually nothing to wear or anything of my own," I said.

There were shops all throughout Hampton Hills, but Cain didn't mention this as he peered over at his men. An unspoken conversation passed through them before he settled his attention back on me. He was the boss. He made the rules and called all the shots.

But that didn't stop Vino from stating the obvious. "She can buy clothes and shit here," he threw out.

"I'm aware, but let's humor her," Cain responded calmly, his attention stuck on me.

Vino didn't argue. Beans opened the door and led the way out to the hall. I inched forward to follow but a hand on my middle stopped me. Cain stepped forth and his chest brushed against the back of my head. Immediately something dug into my back.

He was hard.

"I can play nice," he said gently in my ear.

His proximity made me dizzy. Almost making me lose track of my mission.

I stepped away. "I'll have to remember that once we get to my next prison."

My snappiness made Cain chuckle, a rich sound that sent a dangerous thrill down my back.

Beans and Vino went down first, to collect Cain's car. After a moment's pause, Cain took me down to the lobby. It was a busy morning with guests entering and leaving the building, tourists getting ready to sightsee, parents guiding children to the pool, but no matter the situation, hotel staff still made it a point to speak and attend to Cain.

It was fascinating watching the way he moved publicly. The quiet charm he held that pulled people in.

"We hope you enjoyed your extended stay," the girl at the front desk said with a chipper tone as she grinned big at Cain.

His response was a polite smile as he told her he did before he ushered me out of the building.

The opportunity to scream, to call out for help vanished as we crossed from the lobby out onto the front sidewalk where Vino had pulled a large black truck up to the valet lane.

Cain opened the back door for me, and there was no going back as I slid inside. No matter how luxurious the Range Rover was with its buttery soft beige leather seats, or new expensive scent, I felt uneasy. Boxed in, even.

No one spoke to me the whole hour it took to get to Bedford Heights. An awkward silence filled the car, making it hard to adjust and get comfortable. With each passing mile, I felt hope grow in my chest. That there was a sense of humanity in Cain that would make him let me go.

"It's the apartment building on Clark Street," I said as we drove into the city limits.

Vino took my directions and pulled up front at the curb ten minutes later.

And then I was home. Somewhat.

"Ay, D." Vino turned around and looked at Cain. "Ain't this ya old stompin' grounds?"

With his eyes on me, Cain answered. "Couple of blocks over from here, yeah."

He'd grown up in Bedford Heights?

I couldn't wrap my head around the idea.

Ever the gentleman, Cain stepped out first and extended his hand my way to help me out next. I only took his hand because I was eager to be on the sidewalk. In front of my home. Almost safe and sound.

Life around me was in play, no one noticed the expensive vehicle parked in front of my building. Or the three men in different variations of designer suits. No, on the sidewalk across the busy street, people were coming and going, riding bikes, on a mission. On the sidewalk on my side, people kept on by, not at all fazed or interested in the scene I was in.

No one I knew was out and about. No one I recognized enough to signal for help.

But then, coming down the street was a police cruiser. The mere sight of it sent my mouth dry and my hope expanding.

Chuckling drew my attention behind me. Vino was watching me—they *all* were. "Go on, flag 'em down."

He was challenging me. The gleam in his dark eyes told me all that I needed to know. It would be no use.

I turned and gaped up at Cain, who was staring at me silently.

As if reading the question in my eyes, he nodded. "You never know when it's going to rain." He shrugged simply. "So, I always pack an umbrella."

The police were in his pocket. There was no end to his reach.

My hope deflated and my stomach sank in defeat.

"Stay back, Vino," Cain instructed. "Keep watch. Beans will walk up with us." He peered down at me. "You on the first floor or high up?"

"Fourth floor," I said.

Cain accepted this and showed a hand toward the front entrance. He made no move to let me have my purse back. Instead, all I had was my bag I'd brought along to swap out my street clothes and hold my makeup kit, and the gift bag Cain had given me with my new outfit.

I didn't fight him. I let him continue to hold on to my purse as I led us inside. Straight to our left was the stairwell leading up, and around the corner was the bank of elevators for those too impatient to walk. Most days, I didn't mind walking; I enjoyed taking my time coming or going. Today, I rode the elevator, my legs unsteady beneath me as we soared up to the fourth floor. I was too hyperaware as Cain and Beans flanked me on either side.

Anxiously, I led us over to my door. Apartment 405. My hands began to shake as I faced Cain. "I...I need my key to get in."

Still, he didn't give me my purse. He simply dug inside it, procured my keys, and handed them over.

It wasn't a good sign that he'd let me go.

Placing my key into the knob, I eased out a breath and began turning—

The door gave before I could even push, opening up and revealing who was waiting on the other side.

"'Bout time your pretty ass showed—" Duane's reprimanding skidded to a stop at the sight of who was with me.

My roommate stood before us, hand on the knob, taken aback at my arrival with *guests*. Duane took in Cain and Beans, blinking in sheer confusion, before settling his attention on me.

"Where have you been?" he demanded to know as he pulled me into his arms. "Jenesis's ass out here acting clueless. Nobody at the club don' seen you. I went by the police station on Tuesday and they wasn't hearing me."

My heart softened at the thought of him so worried he'd gone to file a missing person's report.

Heat burned my back and I could *feel* Cain's gaze on me and where I was embracing Duane back.

Duane was tall. He had no trouble seeing eye-to-eye with either Cain or Beans as we separated and he set his focus on the two strangers in the doorway. While he was all things a sweetheart, Duane had no problem taking up for me when he felt I needed it.

There was no denying his slim build among Beans's larger body, and Cain's heavy presence. But Duane showed no fear as he folded his arms and stood erect, staring them both down.

"What's going on?" he demanded to know.

Cain measured the way we were standing, the closeness, and then he studied Duane. Curious. "Eden needed to come get a few things."

Duane arched a brow, coming back to me. "For what?"

I couldn't look at him, or else I'd tell him everything and he wouldn't let me go.

"Doll." Concern filled Duane's voice as he spoke to me, trying to get me to look his way.

"I-I'm going to be staying with Cain for a while," I spoke up, finding some strength to face Duane.

He wasn't buying it. "Uh-uh."

"She wasn't asking." Cain stepped in. He lifted his arm and peered at the watch on his wrist. "And time's a factor."

Duane snorted and whirled around, sizing Cain up. "I don't give a damn what time it is. Who the hell are you, and what the hell is going on?"

Cain blinked, and even if I barely knew him, I could tell he was practicing patience he didn't have. Something about him, right away, told me no one stood up to him. Told him no. Defied him.

Duane was just looking out for me, but he had no idea what he was up against.

I tugged on his T-shirt. "He's just someone I met at the gala I worked. We kinda hit it off."

There was no passion or joy in my voice. I couldn't even convince *myself* I was willingly with Cain.

Duane held up four fingers in my face. "Four days. You've been gone for *four* whole days. I've been calling you, texting you, and you never picked up. Now, I'm supposed to believe you just met someone all willy-nilly and stayed out without letting me know?"

It wasn't like me to stay out all night, or be gone for days on end. Beyond the fact I had nowhere else to go or be, it wasn't my style to worry Duane.

"I'm sorry," I said softly.

"Eden." The warning in Cain's tone was new. I felt it in my bones. I saw it in his eyes. Annoyance. Impatience. And something I couldn't place.

I was loyal to Duane, but it was easier to appease Cain. Without another word, I grabbed Cain's hand and led him through our tiny living room and over to my bedroom where I walked us in and shut the door behind us. Instead of begging Duane to let me go, I should've been pleading with Cain to let me stay.

Turning from shutting the door, I jumped back, suddenly all too aware of Cain looming close behind me.

He was glaring at me. "You made the right choice."

I hadn't done it for him, and I wasted no time making that clear. "My loyalty is to Duane, and I don't want him getting hurt over me."

Cain scowled. "You said you didn't have a man waiting for you at home."

He thought I lied to him. A part of me wanted to come clean, but then, being home made me a little more brave. "Would you have fucked me if I said yes?"

Something dark passed through his eyes as he took a step closer, something like...*hunger*, causing me to back up into my door. "You lied."

I shook my head. "He's my roommate, and I'm not his type like that."

It took a second for my words to register, for Cain to understand the meaning of my platonic relationship with Duane. Once he did, he relaxed only a little. "I don't like surprises."

"Well, I have a roommate. Surprise," I threw out with a lazy *tada* motion.

Cain snorted, taking a step back and soon eyeing the four

walls of my bedroom. It was just as I'd left it. Unmade bed with the blinds up in the window beside it. My sleep shorts on the floor and my night shirt on my bed. He took a step around, quietly admiring my quiet corner where my vanity was set up. Makeup was neatly organized on the desktop, and otherwise stored in the shelving beneath it.

He took in my large movie poster of *Sabrina*, a cinematic shot of Humphrey Bogart caressing Audrey Hepburn's face, on the wall by my closet. His attention didn't linger here for long before he set eyes on what was the true prize piece of my bedroom: my wall of floor-to-ceiling bookcases that Duane had built for me and painted white. I hadn't yet filled all four cases, but it wasn't for a lack of trying.

Cain stared at the colorful arrangement of my books, a vibrant wave of reds, blues, purples, yellows, and whites. Intrigue captured Cain's face as he buried his hands into his pockets and finally regarded me. "What do you read?"

"Romance." I wasn't ashamed.

A ghost of a smile had the corner of Cain's mouth curling as he slowly ran his gaze from my feet to my head, staring intently as if he could see right through me. "Of course."

There it was. Amusement. I should've been annoyed with myself at the realization I could *feed* on it.

I snapped out of it, needing to get him to let me go. "So, this is me."

Cain nodded, taking another look around. "So it is."

"I just thought if I took you here, showed you my home, you'd let me go. I have a life here. It's not significant or anything, it might even bore you, but it's mine." Outside of my role as Sabrina at Crazy Legs, I wasn't an interesting person by any means. I was all things boring as far as Jenesis was concerned. I liked the simplicity of my life: books and movies, quiet nights *in* rather than *out*.

Cain regarded me for all of a minute before he seemed to make up his mind about something. "Pack whatever you need."

He wasn't letting me go.

I wasn't above begging, but I could tell it would do no good. I went over to my vanity and pulled open my top drawer where I kept my eyelashes, and was quick to take five packs out to add to my makeup kit.

Cain watched with interest as I finished collecting extra items to take with me.

"Priorities, huh?" He seemed to tease as he smiled a little.

I turned, batting my faux Minks at him. "A girl is simply naked without her lashes."

Cain stared at me and said nothing. For a moment, we weren't in this ugly situation. I wasn't a woman he'd taken in against her will, and he wasn't some cold-hearted criminal. We were back at the buffet table at the gala. And he was so handsome, I couldn't breathe under his scrutiny. It was easy to see Cain's appeal just then. The air of mystery around him, his good looks, and then the way he looked at you.

I broke away first, caught up catching movement by the window.

"American Joe!" I squealed as I rushed up to greet my furry friend I hadn't seen in what felt like forever.

"*American Joe?*" Cain repeated in confusion from behind me.

I went and opened the window, feeling my soul lift at the arrival of American Joe. My face split into the biggest smile when he let me pet him and even pick him up.

"I think he's an American Curl, so I just call him American Joe," I explained to Cain. Rubbing behind Joe's ears, I couldn't help but laugh. "I almost named him Cat."

"*Cat?*" Cain didn't get it.

I scoffed. "From *Breakfast at Tiffany's*. Audrey Hepburn's iconic character Holly doesn't believe people belong to anyone, but only themselves. So, she doesn't name her cat, she just calls him Cat."

Most people thought I was strange when it came to my love of classic romance movies. No one ever got my references. Except

Duane, who wouldn't mind watching something with me if I were out on the couch in the living room.

Cain didn't look at me as if I were weird, but like I was some phenomenon he couldn't figure out—in a good way.

I focused back on Joe, feeling a sudden tightness in my chest as I set him down and grabbed his food bowl. He didn't belong to me, true, but I liked to think we were friends. That we'd formed a bond beyond his coming to get free food.

"Can't I just come to you whenever you want me?" I begged as I faced Cain. I gestured at Joe who was heartily eating his Fancy Feast out on the fire escape. "He's a stray, like me, and I feed him because nobody else does. If I'm not here tomorrow who's going to make sure he eats? He's never going to know what happened to me. Don't do this. Please."

Cain's brows furrowed. He took in American Joe and came back to me. "Take him with you."

My mouth fell open, but there was nothing to say. I didn't expect Cain to offer to let me bring Joe with me. Beyond the fact that I didn't own any cat accessories or supplies outside of the food dish, maybe I was just like Holly Golightly's character in that I didn't want to *own* Joe and disrupt his independence.

"No, I can't just uproot him." I shook my head.

Cain took a step closer, appearing serious as he took in my emotional state beginning to rise. "Take him with you."

"I'll feed him."

At the door, Duane had stepped in. His contempt for what was going on hadn't lessened as he glowered at Cain.

"Let me talk to my friend." Duane wasn't asking. And shockingly enough, Cain was nice enough to oblige him and step out.

Duane shut the door and folded his arms. "What the hell is going on? And don't lie to me, Doll."

The door was shut, and Cain was still in the apartment. It wasn't much, but it was some form of privacy.

I could've lied, downplayed the messy situation I was in, but this was Duane. "I'm in a little trouble."

"Obviously," Duane responded. He tossed a thumb over his shoulder. "Either he has a gun in his pocket, or he's happy to see me. My guess? That man's never been happy a day in his life."

The circumstances at hand were petrifying, but Duane's humor couldn't have come through at a better time as I was able to finally have a laugh. Cain *didn't* come off friendly, despite his allure. None of his men did.

"It's complicated, but I'll be okay." At least, I hoped I would be.

Duane narrowed his eyes. "Uh-uh, let's go out the window."

Going down the fire escape would be the perfect getaway, but...

"We can't," I said.

Aggravated, Duane asked, "Why not?"

"He's got a second bodyguard, and he's down there." We were, unfortunately, surrounded.

Duane lulled his head back and sighed. "What have you gotten yourself into?"

I don't know.

"I'll be okay." I would've promised, but I didn't want to lie in case...

Duane wasn't convinced, but spared me his disapproval. "At least tell me, do you think the big one is *out*?"

My forehead adopted a crease as confusion set in. "Beans? You think he's...?"

My roommate deadpanned. "Duh."

"What makes you think so?"

"He hasn't set eyes on you since you walked through the door."

I didn't get it. "So?"

"Honey, everyone looks at you. The evil-looking one hasn't stopped looking at you. Even *I* look at you." Duane turned and eyed the door, imagining the two men in our home. "It's all a wonder if this shit is as shady as it sounds."

I backhanded his arm. "Don't be ignorant." Still, Duane *did* have a good tell with people.

Beans was a handsome man. Tall, smooth and pretty brown skin, thick build, and quiet demeanor. Of the three, admittedly, he was the least intimidating.

Not that I wanted Duane with a man who aided in my kidnapping, even if I couldn't tell him.

Duane let it go. "Are you okay? Really? You looked...*terrified* when I opened the door. Something about this man doesn't feel right."

"I was just nervous because I'd been out for days, D," I said with a lame shrug. "Cain may come off scary, but he's not a bad guy." *Lie.* "I'll be back before you know it."

The longer Duane stared at me, the more it felt like the truth was written on my skin. As if he could read through my fibs.

He didn't call me out. He promised to feed Joe and look after him, even let him inside for good while I was gone. And then he helped me pack my belongings.

Out in the living room, I found Beans still standing on guard by the door while Cain had helped himself to sit down on our sofa. He was on his phone, but immediately stopped once he saw me with my things.

Once more Duane was glaring at him as he stood and came over to us.

I handed over one of my bags, and thinking it was filled with clothes, I watched as Cain instantly leaned down at the surprise of the weight.

"It's my favorite books and movies," I said of the bag he was now holding with more support. I never went anywhere without a book on my person, and not knowing how long I'd be with Cain, I'd decided to pack a few to keep me company.

"I have streaming," Cain said.

"Not all my favorite movies are available."

Cain was getting his way while I got no say in anything. Squaring my shoulders, I stood firm and lifted my chin in his direction, holding his gaze. "I don't know how long we'll be together, and it's not fair to stick Duane with *all* of the rent and utilities. Pay him for the inconvenience."

It was a bold move on my part, but I made no apology as I continued peering into Cain's eyes.

He raised a brow, visibly impressed. He turned toward Beans and nodded.

In another second, Beans dug into his suit and pulled out a stack of bills. Duane blinked as the man walked up to him and lazily leafed through the thick pile of hundreds and passed over what was *more* than my half of everything.

Duane gazed down at the money as Beans set it in his palm. He eyed Cain, letting out a breath through his nostrils as a muscle in his jaw tensed. "Hurt her, and I'll come find you."

Cain wasn't a man who was threatened often. This I could tell as Beans sized Duane up, seemingly waiting on word to strike.

Cain gave no order. He simply tilted his head in Duane's direction. "Noted."

Duane pulled me into a long hug before grabbing my bags and following us down to the first floor. Vino was leaning against the Range Rover when we came out. He stood at once, curiously taking in the scene.

"Everything copasetic?" he asked, his eyes on Duane.

"Everything is everything," Cain said as he went and began stowing my belongings in the trunk.

I hugged Duane long and hard, burying my face in his chest. This wasn't supposed to be goodbye, but it felt like it.

"Call me as soon as you get settled," he demanded as he smoothed back strands of my hair from my face.

Despite the fact that I didn't have possession of my own phone, I agreed.

Duane knew me well, but I liked to think I held it together as we said our *see you laters* before I climbed back into the truck. I liked to think he couldn't see that I was breaking inside and unsure of what was about to happen to me. I liked to think he could at least remember the last time he saw me with a sense of comfort that I was strong.

Vino was back behind the wheel and taking off for the highway. My spirit dropped as I sank in my seat beside Cain. It wasn't just the fact that I was leaving my home and going back to Hampton Hills, no, it was where we were and the street Vino was taking.

Bedford Heights was somewhat of a large city, but not large enough.

No matter how high I held my head and knew I deserved better, no matter the time of day, every time I was on Singleton Avenue and passed that familiar one-story beige stucco-textured house, I always looked. Always checked to see if that old 2010 Honda Accord was still parked in the driveway. Always made sure my mother hadn't left without a word.

Starvation clung to my insides as melancholy claimed my heart.

The Accord was still there.

Cain pressed a button between us and the sound of sliding drew my attention over. In front of us, a glass partition wall was going up, blocking out Vino and Beans as a black curtain closed next.

Cain sat up and I went on alert. He dug into his jacket and pulled out a chrome pen. Twisting it, he removed the end and revealed a sharp knife.

Uneasiness took over me as I squirmed in my seat.

Cain held out the secret knife between us. "Take it."

I looked from the weapon to his dark eyes, finding them empty of a tell. "W-What?"

"You seem to think you're in danger, and perhaps you'll find comfort if you had a weapon. If you knew you could defend yourself should I attack you."

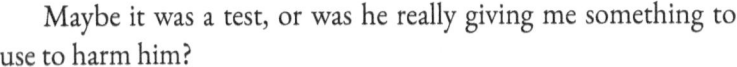

Maybe it was a test, or was he really giving me something to use to harm him?

I could take it and slit his throat, ending this whole thing.

But even the thought made bile rise to my throat. I shook my head. Weak. "I don't want to hurt you."

Cain's other hand was on his lap, his finger began tapping his thigh. "I need you to understand the feeling is mutual."

He wanted me to trust him. Trust that he wouldn't kill me. Naïve or not, I felt a fraction of my walls come down. He wasn't the first man I'd been with, but he was the first to be gentle. To not grab me hard and take it rough. He had the softest hands I'd ever felt, and the heaviest demeanor I'd ever experienced.

I didn't know what to think or feel, but I decided to believe that I wouldn't die.

"You say you won't force me to sleep with you, but you're twisting my arm and making me stay with you," I pointed out.

"I'm not a good person, Eden, make no mistake, but I won't hurt you," Cain swore as he held my gaze. "Take the pen if you want to feel safe."

Safe. I almost laughed bitterly at the thought. I hadn't felt safe my whole life.

Tears threatened to pool in my eyes and I forced my interest out the window.

The pen went away when I didn't take it.

We got onto the highway and I watched the distance between home and Hampton Hills grow.

"I have a proposition for you," Cain began after a while.

A proposition. He already had me. What more could he want?

"Yeah?" I spoke up quietly.

"Since you're going to be with me for the time, we can make the most of it. I'm a busy man, and have to make appearances. That's where you come in. It's good to have a date on your arm, makes people warm up to you. While you're in my care, I'd like for you to accompany me to whatever event I'm requested to attend."

It wasn't as heinous as I'd feared. It was light. Almost innocent. Be his arm candy?

"And if I say no?" I dared to ask.

Cain shrugged. "Then you can stay in while I go out."

He wasn't forcing the issue.

"What would I even wear?" I wondered, thinking of all the women in their designer gowns at the gala last weekend.

"I'd take you shopping," Cain said simply.

Shopping? The idea intrigued me, but didn't add up. "Wouldn't that be counterproductive, considering...?"

"I mostly get invited to dinners and parties, nothing too rigorous," Cain said without missing a beat.

"Still, I'd have to dress up in fancy dresses, right?"

Cain nodded.

I thought about it. "I've never owned a fancy dress before." I'd never had "nice" things growing up. My most prized possession had always been my library card.

Cain studied me, in that long way he often did. "Never?"

I shook my head. "No."

"Then say yes and you can have as many dresses as you like," Cain offered. "Shoes, purses, whatever you need to look the part."

My lips threatened to smile at the idea. "And I get to keep it when you let me go?"

Cain snorted, a corner of his mouth curling. "I don't think we're the same size, so of course."

It all sounded too good to be true.

"What's the catch?" I waited for him to inevitably demand more sex.

Cain frowned. "You'll be doing me a solid. My partner wants me at this art thing on Saturday and insists I bring someone."

He could've brought anyone, why me? "I'm sure you wouldn't be hard up for a date."

Cain didn't deny this. "I'm a one-woman man and I'm satisfied with what I have."

I hated that I felt special then. Special and *confused*.

"Maybe...this'll be our way to even our score?" I suggested. "And we can forget the rest?"

"I'm going to fuck you three more times," Cain said matter-of-factly. He lowered his attention to my body, lingering. "I haven't even gotten to taste you yet."

The want in his voice caused me to sit up and ease out a breath. The mere idea of his handsome face between my legs had me squeezing my thighs together as my sex throbbed in need.

Cain wanted to *taste* me, the same way I had wanted to back at the hotel.

Without even hesitating, I reached over the middle console and went for his belt. Cain watched me attempt to unbuckle him with curiosity.

"This won't count," I let him know, assuring him his *three* had nothing to do with this.

His hands seized my wrists, stopping me. "As nice as that sounds, if you're giving anything away for free, I want *all* of it."

Of course he wanted more.

"Tell me you like it, and I will," I demanded.

Cain narrowed his eyes. "I *own* it."

I matched his stare. "Ha."

A challenge lit his eyes and he didn't back down. Continuing to look at each other, I undid his belt and he let me.

He was heavy in my hands and already erect. Putting up a front or not, Cain was turned on and couldn't deny it. I felt a slickness between my legs as I got up on my knees in my seat and leaned over. I *wanted* him too.

I took him into my mouth and peered up at him beneath my lashes. Cain blew out a breath and sank into his seat. His face contorted in sweet agony as I took him in deeper, squeezing and running my hand down his length. He watched me watch him as my head bobbed up and down until he could take no more and leaned back, groaning at the sensation.

"Fuck," he let out. His hand seized my ponytail and tugged it into a vise grip that made me wetter. "Can I come in your mouth?"

"Mmm." I hummed as I wrapped my lips around the tip and sucked hard and long.

That was all it took to send Cain erupting and spilling down my throat. He buckled beneath me, issuing out more swears as his orgasm took ahold of him.

I settled down into my seat and wiped my mouth, not even hiding my smirk for the rest of the trip.

Back in Hampton Hills, Vino pulled into a parking structure attached to a sleek high-rise that seemed to stretch out of the universe. At the entrance of the parking deck, he swiped his card near a sensor that let us in and he pulled in and drove on to a second level of the three-story unit. He parked near a fleet of luxury vehicles and turned off the truck.

We were here.

Vino and Beans didn't join us as Cain helped me collect my bags and began leading the way toward an elevator. They took off for their own cars, determined to leave us be.

Cain paid this no mind as we boarded an elevator and rode it to the lobby of the apartment building. There, once greeted by the concierge at the front desk, we swapped elevators and soon were soaring toward the top floor. Penthouses and privacy were Cain's domain. I should've known he wouldn't have settled for anything less.

After getting off the elevator, Cain led us up to his door and unlocked it. He pushed it open and showed a hand inside. "After you."

I took a step in and was immediately immersed in Cain's world. Tilting my head back, I was in awe from the entryway alone.

His home was gorgeous. Clean, black wooden floors shined

brightly at our feet, while matte black walls were the interior around us. Black on black, we were cloaked in darkness.

Cain came in behind me and shut the door. He set my bags down by a set of black lacquer stairs that led to a second floor. "Come on, I'll give you a tour of the first floor."

I was too caught up in wonder to be nervous at the idea of being alone with him. I trailed behind Cain, taking it all in. There was a private theater room with large recliners that made the idea of falling asleep during a good film too inviting. He had his own home office where the entire aesthetic was black and gray. I tried to picture Cain behind the executive desk making calls and decisions, and the whole thing seemed so clean-cut for him.

What really captured my heart was his kitchen. It was across from the open space that was his dining room and living room. An area that faced two walls of nothing but windows with a marvelous view of Hampton Hills. I loved cooking and I envied Cain right then for having such a lovely setup. My kitchen back home with Duane wasn't as small or bad as the one I'd grown up in, but Cain's put ours to shame effortlessly.

"This kitchen is immaculate," I said, knowing the word didn't do it justice.

Cain shrugged, facing me with a helpless frown. "I can't cook, but she's a beauty."

He didn't even cook in this wonderland? I shook my head, thinking, *what a waste.* I didn't really have any friends or family, but the sight of the large expansive marble island made me wish I did. So I could cook for them.

In the corner of the living room was a beautiful black grand piano.

"You play?" I asked as I faced Cain.

He eyed the piano. "Sometimes."

I didn't have any talent like that. I thought it was nice that he did. Playing instruments was something I'd always admired in others.

We went up to the next floor where Cain showed me into a

large bedroom with only one wall and the rest windows, giving the room an even better view of the city below. Cain set my bags on the floor by the king-sized bed. By the lack of décor, I knew this was a guest room. Not a speck of dust was in sight as I gazed around the surfaces, letting me know Cain was either extremely neat or had a cleaning person.

"This is where you'll sleep," Cain instructed.

We weren't going to share a bed. I wasn't sure why this took me by surprise, but I liked the idea of having some space. Of him not expecting me to sleep with him.

While the penthouse was set in a black and gray theme, the guest room was a subtle gold and white. I would have my own bathroom whose tub was too inviting to soak in.

I abandoned my things and followed Cain down the hall to another bedroom, one that was a whole apartment on its own. In his bedroom he had a private balcony. I was tempted to go out, but stayed by Cain's side.

Much like the theme of his home, the room was shrouded in black and gray. A step into the closet had my jaw dropping. It was like walking into a department store. All around me hung up, were suits, dress shirts, ties, as well as shoes stocked on shelves, and a smell that could only belong to Cain. Decadent. Smooth. Masculine. A spicy blend of nutmeg and cedar.

This was only one *room* of his closet; in the next room, the other was obviously for *her*. That side was empty.

Back in his bedroom, I helped myself to sit on his bed, at once moaning at the softness beneath me. "What if I don't want to sleep with you for a month?"

Cain smiled, staring down at me while I lay back on my arms. "Then I hope you get comfortable. Although, I don't think either of us can go that long."

Arching a brow, I couldn't help but snort. "Think so?"

Cain nodded without missing a beat. "I haven't been able to concentrate knowing how naked you are under that shirt."

He'd noticed.

"Just because *you* have no self-control, doesn't mean I don't," I said with a faux sense of confidence like I hadn't just given him head on the ride over here.

Cain wasn't buying my act at all. "I seem to remember how much *you* enjoyed our night as much as I did. How hard you came like I did. How much I'm willing to bet you want it again like I do."

I pretended to scoff at the accusation. "I'm an entertainer; I know how to fake it."

Calling my bluff, Cain lazily stared me down. "I wouldn't even need five full minutes with my head between your thighs to have you dripping all over my bed."

I said nothing. Because oral always made me want sex too. And knowing how good Cain's sex was, I'd probably do something embarrassing like *beg* for it.

I lay back and stared at the ceiling instead. "Whatever."

Soon, Cain was in my line of vision, peering down at me. "I really only have two rules: always come back, and don't tell anyone my business."

I sat up at the mention of the first rule. "I can *leave*?"

"With Beans or me as a chaperone," Cain corrected. "You can go wherever you want to shop or explore. Beans will have my credit card. Just come back."

Freedom. Somewhat.

Chewing on my lip, I pushed to see how far he'd go. "What if I bought a car?"

Cain wasn't fazed as he lifted and dropped his shoulder. "Just don't let them swindle you."

Shit.

"You know," I started, feeling overwhelmed suddenly. "I'm beginning to think my sex is worth more than a million bucks with how much you're willing to do for me."

A smirk crossed Cain's face as he angled his head and took a step closer. "Not true." He reached out and cupped my cheek, lifting my head to peer up at him. "You have a million-dollar-throat, too." He ran his thumb across my bottom lip, admiring my face momentarily, before he backed off.

"And I just have to sleep with you three more times?" I made sure to clarify.

Cain angled his head. "Thought we agreed to a freebie in the car?"

We hadn't, but since he was being generous. "*Four* more times and that's it?"

"Four more times and we're even. Unless you want to give it to me more, in which case, I won't fight you."

This setup was too good to believe. I was getting more out of this than he was, but I wasn't about to argue.

"Okay, okay," I huffed as I held up a hand. "Just don't fall in love with me. God only knows what stops you'd take to keep me then."

Cain rolled his eyes, releasing a quiet snort. "I won't." He reached up and loosened his tie. "I'm going to order something for dinner. What are you in the mood for?"

"Doesn't matter," I said.

Cain took off for the balcony and slipped outside, leaving me to fall back into the softness of his black comforter. Unable to resist, I made a snow angel in the bedding, grinning like a fool. This was beyond anything I'd ever experienced.

A girl could get used to this.

8

Eden

IT WAS LIKE WAKING UP IN A FAIRY TALE. THERE WAS no other way to describe the current state of my life. The one where I was living in a gorgeous penthouse with the promise of anything I wanted at my fingertips. Never in my wildest dreams had I anticipated *this* being the outcome of going to model at that Monte Carlo night.

Sunlight poured into the room and bathed me with a new day. The blinds were up, giving me a sight full of Hampton Hills as I rolled over and peered out the window. It was breathtaking, this view.

Nothing could beat the clear blue sky and the pristine horizons before me.

Firm knocks beat on my bedroom door. *Cain.*

I sat up and adjusted my scarf. "Yes?"

The door opened and there was Cain, dressed in a black three-piece suit with a briefcase in one hand. He opened his mouth to speak, but then he simply stared at me. The longer he looked, the more nervous I became.

"What?" I let out a nervous laugh.

Cain shook his head. "You're pretty in the morning."

I covered my face with one hand and waved him off. "No."

"You are," he said. He took in the setting, me in bed, and an abandoned book by the edge. "Sleep good?"

Did I? This bed was even better than the hotel's. The other half really knew how to live. "God, yes." I groaned and lay back down, extending my limbs and burrowing into the sheets. "This is the best bed I've ever slept on."

"Well, you can get up whenever you want," Cain said, admiring me where I was getting cozy. "I have meetings all day, so I'll be back later. Beans will be with you. Whatever you want or need, don't hesitate to let it be known. He's at your disposal."

Cain did something I didn't see coming. He reached into his jacket and pulled out my phone. He held it up, waving it. "Don't give out your location. If you're still here by the end of next week, we can talk about Duane coming to visit."

I didn't know what to say as he came and handed me my phone back. It was fully charged and waiting for me as I pressed the Home button.

The previous evening, I'd gotten dressed and joined Cain down in his kitchen as we ate takeout from Freddy's Fried Chicken, something that made me smile and appreciate Cain for being down-to-earth to not always splurge on fancy meals. We'd eaten and he'd given me space to do what I wanted afterwards. I hadn't been able to call Duane like I'd said. Now, I had a link to the outside world.

Squeezing my phone in my hand, I nodded and looked up at Cain's waiting face. "Thank you."

Cain bobbed his head. "Enjoy your day."

"You too," I mumbled as he walked away.

The house was so quiet, and there were no telltale signs of him walking down to the first floor. He could've been lingering out in the hall, testing me to see what I'd do with my phone back.

No matter, I unlocked it and immediately texted Duane, needing to talk to him.

ME

You home?

Not even a full minute went by before my phone began ringing with an incoming FaceTime call.

I sat up and answered, eager to see my friend. "Hey."

On the other end, Duane was home, sitting back on our sofa in an old Whitney Houston T-shirt. He looked as fresh as Cain had, meaning he'd been up for a while.

"Wait a minute," he responded, sitting up and leaning more into the camera. "Let me see where you at."

I held my phone up and showed him a better view of my bed. More, I stood up and flipped the camera around to give him a proper tour of my room.

I padded over to the bathroom to end it so I could wash my face and freshen up.

"Low key, it's giving very much kept woman," Duane remarked as I set the phone against the mirror so I could clean my face.

"Tell me about it. This is way too good to be true," I said.

Duane was quiet as I brushed my teeth and washed my face, choosing to resume the conversation as soon as I was done and back in my bedroom. "You didn't call last night and I was worried."

"Sorry," I said. "There was just a *lot* to unpack, literally and figuratively."

"You okay?" Duane asked gently. "I mean, I still don't understand how this all transpired."

"I'm okay," I said as I sat down cross-legged on my bed. "It's just a lot to take in. I got myself in a jam, and one thing led to another, and I hooked up with Cain to get out of it."

"Doll." Duane gasped.

There was no judgment between us. Ever. Duane was just taken aback as I confessed my troubles.

"Now we have a deal where I'm going to be his arm candy for a while," I explained.

"Don't blame 'im, you *are* candy," Duane teased. It was the reason he called me *Doll*, saying I was too pretty to be real. He sat back on the sofa and reflected on my words, shaking his head at my predicament. "How is he? Really."

Duane knew me better than anyone. I was a homeless runaway when we'd met. I had just been starting out at Crazy Legs, paying daily fees to stay at the local motel because my last boyfriend stopped telling me he was sorry when he hit me. I was hungry and tired and stopped to try something to eat at the bistro where Duane worked. Naturally, he was my server, and he took one look at me and just saw me.

He'd gone on break and joined me at my table and we talked about music, which he was obsessed with, all the R&B and pop divas, not to mention the soulful men of '80s and '90s.

Duane was a different type of person. He was kind, understanding, and easy to trust. It didn't take him long to get my story out of me about my terrible ex and the motel. When Duane offered to let me crash in his spare bedroom, I'd turned him down.

After Duane's shift, we'd walked to his apartment and he told me about himself. About how he knew what it was like to be hurt by the ones you trusted. About how *his* ex was also abusive. Duane's ex-boyfriend hadn't been as comfortable as Duane was in his skin, and as a result he took it out on Duane.

Growing up, all I'd known was ugly and disappointment, but there that day with Duane, was the start of something new. I didn't have the best track record with people, but something in my gut told me he was okay.

I didn't have anyone I could count on like Duane, and for that, I never lied to him. In some ways, we were a lot alike. He wanted to be loved as much as I did. And we didn't shame each other for that.

"Cain is different," I said as I got back to our conversation. "He's not like any man I've ever met."

Everything about him was scary, but then he had a softness to him, too.

"Be careful," Duane warned. "I don't want you getting hurt."

That was the thing, despite the circumstances, I *knew* Cain wouldn't hurt me. I couldn't explain it, but there was just something about him that let me know he'd never lay a hand on me. That he wouldn't even allow his men to do it.

"He won't," I said. "He's not like that."

Duane wasn't convinced, but he didn't push the narrative. "You're more than my friend, you know."

My heart warmed and I smiled. Duane taught me one thing: sometimes, you got to make your own family. We'd both been lonely and bruised, and finding each other that day at the bistro was kismet. Even if I had no one else, I knew I had Duane and vice versa.

"Thank you," I said. "You be safe, too. And make sure American Joe is comfortable."

Duane huffed, soon flipping the camera around to reveal where American Joe was sitting like a loaf on the floor by the TV stand. "He is living the dream, just like his momma."

If this was a dream, I wasn't sure I wanted to wake up yet. "Don't be jealous."

Duane came back to the camera and sized me up, making a face. "And the sex is good?"

The sex. The thought of it brought me back to the suite.

"Look at me," Cain had said from the moment he was inside me. *"Can you handle it?"*

It had been the most intense sex I'd ever had. What really made it overwhelming was Cain being there with me, cradling me against his body as his drove mine over the edge. I wasn't an object he was getting off on, but an equal he *wanted* to please back.

"Yes," I admitted with a vigorous nod of my head. "Too good."

Duane cackled over on his end. "Well, you enjoy it. He got

you swept off your feet. You better milk that situation for what it's worth. You in the big leagues now, Doll."

The woman from the gala came to mind, her and all her coveting and saying how Cain was the most sought-after bachelor in Hampton Hills.

If they only knew.

My stomach grumbled and I realized I was hungry. "I gotta get something to eat. I'll call you back later."

"You better," Duane ordered with a playful mean mug.

We hung up and I went and used the bathroom before taking the steps down to the first floor.

I shouldn't have been surprised to find Beans down in the kitchen. He was watching something on the TV in the living room. A tumbler of coffee was at his side.

"Morning," I said brightly as I padded into the room.

He tipped his head and kept on watching TV.

It seemed that we were going to be together for a while, and I decided to make the most of it as I went over to the island and sat a stool down from him.

I took in his ill-fitting suit, a size too big, but just as pricy as Cain's no less. Beans was groomed and very put together despite his clothing. His bored eyes watched some sports news on the TV and he barely acknowledged me.

"So, you're my bodyguard, huh?" I asked.

"Babysitter," he seemed to correct.

Honestly, I couldn't blame him; it felt that way. "Do you have anyone special waiting for you at home? I won't tell if you leave."

Beans slowly turned and faced me, his face a blank mask. "No, on all fronts."

"So you're single?"

He kept on staring at me.

"What do you do when you're not with Cain?" I wondered next since he wasn't about to talk about his love life.

Beans narrowed his eyes. "Dig very deep holes."

He was trying to scare me. And maybe if this was the first day, I would've been.

"Ah, it's always good to have a hobby," I quipped. My belly rumbled again and I noticed Beans didn't have any food either, just his coffee.

Duane's words came back to me. I knew I wasn't in any danger, and I should've enjoyed the moment for what it was. For the first time ever, I kinda got to just *exist*. There were no worries over bills or going in to Crazy Legs. I had freedom to do as I pleased.

"So," I started as I got up from the stool. "I have an idea."

Beans raised a brow, saying nothing.

I met his stoic expression with a bubbly smile. My babysitter and I were going on an adventure.

9

Cain

I LOVED IT WHEN THINGS WERE IN MY FAVOR. WHILE I didn't want to go to the art gala Saturday night, I was relieved to at least hear through the grapevine that Sinclair wasn't in the city. That a blog had caught him out in Miami on a yacht with some flavor of the week.

The less I had to deal with my cousin, the better.

It was well into the evening when Vino and I returned home to my place.

In the parking deck, Vino got out of the car and instead of heading to his Camaro, he seemed intent on coming inside with me.

"Need something?" A part of me wanted to stay out as long as possible, to have time to think about whatever the fuck I was doing with Eden.

Vino didn't bother hiding his smile as he walked with pep in his step as we made it inside and walked over to the elevator that would take us to my penthouse. "Five stacks Beans finished her off."

I sighed, shaking my head as he pressed the call button for my place. "There's a reason why I chose Beans."

Vino boldly snorted. "You be thinkin' Beanie Baby the 'nice' one. He don't even think you should let this one live when you're done doin' whatever it is that you're doin'."

I couldn't exactly fault Beans for thinking rationally about the bigger picture. But of the three of us, I trusted Beans to be the most responsible, the most levelheaded, the most *sane*.

We stepped off the lift and went over to my front door. Before I procured my key to unlock it, I reached into my jacket and grabbed my dice and gathered them into my palm. Unlike my profession, I wasn't a gambling man, but once in a while, I liked to humor my crew.

"Fifty thousand they're in there doing just fine," I challenged.

For a moment, Vino considered the wager, but then he shook his head, wagging his finger at me. "Them joints is loaded, and you know it."

I laughed as I dug my keys out next and stuck them in the door. My dice weren't loaded, I just had an unbeatable lucky streak with them.

The first thing that hit me as I opened the door was the fresh scent of Italian herbs and spices and cheese. The smell traveled all the way from the kitchen to the front entryway, making me realize how starved I was.

Vino whistled. "Yes, they ordered somethin' good."

Music was playing and I could hear the sound of *her* laughter.

I set my briefcase down by the door as I shut it behind us. Vino was already on his way to the kitchen as he rubbed his palms together.

Briefly, I wondered if they'd ordered a pizza, but then I had my answer as I stepped into the kitchen and spotted pots and pans lining my stove and Beans sitting at the island eating. Vino was at the other end looking for a plate while Eden was behind it smiling about something as she spoke to Beans. The TV was on in the living room, some live performance they'd pulled up with an old '90s rapper.

Heat radiated in the room, evidence from the recent use of the oven. My eyes went from the pots and pans to the way Eden was guiding Vino on what was what. The way she was dancing to the music, making Vino smile.

"Beans." I spoke up, an edge in my voice I couldn't contain.

Immediately he stood, on alert as he turned and faced me.

"Look who's home," Eden said with a friendly smile.

I ignored her and focused on Beans. "My office. Now."

I didn't wait for him to follow as I took off back down the hall toward my private home office. When I'd moved to Hampton Hills, I'd wanted this space for my weekly conference calls with my staff back in Vegas, but these days, I worked in the provided office space Damon and Phil had given me at their Nichols & Wagner building.

Beans's heavy footsteps sounded into the room just as I shrugged off my jacket and took my place at my desk.

"You wanted to see me," he said, not at all intimidated.

I pinched the bridge of my nose. "Mind telling me what the fuck you're doing out there?"

Beans turned, peering out the room, imagining the scene we'd just left. "She made some lasagna."

My finger began tapping my desktop, an uncontrollable tick of mine. "And you're *eating* it?"

Beans shrugged, not getting it. "Yeah."

Blinking, I tried to rein it in. "Have you forgotten why she's here?"

Beans began to think about it, but it wasn't quick enough.

"She's not here by choice," I snapped. "What reason do you have to just trust anything she cooks? That she wouldn't try to poison you?"

At first, Beans squinted, not getting what I'd said. And then he did, and he laughed.

"I know we come from fucked-up places and situations, but you're overthinking," Beans responded. He thumbed a finger over his shoulder. "That girl wouldn't hurt a fly."

It was something I suspected the moment I first looked into

her eyes. But I wasn't that thoughtless. "Maybe that's what she wants you to think."

Beans made a face. "First of all, I was with her *all* day. I took her to the supermarket, I watched her pick out all the ingredients, and then I watched her come here and put everything together. If she was trying to kill us, she never would've gotten a chance." Once more he gestured out of the room. "She ate *with* me for fuck's sake."

I massaged my temple, trying to calm down. Instinct told me Eden wasn't able to harm anyone—she wouldn't even take protection from me when I'd offered it, but I didn't want to let my guard down. "And you watched every step?"

Beans scowled. "I'm not new to this, Dice. Shit, the girl made lasagna—no one makes that. They always complain it's too much work."

I wouldn't know. I'd only ever had lasagna from a frozen box when I was in the system, and a few times at a restaurant here and there since.

"She's not like that," Beans reiterated. "When she said she wanted to go out, I thought for sure she was going to run up a tab, but nah..." He shook his head, frowning a little. "She just wanted to get food to make us lunch, and then dinner." Something suddenly made him chuckle to himself, a memory of their trip. "She literally spent, like, ten minutes in the book aisle at the store browsing books."

That was the one thing that stood out about her bedroom at her apartment. That bookcase. I lived in Hampton Hills; every shopaholic's dream was to hit up all the shops on Townsend Boulevard.

The fact that Eden had decided to *grocery* shop instead and cook... I couldn't wrap my head around it.

"And she cooked everything?" I pressed.

Beans nodded. "It's good, too. Really good."

It smelled incredible.

I opened my mouth, needing to know—

"Leave him alone."

Standing in the doorway, with her fists trembling at her sides, was Eden.

I didn't like people intruding in on my meetings, but just then, I didn't care.

No longer in that hideous T-shirt I'd picked out from a gift shop, Eden was wearing a black strapless top and leggings. She was barefoot, her white painted toenails on display. I worked my way back up, finding her worried for Beans and glaring at me.

This was a sight to see.

Leaning back in my chair, I thumbed at my bottom lip, amused.

"Take a plate and go," I ordered.

Beans bobbed his head and saw himself out of the room.

Eden remained standing in the doorway. "It's not his fault. I was the one who wanted to go out. You said I could leave."

I didn't care if she left, so long as she came back. And that she'd done.

Looking at Eden, I could see her mind racing to conjure up a defense for Beans. Never in my life did I imagine being *jealous* of the guy.

"And I won't apologize for it," Eden concluded with her chin raised. "You've fed me takeout for an entire week. I wanted something cooked with love, not something made on an assembly line in a cold kitchen."

So she'd cooked.

Angling my head, I studied her more. "Come here."

Slowly, Eden padded over to my desk, stopping in front of it.

"All the way," I instructed.

Eden looked over her shoulder, at the open door, before following my words and coming around my desk. She didn't need guidance to sit on my lap. She perched there on my knee, not fully committed to the position.

No dice.

I pulled her farther onto my lap until she had no choice but to straddle me. Grabbing her jaw, I steered her line of vision until she was staring directly at me. "Beans works for me."

Eden nodded. "I know."

"So when I'm reprimanding my men, don't you dare throw yourself over the coals for them."

It was in her nature to stick her neck out for people, or else she wouldn't have opened her mouth to protest.

"What did he do wrong?" she wanted to know.

Telling her I'd considered the idea of her poisoning me would only give her an idea to do such a thing. But then, I marveled at the thought of her being bold enough to go through with it. Beans was right; Eden wouldn't harm a fly. Despite the circumstances that got her here with me, she was the prettiest angel who had fallen into the hell that was my life.

"Nothing. I overreacted," I confessed.

She frowned and shook her head. "Is it okay that I cooked?"

I moved a strand of her hair out of her face. "Yes."

"And you're not mad?" Eden pushed further.

She didn't like people mad at her. Her heart couldn't take the simplest rejection. If I could teach her anything, it would be to not give a fuck what people thought.

"Not mad." She wasn't wearing makeup, outside of those lashes she swore by, and I took the time to regard her face, dragging my thumb down her lips. "I appreciate the gesture, thank you."

Eden's mouth fell open as she sat up on my lap. "*Oh.*"

The closeness. The smell of her strawberries and pomegranate scent. The softness of her skin and person. It was getting to me.

Eden peered down between our bodies before coming back to my gaze. She grinded into me, grinning big. "You're easy to impress."

I wasn't ashamed of how hard I was. In a bold move, I reached out and grabbed the top of her shirt, yanking it down and freeing her breasts.

Leaning over, I licked her already hard nipple and brought it into my mouth and sucked. Eden gasped and jumped just a little.

It wasn't enough.

I reached for her leggings to feel her, too. I slipped my hand in and felt along the thin material of her panties as I continued to suck on her breast.

Eden whimpered, rubbing herself against my palm.

"You're not so hard to impress either," I noted of her wetness.

"Wait, wait," she seemed to beg as she pushed against my chest for space.

I halted, her nipple in my mouth and her pussy in my hand.

"Your dinner," she said.

I traveled to her other nipple and traced my tongue around it. "Thought I'd have dessert first."

Eden whimpered some more, half riding my hand and half trying to squirm away. "It'll get cold."

"Thank God I own two microwaves."

"Cain," her soft plea drove my dick harder.

I rubbed along the seat of her panties. "I need to know if it tastes as sweet as it looks."

Desire coated her dark eyes as her lips trembled. It wouldn't take much to make her come. I just wasn't sure if I preferred my hand or my face.

Eden continued to ride my palm, causing her breasts to bounce. "Oh please."

I slipped one finger past the side of her panties, into her.

Fuck, she was wet. Eating her wouldn't be enough. I needed to *feel* her too.

But Eden resisted, shaking her head. "I wanna know if you like my dinner."

"I don't care how it tastes; I'll eat it because you made it," I let her know.

She pouted. "One bite and I'll give it to you for free."

That got me up. Eden had just enough time to fix her top as I wrapped an arm around her waist and kept her close to me as I walked us back out to the kitchen. Vino was just leaving with a container. Beans wasn't around, probably having gotten his food and left as soon as I gave the order.

As if what we'd been doing was evident on our faces, Eden leaned into me as Vino passed us with a knowing smirk.

Licking her juices off my finger, I kept my eyes on Eden as I spoke. "I'll see you in the morning."

Vino whistled loudly as he strode over to the door. "Have a good night, you two. Don't do anything I wouldn't."

That wasn't much.

Eden was shy as she hurried to the kitchen and tried to put space between us.

Just one bite, that was her rule.

Easier said than done before I saw the spread before me with a better view.

Eden had pulled out all the stops in this meal. Beyond the lasagna, there was a salad, garlic bread, and a dessert that looked like strawberry shortcake. Beans wouldn't lie to me. In the past, I'd had women attempt to pass off takeout as their own cooking, but if Beans said he watched Eden make every item, then I knew this was all homemade.

"You made all this?" I couldn't stop myself from asking as I finished taking in every dish.

Eden nodded, standing back, nervous. "I should've asked if you even liked lasagna."

I went back to the food. Even the salad was homemade as I spied chopped-up carrots instead of the shredded stuff that came in premade bags. "No one's ever cooked for me before."

Eden's brows furrowed. "*Never?*"

I shrugged, rubbing at my bottom lip. "I've never had a home-cooked meal before." I tossed her a small smile. "I didn't exactly have the luxury of a childhood."

Sympathy clouded Eden's eyes, and with anyone else, I would've hated it, but with Eden, there was something more. Almost a sense of understanding.

"Thank you," I said again, holding her gaze. "It means a lot."

That shy side of hers took over as she ducked her head and busied herself with grabbing a plate. "At least see if you even like it."

I placed my hand on hers and squeezed. "Doesn't matter."

Everything made sense as I went and washed my hands at the sink. I understood why Beans had eaten. After growing up in foster care as well, he didn't know a thing about something made at home either.

When I took my place at the island, Eden had already prepared a plate for me with a portion of lasagna and garlic bread, and then another plate with a helping of salad.

In a rare moment, I felt like a kid in a candy store as I grinned down at the food. I didn't enjoy too much in life, but food was top tier for me.

Eden hung back behind the island, waiting and watching for me to take my first bite. Really, I didn't care how it—

"*Mmm.*" I moaned after the first taste. All I needed to do was take one bite and I could have her, but one bite wasn't enough. I went in for another, needing more. The seasoned blend of the sauce and meat combined with the buttery pasta and cheese had me focusing on my plate. *If* she'd poisoned me, this would be one hell of a way to go.

"You like it." Eden was grinning, and there was no downplaying it. Not that I would.

"It's amazing," I let her know. I hadn't even finished my first helping and I was already eyeing the pan, hoping there was plenty left.

Eden tracked my movement and went and grabbed the spatula. "Here, I'll give you more now so I can start cleaning up."

"No," I sat up and put my fork down. "I'll clean."

Eden brushed it off. "It's not a big deal. I made the mess."

"You cooked for us," I said. "I'll wash your dishes."

She wanted to fight me on it, but didn't as she set the spatula down and leaned against the island. She stared at me and my plate. "Well, I'm glad you like it."

"Where'd you learn to cook like this?" I stood from my seat, needing some wine to go with the food. On one side of my back counter was a rack of wine, and I went and grabbed my favorite bottle of red.

Eden drew a tiny circle onto the island. "We had, like, one TV when I was growing up. And it was so old it only got two channels. One for classic movies, and the other for cooking. Naturally, I love both now."

It put a reason to her *Sabrina* poster in her bedroom at home and her mentioning *Breakfast at Tiffany's*.

I sat back down at my place and helped myself to her salad. You couldn't mess up a salad, but still, I gave her a thumbs-up as I ate another bite.

I'd never known what it was like to come home to a hot meal. Something fresh out of the oven, made with tender care and soul.

It was my first home-cooked meal, and I wasn't sure when Eden would leave, but a part of me could already get used to this.

IO

Cain

A SWEET SMELL GREETED ME BEFORE I OPENED MY EYES. I knew she was here before I woke up fully. The familiarity was both soothing enough to dive deeper into my sleep, and yet foreign enough to drive me awake.

Red hair spilled across the pillow beside me. Her tiny body was in a ball, not quite relaxed, but not too stiff. Even with how silly she was being last night, Eden wasn't comfortable here in my bed. The only reason she'd slept in it was because I'd been too tired to do anything after eating good and cleaning the kitchen. Like teenagers, we'd crawled into bed after my shower and kissed all night.

Now, waking up and seeing her rigid posture unsettled me. I wasn't a good person, but I wasn't going to hurt her.

Reaching out, I gently pressed my hand on her shoulder, as if to calm her.

It had the opposite effect.

She curled into herself more before looking over at me with one eye open. Frowning, she said, "Can I have ten more minutes before we…?"

Disgusted at what she was alluding to, I grimaced. "I understand boundaries."

Being brought out of your sleep could be a terrifying experience. This I knew. Eden didn't strike me as someone who'd been kept safe her whole life; waking her up and demanding sex would be repulsive on my end. Captive or not, I didn't want to set the pace as if I could command sex at the snap of my fingers. It was the main reason I'd given her her own bedroom.

Eden rubbed at her eyes and sat up.

"Go back to sleep," I told her. "You were looking a little stiff. I just wanted you to relax."

"Oh." Eden chewed on her lip. "I'm okay."

Still, she softened up and smiled as she bundled up under my thick comforter.

I got out of bed, already mentally going over the day's hefty itinerary. "I'm going to go get ready for work. Did you buy anything yesterday for the show tonight?"

Eden shook her head. "No. What kind of show is it?"

"It's an art gala. You walk around, buy some pretentious art, and if you're me, unfortunately, you have to network. Form business relationships."

"Sounds boring," Eden concluded.

They usually were. "I'm sure you and I can manage to survive."

A devilish look crossed Eden's face. "*If* I decide to go with you as your date."

Her teasing caused me to smile. I took in the way she was laying there, peering up at me, a glow beginning to bless her person and skin. Having just woken up or not, she was as beautiful as ever.

Feeling playful, I asked, "Anyone ever tell you that you have a spankable ass?"

All at once, Eden's eyes enlarged as she stilled and went silent. Curiosity and hesitation took over as she appeared thoughtful.

Before things could escalate, I took a step back, determined to leave on time. "I have a full schedule today, so I won't be able to pick you up and bring you with me to the show. Beans will drop you off and I'll meet you there."

Worry caused Eden's pouty lips to turn downward. "Meet you there?"

I collected my watch from my nightstand and checked the time. "My office is right near the venue. More than likely, I'll be there first." I regarded Eden where she remained nervous and anxious. "You'll be fine."

She didn't seem convinced. "What if...I don't fit in?"

I almost could've laughed at the question. But I didn't, not wanting her to think I was laughing *at* her. "Then we can not fit in together."

I left her with this idea before going and slipping into my master bath.

Twenty minutes later, I met Beans down in the kitchen. If anyone had a key to any of my properties and vehicles, it was Beans. Partly for insurance, and partly because if I ever were to meet an untimely demise, I wanted him to have it all.

"Please see to it that she goes and buys something to wear tonight," I said as I dapped him up in greeting.

Beans made a face. "Sure that's a good idea? What if she sneaks off and buys a gun to shoot us?"

He was mocking me. And I deserved it.

I ran a hand down my face to stifle my smile. Perhaps I was being ridiculous last night.

One thing about Beans, he was hardly ever wrong.

Pounding started down the hall at the front door and I knew Vino was here.

"You got jokes," I said to Beans as I took off to get the door.

I met Vino outside and we climbed on the elevator to head down to the parking deck.

"How's Curtis doing?" I asked of one of my runners.

Vino bobbed his head. "It's snowing in Calabasas."

That was one front squared away, and as we rode down to the

ground floor, I sighed, mentally preparing to make nice and blend into the corporate world of Hampton Hills.

One of the main reasons I took over my late father's casino was to prove a point. Outside of revenge, I kept myself as CEO of Cartier simply because I wasn't wanted there.

After the dust had settled, and the lawyers had combed through the documents and testaments realizing there were no loopholes to be found, my father's brother, Sandford Carter, had approached me. He was one of the top property developers in the West. Rich enough he had no problem offering to buy Cartier from me, to "keep it in the family."

Right from the start, I was donned a bastard. A black sheep. An enemy. My seat in their billionaire boys' club wasn't welcomed, but I graced it with dignity and my head held high.

My whole life was a montage of being unwanted, so this was nothing new to me. I could handle the elite's judgment and bullshit. Years of training had taught me how to move in a room full of vultures.

An old Shakespearian quote came to mind at the thought of navigating life in the Hills: "*Love all, trust a few, do wrong to none.*" I practiced this mantra tenfold to keep up appearances, and it saw me through gracefully every time.

I made it to the gala first, as expected, and I hung around the front of the showroom, forcing nice as men after men would approach me.

That first year after James's passing had been spent in exile with nothing but cold shoulders being cast my way. Now that I'd shown I wasn't going anywhere, that I was going to run Cartier and make moves of my own, the people who'd shut me out, now flocked to me. Call it ego or pride, but I rarely accepted any deal brought my way.

Until Damon Nichols.

Naturally, Damon wasn't here at the exhibit at Muse, so that left the door open for other investors to approach me.

In the large open space of the front room, nothing but white walls and white floors with colorful portraits hung up, I stayed by the front, hoping to catch Eden as soon as she walked in the door. Catering was around, offering glasses of wine and appetizers. I accepted a bottle of water to start off with.

Chatter filled the air and hearty laughter, too, competing with the musical sounds of old-school Black pop and R&B.

I was alone, musing over a painting of a naked Black woman laying on a rug. Against the royal blue backdrop, her bronze skin radiated off the canvas as she lay on her side, staring straight ahead. Her jet-black hair was long, stylistically covering her breasts and torso, leaving much to the imagination as her long legs were curled delicately beneath her.

It was a tasteful portrait, one that caught the eye and held it. The woman's expression was bored, yet powerful as you peered into her eyes and saw no fear or worry. Studying the painting, I wondered how Eden looked whenever she'd danced at that sleazy strip club.

Even without taking her clothes off, I couldn't take my eyes off her. I bet she'd commanded the room every time she entered it.

"Look who's here!" A strong voice greeted my ear and turned me around to catch Wade Marsh standing beside me. A huge grin split his round face, showing how happy he was to see me. Wade worked in the entertainment industry. He'd been distant when I'd first come around, but never rude. For that, I often tolerated him.

"Wade, what's up?" I shook his hand and put on a smile, playing my part.

Wade took a sip from the cognac glass he was holding. He was too higher-up to settle for wine. "Not much, not much, just... around, you know?"

Chuckling, I thumbed at my lip, knowing he was beating around the bush. He wanted something. "Yeah? And how's that going?"

Wade laughed and patted my back extra hard, in that way older men liked to do when they wanted to *son* you. "Listen, I'm not going to bullshit you; people been talking."

I looked around the room, finding Vino in a corner talking to some model I vaguely recognized. "That's the thing about this town, Wade, people always talk." I got back to him, wanting it straight. "What are they saying?"

A corner of Wade's mouth curled as a sly grin captured his light brown face. "You're trying to bring primetime fights to LA."

For once, the gossip was semi accurate. It was an idea I'd been considering now that things were on the up with The Residence at Cartier. Since old Hollywood and beyond, Las Vegas has held premium boxing matches. To bring that kind of entertainment to our establishment in LA would make us major numbers.

"It's just an idea," I said with a shrug. "Every good draw has a main attraction, and that's what a show in LA would need."

Wade scratched along his neck, soaking in my words. "Jaguar Jones is about to be next. Give him a huge pay-per-view event..." He whistled, shaking his head. "And he's out of there."

"Yeah, if you can get ahold of him," I agreed. "Would be nice to see."

Wade wasn't buying it. "Bullshit. Every time you're in Vegas you're with Jaguar."

To that I had to laugh, because it was almost true.

Justice "Jaguar" Jones was on the come up. A boxer out of the mud with a story many underdogs could relate to. He had a certain charisma you couldn't find anymore in a world so disingenuous. He came from nothing, something I knew all too well, and whenever we ran into each other and talked, the conversation was always real and thoughtful.

All it would take was a phone call to set him up in LA doing a fight, but that was a call I wasn't intent on making just yet. Getting into boxing was just an idea. I already wore two hats, and I wasn't sure about a third.

"We'll see, it's just a—"

Wade wasn't listening to me. His eyes were glued past me, at the door. I turned and knew why.

She was finally here.

Michael Jackson's "The Lady in my Life" was beginning to play and I could barely hear the iconic melody as all went radio silent as I zeroed in on Eden.

The first thing I noticed was her hair. Eden's hair was no longer red, but black, and pinned up in an updo.

I liked the red, but the black... I took in the way the long loose locks framed her angelic face, making her look prettier, calling attention to her large eyes.

My gaze trailed to the dress—if you could call it that. Like something out of Greek mythology, it was a lengthy cream one-shoulder gown. Skintight and had a section missing in the middle, causing the top and bottom half of the gown to be connected by a gold ring, exposing the fact that she was wearing a thin gold garter belt chain that attached at her thigh.

Beneath the gown, it was clear Eden wasn't wearing a bra or panties. The high slit up the side gave a vivid view of her leg up to her naked hip. The sight made me clutch my bottle of water. That and the way Wade was looking at her. The way almost *all* the men in the vicinity was looking at her.

Wade whistled, rocking on the heels of his feet. "Shit, why they ain't make 'em like *that* when I was your age?"

He went on to mumble a few choice words that had my grip on my bottle tightening until it crumbled in my fist.

Trying and failing to calm down as I took in the scene, I questioned how long I could go the entire evening without shooting anyone.

11

Eden

It felt like all eyes were on me as I entered Muse, the art gallery Beans had dropped me off at. Other people were entering the building, but it felt like everyone was focusing on *me*.

It was one thing when I'd been playing model and server at the Monte Carlo night, because then I'd at least served a purpose. Here, as a *guest*, I wasn't sure I belonged. When I'd gone shopping that afternoon with Beans for dresses, I'd never felt more out of place browsing through all the shops holding nothing but designer. Back in Bedford Heights, it wasn't rare to see someone wearing high-end clothing, but it had never been *my* style.

I honestly didn't feel right even considering the five thousand-dollar Oscar de la Renta dress that had caught my eye.

"They'll probably see right through me." I'd pouted as I gave up ten minutes into our stint in a shop called Rare Luxe.

Beans wasn't a fashionista. He'd looked bored out of his mind the entire time I'd sat at the local salon having my hair dyed dark, and even more so now that we were shopping for clothes. But he took me by surprise when he peered straight into my eyes and willed me to be strong. "Then let them see you're fearless. You're a beautiful woman, and you can't shatter diamonds, remember that."

You can't shatter diamonds. I'd liked that mantra right away. It served to help me shop with my head held high as I eventually found what I'd deemed the perfect dress.

At first, I didn't think I could pull the dress off, but I loved the way it looked on me as soon as I put it on. My breasts were sitting high and my ass looked great. I couldn't wait to be seen in it.

Now at the gala, I wasn't so sure.

Letting out a nervous breath, I took a step farther into the entrance and looked around, searching for—

Within a blur, he'd materialized in front of me. Cain came out of nowhere, and didn't look an ounce happy to see me.

I had just opened my mouth to greet him when he took my hand and whisked me away, out of the entrance and through the front room filled with paintings I didn't get to really see. It was a blur of people and things as Cain walked with determination to get somewhere in the gallery.

He didn't stop to respond to any of the people who spoke his name or attempted to start a conversation. No, Cain kept walking until we'd hit the back of the building where there was a back hallway leading to a restroom, an exit, and an office. For a moment, Cain paused, meditating as he swung his attention from the restroom to the office. In the end, he chose the office as he ushered me inside and shut the door behind us. The soft *click* let me know he'd locked us in.

I hung back, confused, worried, uncertain.

Tension was steaming from Cain as he turned from the door and faced me. Impassive.

I took a step back. "Is something wrong?"

Cain blinked, a smug smile turning one side of his lips up as he tracked my movement and took a step forward. "What do you think?"

Quickly, I looked around the office, searching and failing to find a way out. There was just a bookcase, a small sitting area, and a desk in the room. The window above the sitting area was made of glass cubes with no way to open it. The only exit was the door. And I knew there was no way I was getting by Cain.

"I don't know," I admitted as I got back to him. "I don't understand."

Cain's eyes raked over my body and heat crept under my skin at the sight of his exploration.

"That's some dress," he remarked dryly.

I frowned. "I thought I looked pretty." I looked down at myself, patting my middle. "Do I look ridiculous?"

A simple shake of his head was all I got as he kept advancing closer. "You're beautiful."

I backed up until I hit the desk behind me. There was nowhere to go. I was cornered.

Cain's hands came down on either side of me, blocking me in. "Let me show you how much I *like* this dress."

In seconds he was leaning down and grabbing me by my waist, picking me up as if I weighed nothing before setting me on top of the large wooden desk. His hands slid beneath the open fabric of my dress and seized my hips, thumbing my flesh. His intentions were clear and a violent surge of need pulsated between my legs as I looked into his eyes.

"Cain!" I let out at the sudden feel of his hand on me.

"This doesn't count," Cain snapped as he played with my clit.

Gaining some semblance of control, I spoke up, "Say you want me and I'll consider it."

Cain gripped my thigh, dragging me to the edge of the desk. "I'm taking it for free."

I jerked away and shook my head. "Uh-uh, say it."

Cain pushed the material of my dress up to my waist, exposing my bareness to him. Soon, he lowered himself to his haunches and spread my thighs.

My chest was heaving up and down, peering over at him. The door was locked, but anyone could be on the other side, and here I was, spread open for Cain with no shame to be found.

Cain peeled his eyes from mine and focused on what was in

front of him. He leaned close and the feel of his breath on me caused a tingle to dance down my spine.

"Shit!" I squealed at the feel of his tongue doing a hot, wet sweep from my clit to my entrance and back.

He did it again and I bit into my lip hard to keep from screaming out at the sensation. Cain wrapped his lips around my clit and licked it slow and hard, causing me to jolt forward.

Fuck. Fuck. Fuck.

His hands crept up my body and slid beneath the top of my dress, going and taking my breasts in their grasp and massaging them.

I moaned. "You want me."

"Of course I want what's mine," he responded.

What's his. Somehow, the tone of his voice, the edge he'd packed into his words, as if daring me to argue, it all turned me on more.

Cain went back to tasting me without abandon. No one had ever gone down on me like this before. With such passion, such fervor, such *enjoyment.* Cain licked me slow and sucked me gently, taking his time to really savor the act. This was more than returning the favor. He was going down on me because he *wanted* to. With the tactic he was using, I'd dare to say he *needed* to as well.

An ugly sound escaped me as he stuck his tongue inside me, sending me to the brink.

I squeezed my eyes shut and tried to crawl back, unable to take it.

Cain's grip on my breasts tightened. I looked down to find him glaring at me. "Don't run from me."

His mouth was back on me, his teeth grazing my clit threateningly.

"Fuck," I whined, trying not to do something pathetic like cry.

It was too much. His tongue lapping at my clit. His hands kneading my breasts. It was sensory overload as I threw my head back and cursed, rolling my hips into his face, riding it to chase that special high.

My vision blurred as my mouth fell open. I reached out, tangling my hand with one of his, feeling grounded when he squeezed my palm.

A tsunami of pleasure burst inside me and I rode out the tidal wave as my orgasm took over. Gone was any sense of etiquette as I let loose and moaned as loudly as my soul allowed, flattening my back against the desk, all too aware that Cain was still licking me.

My right eye was twitching and my body was shuddering as I came back down to Earth.

Weak or not, I sat up as Cain hovered over me. I was glistening on his lips, and I wasted no time in leaning close and licking the evidence from the corner of his mouth. He held my face in his hands and kissed me, the taste of me prominent on his tongue.

Hastily, I went for his pants, needing more, needing to feel him inside of me.

Cain's hands came down on my wrists, stopping me as he pulled away. "I don't have protection."

"I'm on birth control," I let him know.

All at once the moment cracked as something like mistrust passed through Cain's eyes. He took a step back and shoved my hands away. "I've heard that before."

I closed my legs and slowly pulled myself together, feeling embarrassed for how desperate I'd sounded. The only reason we were in this situation was because I'd stolen from him. Of course he wouldn't trust me when I said I was on birth control. I'd seen it before, some girls at the club who'd caught the eye of a big spender and their first instinct being to get pregnant and secure their future. It was a means of survival, but it wasn't for me.

Smoothing my shaking hands down my dress, I bowed my head. "The first thing I did when I got on my own was go to the clinic and get on birth control." Bravely, I looked over at Cain. "I could barely take care of myself. I didn't want to chance being responsible for another life. I know what you think of me, but I wouldn't try to bring a baby into this."

He scowled, shaking his head once more. "You have no idea what I think of you, Eden." He ran a hand down his tie, adjusting himself to be presentable. "It's not about the money. I can afford a kid. I just don't want one."

"Why not?" I wasn't sure if I ever wanted to become a parent myself, but someone in Cain's position had a much better shot than I did of providing stability.

He regarded me for a long while as he stood at the door, as though he were deciding on what to say. "Any time I walk out of my house, there's a high chance I won't come back." He hung his head. "I told myself a long time ago I'd never put a woman in a position to raise a kid alone. I've lived that life and it kills."

My heart ached in my chest at the revelation. "You were raised by a single mom?"

Cain nodded. "Yeah. Wasn't fun one bit."

"And your father...he *died*?" I asked.

A muscle in Cain's jaw tensed. "Yes."

It was probably sensitive territory, but I couldn't stop myself from asking, "How?"

"I killed him," Cain said matter-of-factly. He reached for the knob and wrapped his hand around it. "Can we go?"

He'd dropped a major bomb on me, freezing me in place.

Something had told me Cain was dark. A criminal. But to hear him confess to really being a killer? I didn't know what to think.

Swallowing the lump that had lodged in my throat, I slid off the desk. I turned and fixed up the paperwork we'd rearranged. The photos we'd knocked over. The pens we'd scattered. Anything not to face him.

"I...I need to use the restroom," I told him.

"Okay, I'll be out in the gallery waiting," he said before slipping out of the room.

I practiced taking deep breaths as I turned back around and

saw that I was alone. Over in the restroom, I fixed my hair and dress in the mirror after doing my business. My mind was racing. There was an exit right there. I could slip out and take off. Rid myself from this situation once and for all. He knew where I lived, but I could take Duane and...

Where would we even go? Cain had my thirty-one thousand dollars. Going on the run with no money would be reckless.

The thought of running was only halfhearted, though. Even if I was taken aback by Cain's confession, fear didn't consume me. Nor disgust. Once the momentary shock wore off, I didn't feel any sense that *I* was in danger.

It was because of this that I ignored the idea of sneaking out.

Not that I would've had a chance. As I opened the door to the restroom, I immediately caught Vino leaning against the wall opposite me, waiting.

He took one look at me, starting at my gold heels and working his way up. He shook his head and let out a low whistle. "If my girl was out dressed like *this*, I'd cop an attitude, too."

A small smile lightened me up. "You like it?"

Vino took the lead back down the hall out into the gallery. "Hell yeah, it's sexy."

Cain was talking to a group of men when we made it into the front room. All of them looked my way, but only Cain's attention sent my body on alert and made my brain hazy.

An old soul song was playing throughout the gallery. A man singing, *begging*, someone to stand by him. I could feel the familiar sensation of being watched by others, but none of this mattered as I crossed the room and met up with Cain. He excused himself from the men and covered me with his presence, cloaking us into our own little bubble.

He showed me around the gala, pointing out portraits that interested him as he wrapped an arm around my waist. I clung close to him, listening to him speak about the photos and paintings, hanging on to his every word. The outside world of the other guests in attendance disappeared and it was only Cain and me as we went in room and after room, taking in the art.

Cain told me he killed his father, and I let him take me home and rip me out of my dress. He held no remorse for the murder, and I let him lay me down and fuck me slow. He had probably killed many others, and I let him come in me as he held my trembling body close and sucked the soul from my lungs with his mouth. His hands were dirty, and I let him pull me into his shower and wash every inch of my body under the hot spray of water. He'd done the most unforgivable thing, and I let him dry me down and rub lotion into my skin. He wasn't a saint, and I went to bed with him, engulfed in his arms.

And I slept soundly.

12

Eden

"HOW MANY OTHERS HAVE YOU DONE THIS WITH?" I asked Sunday afternoon.

"Just you," Cain responded, clarifying he wasn't some serial kidnapper.

I should've been relieved that no other girl had been forced into my position, but instead I felt special. One week with this man and I was already ditsier than ever.

I sat on the corner of his desk cross-legged in his shirt from last night. He was in his chair, dressed properly. He'd chosen to work from home today. And I liked that. I liked the steady sound of his voice as he spoke on the phone and called all the shots.

I liked the way he was blasé about dealing with millions of dollars. I'd brought him a sandwich for lunch, wanting to quickly leave after handing over the plate, but Cain had reached out, taking my hand and holding me back. He spoke of thousand-dollar contracts and expansions as he wrapped an arm around my waist and held my body close.

He didn't mind that I was around.

While he was on the phone all morning with his calls, I laid on the sofa in the room, lounging and reading a book until he was finished for the day.

Now, there was no Beans, no Vino, just us.

We were playing a game of Twenty Questions. Unlike anyone else I'd ever known, outside of Duane, Cain was above all honest. Whether good or bad, he didn't lie.

For most of my life, I'd felt like a burden. Annoying. In the way. Cain didn't seem to mind my ramblings and questions. He sat back in his leather chair, amusement clear on his face as he looked at me as I perched on his desk in just his shirt.

"How old are you?" I wanted to know.

Cain sighed. "Twenty-eight. I'll be twenty-nine in September."

I breathed a sigh of relief. "Oh thank God you're not a Sagittarius. Like, I've heard Virgo men aren't the greatest, but lesser of two evils, you know?" I said, thinking of some of my talks with the girls back at Crazy Legs.

Cain chuckled, shaking his head. "I don't believe in that shit, Eden."

"So you don't believe in fun?" I challenged as I arched a brow.

Cain only grinned at me, and it felt like the rays of a million suns warming me internally.

He sank deeper into his chair, peering over at me as his thumb began to tap against his armrest. "There are nine years between us. Does that make you feel uncomfortable?"

I shrugged. "I've never been with a man my own age."

Cain's eyes narrowed. "Never?"

I fingered my white nail polish on my big toe. "Most guys who took interest in me were always older. Does my age bother you?"

"I don't take pleasure in the fact that you're so much younger than me," Cain stated earnestly.

I thought of Keith from back home. He was older, wiser, and I could tell because of this he only tolerated me. He thought of me as just a kid. I didn't know much, but I didn't want to be tolerated in love. Didn't want to be a burden ever again.

"But you won't let me go," I pointed out, looking at Cain beneath my lashes.

He angled his head, admiring me. "I'm not the hero in this story."

He had traits of being a bad person, but I didn't buy it. He had taken me into captivity, and yet he was still one of the nicest men I'd ever encountered. Considerate, kind, gentle—he was far better than the men I'd known before him.

"I'll be twenty in July," I said.

"I'm aware."

"I'm a Cancer," I offered.

"That you certainly are."

Cain was teasing, and I hated how it lifted my mood so easily. I took a pen from his holder and flung it at him, causing him to let loose a laugh that echoed deep in my chest.

Because of the way I'd grown up, my love language was Words of Affirmation. A weakness I couldn't shake. "Do you like anything about me?"

Cain blinked a few times, as if the question was silly. "I *like* many things."

"Name one," I said.

Cain's lips twitched to smile. "We're never using a condom again."

I rolled my eyes. *Of course.*

I'd never tell him, but I liked his sex. His oral. His caress. His demanding kisses. In the moment, it was so consuming with him. Swallowed. Devoured. And I couldn't get enough. Right away last night I could tell the difference in going without protection. He groaned louder, he stroked deeper, and his touch lingered on my body. He was so big, so much, I loved that he took his time, dragging my orgasm out of me as he watched me teeter out of the universe beneath him. And when I was listless and spent, he'd stare at me for a moment before leaning down and kissing me softly until I was moaning all over again.

He was the best lover I'd ever had. So attentive and in tune with me. If I ended up spending another week with him I didn't mind.

"Tell me something real," I wanted to know as I brought my knees to my chest. "That you like about me."

Cain didn't hesitate to come up with an answer. "Your smile."

Blushing, I rested my chin on my knee. "Same."

"Isn't that cheating?" Cain joked of my copied comment.

I shook my head. "No. You can come off scary, unapproachable, but then you smile and you're just...classic handsome, boyish, and bright. I like seeing you smile."

Cain took in my response and remained quiet.

I got back to our game, not wanting to miss a beat. "What's your favorite meal?"

"Meatloaf," Cain confessed. "Something about it...it feels like home, or what home should be. Growing up, watching cartoons, that's mainly what they'd eat. That or chicken."

His words tugged at my heartstrings. I knew what he meant. Of wanting a meal that brought comfort and reminded you of home. Or the idea of one. It was why chicken noodle soup was so popular when sick. The placebo effect it brought you.

"I'll make you meatloaf," I told him.

Cain frowned. "That's okay."

"You don't like my cooking?"

"I love your cooking," he declared. "But I don't want you to feel it's expected of you."

"It's nothing," I assured him. "When I leave here, I'll never be able to cook in a kitchen like you have. It's fun for me."

Cain still didn't look comfortable at the idea, but he didn't reject it. "Okay."

I smiled. "Okay."

"Why did you strip?" It was Cain's turn as he asked me of my previous occupation straightforwardly.

"It took care of me. Easy money when I needed it most," I said without shame. Since we were on the subject of our less-than desirable career paths, I finally got the courage to ask him what had been brewing in my mind for days. "Why do you sell drugs?"

A spark passed through Cain's eyes, but he didn't break and admit it. "Why do you assume I'm a drug dealer?"

He was denying it. I snorted. "I know a drug dealer when I see one. All types come in Crazy Legs. You have it on you. Beneath the fancy suits and big casino, is your true occupation."

Cain tilted his head, relaxing his jaw on his hand. "Ever date one?"

I wrinkled my nose. "I never wanted to get mixed in any trouble."

That got Cain to chuckle loudly. "No, not you, the thief."

I looked down at his desk, forcing interest in his large calendar that had a few dates penciled in with his surprisingly neat handwriting. I'd made a few poor choices in my life, but I wasn't always stupid.

"It's a force of habit," Cain said gently, getting us back on track. "I started when I was young."

I looked up, finding him watching me. "Why?"

He looked away from me and scratched along his jaw. "My mom died when I was twelve. My father didn't come forward, and there was no other family around to take me in. I was put into the system, and as you can imagine, that place was the stuff of nightmares. Some of my homes didn't feed me and I had to eat." He shrugged in a what-can-you-do manner.

Survival. At an early age, he'd done what he had to do to survive. Just like me.

We stared at each other. No judgment passing from either of us. He didn't like that I danced, simply because of the perverted occupants that frequented my world, but he didn't care to shame me for what I'd done. I wasn't a fan of drugs, but I understood being so hungry your belly hurt and all you could do was cry yourself to sleep.

Maybe this was why he'd killed his father, for leaving him in the gutter. I'd never even known mine.

"Your education?" Cain prompted next.

I shrugged. "I stopped going to school before I could graduate. I got my GED last summer." Being a runaway, things got messy after a while when I'd been living with my boyfriend. Not that my mother had ever looked for me or filed a report.

Cain took a deep breath, appearing thoughtful. "So if I were to present you with a contract to honor our arrangement, you'd just trust me and sign it?" he asked coolly. "Without reading the fine print?"

I felt dumb just then, as if I were too illiterate to understand anything, and I hated him for it.

"Fuck you," I breathed out as I climbed down from his desk and took off out of the room.

I went up to my bedroom and sank into my chair in the corner of my room. Peering out at the city below, at the bright blue sky and the sunny day out, I told myself not to cry. Not to feel inadequate.

Knock. Knock.

Cain was leaning in the doorway. His arms were folded and concern was written across his dark face.

I didn't need his pity.

I dabbed at my eyes and looked off. "Go away."

"Eden..." He paused, collecting his words. "It wasn't my intention to make you feel any way. I didn't mean to push you so hard. I'm sorry."

Chewing on my lip, I faced him. "Thought you didn't make apologies."

"I do when I hurt someone I care about," he said softly. He ran a hand over his head and sighed. "Look, when this is all said and done, outside of Duane, do you have any family you can go back to? A way to start over?"

Bitterly, I laughed and sniffled. "Why do you think I was dancing at fifteen? I ran away and moved in with my boyfriend. My mom didn't even report me missing. She just let me go." My tears dried up because I refused to break over her as my heart hardened. "She doesn't like girls. She doesn't like *me*. She's got this boyfriend who'd pick with me. Nothing I ever did was right for him. I was always in the way. And she always was on his side.

"It was him or me, and she chose him. I moved in with this guy I was seeing, which was good until it wasn't, and then I had nowhere, so I used what little money I had for that first fake ID, and got a job at Crazy Legs."

Click. Click. Click.

Cain stood impassively clicking a pen at his side. "Do you *like* stripping?"

I shrugged. "It's okay. It takes care of me. Last year I tried to go back home to my mom and..." I rubbed at my cheek, remembering my bruise, remembering the rejection. "...got a reminder why I left."

"Who hit you?" His voice was eerily clipped, yet demanding.

I bowed my head and focused on my fingers. "Him."

"And what did *she* do?"

I should've been numb at the truth of the matter, but still my voice cracked as I answered, "N-Nothing."

A hot tear rolled down my cheek and I quickly wiped it away. It wasn't worth it.

It's okay. You are *okay. You don't need those people.*

The silence was loud, suffocating, causing me to look over at Cain.

He was studying me. No longer clicking that pen. He stared at me a beat longer before simply turning and walking away.

I let out a breath, unable to shake the intensity of the moment.

I wasn't even aware he'd gone downstairs until I heard the front door open and shut a minute later.

He was gone.

13

Cain

THE DRIVE INTO BEDFORD HEIGHTS WAS QUIET, SAVE for the radio. I'd given myself ten minutes to decompress down in the lobby of my building before Vino and Beans showed up.

No amount of space or time could convince me to change my mind. All it took was the sight of Eden's eyes to do me in. My biggest weakness: *tears*. And not the bullshit kind for manipulation and attention, but the kind from deep within the chest: sorrow.

Tears reminded me of *her*. Of all the agony and tragedy that was age twelve.

"You sure about this?" Vino probed, glancing my way as he drove into the city.

Quietly, I nodded.

The energy in the car was volatile, heavy and doused in butane. One wrong move or word, and things would go up in flames. I hadn't been this riled up in ages, it felt.

"I mean, she's just some skin. Why bother going the extra mile?"

"She's a castaway, like me," I said more to myself than anything. She'd grown up in a home that rejected her, casted her out, leaving her to go to extremes to survive. Just like me.

I hadn't said much when I called up Beans and Vino, telling them we had some business to take care of on Eden's behalf in the Heights. Because they knew me so well and could read me on sight, they hadn't said much when Vino pulled up to my building to pick me up. Beans occupied the back of Vino's S-Class while I sat up front next to Vino.

In their eyes, I was just fucking Eden for payback, to pass the time—because I could. Going out on a limb for her...it probably didn't make sense.

Eden's problems weren't my concern in the long run, but hearing her story, or part of it, ate at me.

"Eden's five-three," I said of her height I'd read from her ID.

"That *all*?" Vino remarked of her short figure.

I ran my thumb across my bottom lip. "Now, imagine this five-foot-three person telling you that they ran away from home because some man probably your size was putting their hands on them. That their own mother didn't do anything to stop it."

Vino continued to drive, bobbing his head to the Killer Mike song playing. He was quiet for a minute before he slid his gaze my way. "Can I kill him?"

I shook my head. I didn't know Eden to say that this was personal, but that's how it felt, *personal*.

If she had a better mother, a better home—was *protected*, she wouldn't have fallen into *my* path.

"Sure this is the place?" Vino asked as he pulled his car to a stop a few houses down on the opposite side of the street of our target.

Vino had a photographic memory. He remembered the exact route he'd taken from Eden's apartment. Just like *I* remembered the house she'd stopped to look at on the way to my place. To some, it may have been a fleeting glance, not much to think about. But I couldn't miss the look in her eyes, the raw emotion clouding her features. *Longing*.

"Call it intuition." I held my hand back toward where Beans sat behind us. Instinctively, he passed me a burner and I brought it to my lap to inspect it. "Be ready to make some calls," I ordered as I checked the clip.

Beans snorted. "Think I would hand you an empty piece?"

He had been exceptionally silent the whole way here. Meeting his eyes in the rearview mirror, I asked, "Got anything to say?"

He shrugged lazily. "Can we make it quick? I'm starving."

Vino chuckled and the mood shifted, becoming less tense.

Between the three of us, this was just another day at the office. We all had dirty hands, and this wouldn't be the last time any of us stained them.

I eyed the house, the small one-story beige home with the Honda Accord in the driveway. From the outside, it blended in with the other houses on the street. Nothing out of the ordinary stood out. The lawn was cut, there were a few flowers in the beds by the front steps, and a peek at the back saw there was a healthy white fence up.

Daylight was still visible, not my preferred setting for what I was about to do, but fuck it. I had enough reach in Bedford Heights that I ultimately wasn't worried in the long run.

As pissed as I was, a part of me wanted to drag this motherfucker out into the street and shoot him like a rabid animal. But we lived in a viral world and I couldn't chance it.

Tucking the gun into my suit, I unbuckled my seat belt. "Let's go."

A few kids were on bikes farther up Singleton Avenue, the smell of chlorine was in the air, echoes of pool water splashing could be heard from a house behind us, and a nearby radio blasted as we got out of the car and crossed the street. The neighborhood was in play, and for that, we kept it casual as we approached Eden's mother's home.

Beans went and rang the doorbell, standing back beside us and waiting patiently.

The dark brown wooden front door pulled open just a smidge, a chain lock in place. A woman's face appeared in the crack of the door, eyeing the three of us curiously. "Hello?"

All I needed was one look at her to see an older version of Eden and I snapped.

"Go," I ordered, signaling for Vino to make a move.

BANG!

In seconds, he had kicked the door in, breaking the chain lock, and sending Eden's mother flying back across the foyer.

The house opened into a living room with polished wooden floors, decent furniture, and my mark sitting on the sofa. The stench of alcohol and weed permeated the room, as I caught the man rolling a blunt over the coffee table.

Old-school music was playing from a speaker in the corner. The Isley Brothers.

"Bobby!" Eden's mother hollered from her place on the floor, shaking in terror. She was dressed down for the day in a tank top and sleep shorts, her hair all wrapped under her scarf. Blood lined her mouth, evidence from her collision with the door.

I didn't give a shit.

My attention focused on "Bobby." He'd leaped to his feet, eyes going from his woman on the ground to the three men entering the house. I took in his build: on the taller side, slightly muscular, but not too much, as though he had a problem with beer or portions. It was his arms that really stood out. Thick, muscled, and covered in ink.

Eden had been no match.

One glance around the room and I didn't see a single photograph of Eden up on the wall. No baby pictures, kiddy photos, or anything from school or out in the yard. It was as if she hadn't existed.

"*Bobby.*" My voice was calm, despite my rage. "Let's take a walk."

He looked at me crazy. "Who the fuck are you?"

"We'll get to that, on our walk," I told him.

Bobby wasn't hearing me. He made a move to reach for something, the phone on the coffee table.

Vino whipped his gun from his jacket, extending his arm out as he aimed at Bobby. "Ah ah ah."

"AHH!" Eden's mother screamed. "Take whatever you want! Please!"

A robbery? I almost laughed at the insinuation.

Her pleas fell upon deaf ears.

"A walk, Bobby, that's all I want," I said as I peered into the man's dark eyes.

He glanced at Eden's mother, being the strong one of the two of them. "It's...it's okay, baby. It's okay."

The soothing tone he'd used worked like a charm as Eden's mother calmed down just a little. She had crawled until her back was against the wall, shaking as she peered at all of us with uncertainty.

I craned my neck to look at her, disgust turning my lips down. "What's your name?"

Her eyes went to Bobby, like she needed his permission to speak. "T-Toni."

"Edwards?" I asked through clenched teeth.

Toni's eyes enlarged as her mouth hung open. Reality set in. This wasn't random. "H-How do you know my name?"

Closing my eyes, I breathed in through my nose. Every second here in this house was a reminder of the girl back at my home.

My attention flashed to Bobby. "Let's go out back."

"How do you know my name?" Toni begged, her voice strained.

No one paid her question any attention as Bobby led the way out of the room.

"Stay right there," Vino spoke up from over his shoulder at her. "Make us chase you, and I'll empty the whole clip in you."

Her cries greeted my back as Bobby entered the next room, a kitchen. Food was on the stove, a meal of chili. A cutting board sat on the counter by the back door. A knife in perfect view.

A corner of my mouth curled. I hoped he'd grab it and make this even more interesting.

Bobby's gaze lingered on the knife as we passed it on our way out the back door. The privacy of the surrounding white picket fence was all I needed to pull out my burner and dig it into Bobby's back.

His hands shook as he raised them in the air, slowly turning to face me.

"Whatever you think this is, you're mistaken." Tears lined his vision and I thought he'd do something pathetic like break down and cry.

Shaking my head, I sized him up once more. "No, I'm not mistaken."

The sharp clink of metal alerted us to Vino's Zippo shutting as he lit a cigarette. Beans hung by the back door, staring on at the scene coldly.

I got back to Bobby.

"Answer a few questions for me," I told him. "Answer them right and I'll let you go. Answer them wrong?" A sinister smile took my lips. "And Toni's going to become a lonely party of one."

"Man, I ain't do nothin'!" Bobby shouted. He was a grown man, trembling before me in fear like a child. Of course he wasn't willing to fight someone his own size. Not even to spare his life.

My grip on my gun was firm as I aimed at Bobby's chest. "How long have you been with Toni?"

Blinking rapidly, Bobby's words came out rushed and desperate. "Ten years. We been together for ten years!"

Eden had spent five of those years at a strip club to make money to feed herself.

"Get on your knees," I ordered.

"Man, whatever you think we did, we ain't do!" Bobby pleaded as tears rolled down his cheeks.

"On your fucking knees," I snapped.

Bobby sank down to his knees, his shoulders shaking, sweat beading his temples, and piss lining the front of his jeans.

"Next question, do you and Toni have any kids?" I prompted.

Bobby shrugged. "She got a girl somewhere and I got a boy with my ex."

Somewhere.

"Do you know Eden Edwards?" I pressed on.

"Y-Yeah," Bobby's voice faltered. "That's Toni's kid, man. Is that what this is about? I ain't got nothin' to do with that little bitch."

A dry chuckle sounded from Vino's direction. If I'd let him play this his way, Bobby would be going out slower, and more painful. But I never had a flare for dramatics. I had someone to get back to.

"I let *men* die on their feet, but cowards..." I eyed Bobby smugly. "...they go out beneath me."

"Yo, please!" Bobby's voice cracked. "That bitch ain't nothin' but trouble. Whatever problem you have with her, take it out on her! I'm tellin' you, she couldn't do shit right around here. I tried knockin' some sense into her and it ain't ever stick, man. Do what you gotta do wit' her. S-She's worthless. She—"

I pulled the trigger, once, twice, three times, ridding the scum from the earth, baptizing myself in his blood as a hot spray hit my face.

Bobby's lifeless body slumped over, leaking thick red blood onto the green lawn.

Taking my pocket square out, I wiped at my face to clean up.

"Wanna hit up the cleanup crew?" Vino asked as he strolled up beside me.

"Nah." I shook my head. "It's not worth them making the trip."

Being that it was only three of us, when shit really hit the fan, I had insurance policies in place. If a deal went south and we wound up with a body or two on our hands, we used our cleanup crew—forensic-level cleaners who could erase any crime scene in record time. Or, if something felt sketchy, or I'd been crossed, I had the hit squad on standby. A team of no-name hitmen who were only a phone call away. If you wanted your problems to disappear—without getting your hands dirty, there was no better help than the hit squad.

It was amazing what connections you could make in the underworld.

Bobby, though, wasn't worth the effort. This was Bedford Heights.

Nobody would give a fuck he was gone.

"Call up someone local to come clean this up, make it worth their while," I instructed as I rubbed at my face some more. "Maybe a young one, someone trying to prove their rank."

I didn't have an army, but a few soldiers who did some impressive work for me. Any coke sold in Bedford Heights went through me. I knew the ins and outs of the city too well after my time growing up here. Gaining some control of it hadn't been hard at all.

Vino gathered his phone. "Five is a good starting point, but ten would be better."

I finished with my pocket square and shoved it inside my jacket. "Think so?"

"I'd do it for five," Vino said with an easy shrug. "That'll get you admiration. But ten thousand would get you loyalty. Especially from a kid who ain't never had shit."

I regarded Beans for confirmation. He nodded.

"Fine, make it ten. Pick someone who can handle getting their dick wet for the first time without telling everyone who can listen." I eyed our surroundings, catching a curtain moving next door in the back window. "And give five to the neighbor."

My gaze flickered toward the house behind us, imagining Toni inside. "One last thing."

I left Vino to sort out the cleanup while Beans trailed me back inside. Toni had only moved to sit on the couch.

"Please." She was a blubbering mess as she held up a hand, trying to shield herself.

Rolling my eyes, I sat down on the coffee table in front of her. "Shut up and listen."

Toni squeezed her eyes shut and tears fell down her face.

I felt nothing.

Rudely, I reached out, wiping Bobby's blood onto the material of her shorts. "The way I see it, you've got two options." I tucked my gun away and leaned over, propping my elbows to my knees as I stared on at the pathetic excuse of a mother in front of me. "You're either going to switch to eating pussy, or you're going to join a convent, because if I ever hear about you fucking another man, I'll come back here and kill you both."

"I'm so sorry," she whined as she visibly trembled. She didn't even know *what* she was apologizing for.

"Shut. Up," I ordered once again. "Now, I welcome you to call the police, because then they'll come here and make it look like a domestic dispute, or a robbery gone wrong. Either way, it's no sweat off my back."

Toni looked at me with her wet eyes and swollen mouth. My heart was cold because I couldn't find it in me to sympathize with her. To try to put myself in her shoes and understand why she'd chosen some dick over her own kid.

The back door opened and shut, and soon, Vino's heavy footsteps were entering the room. He simply nodded at me. It was taken care of.

I stood from the coffee table. "I hope we've come to an understanding."

Toni shook her head. "I don't...I don't get it. What did we do?"

"It's not about what you did, but about what you *didn't* do," I clarified.

Beans led us up to the door, going and opening it for me.

Turning, I regarded Toni one last time. Narrowing my eyes, I frowned at just how similar they looked. "Next time, choose your daughter."

14

Eden

No matter how many times I restarted my chapter, I couldn't soak in the words on the page. My mind was racing, too distracted, too anxious, too hyperaware that *something* was going on.

Night had fallen and Cain was nowhere to be found as I sat on the bottom step by the front door, trying to read as I waited on bated breath for his return. *Night Changes* by Eleanor Patrick was my favorite book. A comfort read that never failed to lift my mood whenever I was down or lost. That Sunday evening, rereading the familiar passages about Dixie and Darius worked to no avail. I was stomped. In the end, I bookmarked my spot with a recipe for clams and linguine and gave up.

My book dropped from my hand, landing in a *smack* on the floor beneath me. Keys were jiggling just outside the front door. He was home.

The knob slowly twisted and I stood just as the door pushed open and Cain appeared behind it.

Blood. It was the first thing I noticed as I got a good look at him. Along the collar of his white dress shirt were splatters of blood and what looked like pieces of *flesh.*

Oh God.

Immediately, Cain noticed me, stopping in the doorway to peer into my eyes solemnly. And then he set what he was carrying with him down.

My eyes lowered and enlarged. From the front, the beige duffle was just a bag, but a peek at the side revealed mesh material showcasing *what* was inside.

"American Joe!" I squealed as I rushed down to see my furry friend.

Silently, Cain went out to the hall and grabbed the remaining items he'd brought home. A bright blue plastic litter box, a bag of litter, dry cat food, and something else in a gray shopping bag. He set all this down at the door, looking at me briefly, before going by me up the steps without a single word.

As happy as I was to see American Joe, to be reunited, I couldn't get over the sight of Cain. The undeniable fact that someone had gotten seriously hurt. That the blood on his clothing could only belong to...

I unzipped the pet carrier and let Joe out. Nervous, he huddled in the corner by the door, unfamiliar with this place.

"I know, Joe, I know," I assured him. I reached out and petted him softly, letting him know I had his back. That we'd brave through this together.

Curiosity got the better of me and I stood up, looking over at the staircase where Cain had gone.

I had to know.

Lead lined my belly and my legs were heavy, making my steps a challenge as I struggled to climb the stairs. At the top, I contemplated going back down and minding my business. But the brutal image of blood and matter drove me forward. A shiver went down my spine as I made my way up the hall to Cain's room.

The bedroom was empty. Across the space, I saw that the master bathroom light was on. I padded over, my heart beating violently in my chest.

Cain was naked, having discarded his clothing in a black bag in the middle of the marble floor. There was a laundry hamper against the back wall by the shelf full of towels and washcloths. He didn't intend to clean his clothes, because they were covered in evidence.

Taking in Cain's lean figure, I saw no signs of injury. He had come out the victor in whatever he had done.

Swallowing the lump in my throat, I managed to speak up. Needing to know the truth. "Did...did you kill...my mom?" I didn't recognize the softness of my voice.

Cain didn't face me as he gripped the handle of the glass door to his massive shower. "No."

Something like relief passed through me. "Why not?"

"Because I know what it's like to still love the person who hurt you the most." With that, he stepped into his shower and shut me out.

I waited for him on the edge of his bed. So many thoughts and feelings were circling my mind, but only one overpowered my entire being.

His presence washed through the room before he entered it. Cain appeared in the doorway of his bathroom dressed in only a pair of silk gold pajama bottoms. The color did nothing but complement his dark brown skin.

Cain spotted me and paused. "Eden."

There were no words, so I went on autopilot. With trembling hands I unbuttoned two buttons on his shirt I was still wearing, allowing my cleavage to spill out. I leaned back on my arms, willing.

Cain raked his gaze up my bare legs, over my body, and collided with mine. "What is this?"

"You can have me," I said, holding his gaze, hoping he didn't see me shaking.

Cain let out a breath through his nose. "You don't have to do this because of what I did."

He didn't expect it, which did something to my chest as my heart beat harder. "I want to."

Cain shook his head. "Not tonight, Eden."

"Please," I breathed out, feeling like I needed this somehow.

Cain's eyes flashed to mine once more, annoyance visible within them. "You don't have to spread your legs because I did something nice for you."

His words lashed at me as if he'd struck me. As if he put me in my place for behaving like a child. Like some silly little girl.

I leapt to my feet, my throat swelling with hurt as an icy burn skidded all over my skin. "Fine, I'll go spread them for someone else."

"Eden." He said my name the hardest he'd ever spoken it.

I didn't listen. I marched right over to the door, prepared to get dressed and go—

A vise grip seized my upper arm and whirled me around to a seething Cain. He had a hold on me that there was no shaking as he lifted me from my feet with ease. "You're not leaving this fucking room."

In seconds he'd dragged me kicking and struggling to his bed, where he threw me down. My body bounced for a moment, my head dizzy, but my anger was unrelenting. Cain soon hovered over me, his hands coming down on either side of me, blocking me from getting up and leaving.

I shoved at his chest. "Get off me!"

He only stared down at me, not budging.

Beating on his chest, I tried again and again to get him to move. When it didn't work, I was left peering up at him gazing down at me. Locked in, there was no running from the humiliation. Cain looked down at me as my emotions bubbled to the surface, choking me.

Weak and pathetic, I let out a cry I couldn't hold. "He hurt me." Tears pooled in my eyes and rolled down my cheeks as I began to sob until my throat throbbed. "He hurt me and she didn't stop it. She didn't help me. She didn't care."

I wanted to run and hide my ugly, but there was no getting away from it. Not with Cain facing it head-on.

Cain's dark eyes swam with a look I couldn't decipher. His soft hand cradled my face, thumbing at the tears leaking out of my eyes. "He's dead now." His voice was raw, strained, filled with compassion. "Look at me."

I didn't want him to see me like this. To go to that house and see where I'd come from. To know how outside of Duane, nobody cared about me.

"Look at me, Eden," Cain demanded.

There was nowhere to go. Grudgingly, I looked at Cain, finding a serious expression marring his face. "No one is ever going to touch you again. If anyone so much as looks at you funny, I won't hesitate to kill them. Do you understand?"

My sobs took over and all I could do was stare at him. This man who had done something most would consider heinous.

Neither disgust nor judgment radiated from Cain as he angled his head, wiping at my face, cleaning me up, focusing on the task. "You take punches because it's all you know. What you think you're supposed to do." He shook his head, going back to peering down into my eyes. "This fucking martyr shit dies now."

"Why...why do you care?" There was no fight in me as I lay there beneath him. His rich scent of masculinity, spice, and power somehow cocooned me in a comfort I hadn't ever known. A warmth I could crawl into and never come back out of.

Cain frowned. "Once upon a time, I was the smallest kid in the system and I took some punches too."

I couldn't imagine him as small. Not ever in this life. "You did?"

Cain nodded. "Sometimes it was the kids, and sometimes it was the parents."

My chest caved at the thought of a little boy being beat on. "Did you fight back?"

Cain shook his head. "Only when I was feeling big, and that wasn't often."

My heart twisted up and my eyes ran to the scar on his bottom lip. Tentatively, I reached out and touched it. "Is that how you got this?"

Cain took in a breath, his body going tight before me. "She didn't mean it."

I looked from his scar to his wounded eyes. "*She*?"

Pain slashed across Cain's face and he didn't try to hide it. Didn't try to change the subject. Didn't tell me to shut up. "My... my father was a married man. One of the biggest most influential people in old Vegas. My mom was just a young woman with a dream. He preyed on her and that's how I was conceived. Fed her a dream of love and money, and when she turned up pregnant, he switched up.

"So, she came back here. Settled down in Lindenwood and raised me with the little scraps he'd given her. When I was six, he came to visit, to shut her up, to smack her around, to threaten her if she ever contacted his wife. He walked out of our little house and she ran to the screen door, screaming, watching him leave. I... I went up beside her at the door, to see him go. And she was so hurt, so upset she..." He raised his hand, curling his fingers. "She grabbed the back of my head and just...

"She didn't know what she was doing. She was hurt, and she just reached for something...and it was *me*. She bashed my face into the door over and over until it opened and I fell through." Cain's face was empty as he told the horrible tale, detached from the horror he was telling. "My lip was cut and I lost a tooth."

My eyes rushed to the scar, the jagged imperfection that started on his lip and ended below it. His own mother had given it to him. I couldn't imagine carrying around such a reminder.

"She loved someone more than me, too," Cain spoke softly, finishing his story.

My eyes widened, taking in his words. The revelation. And then I saw him, saw him like he was seeing me.

Leaning up, I pressed my lips gently to his scar and lingered. Mothers were supposed to kiss boo-boos, not make them.

Closing his eyes, Cain kissed me back chastely before moving away. He settled down behind me, and missing his proximity, missing being caged in, I rested back against him. His arm came around me and held me close, and I looked down at his hand on my hip. The one with the rose tattoo. His only tattoo.

"Does your tattoo mean anything?" I wondered.

"My mother's name was Rose," Cain explained.

I ran my thumb over the ink, nodding at the fact.

He loved his mother, despite it all. The same way I loved mine.

Silence fell over us as Cain held me close and I relaxed into him. A comfortable quiet where nothing really mattered.

My belly grumbled, interrupting our moment and a smile curved my lips up. I hadn't eaten since that morning.

Cain squeezed my waist, having heard my body's protest. "I'm going to order some takeout. Make me breakfast in the morning?"

He could ask for a vital organ and I'd give it freely. "Yes."

Cain rolled me over onto my back, coming and leaning over me once more. His hand caressed my face, tilting my head back so that I could see into his eyes. "Are you okay?"

I felt nothing at the fact that Bobby was dead. "Yes."

Cain remained staring at me, stroking my jaw as he did so.

He touched me with hands that had just stolen another's life, and I had never felt more safe.

15

Eden

MY FIRST WEEK ALONE WITH CAIN FLEW BY AND I became adjusted. We settled into somewhat of a routine. In the mornings, Cain would leave for work, and I'd sleep in. Some days I'd make him breakfast, and some days I didn't. He didn't mind either way. Every other morning, he'd go down to the building's gym to work out and come back up to shower before work.

The days he stayed home I'd lounge in his office wearing one of his shirts and read. He'd spend hours on the phone or on his desktop. I liked sneaking peeks at him, finding him discussing deals and punishments with a straight face. He could sign a million-dollar contract and fire an employee all under the same mundane expression. He hardly ever lit up when he was in work mode.

But it wasn't all casino business. When it was drug related, he'd switch phones and speak in a funny code I couldn't understand. His side business dealings could last as long as his casino talk, or be significantly shorter depending on the day.

At noon, Cain would take a break for lunch and we'd eat something light: a salad, a sandwich, a bagel—Cain wasn't picky and he *never* complained.

He'd go back to work after and I'd return to my book. Eventually, I'd venture off to get started on dinner.

Dinner was a process I loved the most because Cain was such a big eater. He'd eat whatever I made. Even when I was experimenting. After, he'd clean, and when he was done, he'd pick me up and take me to bed.

"You could go out to the club," he told me one night while we lay in bed.

"I'm not a club girl," I responded honestly.

"Still," Cain insisted. "You don't have to be so cooped up in the house all day."

I had never known freedom and stability like this, and considering the circumstances, I couldn't help but laugh. "I think you need to read the kidnapping handbook to understand how this works."

Cain rolled over on top of me and kissed me quiet then.

Still, these days, life was like that old Sinéad O'Connor song. Since I was with Cain, I could do whatever I wanted. I could come and go as I pleased, but I didn't really exercise this right. Beans was also the closest thing Cain had to an assistant, and sometimes I'd tag along with him if he were going out to run an errand.

As much as I wanted to explore Hampton Hills, I otherwise stayed home. Maybe it was the romantic in me, but a part of me longed to go sightseeing *with* Cain.

But he was always busy.

As nice as Beans tried to be, and as much as I loved having American Joe, I was still lonely. It was a Monday when I finally reached out and called Duane to come over. Cain and I hadn't discussed it in depth, but it wasn't like he was around to ask. I didn't even have his phone number, and I wasn't going through Beans to talk to him.

Duane came over and my mood immediately lifted as I pulled the door open and saw his familiar face.

"Duane!" I squealed before throwing myself against him in a hug.

Duane's hearty chuckle rumbled from deep within his chest, causing my cheek to vibrate. He smelled good, reminding me of home.

He stepped back and examined me at arm's length. "Well, I don't see anything outwardly wrong." His eyes went to my head. "Outside of your hair change."

"Oh, stop," I said as I waved him off. Touching my now dark hair, I explained, "I wanted to blend in here."

Beans was standing beside us quietly. On guard and present if needed.

Duane took in the entryway and tilted his head back. "We are not in Kansas anymore."

"Definitely not," I agreed.

Duane came back to me, perking a brow. "So, you get to live in this nice-ass penthouse, have good sex, *and* get princess treatment?" My friend frowned. "Does he have a brother?"

At first, I started to laugh, but then I paused, unsure. "I don't...I don't know."

"He doesn't." Beside us, Beans spoke up, his eyes glued to me.

Duane sighed. "There goes that."

I took his hand. "Let's go see my room."

"Eden." For the first time, Beans's tone read of a warning. "Just *your* room."

I wouldn't have shown Cain's room anyway, understanding there was a line. Cain was generous despite the circumstance, and he really only had two rules.

Always come back, and never tell anyone his business.

Duane followed me up to my bedroom where he ooh'd and ahh'd at the site, furniture, and amenities. I showed him the downstairs as well, the theater room I was dying to use, the kitchen I was obsessed with, the balcony with the opulent view of the city, and the cozy entertainment area where we settled down inside. Beans hung back at the island in the kitchen, within hearing and seeing distance.

Duane relaxed on the love seat, moaning as he melted into the butter-soft fabric and material.

"I know," I agreed as I sat with my legs curled beneath me on the sectional. "I love reading in here."

Duane peered around, taking it all in. "You're certainly set up nice." He leaned over and helped himself to one of the appetizers I'd made for his visit for us to snack on. Pizza pinwheels, and sausage balls. He ate a pinwheel and smiled at the taste. "I've missed this. I'm basically starving now."

While he was good at his job, Duane wasn't much of a cook at home. Like some men, he would cook or grill some meat, but was terrible about preparing starches and vegetables.

"Sorry," I pretended to apologize. "Guess I could meal prep you some stuff while I've got the time."

"You playing, but I'll take it," Duane said as he swiped up a sausage ball. And then, because all of the food was with us, he looked over and observed Beans. "Hey, you want any?"

I'd made Beans his own mini tray, and because of this, he declined. "I'm good, thank you."

Still, Duane looked on at him. "What's your real name?"

To that, Beans quietly stared at Duane, offering nothing. It all made me curious. "Beans" and "Vino" weren't their *real* names. They even called Cain "Dice" whenever they spoke to him.

Duane snorted when Beans didn't respond. "Y'all came to my place covered in blood and I took your hush money." He palmed at his chest as he lounged back against the cushion. "I'm pretty sure that's a crime on my part, but I kept my mouth shut. Trust me, I'm not about to blab to the police or anything if I know your first name."

Beans continued staring at Duane silently. His tongue prodded the inside of his cheek as he appeared thoughtful. I didn't think he'd answer, but he did. "Malcolm."

Duane took this in and nodded. "Do you prefer Beans, or can I call you Malcolm?"

Beans raised a brow and tilted his head slightly to consider it. "Malcolm is fine."

Duane didn't push further before coming back to me. "How long you staying, Doll?"

This was where things got tricky on *my* end. It should've been simple. Three nights at the most, since I "owed" Cain three more rounds in bed thanks to his petty revenge. But it didn't turn out like that.

We'd had sex all last week, and I hadn't made an effort to count any of it toward my freedom. That night at the hotel, I'd been desperate to go, for fear of my life, but now... Duane said it best, Cain treated me good, I had a nice place I was currently staying, and I wasn't complaining about the sex. *Couldn't* complain about the sex. Cain could make me come with little to no effort. I loved that he worshipped my body until it was truly spent.

Sure, we weren't intimate in the way I'd prefer to be with a man, but the arrangement wasn't so bad. If I had to stick around for another week or two, it wouldn't be the most awful thing in the world.

Chewing on my cheek, I picked at a pinwheel, refusing to meet Duane's eyes. "I don't know."

He didn't judge me and I loved him for never breaking our bond. "Be careful. We both know how you operate, what you *want* in life, and I couldn't stand to see you used up and hurt."

It was what I needed to hear. This wasn't some warped, twisted fairy tale, and I needed to remember that.

He killed for you, my subconscious poked through.

And then there was that.

That night we'd bled our truths out loud and he'd held me close.

I popped the pinwheel in my mouth and focused on chewing. The worst thing I could do was get silly and believe this could turn into more. That anything good could come out of blatant kidnapping and sexual blackmail. That I should let my guard down and actually *fall* for the guy.

"My head is screwed on straight," I told Duane with finality.

He offered me a lopsided smile. "I support you no matter what."

"I know." I had no one else but Duane, and I cherished him fondly for always being there when no one else was.

Half an hour later he stood and rubbed at his middle. "God, the way I could stay right here all night. Just give me a beer, put on the Chargers game, and I'm set."

The TV came to life and I turned to find Malcolm standing among us now. He flipped through the channels until he found the latest sports news segment.

Duane laughed. "I was kidding."

Malcolm regarded him briefly before facing the TV. "I like the Chargers."

A corner of Duane's mouth quirked up. "Yeah? That's sacrilege where I'm from."

Malcolm shrugged. "I tried to keep it loyal and local, but that Rift Taylor made me a fan."

"Definitely feelin' The Rift Shift," Duane seemed to agree. "He's the future of the NBA."

Malcolm cut back to Duane. "Definitely."

I groaned. "Ugh, not basketball talk."

Duane chuckled. "As much as I put up with your romance novels *and* movies, you owe me a shit ton of guy talk."

Even if it was true, I made myself busy by collecting our dishes and walking them over to the kitchen. It was time to start on dinner anyway. Once Duane started talking basketball I couldn't keep up. And don't get me started on the confusion that was the whole concept of *fantasy* basketball. None of it made sense to me.

I let the steady chatter of Duane and Malcolm's basketball ramblings keep me company as I went about getting out pots and pans to prepare a dinner of ham, scalloped potatoes, and asparagus.

Duane couldn't stay long, not with his shift at work nearing. He came and kissed my cheek before I walked him to the front door. He hugged me close and tight, giving me all the positive vibes I needed to keep my spirits up.

After Duane left, Malcolm settled in front of the TV to get ready to watch the night's game. American Joe lay on the floor in a loaf between the dining room and entertainment room. I wasn't a fan of sports, but something about the atmosphere of Malcolm watching a game and me cooking dinner felt homey. And I liked it.

Cain didn't have a set schedule. Some nights, he came home around seven, other nights eight, or at the earliest six. As the time winded down and the clock struck nine, I began to worry.

While he never expected dinner to be ready by the time he got home, I liked having it hot and fresh for him. But as the night went on with no sign of him, I was forced to put everything up and clean after myself before joining Malcolm in front of the TV to mindlessly watch the game.

Sometime in the night, I awoke to the feel of Joe's paws digging into my legs as he walked over me on the sofa to find a place to lay.

Rubbing at my eyes, I lifted my head to see that the downstairs area was drenched in darkness, save for the TV. Some movie was playing and Malcolm was up in the chair across from me watching it.

At the sound of my stirring, he turned my way. "You can go on up to bed now. He's not coming home tonight."

My stomach leapt to my throat as my eyes tripled in size. Had something happened?

While this whole thing was still fairly new, it wasn't like Cain to *not* come home.

Reading the fear on my face, Malcolm simply shook his head, alleviating my worry and arousing my curiosity.

Sensing he wasn't about to answer any questions, I did as told.

My phone said it was midnight. Cain wasn't coming home. So I went upstairs, and for the first time in a week, slept in my own bed.

16

Cain

REPUTATION WAS EVERYTHING, WHETHER IN THE cutthroat business world, or the ruthless underworld. Your name and modes of operation, was everything.

In the eyes of many I wasn't competent to run Cartier. Something I couldn't fix, nor was I interested in attempting to. But in the drug trade, I made it my business to be on top of my shit. It was my bread and butter long before I ever donned the role of CEO of a billion-dollar company. I sold the purest coke money could buy, and I intended to keep it that way. Which was why I was beyond aggravated to learn a dealer of mine in LA was lacing my product with fentanyl—the lethal buzzkill.

Fentanyl meant one problem: the police.

While I had cops in my pocket, there was no getting around the ones who were trying their damnedest to crack down on the fentanyl epidemic. The last thing I needed was an honest badge on my trail.

So, reluctantly, on Monday, Vino and I took off for LA to permanently correct my LA contact Semaj.

Coming back home after dealing with that, I was a little on edge.

It wasn't regret plaguing me. I could still sleep like a baby last night after giving the order to end Semaj's life. The blood on my hands didn't deter me, but really it was the consequences of the turn of events that bothered me most. Running the casino was stressful; this side of things was a headache all its own as well.

We had just gotten out of Vino's car after he'd driven me home and parked in the parking deck of my building, when I paused at the trunk of the car.

We hadn't drunk or smoked, but it felt like I was dealing with a hangover.

Before I went in and faced Eden, I took a moment to stand back and decompress. I needed a second. I didn't want to carry this energy inside with me. Didn't want to burden her with my grievances.

We had just finished the deed when Beans's text came through on my phone last night.

B

She fell asleep staying up waiting for you

It was a small thing, but I didn't miss the meaning.

Eden had a soft heart, otherwise she had no business staying up waiting for me. Being worried.

Before, I never cared about my work hours, until her. Now, I looked forward to cutting my day short and making it in. I liked coming home because there was hot food and *her*.

Vino came and leaned against the trunk beside me. He pulled his pack of cigarettes from inside his jacket, hit the bottom with his palm so that one jutted out, and grabbed it. He lit up and took a drag. The potent smell of nicotine filled my nose soon after.

"You made the right call," Vino spoke up.

Shit like this was easy for him. It was why he was the perfect confidant. He could take a life without blinking or feeling one way about it. Business was always just business. Never personal.

It wasn't exactly personal for me either, but taking out Semaj disrupted our whole LA system. And I wasn't a big fan of change.

Massaging my jaw, I let out a heavy breath. "I'm not so sure about that."

"He was bad for the brand."

"He had a lot of connects."

"And he was killin' them, or, they were gettin' him to kill our customers." Vino inhaled his cigarette as he lifted and dropped his shoulders. He blew out a stream of smoke. "People buy your shit because they know it's pure. Semaj was fuckin' that up for you. He worked *for* you, and he should've run his little bright idea past you before he took it upon himself to make change."

Vino was right, but still, now I had to figure out a replacement.

I rubbed at my jaw once more. "I just don't like having to go through the motions of getting someone to take his place."

Vino sympathized. "I know. Shit was running smooth as it was."

Until Semaj messed it up.

Taking a final moment, I composed myself as best as I could. I shed my angry disposition like a second skin and released a calming breath. I was home now, and there was no room for irritation.

Vino and I headed inside and went up to my penthouse. One step inside the door and I could already hear the sounds of her existing. Something about just knowing she was up and around made my mood lift. Every minor error over the last twenty-four hours dissolved as I crept down the hall and set eyes on Eden.

Beans was in the living room, watching basketball highlights, paying Eden no mind.

I got back to her and took in the setting.

All I could do was stare at her as a tightness clenched in my chest. Dinner smelled heavenly, something beef. By some intuitive instinct, I knew it was meatloaf. Jazz and old R&B music was playing and Eden was singing along to Mickey and Sylvia, doing a little wine as she looked down at something on the floor—probably Joe. She went back and forth from dancing to chopping

up something on the counter. She was floating like a fairy—
Tinker Bell—and it was the most ethereal thing I'd ever seen.
Coming home to *this* was something out of a dream.

I was so transfixed by the sight in front of me, I barely
registered Vino talking to me until I felt his hands come down on
my shoulders. He gave me a brief massage as he came into view.
"You've got it made, D."

Blinking, I shook my head. "Too bad I can't keep her."

Vino frowned. "We make way too much money to be told
what we *can't* do."

It could be that simple, except, my moral compass was
actually working.

Vino and I went farther down the hall and into the kitchen
area. Eden was singing along now, off in her own world. Her hair
was secured at the back of her head in a bun. Her pretty face was
bare, save for her faithful eyelashes. I loved this look on her: lip
gloss, clean face, and lashes. The top she was wearing barely
covered her midriff, and those shorts—that tattoo below her ass
was on full display.

Vino knew better than to look at the women I messed with.
As much as I would've rather preferred Eden be more covered, I
kept quiet. For once in my life, I had something to be happy
about, to look forward to.

Truth be told this was my favorite part of coming home now.

I went around the counter and up behind her. She was
preparing a plate of meatloaf, peas, and mashed potatoes. A large
bowl was out for a homemade salad, a tray of rolls was near, and
bottles of dressing were out as well.

We could've made our own plates, but I admired how Eden
went all out.

"Oh." She jumped a little as I pressed a kiss to her shoulder.
God, she smelled good.

Eden angled her head to peer up at me. "You're home."

"I am," I responded.

Vino and Beans came and sat at the island. Eden handed

Beans a plate and he quickly dug in. Vino was next as he greedily reached for the plate she was offering.

A gasp escaped Eden's lips as she took a step back.

Vino paused, confused. "You good?"

Eden's eyes doubled. "Y-your sleeve."

And there it was.

On the ends of Vino's sleeves were rust stains—*blood* stains. Evidence of what had gone on last night.

Vino simply shrugged. "Comes with the trade."

Beans went back to eating and Vino was quick to join him.

By Eden's stiffness, I could tell this was a lot for her to take in. Unlike the women I was with before her, Eden had gotten closest to me. She *knew* me beyond the surface, so I had nothing to hide. There was no need to put up a front.

"You are among wolves," my words were in her ear, for her only. "Never forget that."

Eden stilled beneath me, as if unsure what to make of that statement. She reared back and gazed up at me. "What does that make *me*?"

"Someone who needs to decide whether they're going down with the slaughter, or going to howl with the pack." I kept my focus on her eyes, reading her in this moment, deciding what *my* next move would be.

I'd never hurt her, but I craved loyalty, to know that I could trust her. It wasn't until this moment where the music faded into the background and I hardly noticed Beans and Vino eating their meals that I realized that I already did. Unlike anyone before her, I'd let her in.

Eden peered up at me, her soft eyes reading my soul it felt like. The silence stretched between us and the more I stared at her, the more I couldn't find judgment. But more, acceptance.

"Ahem."

Obnoxiously, Vino cleared his throat. "It's rude to be all up on each other like that in front of company."

Whatever spell that had befallen us broke at that interruption.

Slowly, I peeled my gaze from Eden and focused on Vino. "If we're being honest, I'd rather you take your food and go. I don't care for the pleasantries. I'd rather come straight home and fuck her."

Vino bore a smile just as Eden sucked her teeth and swatted at my chest for my crassness.

I braced my hands on the counter on either side of her. Her sweet scent washed over me, competing with the delicious food she'd prepared. "Dinner smells good."

"Uh-huh." Eden went about making a third plate. By the time I was around the counter and finding a seat next to Beans, she slid the dish to me.

"I made a ham last night. I'll have to give you some to take home," Eden was speaking to Vino. "Malcolm and I had ham sandwiches for lunch. It was really good."

Malcolm.

It took me a beat to realize she meant Beans. It had been so long, I had honestly forgotten his *real* name.

Vino angled his head, swinging his attention from Beans to Eden. "Well shit, y'all got close, didn't ya?"

Eden lifted and dropped her shoulder lazily. "Kinda. Is Vino short for something?"

A wicked smile stretched across my left-hand man's face. "It does." He wagged his finger at her. "But if I tell you, I'll have to kill you."

Eden blinked, not finding the comment in the least bit funny. Neither did I.

Vino was just playing the game smart. The less Eden knew about him, the better. A crew of criminals, we rarely let anyone get this close to us.

Though I understood him, I still corrected him for Eden's benefit. "Vino."

He tossed me a smile and went back to his meal. "I'd appreciate the ham, Eden. Thank you."

Eden didn't join us. Instead, she began wiping down the stove and area she'd prepared the meal and gathering Tupperware. Even as I ate her amazing meatloaf topped with tomato sauce liked I preferred, half listening to Vino and Beans's chatter, I kept my eye on Eden, measuring her movements.

Something was wrong. It was hard to miss, especially when dinner was done and Eden disappeared from the room.

In the week since she'd been staying with me, we'd established somewhat of a routine. She'd cook me dinner, I'd happily eat it and clean every dish, and as I did all this, Eden would hang around the kitchen. Sometimes she'd ask me about my day, other times we spoke about hers. Tonight, she'd ditched me.

It was even more clear when I went up to my room to shower before bed. Eden wasn't anywhere to be found. Even if there was no sex involved, she'd taken to sleeping in my bed.

Tonight I came back from my bathroom to an empty bed. Not even American Joe was around.

I could've let it go, but an itch developed beneath my skin. The longer I gazed at my vacant bed, the longer the itch lingered.

My gaze roamed to the hall once before I took off to find her.

The light was on in Eden's room and the door was ajar. I rapped my knuckles against the clean white wooden door a couple of times before pushing it open.

Eden was in bed. American Joe was at the foot of the bed curled up and asleep. Eden was fresh in an olive-green slip and a black scarf on her head. She sat up against the plush cream headboard as she read a book.

Over the last week she'd made herself at home in my penthouse, leaving a piece of her in every room by way of books. Every book I picked up I discovered was bookmarked with a recipe the size of an index card. She'd start reading several books at a time and save her place in each with a recipe. Something that I admittedly found adorable. And, albeit, made me hopeful too. The recipes always sounded good, especially the orange and lemon butter cookies I'd found in the last book I'd picked up.

At my arrival she wrinkled her nose and grimaced as she pulled her attention from her latest book.

"What are you doing in here?" It was obvious, but I wanted her to talk to me.

Eden frowned and went back to reading. "I'm not in the mood. I'm reading."

Her not being interested in sex didn't bother me a bit. It was her very deliberate choice to sleep in her own room that did. As far as I knew, she'd only slept in her bed the first night before she started crawling in mine.

I rounded the king-sized bed, going and pulling back the thick dusty-gold comforter and climbing in beside her. The mattress dipped beneath my added weight. American Joe didn't stir and Eden made no effort to scoot away. Her nostrils flared but she said nothing as she kept her gaze on her book.

The silent treatment? Huh.

In the past, with other women, I wasn't much for affection. It was always mechanical. Public appearances, dinner dates and outings, and a couple rounds in bed before we fell asleep on different sides.

But not with Eden.

Eden continued to read and I continued to stare at her. A game of wits.

As much as I could stare at her pretty face all day, I broke first.

"You know, you can read in my room," I said.

Without taking her eyes off the page she was on, Eden shrugged. "I'd rather be in here. *Alone.*"

She was breathtaking when she was happy. Glowing and full of life. When she was irritated like she was now? Fucking adorable. I almost wanted to rile her up just to see her nostrils flare again.

"Something the matter?" I pressed, not wanting to beat around the bush.

Slowly, Eden turned and faced me. In her eyes, I didn't see

anger, just hurt. "This is a regular occurrence for you? Coming home late covered in someone else's blood?"

I suppressed the urge to snort. "Only sometimes."

She looked at me a moment longer before going back to her reading.

It felt like she was shutting me out. "Eden."

She sighed, going and closing her book. "I don't even know your phone number. You were gone all night and day. You spoke to Malcolm, not me, letting him know you were all right."

Her genuine concern over my well-being was palpable. And foreign to me all the same.

"Eden," I began calmly. "If something happens to me, you're free to go."

Those nostrils flared. My one true warning before she reached out and shoved me in a loud huff. "Be serious."

"I am," I responded, holding her gaze. "I've made my bed and I understand the path I chose. If something happens and I don't come back home—*ever*, it is what it is."

Eden shook her head. Of course she didn't understand. "Aren't you a millionaire?"

"Try *billion*," I corrected.

She seized me with a pleading look. "Then why do you have to still deal drugs and be in that life?"

It was times like last night with Semaj that I asked myself the same thing. Why I still built houses when I could sit comfortable with the revenue that came through from Cartier. I guessed the timeless adage of old habits dying hard had something to do with it. Not to mention there was a moment in the beginning after I succeeded in becoming owner of all of Cartier holdings that I wasn't sure if I would retain it all for long. The threat of litigation was very real when Sandford hadn't taken my turning down his offer to buy the business from me well.

Drug money made me. It was something like a safety net to fall back on when I thought about my intent to wear two masks from the start.

Eden wasn't judging me. Worse, she cared and worried.

"I wouldn't be where I am if it wasn't for dealing," I admitted. "The only way I survived the system was making a way for myself. The first time I touched a roll of money I bought myself a nice shirt and some pants and went to a restaurant and ordered a steak." A bitter smile curled the corner of my mouth as I glanced over at Eden, who was hanging on to my every word. "Think that was the last time I ever cried."

"It was that good?" she wondered innocently.

I shook my head, silently recalling that moment I'd sat alone at a table with tears rolling down my cheeks. "It wasn't about the taste, but about what it represented. Coming from the very bottom, being overlooked and neglected—to *still* make it despite all the obstacles. That's what dealing did for me."

In a way, it kept me humble, in another, it was a habit I couldn't shake. It came with unneeded stress I would admit, but I'd always managed to deal with it.

Her soft hand sent goose bumps across my body and a chill down my spine. It was unexpected. Eden had reached out and caressed my face, frowning as she peered at me.

"You survived, you know," she said. "You made it. You don't have to keep up with that life anymore."

"Guess I haven't found a reason to get out of the game," I confessed with a shrug.

She stroked her thumb across my cheek as she gave me a lopsided smile. "Maybe someday you will."

Who could call it?

Still, to right my wrong, I apologized for my absence. "I'm sorry I didn't talk to you last night."

My words took her by surprise. "Thought you didn't like saying *I'm sorry*?"

I didn't, but for her, I would.

In another moment I reached out, taking her into my arms and soon hovered over her. "I don't like you upset, Tink."

Confusion had Eden blinking. "*Tink?*"

"Like Tinker Bell."

She quirked a brow suspiciously. "Is that a short joke?"

I held her face in my hand. "Nothing about you is a joke to me, Eden."

A deep blush had her squirming and looking away from me.

Staring at her and holding her, it really was a pity I couldn't keep her.

17

Eden

MY BODY WAS COMFORTABLY WARM WHEN I WOKE UP. A stark contrast to waking up Tuesday alone in my room.

It was kind of funny. All it took was a week for me to become accustomed to life with Cain. Going to bed by myself made me feel cold and lonely. As my eyes opened Wednesday morning and I rolled over and saw his sleeping form beside me, I let out a contented sigh.

Cain lay next to me, eyes closed and sleeping quietly. Despite his troubled past and heinous deeds, he was a beautiful man. The scar on his bottom lip couldn't take away from his otherwise flawless ebony face.

Unlike when he was dealing with work, he was at peace as he lay facing me.

My eyes roved to his hand where it lay between us on my dusty gold sheets. While it was clean, I still imagined the blood on them. I wanted to believe he'd done what he did for a good reason. If there *was* a good reason to take a life.

Instead of dwelling on the matter, I climbed out of bed and tiptoed over Joe's sleeping body on the floor. Since my second night here I'd basically been sleeping in Cain's room. That's where I kept my toothbrush and other toiletries. I crept down the hall, the cold hardwood floor greeting the pads of my bare feet. Once in Cain's room, I made my way to the attached bathroom. I had just grabbed my toothbrush when Cain appeared in the doorway behind me.

There was his and hers sinks. I took one and Cain took the other. Together we brushed our teeth and washed our faces. The silence stretched between us was nice. A calm stillness that I found comforting.

When we were both done, Cain chanced a step closer and flicked his finger at my scarf. "Morning."

"Morning," I responded. Considering the time, I mentioned, "Aren't you running late?"

Cain leaned against the counter. "I pushed back some meetings and conference calls."

Whatever had him out all night must've disrupted his whole schedule.

Cain was watching me, and soon, he was in front of me, caging me in as he placed either hand on the counter beside me. "What's on your mind?"

I should've tread lightly, but curiosity got the better of me. "How...how many people have you killed?"

Cain didn't even flinch. "Lost count."

There'd been many. "More than a handful?"

A ghost of a smile threatened to break across his face. "Wasn't exactly keepin' score to give a figure."

There'd been many and he didn't even reflect on the matter. There wasn't a hint of a guilty conscience peeking through as I brought up his crimes. He was unremorseful.

"Okay," I decided.

"Okay?" Cain took another step closer, crowding my space. "That all you have to say?"

I didn't know what to say or think. He'd killed one of his men because they'd tried to kill him. He killed his father for using and abusing his mother, and for abandoning him. He killed Bobby for hurting me. There was always a reason, it seemed. A method to his MO.

Sometimes...sometimes things weren't so black and white.

Cain studied me closely. "What's your next move?"

"Breakfast," I stated simply.

My answer took him by surprise. Briefly, he did smile, but it washed away quickly as his hand came around my throat. He tilted my head back to where I was staring up at him. He brushed his thumb along the column of my neck. "Why aren't you afraid of me?"

I had every reason to fear him for the things that he'd done, but I wasn't afraid. "Because I don't believe you'll hurt me."

Cain quirked a brow. "No?"

I held his stare. "No."

Once more he stroked my throat, snorting softly. "So naïve."

I slapped his arm. "You're just trying to scare me because I see through you."

"Is it working?"

"No."

Cain let me go, letting loose a smile as he did so. "Too bad."

I rolled my eyes, something that made Cain laugh. He had the most handsome smile. I could stare at his smile all day.

His hand came up once more and he caressed my face, running his thumb behind my ear. "Why Paris?"

He was talking about my Eiffel Tower tattoo I'd gotten this past January.

"It's where Sabrina goes to find herself in my favorite movie," I explained.

Cain's forehead adopted a crease. "What movie?"

"*Sabrina*, the one from 1954. Although the '90s remake is good too," I told him.

"Haven't seen it," Cain said.

It wasn't a shocker this man didn't watch classic romances. "You should, it's really good. Plus, Paris is the city of love."

"So I've heard," Cain mused. "You planning on going?"

I frowned a little as I rested against the counter behind me. I glanced down at my empty nailbeds. "It's probably not that expensive, but I never really saw myself going there. It's just, you know, one of those things," I said with a helpless shrug.

Cain tilted his head to the side. "One of those '*things*'?"

"Yeah, one of those things you just can't have." I chewed on my lip, wondering. "Since you've become a 'billionaire,' hasn't there still been one thing you wanted you couldn't have? I mean, money can't buy everything, right?"

Cain leaned back against the wall opposite the sink, appearing thoughtful. "Last year...there was something I thought I wanted —*needed*, but I was wrong." He looked back at me, trailing his eyes up my person and meeting my gaze. "Very wrong."

I wondered what it was. At the same time, it sounded like he hadn't gotten it either. While a part of me was bummed about never seeing Paris in person, Cain didn't seem all that caught up on losing his desire.

"*Aimer et être aimé*," Cain recited in near perfect French of my other tattoo. "*To love and be loved.*"

It came from a quote from a French novelist, George Sands. "There is only one happiness in life: to love and be loved."

Outside of Paris, that was my biggest want in life.

"You're big on love, huh," Cain marveled.

I nodded without shame. I read about it and watched it, wanting it more than anything. "Yes."

"That what you want?"

"I want the fairy tale."

A humorous gleam passed through Cain's eyes. "White picket fence and all?"

"It doesn't have to be that cliché. Just honest, true love," I said. I'd come from the coldest household, worked in the harshest environment, and yet I still believed that it was possible that someday I could find warmth, love—a *home*.

"And what do you think love is like, Tink?" Cain pressed on.

A shy smile touched my lips. "A blessed duality, where one

minute your person makes you feel like you can fly, and the next they're keeping you grounded, safe, secure." I either sounded totally naïve or helplessly optimistic. I leaned toward the latter. I was a romantic after all.

"Cute," Cain said with a small smile as he folded his arms.

With anyone else, I would've thought they were mocking me. Looking on at Cain, I could tell that wasn't the case.

"Don't you want that too?" I asked. "Love, I mean."

He himself had come from Hell. Surely he had to want to be loved as well.

Cain bit his lip and seemed to think it over for a moment. "I don't know. I've never had a family, at least a real one."

It used to burn me at the reality of my homelife. Of having a mother who didn't care whenever her boyfriend would bully me or hit me over the littlest thing. "Do you ever just feel...broken? Unfixable?"

Cain regarded me. "All the time."

"It never goes away, huh?"

Cain shook his head. "I kinda just accepted it's not in the cards for me. Happiness. Love and all that."

My heart dropped at his words, at how defeated and final they sounded. "Why not?"

He gave me a lazy smile. "Who could love a monster?"

I could.

The realization stunned me. Luckily for me, Cain went on before I could say it out loud.

"I don't really buy that Disney bullshit anyway," Cain said.

A frown tugged on my lips. "Why don't you believe in happy endings?"

"Because I've done some bad things."

"So?" I challenged. "There's still room to grow and change."

Cain only stared at me. "Guess we'll see how the dice roll."

He didn't sound convinced, and I hated that for him. Bravely, I took a step closer to Cain, bridging the gap between us. I placed my hand on his chest, so tiny in comparison to his stature. "Even the ugliest of monsters have a heart, and they deserve to be happy and loved, too."

A quiet formed between us. Cain stared down at me as I peered up at him.

I didn't see a monster. I saw a man who treated me better than almost everyone I'd ever known.

Cain broke away first. He turned for the door, ready to leave and end this moment. "I've got calls to make and sit in on." Before he walked out, he faced me one final time. "Thank you, for dinner last night. It was amazing."

And that was it.

After brunch, I curled up on the sofa with American Joe. I read a book as he rested against my thigh. He had adjusted so well to this new setting. In a way, so had I.

Sure, the circumstances were murky, but there wasn't much to complain about—there *wasn't* anything to complain about. I didn't have to work, I got to cook all the time and hone my skills, I got to read more often, and I was having mind-blowing sex.

I was almost positive when I left this penthouse and returned home Duane would have me committed, because clearly, I was losing it.

The sudden arrival of fingers lodging in my hair caused me to jump as my heart skipped a beat.

My hand flew to my chest as I whirled around in time to see Cain standing there behind the sofa. Dressed in a white dress shirt with black slacks, he was on the phone, staring at me impassively.

He placed a finger to his lips, signaling me to be quiet before he held the device away from his ear. "Get dressed. We're going out."

With that, he turned and walked away.

We hadn't attended any events last week, but I guessed it was back to business.

I saved my spot in my book before heading up to my room to

get ready. With no clue in where we were going, I browsed my selection of outfits I'd gotten from the shops in town and drew a blank. Taking a chance, I grabbed a little beige dress and decided it would have to do with wherever we were going.

I'd loved the piece as soon as I set eyes on it. Its bodice was butterfly inspired, bejeweled with the material cut out at the sides and backless. The flowy skirt and tight top made me feel pretty when I'd initially tried it on.

It didn't matter where we were going. As soon as I put on the dress, I knew I was wearing it out.

When everything was in place, my hair and makeup done, my dress snug on my body, and my heels giving me a boost, night had already fallen. I went down to the first floor with American Joe trailing behind me. I liked to think of us as two peas in a pod. Where I went, he went. We were both strangers to this new world of Hampton Hills, and it felt good to have an old friend having my back and vice versa.

I'd made it downstairs just in time as Cain was down the hall exiting his office. He'd been on his phone, but one look up and he froze. His gaze fell to my feet, soon doing a long and slow sweep up.

A bubble of anxiety blossomed in my belly and I nervously shifted from one foot to the other.

Cain hung up his phone without so much of a goodbye. He came over to me, examining me further. Quietly and thoroughly.

"Is it okay?" I wondered of where we were going.

Cain himself was in a fitted rust-orange three-piece suit with a beige accent tie and pocket square. We hadn't done it on purpose, but the reality of us matching brought me comfort.

Cain went past me, as if making up his mind about something. "It's fine."

Fine? I thought I looked more than fine.

I whirled around and watched him head over to the front door. "Are Malcolm and Vino coming?"

Cain shook his head and opened the door, holding it out for me to exit first. "I gave them the night off."

Oh.

I bent down and quickly petted Joe before heading out. Even as I followed Cain down to the parking deck, I still couldn't imagine what we were up to. We passed a row of a fleet of vehicles until Cain came to a stop in front of a black Audi. Being chivalrous, he opened my door for me and helped me in before shutting the door, rounding the car, and climbing in beside me.

The whole time Cain drove, he gave no tell on where we were going. Instead, he let the radio play, a station dedicated to old-school R&B, as I recognized classic Marvin Gaye singing about a distant lover.

The drive wasn't long. A good ten minutes later Cain was pulling up to a valet line in front of a building with a marquee over the entrance. The glowing yellow sign told me this was Lucky's Blues Lounge. Other couples were heading inside, hand in hand, or arm around arm. They, too, were dressed up.

Cain exchanged keys with the valet as another man came to my side of the car and opened the door for me.

A gentle breeze danced past my body as I stood on the front sidewalk taking it all in. The street was busy with cars going back and forth, the surrounding businesses were restaurants, cafés, and a lone movie theater.

"Ready?" Cain was at my side, placing his hand on the small of my back, prepared to lead me in.

I wasn't sure what was going on, but I was excited. "Yeah."

Cain led us inside and at once it was as though we traveled back in time. Blues was playing from the speakers, and straight ahead of us I spotted a stage with abandoned instruments and a microphone. The men and women walking around waiting on the tables and booths in the room were dressed to the nines in trousers, dress shirts, or skirts and dresses. The dimly lit room and the swing of blues music reminded me of the old paintings I'd see at the hair salon growing up, like something out of the Harlem Renaissance.

Wow, I mouthed to myself as I took it all in.

Cain leaned close to say, "I own this place. There's some paperwork I need to check in on, and since you like old movies, I figured you'd appreciate the club."

He read me right. Night clubs in Bedford Heights were filled with raunchy rap music or R&B without emotion or love. I'd never liked that environment, no matter how many times Jenesis dragged me out to have "fun."

Lucky's Blues Lounge was the exact opposite. Delicious smells of food hung in the air as waiters and waitresses served guests at the tables and booths, the current blues song had couples on the dance floor slow dancing and clinging close, and the steady chatter from the second-floor area provided a sense of no drama but a calm setting.

"I like it!" I perked up, causing Cain to break out in a small smile. "Thanks for taking me."

All at once he was serious again. "I like seeing you happy."

I bit my lip to contain my smile and blush. I held his hand as we were brought to a booth in a quiet corner. We had a view of the entire first floor, something I could tell Cain liked as he surveyed the room before returning to our table. He ordered himself a glass of wine and I requested a lemonade.

Once our waitress was gone, I turned back to Cain, finding him skimming the menu. The menu was adorable, shaped like old school vinyl with a list of items the lounge served on both sides.

"What sounds good?" Cain wanted to know, not taking his eyes off the menu.

I gave mine another once-over before settling on the blackened salmon topped with shrimp and crab and served with collard greens and basmati rice.

Really, I was too excited to eat, but even if Cain was a *billionaire*, I wasn't about to be wasteful. I hardly got to go out to places. Back home, my life was an endless routine of work and home, or occasionally the bookstore.

Our waitress swooped by, depositing our drinks before collecting our orders and leaving once more.

I sipped on my lemonade and soaked in the music. It reminded me of my favorite films. Of romance. Of love.

My eyes glided over to Cain. He was caught up on his phone, lost to the music as he occasionally bobbed his head.

If I let myself get carried away, I would say this was a date.

The thought made me blush harder.

"Something funny?" Cain's attention was now on me.

I shook my head. "No. I was just wondering, why blues? Why this place?"

Cain gave a small shrug as he looked around. "One of the nicest homes I stayed in was run by an older couple. I was only there for a day, but I'll never forget the experience. The wife was kind and the husband loved jazz, the blues, old music that held soul." Cain spoke with his hands, gesturing to his heart as he explained it. "Ever since then, I've been in love with the sound. It reminds me of the one nice stop I had in the system."

I hated how he grew up. It was so similar to my own upbringing, but far worse when I thought about it. Going from a broken home to a cold and cruel system was something no child should have endured. But somehow, someway, Cain had persevered. Of course he had. He was probably the fiercest person I knew. I couldn't imagine anything getting in his way or stopping him. Even sitting across a table from him I could feel his presence, feel his power and strength.

He likened himself to a monster, a villain, but even with the blood on his hands, I still saw the good in him.

"Whenever I'm having a hard day, I like to just sit back and listen to the blues. It's my calm," Cain said of his favorite genre of music.

Whenever I was in a funk, I liked curling up and watching my favorite movies, or reading a book. We all had our own ways to escape, and I liked Cain's the more I listened in on the songs that played throughout Lucky's.

Our food came and I ate my salmon while Cain enjoyed his marinated chicken. As delectable as the food was, I couldn't stop my foot from tapping on the floor to the beat of the music. The trumpets echoed in my heart and the slap of the piano keys made me want to bounce.

It wasn't long after our meal that I stood from the table, grinning down at Cain. "Let's go dance."

His brows furrowed as he shook his head. "I don't dance."

I pouted, not even sure if it would work. "Please."

"Not my thing, Tink."

Tink. I'd never tell him how much I liked the nickname. "Come on, it'll make me happy."

Half a beat later Cain was up out of the booth and pulling me close. "You are a brat, you know that." He pressed the words into my ear, sending goose bumps down my spine. The seductive tone of his voice, the feel of his hot hands on my body, I felt delirious just then.

Out on the dance floor, other couples made room for us to join them as we fell in step to the sound of a woman singing about foolish things. Cain's arms came around my body as I wrapped mine around his neck.

"Thank you," I said as we swayed along to the music.

"Anything," he responded of what he'd do for me.

My cheeks hurt from smiling too much. "What makes *you* happy?"

Cain bit back a smile, as if he was in on a joke I wasn't privy to. "Little things."

It was a vague answer and I wanted more. "What do you want most?"

He came closer, stroking my jaw with his thumb, watching the action. "Light." He said this so lowly, I wondered if I'd imagined it.

He spoke in mystery, but I didn't care. I liked this. This

moment between us where we were just a man and a woman out on the town. Where the violence of our pasts wasn't out to haunt us.

I reveled in Cain's gentle touch. Next to Duane, he was the only one who handled me that way.

Staring up at him looking down at me, I shivered internally. What did I want most? To kiss him. Right then and there, in the middle of the dance floor. In this darkened room, crowded space, along the buzzing stir of jazz. I wanted nothing more than to get lost in his taste, his arms—him.

In one way, Cain was my captor. A man holding my freedom over my head. In another, he was my savior. A man who was hell-bent on protecting me from my adversaries. A paradox, I knew, but I accepted all the same.

I felt so much as he continued looking down at me. Before I did something foolish, like go through with kissing him, I leaned close and rested my head on his chest.

His heart beat steadily, and it only served to remind me of his place in my life. Despite it all, Cain kept me steady, whereas before everything was unpredictable and uncertain. Here, with Cain, everything was a smooth flow. A calmness I'd never known before.

"You're not so bad," I murmured against his chest.

Either he wasn't so bad, or I wasn't so good, because I didn't care to judge this man for his crimes or deeds.

Cain probably had work in the morning, but after settling whatever paperwork he needed to go over with the manager, he let me stay all night. He let me go up on stage and touch all the instruments. He let me go up to the second floor where I explored. He let me do whatever I wanted. And I was happy.

18

Eden

It was late when we got in from Lucky's. I'd had the time of my life slow dancing to jazz and the blues, feeling the heat of Cain's stare as I roamed the place long after it closed.

I had never smiled or laughed so much in my life.

I should've been tired by the time we'd made it home, but I was oddly wired.

Instead of sharing the shower in Cain's room, I'd gone into my own to free my face of makeup. Wiping my face clean, I hummed along to the memory of the Dinah Washington song I'd danced to with Cain.

Showering solo was noticeably different. The whole process wasn't as fun without Cain. Honestly, I loved the way every time we showered together he'd lather me up with soap and clean me, and then when we were done, he'd dry me down and rub lotion into my skin until I smelled like a mix of cocoa butter and berries. At this point, I was too lazy to do it myself.

After my shower I found a discarded shirt of Cain's and slipped it on before heading down to the first floor. Hours had passed since I'd eaten my blackened salmon. While there were leftovers in the fridge, I opted for grabbing a couple packets of ramen to boil on the stove to eat. The entire downstairs area, save for the kitchen, was bathed in darkness. American Joe wasn't around to keep me company as I cooked my ramen.

Cain's stainless-steel refrigerator held a touch screen on one door. I logged on to my Spotify account and found a blues and jazz playlist to play to keep with the night's theme. Soon, Nina Simone began singing about a new dawn, a new day, and a new life.

I hummed along as I padded over to the counter to lean up on my tiptoes to reach into the cabinet for a bowl.

A hand beat me to it, startling me and making me land back on my feet, stumbling until my back collided with a solid chest. Warmth pressed against me before I whirled around to find Cain standing there. Amusement sparkled in his dark eyes as he peered down at me.

"What's all this?" he asked.

I accepted the bowl he'd grabbed for me and went by him. "Thanks."

At the stove I helped myself to a portion of the noodles after mixing in the beef-flavored seasoning from the provided packets.

I grabbed a bottle of hot sauce from the pantry and Cain watched as I settled at the island with my bowl and condiment.

I knew he was from Bedford Heights and beyond thanks to being in foster care, but since then he'd become a billionaire. His palate was far expensive now after wining and dining at five-star restaurants. Even with his Black Card in my grasp when I'd been out shopping, I couldn't stop myself from sifting through the grocery store until I found an aisle that held ramen noodles. Something the cashier had raised a brow at when I'd been checking out.

"Have you ever wanted something cheap and easy?" I asked as I looked up from my food.

Cain ran a hand down the front of his black T-shirt, smoothing out the material. "Once in a while I'll eat a burger."

I stirred my noodles with a smile. Something about this detail was adorable to me, trying to imagine Cain pulling up to a local drive-thru to purchase a greasy burger, fries, and a Coke or shake. "I'd love to watch you eat a burger."

Cain sniffed the air and I flicked my gaze to him, finding him eyeing my bowl. "Want some?"

"Yeah, if it won't put you out."

I shrugged and stood up. "No trouble."

I quickly went and grabbed a second bowl and fork and gave Cain his own portion of the noodles. He remained on the opposite side of the island as I settled back down on my stool.

Cain studied his bowl with a boyish smile that made my heart skip a beat. "Now this is five-star dining."

Of course I'd been wrong about his tastes. He appreciated food in all qualities due to his brutal upbringing where he often starved.

"Sometimes I add a little hot sauce for the razzle dazzle," I said as I tipped a few drops of Devil's Red into my bowl.

Cain held his out. "Don't leave me hanging. I want the works."

I went and added some hot sauce to Cain's bowl and he grinned even more.

Together, we began eating our ramen across from each other. Him in his T-shirt and pajama bottoms and me in just his dress shirt. There was something so homey about it, that I ate my noodles with a goofy smile.

We'd skipped dessert at the lounge, and a part of me was craving something sweet to top this late-night meal off.

"What's your favorite dessert?" I asked as I looked up from my bowl.

Cain chewed and swallowed, appearing thoughtful at the question. "Honeybuns."

At the admission I perked up on my stool. "Oh my God, I *love* honeybuns! But they have to be from the corner store or gas station. The ones from the supermarket don't taste the same."

Cain chuckled, his broad shoulders shaking as he did so. "Thought I was the only one who noticed that."

I blushed and went back to my food.

"Oh, before I forget, I bought an air-fryer while I was out with Malcolm," I mentioned between bites. "It's the best way to reheat pizza or wings. And it's a little healthier than deep-frying everything."

Cain bobbed his head. "That's fine. You can take it with you when you go home."

I frowned. While it was more top-of-the-line than the one I had back at home with Duane, I'd bought it for Cain since his kitchen was almost bare of appliances. "Why don't you keep it? I'm sure you'll figure it out. It's not hard to use one."

A corner of Cain's lips curled as he ate a forkful of noodles. He regarded me, giving me a sheepish shrug. "I burn cereal."

For someone who loved to eat, it was a pity he didn't know how to cook. God, his kitchen was a playground for me. It was never a hassle cooking meals every day to feed the two of us along with Malcolm and Vino.

I shook my head. Even if he didn't cook, there was no missing how spotless his kitchen was, or his home for that matter.

"You don't have a maid?" I wondered.

"She comes once a month. I try to keep up after myself until then," he explained. "Given the lifestyle I lead, I try not to have too many eyes and ears around at all times."

That explained why he didn't have a real assistant outside of Malcolm. No wonder to the outside world he came off as an enigmatic billionaire and bachelor. He guarded his private life very well, because what was done in the dark couldn't afford to come out in the light.

"I won't tell, you know," I said as I forked at the remains of my noodles. A heavier blues song was playing in the background, filled with harmonica and guitars, and a man singing his heart out.

A grim expression crossed Cain's features as he squinted a little at my words. "That so?"

"Uh-huh." I nodded. "I won't tell any of it. What you do and what you've done, is safe with me."

"Hmph." Cain hummed as he grabbed his bowl and walked it back to the counter.

I bit my lip, wondering if that was a bad thing to say. Grabbing my own bowl, I walked it over to the counter and abandoned it there after scraping out the remains of the noodles in the trash.

Cain placed his bowl in the sink before leaning back against the counter to study me. "Got any more plans for the remainder of the night?"

His face was void of a tell of what he was thinking. A shadow had passed over him suddenly, almost as though he was shutting down.

I looked down at the tiled floor and shrugged. "I was thinking about staying up a little late and watching a movie in the theater room."

"Mind if I join you?" Cain surprised me by asking.

My head shot up at that request. "Sure!"

Together we left the kitchen side by side as we entered the hallway. Cain was quiet, his features betraying nothing.

"You know, if you don't end up liking it, we can't be friends," I teased as I peered up at him.

Cain peeked at me from the corner of his eye. "'Friends.'" He briefly snorted and shook his head.

I narrowed my eyes. I was almost, *kinda*, serious.

We kept walking in silence and I stewed in my head, wondering—

Within a second, Cain had stopped, faced me, and whirled me around. My back met the wall behind me in a solid *thump* as my breath escaped my lips. I had just a second to blink before he came capturing my face in his hands and kissing me hard. And I melted, caving against the wall as he held my face and kissed me raw.

"Mmm." I moaned without shame as I wrapped my arms around him and pulled him closer, seeking his heat, his body—him.

This was everything I'd wanted back at Lucky's. Just him and me, lost in each other, as we kissed without abandon.

Cain pressed himself against me, his hardness digging into my belly and his touch igniting my soul on fire. I was all need as his lips lingered on mine, his tongue finding solace in my mouth.

His hands slipped from my face and traveled to the shirt I was wearing, beginning to unbutton it. All too soon he broke away from my lips and kissed a path down my neck, past my breasts, following where his hands were going at a pace that left me squeezing my thighs together. I could feel my heart beat down below as an almost painful throb began to pulsate.

I needed him. So, so badly.

Cain sank to his knees before me, going and staring at where I was clutching my thighs together with a sexy smirk that only made me wetter. He shook his head, peeking back up at me. "That's not going to work."

He unbuttoned the last button and exposed my nudity beneath the shirt to him. His eyes glowed with want and pure lust. His hands trailed down my thighs, gently guiding them apart just before he buried his face between them.

My back arched from the wall as I let out a strangled cry of pleasure. God. His mouth, his tongue, his expert ease at bringing me to the brink with just enough pressured flicks.

My hand landed on the top of his head, steering him more into me as I rolled my hips into his face. "Please," I begged as my eyes slipped shut.

I could feel my release building, more and more as Cain spread me and ate like his life depended on it. His moans turning me on more as he pulled my clit into his mouth and sucked on it hard.

Unable to hold back, I screamed out as my orgasm took over

me. All I could do was ride it out as Cain kept going, getting his fill of me.

When I could take no more, I pushed him back, dropped to my knees, and yanked his pajamas down. Looking up at him watching me, I stroked him once before taking him into my mouth. I had only gotten to suck him for a moment before he was pulling me up to my feet once more. Cain took a dangerous step close, the stormy look in his eyes my only warning before he picked me up and slid inside of me halfway.

"Fuck." He pressed his forehead to mine, groaning at the sensation of us. He pulled back and looked me in the eyes lazily. "I have enough 'friends.'" He thrust into me more, until I was fully seated on his length and gasping at the stretched feeling. "Understand?"

With my mouth open all I could do was nod.

Cain perked a brow. "What number is this?"

Number. What number were we on in his sneaky game of sexual payback?

Lulling my head back until it rested against the wall, I racked my brain for a figure. When an answer came to mind, I stared back at Cain. "I stopped counting."

He smirked, thrusting once more. "Same."

He began fucking me, right there against the wall in the hallway. Hard, full-force, as if he were sending me a message.

I was a mess of whines and moans, clinging on to his shoulders to find some sense of gravity.

The pressure was building back up as he slipped in and out of me, my wetness evident by the *splish-splash* of his strokes. Cain looked down between us, watching himself enter me over and over again.

"Fuck." It had never been this good before with anyone else. Only Cain held the power to make me a wreck like this. It was as if there was a deep ache inside of me that only he could reach.

Sex with him was always a heavenly experience where he

pushed my body to its limits, and when I was spent and shattered, he held me close in the aftermath.

Breathing hard and heavy, I stared down at Cain, feeling that *need* again. I unclasped my hands from his shoulders, going and caressing his face. His eyes and his want were only for me. Leaning down, I devoured his mouth with my own. Kissing made the sex more intense, with heavier consequences.

I had to agree with Cain. I had enough friends, too.

19

Cain

A SHARP BUZZ FILLED MY OFFICE, FOLLOWED BY BRIEF crackling over my desk's intercom.

"Mr. Carter, Beans is here to see you," my secretary's—LaShanti—voice spoke up just as Beans made his entrance in the doorway.

I pressed the Talk button as Beans shut the door behind himself for privacy. "Thank you."

I settled back into my plush leather chair behind my executive desk I held in my private office at Nichols & Wagner's Hampton Hills location. Before me, on my left where a gray suede sectional sofa lined the wall, Vino was sitting back. It'd been a dull day at the office and he hadn't minded stopping by and hanging out while I went over contracts and checked in on the progress of The Residence at Cartier out in LA.

Beans's arrival was a welcome surprise and break in the monotony.

Still, I couldn't pass up giving him shit. "If it isn't Malcolm."

Vino cracked a grin, sizing our friend up. "XL."

The joke caused us to laugh as Beans was quick to make a face and flip Vino the bird before coming and taking a seat in one of the black chairs in front of my desk.

It was evening, going on six thirty, and I was about ready to call it a day. Whatever he wanted left me curious, though, because it wasn't long before I was due to head home.

"What brings you by?" I asked, cutting to the chase. "Something wrong?"

It had been weeks, and I still had him on babysitting duty as far as Eden was concerned. Even if I didn't believe for a second she'd run off and make trouble for me. I liked knowing she had someone with her, someone who wouldn't hesitate to protect her if she needed it. Hampton Hills was mostly harmless, as close to perfect as a city could get. But I never wanted to be caught lacking.

Beans shook his head. "Everything's fine. I just stepped out to talk to you before you left for the day."

"And Eden?" I pressed.

Beans shrugged. "Is at home roasting a chicken and making homemade gravy."

My stomach threatened to growl at the thought of the meal. For once in my life, I felt spoiled.

I thumbed at my lip, feeling a tightness in my chest. *I should get her some flowers.* Eden was as pretty easygoing as they came. She didn't make any demands or wants. Even with access to my Black Card and my never-ending bank account she didn't splurge.

Maybe a trip to the bookstore, too.

"So, what's up?" I asked, feeling comfortable knowing that Eden was accounted for.

Beans looked back at Vino before returning to me and lifting his chin in my direction. "Can you get tickets for the NBA Finals?"

At once Vino clicked his tongue and scowled. "Tell 'im no."

Beans snorted, looking back at him. "Doesn't matter whether I'm there or not, Golden State isn't beating the Chargers."

"Fuck the Chargers," Vino snapped.

I didn't get wrapped up in sports too much. In Vegas, I'd go and see a Jaguar Jones match if he had one, but that was only out of respect and loyalty. Football, basketball, and the rest? I was hardly a casual fan to form an opinion like Vino and Beans.

Beans loved the Chargers and their rookie All-Star, Rift Taylor, and Vino was loyal to the soil as far as California teams went. Being from LA, Vino was rooting for the Lakers first and foremost, and then he still threw support to the Kings, Clippers, and Golden State.

Their usual bickering drew a smile to my face. Beans didn't ask me for anything, and because of that, it was never a problem to oblige him if he ever did have a request.

Being one of the top companies in Hampton Hills, we often were afforded many amenities. Free samples from clothing brands, tickets to red carpet releases, or backstage passes for the latest concert. And one luxury many at the office coveted, was the access to free tickets to sporting events. Damon and Phil were gifted the sports tickets, and being their partner in our joint venture, *I* was now able to pull rank and get tickets too. But again, it wasn't my thing. When the Long Beach Sharks and the Kansas City Chiefs went head-to-head at this past February's Superbowl, I'd been in a generous mood and raffled off my share of the tickets to the staff on my floor.

I'd been considering doing the same for next month's NBA Finals.

"Done," I told Beans.

Vino rolled his eyes. "Gon' and take ya ass to nowhere-ass Ohio."

Vino's saltiness made their exchange that much funnier.

"Anyway." Beans returned to me. "It's a month away. Think you'll be done with Eden by then?"

My eyes fell to the large calendar on my desk, the one telling me of the many weeks Eden had been in my home. Neither of us spoke about her going home, returning to Bedford Heights and being done with my payback. At this point, we were fucking because we wanted to.

Vino dropped his humor, turning serious. "That is a million-dollar question, D." He sat back and steepled his fingers together, musing over the idea. "You gon' let her live?"

My office was soundproof, and once every two weeks I had a guy come in and check for bugs. I played the business game clean, but being young, rich, Black, and successful, didn't mean the feds weren't watching.

I thought over Vino's valid question, going and looking out one of my floor-to-ceiling windows that lined the left side of my office.

For all intents and purposes, I *shouldn't* let Eden leave alive. But the thought of snuffing out her light didn't bode well with me.

Still, she knew too much. "I'm having Rob draw up an NDA as we speak."

Vino's lips twisted into a smirk.

Yeah, I knew it was bullshit. My lawyer was worth every penny, but even I knew an NDA wouldn't protect me in the long run due to Eden's knowledge of my crimes. She was a liability.

My finger tapped rapidly against my desktop. This line of conversation was necessary, but I hated to have it. "You want to do the honors?" I asked Vino.

He shrugged. "Nothing personal." He glanced at Beans. "We all know this one won't do it. Not with him giving his name out and everything. Becoming best friends with her and shit."

Beans didn't deny his inability to kill Eden.

Beans watched me. "It's not happening."

"Oh?" Vino challenged.

Beans regarded him, gesturing toward me. "He can't do it himself. You really think he's going to let one of us do it?"

Beans wasn't wrong. The ease with which Vino was willing to go through with it tempted me to reach for my gun. And he'd only been doing his job.

I scrubbed a hand down my face. "She doesn't die."

I had my principles when it came to taking lives. Even if there was a possibility Eden was playing me and planning to turn me in —I'd let her.

"Hey, I like her, I do," Vino spoke up once more. "But you gotta figure out what you're going to do with her. The longer you drag this out..."

"You're not going to want to let her go," Beans pointed out.

I dismissed his remark. "I always let them go. Sooner or later, they always walk."

Beans didn't back down. "This isn't that."

Rolling my eyes, I looked to Vino for backup, but he didn't look too convinced.

"She wants the impossible. The 'fairy tale.' Someone on the straight and narrow," I mused more to myself than to them. We could never work.

Eden was a naïve little romantic.

This Big Bad World would eat her type alive, and as much as I shouldn't have cared, a part of me wanted to cloak her from it all. In all my years looking out for myself solely, I'd never had a weakness, a soft spot for enemies to see—now, I wasn't so sure if that were true anymore.

"Nothing is 'impossible' for you," Beans responded. "You beat the odds every time. *This* would be no different."

I loosened my tie and sank back in my chair, glowering at my closest and oldest friend. "All right, in the meantime, when are *you* going to get some business of your own? When was the last time you saw a man?"

Beans frowned and I wondered if I'd crossed the line. Ever since we were kids, his self-esteem had been in the dumps. He wasn't hard on the eyes, as many women had had the misfortune of finding him attractive. "I'm committed to the cause."

I snorted. *Too committed.* "I never saw something like a happy ending for myself, but you, you deserve it. Something nice and stable."

Beans wasn't convinced by my deflection. "You're really not this evil person you make yourself out to be."

I waved a hand out the room, alluding to where Eden was back at my penthouse. "No?"

Beans smiled. "Rocky start, I will admit, but this is more than repaying a debt. The sooner one of you accepts it, the better. Although, it is entertaining to watch."

Rolling my eyes, I focused my attention out the window.

She wasn't afraid of me.

Unlike many before her, Eden ate up my anger with a playful smile that left me mystified. Kennedy had held an attitude with me, but she was still intimidated—*afraid*. Eden was no such thing.

"D?" Beans spoke, bringing me out of my thoughts.

I looked his way. "Hmm?"

"Quit playing with your food. Either swallow or spit it out."

I released a heavy sigh, knowing he was right. I needed to figure out my shit, and fast. The longer Eden stayed, the more chances she'd end up corrupted—or dead.

I stood from my desk, ready to head back home. I knew in the end this would complicate things more. All it would take upon coming in the door was smelling her dinner, hearing her around somewhere, and seeing her face. Those large eyes that glowed with affection for me, and that pretty-ass smile that made my heart beat hard in my chest. I'd seen a lot of beautiful women in my life, but none *this* sweet.

Fuck, I needed to plan my next move.

Leaning over, I pressed the Talk option on the intercom once more. "LaShanti?"

Static sounded out and I heard my secretary respond back. "Yes, sir?"

"I'm heading out. Anything else on the itinerary before I go?"

A moment passed, surely she was typing away at her Mac and pulling up my schedule. "Yes, your uncle called and wants to meet up with you for drinks at seven. It's downtown at Bellaire. So sorry for the short notice. It must've gotten lost in my notes."

Closing my eyes, I took in a deep breath. Sandford could only bring me stress. Still, he was a welcome reprieve than running into his son. I still had to hear him out at one point. Thankfully for me, the last I'd heard he was in Aspen fucking some resort director.

Opening my eyes, I exhaled and attempted to remain calm. I pressed the Talk button. "No problem." I checked the time on my Richard Mille. It was six forty-seven p.m. "Anything else coming up?"

"Yes!" LaShanti said, ready this time. "You have a meeting over dinner this Friday with a Mr. L. Cairins. It's at seven, and you'll be meeting him at The Sheridan."

L. Cairins. The name didn't ring any bells and I made a mental note to look into who he was. For now, I was running late. While I didn't give a fuck about Sandford, I still had enough sense not to keep him waiting.

I pressed the Talk button a final time as I rounded my desk. "Thank you, LaShanti. Have a good night."

Vino and Beans stood, both mirroring the same concern.

I went over to the mirror by my door and fixed my tie. "I'll be fine."

"You sure?" Vino wanted to know.

I had no clue what Sandford could want, but I wasn't going to hide from him. Going and gripping the door knob, I faced my men. "Yes. Vino, you can drop me off, and Beans, get back to Eden."

I should've texted her, but chances were this meeting with my uncle wouldn't be long. Given my history with Sandford, I'd be in and out of Bellaire in twenty minutes top.

At exactly seven oh-one I walked into Bellaire, a ritzy pub and grille in downtown Hampton Hills. The smell of freshly grilled steaks filled the air as I passed the maître d' and stepped into the establishment's front room.

Soft jazz was playing amid the chatter in the room at all the nearby tables. It was only Tuesday, but the place was full of older couples, and a few younger ones. Straight ahead of me at the bar I spotted Sandford nursing a crystal tumbler of dark liquor.

Tall, in shape, and still possessing all of his hair, my uncle was nearly the spitting image of my late-father. Meaning, we looked alike as well. Fortunately for Sinclair, his look was all his own.

I took the strides over to the bar where Sandford held the left end all to himself.

"Uncle," I greeted him before taking the stool farthest from him, leaving two between us. I flagged down the bartender, going and ordering a glass of Château Corton Grancey. Sandford smirked at my request and helped himself to a sip of his liquor.

"Nice of you to join me," he noted as his steely eyes bore into mine. In the almost nine years that we'd known of each other, we didn't make it an effort to meet up at family reunions.

"I was at the office." I shrugged. The bartender set a coaster and wineglass in front of me and poured my red before leaving the bottle and going and helping patrons on the far end of the bar.

Sandford hummed. Soon, he furnished a thick cigar with a gold wrapper around the end from his jacket pocket. With his chrome guillotine cigar cutter, he cut the end before commencing to light up. Bellaire wasn't exactly a smoke-friendly place, but when you were the richest man in the room, nobody told you what to do.

My uncle took a drag from his cigar and blew out a stream of smoke from his nose. "Want one?"

I shook my head. Even in my youth when I'd sold dime bags for lunch money, I hadn't partaken of my product. I liked to keep my wits about me.

"'Course not," Sandford said loudly, eyeing my glass of wine. "Not a man who drinks wine like a woman."

His jab bounced off of me. "Did you invite me here to insult me, or to talk?"

A snarl crossed Sandford's face. "I invited you to talk, business."

Maybe I was better off dealing with Sinclair. At least he tried to suck up to me.

I took a sip of my wine, admiring the notes of blood orange, dried raspberries, and baking spices. "What's there to talk about?"

Sandford bared his teeth. "Cartier."

I tried and failed to suppress my smirk. Swiping at my brow, I sat up and ran my finger along the thin stem of my wineglass. Coltrane was playing in the background, a soothing sound among people enjoying their meals.

"What about it?" I asked for the sake of humoring my uncle.

He stole another pull from his cigar. "I want it."

"We talked about this."

"It belongs to me."

"Not according to dear ol' Dad's last will and testament."

Sandford's grip on his tumbler tightened. He was shaking as he narrowed his eyes, venom lodged deep in their dark depths. "You're my brother's bastard seed. Nothing more, and nothing less."

I let him have that one. After all, it was true. "Still doesn't take away from the fact that Cartier is mine."

My uncle turned smug, swishing around the contents of his glass as he stared ahead at the back wall of liquor. "I knew about the whore. Jimmy wasn't exactly secretive about his extramaritals." Sandford sized me up, disgust marring his face even more. "He was disappointed when she decided to keep you. Something he regretted until the bitter end."

This was also true.

Sandford turned so his whole body was facing me. He shot a finger in my direction accusingly. "I'll never believe he genuinely gave you of all people his livelihood before me. His flesh and blood."

I schooled my features, refusing to give this fucker any emotion. "Aren't I flesh and blood, too, Unc?"

Sandford snorted at my expense. "I'm not your family, boy. Never forget it. Jimmy didn't want anything to do with you. You know it. And *I* know it. You don't deserve Cartier. You don't even deserve to wear our last name. You're not a Carter."

Sandford was right about everything. When I'd shown up to officially meet my father all those years ago, he wasn't impressed or interested.

This was why it was easy to kill James slowly and painfully with no remorse. My mother had her faults. She'd loved me until she couldn't anymore, until James became her only want in life.

I killed him because he killed her. He may not have been there when she slit her wrists and sank into that bathtub, but he'd been the cause through and through.

As much as part of me wanted to brag about it, brag about making Sandford's beloved big brother cry and *beg* for his life, I didn't.

Tap. Tap. Tap.

My finger bounced against the countertop absentmindedly.

It really was a pity I couldn't kill Sandford too.

When I'd demanded for James to sign everything over to me, I'd fully intended on selfishly keeping it all to myself. I only cut Dorothy a hefty chunk of change because she was at least *innocent* in all this. We'd met at James's funeral, and it was as though the widow had seen a ghost. She didn't welcome me with open arms, but she hadn't outright viewed me as an outcast either.

I couldn't kill Sinclair no matter how annoying and persistent he was. And I couldn't kill Sandford because he was too high-profile to get rid of. With James, I hadn't cared about the risk when the reward was so worth it.

"Say something, boy," Sandford demanded as his hand that wasn't nursing his cigar turned into a fist.

Tap. Tap. Tap.

"You've made yourself very clear on where you stand with me and my ownership of Cartier," I began calmly. "Be that as it may, I'm not relinquishing control of it. Ever. Our stocks are up and I'm about to make a killing with Damon and Phil."

Sandford stood up, leering down at me. "So help me I'll rip

Cartier from your dainty little hands if it's the last thing I do. You don't belong in that chair. You don't belong in this town. You are filth better off in the gutter where you came from."

SLAM!

He slapped his hand down on the counter between us, leaving behind a Franklin before turning on his heels and walking off.

People around us were staring my way, their eyes doubled in intrigue.

I turned around on my stool, bitterly lifting my glass of wine in the air. A toast to the last man seated.

20

Eden

He didn't come home.

After spending all day slaving in the kitchen roasting a whole chicken complete with sides of dressing, green beans, carrots, mashed potatoes, salad, and rolls, I was disappointed as time ticked by and Cain never came home to see my spread. To be silly, I'd even had packs of Honeybuns set out for dessert.

But Cain never showed.

Malcolm wasn't forthcoming on the holdup. He'd gone out to speak to Cain at his office around six, and when he'd come back, he hadn't said a thing.

I gritted my teeth, annoyed that Cain hadn't so much as texted me about his absence. Something I thought we'd spoken about before.

Even still, I found myself in *his* bed, waiting up for him. It wasn't that I was waiting, but more so that I couldn't sleep. I was too plagued with worry as I tossed and turned.

Fed up, I finally flung the comforter aside and got out of bed. In just my thin red nightgown that hung to my thighs, I thought better and grabbed my cream-shaded robe in case Malcolm was around.

Out in the hallway my body went still. The soft notes from a piano's keys echoed in the air from down on the first floor. I stood for a second, just listening to the sad melody flowing around me.

He was home.

In all the time that I'd been with Cain, I'd never seen him acknowledge his piano that sat in the corner of the living room. I almost doubted it was him playing it, but by some instinct I just knew.

It wasn't until I was at the edge of the room that I had trouble believing my eyes. With his back to me and his head down, focused on his hands, Cain was playing the piano. His jacket was slung over the back of one of the chairs in the dining room, and his shoes were abandoned on the furry area rug underneath the coffee table in the living room.

Without fail, Cain's fingers flowed across the piano keys. A somber sound came out of his playing. A sad song that made me frown as I padded over to him.

Cain kept playing as I went and rested with my back against the keys on one end. His face was empty, but for what it didn't show, his melody told me something was wrong.

"Cain?" I spoke up gently.

At once he stopped playing, but he didn't look at me.

I didn't want to push him if he didn't want to talk about it.

"How did you learn to play?" I asked.

It was just after ten p.m., and Malcolm wasn't around. Joe was sleeping on the back of the sofa. The blinds were open in the living room, giving us a peek at the blackened sky outside. Setting the tone for the music Cain had been playing.

Cain pressed a key and a note sounded out. "There's a community center in Lindenwood I used to go to after school. They had a piano in their music room. No one was around to teach lessons." Cain gave a stiff shrug. "I guess sometimes the music is just in you."

He'd taught himself. Which really was incredible, because he was *good*.

I wasn't used to seeing Cain like this. Usually, he was serious, and sometimes, when it was just us, he was silly and upbeat.

Reaching out, I ran my hand over the waves on his haircut. "What's wrong?"

"You were right." His voice was noticeably different, low and filled with defeat. As he lifted his head to peer at me, I choked on a breath at the sight of him so sullen. "Even as a billionaire, there are things money *can't* buy me."

It sounded like he wanted something, badly, and he'd just come to terms with the fact that he couldn't have it. "Like what?"

"A peace of mind." Cain's shoulders dropped as he looked past me at something off in the distance, something I would've bet wasn't in this room. "Happiness."

My brows pinched together. "You're not happy?"

Quietly, he shook his head as he returned to me.

I opened my mouth. "Cain—"

"It's whatever. I know what I signed up for when I stepped into this world," Cain said with a dismissive shake of his head at my worry.

He just admitted he wasn't happy and he didn't know peace. I couldn't ignore it. I *wasn't* going to.

I slid closer to him until I was right next to him. A corner of his lips curled and he reached over and tugged on the knot keeping my robe closed. It loosened and fell, leaving my robe to open and expose my nightgown. Cain's hands ran down my sides along the curves of my waist where they rested. His hot touch sending my heart beating hard in my chest.

"Where were you tonight?" My voice came out throaty, evidence of his effect on me.

"My uncle—my father's brother wanted to meet for drinks." Cain's hands fell to his lap as he hung his head once more. "I knew it couldn't be any good, but still I went." He thumbed at his bottom lip, at his scar. "It was the usual with Sandford, 'You're not good enough to control the company.' 'My brother never wanted you.' 'You don't deserve to be a Carter.' Just the typical unwelcome wagon."

I reached out and squeezed his shoulder for support. "Sandford sounds like a real asshole."

Cain fought a small smile. "Doesn't make him any less right."

"Cain—"

"He's right, Tink," Cain cut me off. "I've felt the burden of existing my entire life. For a while there I was waiting...just waiting."

"Waiting for what?" I asked when he didn't continue.

Cain looked up at me with empty eyes and a broken soul. "For the day it goes away."

"Hasn't it?"

Once more he shook his head.

Cain ran his hands down his face and let out a sigh. "Of course I don't give a fuck about Sandford, but a trigger is still a trigger."

Nobody liked to hear they were unwanted.

I went up behind him, going and massaging his shoulders. It felt like there was so little I could do to make him feel better. I could tell him his uncle was wrong, but he'd endured a lifetime of feeling this way, right down to his mother's passing and being put in the system.

"How did your mom die?" I asked gently.

"She killed herself when I was twelve," Cain admitted. "I came home from school one day and found her in the bathroom in the tub. I climbed in and tried to save her, but naturally it was too late."

My hands paused in their movement. Deep in my chest, my heart tore in two for the little boy who lost his mother and never had a father. It wasn't his fault by any means, but still he probably blamed himself, felt not "good enough" for his mother to choose him. It was a pain I knew all too well being rejected by my own mother.

There was nothing I could say, so I started rubbing his

shoulders again. More, I leaned close and rested my head on his as I wrapped my arms around him and hugged him. His hand covered mine and we were quiet.

Not too long later Cain pulled on my hand, wanting me to come down to his level. I sat backward on the bench beside him, and not pleased with this position, he grabbed a hold of me until I was sitting on his lap. The smell of his spicy and powerful scent enveloped me, giving me a rush of him all at once.

The gesture made me smile. I liked being this close to him, too.

It was Cain's turn to touch as he caressed my face and studied where his hand was on me. Out of all the people I'd ever known, he touched me the best. Soft, gentle, as if I were fragile and he didn't want to break me.

"Tell me something," he demanded, wanting to switch topics.

"What do you want to know?"

Cain's hand slipped behind my neck. "How old were you when you ran away?"

I thought back to that time in my life, hard to believe it wasn't so long ago. "Fourteen. I'd had enough of Bobby's bullying and my mother's neglect. My boyfriend at the time was twenty and just so much more supportive. He begged me to move in with him at his place, or, his mom's. At first, it was nice, I was still going to school and he'd give me a little money now and then.

"And then it wasn't so nice. He started talking to other girls and when I confronted him about it, he hit me too. I stuck around for a little bit because I didn't want to go back home. Didn't want to look like a failure to my mom. And then when I turned fifteen, I grabbed my stuff and left. I bought a fake ID and went to Crazy Legs and David took one look at me and said I had one shot to make an impression."

Cain stared up at me, hanging on to my every word. His features were free of judgment and pity. Just the sight of him listening made me feel comfortable and safe enough to continue.

"So, that night as I'm on the brink of tears, I went out there and danced. I was so scared. I didn't want to show my body. Didn't want to get completely naked." I could still vividly remember how my hands were shaking and I felt on the verge of vomiting. Somehow, someway, I'd made it out to the stage without making a fool of myself. "Thankfully, I didn't have to. I'd danced down to my underwear and they were just throwing money at me. I made seven hundred dollars that first night. David took two hundred and said I could come back. I used the rest of the money to rent a motel room and bought a burger."

At the time, I'd been relieved and excited over my first night's earnings. I never had to look back at Alex or my mother again. My second night dancing I made around four hundred, but I made it work for me. That's all Crazy Legs was for me, a means of survival.

Cain's hand fell from my neck and settled on my hip. "Did you ever consider selling yourself?"

There were no walls here. We didn't lie to each other, no matter how ugly the truth was. "Yes." I looked down at my lap, not meeting his gaze. "I told myself if I didn't make any money on the stage, I'd let the first man who approached me with the right price have me."

I was so thankful for all the money I'd made on the stage that night, and the money I got from doing a couple of table dances. I didn't think I could live with myself had I given myself up for money.

Cain sat beneath me staring up at me as a muscle in his jaw tensed and his left eye twitched. He looked away and shook his head, as if ridding himself of whatever train of thought had come to mind.

"What?" I pressed when he didn't speak.

He came back to me, squeezing my hip. "I didn't kill Bobby slow enough. And now I want to find your ex."

"It's the past," I said with finality, if only to spare him from being angry over what I'd gone through.

Cain wasn't convinced. "Life's dealt you a pretty bad hand, and yet you're so optimistic."

"I have to be," I said for more than him, for myself. "Hope is the only thing we got in a world so cold."

Amusement danced in his eyes and I was happy he was almost back to himself. "Do you think you'll ever get your fairy tale?"

In some ways, *this* was a fairy tale. There was no other way I'd ever get to live in the lap of luxury and do whatever I wanted and not have to worry about bills or responsibilities.

Sadness singed deep in my chest at what reality would be like when I returned home. A bitter smile was all I could offer to keep from tearing up. "There are no horses in Bedford Heights, Cain."

He hung his head, albeit agreeing too. "No, there aren't."

The mood was too dark, too moody, too defeated.

I adjusted myself until I was straddling his lap. This wasn't about me.

Boldly, I took Cain's face into my hands and held his head up until he could only look at me. "Hey."

He smiled, those dimples indenting his cheeks. "Hey."

"Fuck your uncle, okay? And anyone else who makes you feel less than."

A gleam sparkled in Cain's eyes. "Okay."

He thought I was adorable, I could tell, but I was serious. "You're not allowed to be sad around me."

At once Cain's arms came around me, holding me in place. "Okay."

I frowned, still annoyed with his uncle. "You missed dinner."

"I'm sorry."

"I made you a plate."

"Thank you."

And just like that, Cain held my hand as I walked us over to the kitchen where I grabbed the plate I'd made him from the microwave. Just like he always did, he ate every bite and did so with a smile. A smile that burned me deep in my chest.

I took it back.

This *wasn't* a fairy tale. Cain was no prince.

And I was okay with that.

21

Cain

L. CAIRINS.

The name drew a blank. Even a look through Google came up empty. I could wait until Friday night to meet the elusive man— but I didn't like surprises. I liked knowing how to move in every situation.

I leaned over my desk and pressed the Talk button on my intercom. "LaShanti, do me a favor and call up L. Cairins."

A moment later my secretary got through to me. "I'm not seeing his contact info, but I'll keep looking. While I dig around, Sinclair Carter is on line 1 waiting for you."

I glanced at my landline that sat on the left side of my desk. A red light was flashing under *Line 1*.

I wasn't in the mood for Sinclair, especially after what happened with Sandford.

Still, he was the lesser of two evils. I grabbed the phone and pressed the button for Line 1 to quickly blow him off. "Carter."

An easy, husky chuckle met my ear. "God, you're so official with it."

I sank back into my chair. "What can I do for you, Sinclair?"

"Right to the chase, huh?" Sinclair joked with a sharp whistle. "All right, fine. I was calling to see about dinner tomorrow night."

I ran a hand over my waves. "Can't, I've got a business dinner."

"Tomorrow night?" Sinclair questioned.

"Unfortunately." I didn't have the patience to even bother pretending to be disappointed in not having time for him.

"L. Cairins?"

I froze, not missing the humor in my cousin's tone now.

How did he know that name?

"Yes," I responded through gritted teeth as my grip on the phone tightened. "How did you know?"

Once more Sinclair chuckled. "Does an 'anagram' sound familiar to you, Cain?"

Anagram: a word or phrase formed by rearranging the letters of another.

Immediately I sat up and grabbed the nearest pen I could find and scrawled *L. Cairins* down onto my desk calendar. Underneath, I wrote an S, and then an I—

Fuck.

L. Cairins was just *Sinclair* mixed up.

My silence fueled my cousin's laughter. "Took you long enough."

"What do you want, besides wasting my time?" I snapped.

"Easy, don't be so hostile," Sinclair said. "How else was I supposed to get ahold of you when you've been ghosting me for months? Frankly, I'm impressed with myself for pulling this off if I'm being honest."

Fucker was probably over there patting himself on the back.

There was just something about the Carter bloodline that forever ruined my mood and spiked my temper. Truth was, I only had myself to blame for stepping into this world to begin with. But I wasn't feeling accountable, at least above all with Sinclair. "There's one little flaw in your plan, genius."

"What's that?" Sinclair asked.

"You revealed yourself too early. What's stopping me from cancelling right now and not showing up?" I challenged.

Sinclair clicked his tongue. "Oh come on, playboy, it's just dinner."

Even with my threat he was cool, calm, and collected. That was another thing about the guy that annoyed me: he was arrogant as fuck and still the one person in the room who oozed a nonchalant grace.

I leaned back, resting my arm on my armrest as I focused my gaze out the window across the room. Having an office on the top floor came with a terrific view. On tough days, the serene cerulean skyline could calm me when tackling a contract or dealing with a holdup down at the site in LA. Today, having been tricked into a business dinner with my annoying cousin? The cloudless blue sky wasn't doing it for me.

"It's just my time," I said as I got back to Sinclair.

"Hear me out. I promise it'll be worth it," he swore.

Doubtful. "I'll consider it."

Before Sinclair could say anything else to piss me off, I hung up and dialed Beans. Between him and Vino, he was something like a therapist. The first person I talked to when I needed to make a rational decision. Beans didn't care to tell me what I wanted to hear, but what I *needed* to hear, whether I liked it or not.

"What's up?" he answered on the second ring.

I tossed my pen on my desk and sighed. "You remember that business dinner LaShanti said I had on Friday?"

"Yeah?"

"It's Sinclair," I said.

"What?" Beans's confusion was palpable through the phone.

"Fucker set up a dinner with me under a fake name. He just called and admitted it."

Over on Beans's end I heard chuckling. He actually found this predicament funny.

Massaging my temple, I shook my head. "Did I miss the joke?"

"Go and hear your cousin out, Dice," Beans said between laughs. "If he went to this length to get you to sit down with him, at least hear him out."

The sooner I heard Sinclair out, the quicker I could be done with him. In the grand scheme of things, he was harmless. College educated, and something like a socialite, the guy was more known for being caught in the blogs for fucking some model or influencer. As soon as I emerged as James's long-lost son, Sinclair was one of the few people who hadn't batted an eye or cast me out.

"Fine," I relented.

"And take Eden," Beans added.

To that, I sat up, unsure I heard him right. "Excuse me?"

"You heard me," Beans said clearly. "If you take Vino, he's just going to egg you on to put a bullet in Sinclair. Besides, bringing Eden lessens the tension and will make things light."

Tap. Tap. Tap. My finger rapped against my desktop as I ran over the idea. Dinner alone with Sinclair was too tempting. At least with Eden there I would be in a better mood and less likely to just shoot my cousin.

I didn't want to go to the dinner, but I'd given Damon my word on making time for Sinclair...*eventually.*

Reaching into my pocket, I pulled out my old and faithful red dice. They were one of the few things I kept from my childhood home. From my life before. No matter the roll, they always saw me through. I didn't believe in luck. Life was what you made it. And with these dice, I was a made man.

I shuffled them in my palm before releasing them on to my desk. They rolled a few times before coming to a stop.

Seven.

I snorted. "Guess I'm going to dinner."

22

Eden

"AHH!" A GUTTURAL SCREAM SOUNDED OUT, followed by an angry moan and a hiss.

On screen, the camera had just panned on to Holly Golightly as she climbed out of a cab before crossing an empty New York street. Once at her destination, she rummaged through a paper bag and procured a croissant. Content, she stood nibbling on it outside of Tiffany's storefront where she gazed inside at all the items she could never afford. I had just started my movie as I curled up in the theater room when the screaming began.

It was undoubtably a woman's scream. I paused the movie and sat up. Why would another woman be in Cain's home?

I didn't think to be scared, not with Malcolm nearby watching TV.

Slowly I got up from the cozy recliner. In just my socked-feet, I crept out of the room and edged toward the disturbance.

"Where did it come from?" an accented voice screeched from the kitchen.

American Joe.

Quickly, I sped up my pace until I was in the kitchen, walking in on a scene that was too bizarre to be comical. An older woman with short curly hair was waving a broom at a frightened Joe, who was cowering in the corner by the sink and cupboards. Joe's tail was bushy, further evidence of his terror. This didn't deter the woman from wielding her weapon of choice.

Malcolm entered the room, abandoning the TV in the next room, eyeing the woman and soon Joe. He shook his head. "Never seen a cat before?"

The woman held out the broom accusingly toward Malcolm. "I said where did it come from?" She was dressed in a gray uniform dress. The sight of it told me she must've been Cain's housekeeper.

Malcolm tipped his head my way. "He's with her."

At the mention of me, the woman turned and suddenly noticed I'd stepped into the room. She adjusted her glasses with one hand while still clutching the broom with the other for protection. In all honesty, she looked like a harmless older woman —aside from her possessing a weapon, even if it was just a broom. Her tan face was vacant of wrinkles or worry lines. Although *disapproval* was prominent across it.

"And *who* is she?" the woman asked with venom in her tone. "Does Mr. Carter know she's here?"

"Of course, she's a friend of Mr. Carter's," Malcolm explained, swinging his gaze from me to the woman. "Do you mind putting the broom down, Vera?"

Even with it squared away as to who I was, Vera was reluctant to lower the broom. After a moment's pause, she did. She set it beside her and smoothed out her hands across her dress, holding her head high with dignity.

Joe scurried away, his claws scraping against the tile flooring as he ran past Malcolm and me out of the room.

"I wasn't aware Mr. Carter had any *friends* staying here," Vera commented.

I was under the impression that Vera only came once a month due to Cain's wanting as much privacy as he could get. What business was it of hers who was staying here or not?

"Recent change of events," Malcolm said by way of explanation with a limp shrug.

Vera wasn't satisfied with this response. "Well, how is he doing these days? I'll have to bring Cecilia by some time. She's been asking about him."

Malcolm was calm as he stood tall, offering Vera a small smile. "Mr. Carter is doing fine, busy as ever, but fine all the same. I'm sure he'd love to see your daughter and catch up."

Vera went over to the island and made herself useful by straightening out a bowl of fruit. She ran her hand along the smooth marble countertop and raised it to study her palm. She pinched her face when she saw that it was clean.

Vera got back to Malcolm. "She just broke up with that banker." She shook her head, making an effort to pout a little. "He wasn't right for her anyway. Not ready to settle. Not a good one."

She was trying to set Cain up with her daughter, as if I wasn't standing right there.

I opened my mouth, wanting to speak up and say that Cain wasn't single, but couldn't...because he kind of *was*.

Thankfully, Malcolm came to my rescue. "Shame. Maybe Cain can set her up with a friend of his."

Vera came around the counter, going and standing in front of Malcolm. "*He* can do just fine himself."

"I'm afraid that's not going to work. He's already spoken for."

Vera blinked in confusion. "Since when?"

Wasn't it obvious?

"Since me," I spoke up.

At the sound of my voice, Vera grimaced. She had no choice but to acknowledge me. She turned, barely sizing me up before dismissing me again. "You are a child," she scoffed at the idea of my being with Cain.

I wanted to voice that I was almost twenty, but swallowed down this remark for how silly it even sounded in my head.

"She's not," Malcolm said, coming to my defense once more.

"They've been spending a lot of time together and have gotten close. She even cooks for him."

Vera narrowed her eyes, the gesture and distaste magnified by her glasses. "Peanut butter and jelly is not a meal."

There was no doubt I was a youthful-appearing young woman—I was only *nineteen* years old, but still, that didn't give Vera any right to sweep the idea of me under the rug, as if I wasn't good enough for Cain.

Malcolm sighed, his shoulders rising and drooping as if he were exhausted with this conversation. "It doesn't really matter what you think, does it? As long as Mr. Carter is happy with Miss Edwards, that's all that matters. Right?"

Vera didn't answer, prompting Malcolm to get more stern, more serious than I'd ever seen him. He peered at the rude housekeeper and spoke as if he were handling a child and not a woman old enough to be his mother. "Or perhaps Mr. Carter should put a notice out for a new housekeeper. One who'll understand boundaries and their place?"

With the threat of her job being taken from her, Vera squared her shoulders and stood straight. "No, sir, that won't be necessary." Briefly, she looked at me before focusing on Malcolm. "I'll go clean the first floor."

She didn't say another word. She leaned down and collected her bag of cleaning materials I suddenly noticed was on the floor by the island and walked out of the room past me quietly.

Pleased with the situation resolved, Malcolm faced me. "You good?"

I didn't *feel* good. "Yeah. You didn't have to say anything, but I appreciate it."

Malcolm's brows furrowed. "My job is to look after you. That's what I'm here for."

I gave a small smile. "Well, you're the world's best babysitter."

Malcolm snorted, shaking his head. "Yeah, a month from now, this'll all be worth it."

"What happens in a month?"

For once, Malcolm puffed up his chest with pride. A ghost of a smile forming on his mouth. "The NBA Finals. Di— Cain's going to get me tickets."

A month from now he'd be traveling to watch basketball games.

A month from now he'd be free of his duties.

Maybe in a month Cain would be done with me, too.

I felt uneasy as I went and settled back in the theater room. I hadn't eaten much that morning, but my stomach felt oddly full suddenly. A bad taste lingered in my mouth and I no longer had the interest in watching Audrey Hepburn's classic romance. I was tempted to go on up to my room and hide out with Joe, but decided it wasn't worth chancing running into Vera again.

"*You are a child*," her words echoed in my ears, burning beneath my skin. It was bad enough she had no problem trying to set Cain up with another woman right in front of me, but to be viewed as if I didn't even measure up stung. My fists curled in my lap and began to shake. To her I was a silly little girl Cain was toying with. Nothing more, and nothing less.

What bothered me the most, was the reality that she was right.

Cain was free to go out and see whoever he wanted. This whole arrangement was just a means to even the score.

We weren't in a relationship. This wasn't *real*.

I chewed on my lip and questioned my sanity at the disappointment I felt in those facts. In the ugly, green jealousy I felt at the idea of Cain going out with another woman. I'd been out on his arm as well, but with someone else, it would be different. It would mean something.

I didn't like it at all.

My thoughts betrayed me and fed on this realization, driving my heart to beat harder in my chest as my lips drew into a frown.

I didn't want to see Cain with another woman. He had enough friends, and I had enough being nothing to him.

Maybe, just maybe, I *wanted* to be his.

Vera was trying to poison me. I couldn't prove it, but I was certain. After I finished *Breakfast at Tiffany's* I went over to the living room to sit with Malcolm. Only, Vera was cleaning the floor-to-ceiling windows, and by cleaning, she was fumigating the room with whatever chemicals she was using. The strong scent of bleach and pine seeped into my system until I could feel it clawing up my throat, threatening to gag me.

Malcolm began to cough and moved to the kitchen. I went up to my room and discovered Vera had cleaned in there as well. The hardwood floor was shining so much I could see my reflection in its surface. The smell of lemon and soap assaulted my nose and I covered my face.

God, she really was trying to take me out.

I thought to go over to Cain's room and hole up until he got in, but Joe crossed my mind and I wondered where he was in all of this. A glimpse around the room found him to be nowhere in sight.

My bed was freshly made and empty. On some instinct, I dropped to my knees to look under it.

Aha!

Sitting quietly in a loaf under the bed was Joe. He didn't look the least bit pleased with the circumstances regarding Cain's housekeeper.

"Don't worry, she's downstairs now," I assured him.

Joe made no effort to move.

Couldn't blame him.

For the rest of the day, I holed up on the balcony, letting the warm May air circle around me. Being on the top floor, I had a terrific view of Hampton Hills. While I read curled up on a chaise lounge, life was bustling down below. It wasn't much, but it was a reprieve from being inside.

Hard knocks on the sliding glass door drew me from my reading.

In my bedroom at the door stood Cain, staring out at me curiously.

I remained where I was. I could only stare at him, feeling conflicted inside. The last of the sun was shining in on him, bathing his face in a golden glow.

Movement at his side caused my eyes to drift lower—

He was holding a thick bouquet of red roses wrapped in white paper outlined in black. It was easily three dozen with how many buds were poking out.

A gasp escaped my lips.

Clumsily, I rose to my feet and abandoned my book at my seat. One step inside and I was engulfed in Cain's arms as he came in for a kiss that melted all my doubt.

Cain took a step back and held up the roses, offering me a crooked smile. "Was thinking of you."

Excitement bloomed in my chest. He was *thinking* of me. No one had ever gotten me flowers before. Let alone such a lovely arrangement like what Cain was holding out.

I accepted the flowers and took a whiff. *Sweet.* "Thank you."

Cain peered out behind me before coming back to me. "What are you doing out there?"

Just like that, it all came crashing back. "Your housekeeper wasn't so fond of me."

Cain tilted his head to the side, narrowing his eyes. "Vera?"

I nodded and fiddled with my roses. "She wasn't very nice."

My words seemed to amuse Cain. He chuckled and rolled his eyes. It wasn't funny.

"She's been trying to set me up with her daughter for a while," he said with a helpless shrug. "Not interested by the way."

"No?" I questioned.

Cain's hand came up and cupped my cheek. He ran his thumb along my bottom lip, distracted as he watched this action. "I know what I want."

"Do you?" I hated how I sounded desperate for reassurance.

"Yes," Cain responded. He lifted his wrist up so he could eye his watch. "I want you to get yourself together. We've got dinner in an hour."

It was Friday night. Was he taking me on another date?

"At Lucky's?" I asked.

Cain walked off and shook his head. "No, this is business." He didn't elaborate as he kept on out of the room.

I took the bouquet downstairs and placed them in the empty crystal vase at the dining room table with fresh water. Vera was gone and her toxins no longer lingered in the air. Still, I cracked the patio door open to let out her negative energy some more.

In another month she'd be back. And I'd be gone.

For some reason I didn't like this fact. This wasn't my home, but I liked it here. Against all reason and sanity, I liked Cain, too.

It was a time crunch, but I got myself together as thoroughly as I could. I showered and pulled on a little black dress. I left my hair down and went for a natural look with my makeup. After stepping into some six-inch Yves Saint Laurent heels, I went down to the first floor. Cain was ready and waiting in the living room, standing in the center in front of the large TV. One hand was deep in his pocket as the other clutched the remote while he looked on at the screen. Instead of a tragic news story or an uplifting one, he was watching some business channel. A series of numbers ran up the screen beside a list of names that sounded like corporations.

"All set?" I asked, making my presence known.

Cain slowly pulled his attention from the television screen and faced me. His eyes started low at my black Saint Laurents with golden YSL emblems for heels, before raking his gaze up my naked legs, to my tiny black dress, until he reached my eyes. He raised his hand and stroked his thumb across his bottom lip, staying silent the longer he looked at me.

He suddenly fell out of his daze as he shook his head. He briefly turned and shut the TV off before crossing over to me.

"You look beautiful, Tink," he noted as he observed me from up close. He came down for a quick peck on my lips that left me wanting more. I was half a second away from tugging him back when he pulled off and began leading us toward the front door.

It was just the two of us as Cain drove us in his black Mercedes over to a restaurant called The Sheridan. Outside a bevy of cameramen were flashing away at the brown-carpeted entrance as people stepped out of luxury vehicles at the valet lane.

"Oh wow," I let out over all the commotion. Just ahead of us I spotted two notable faces. An esteemed hip-hop producer and a major influencer and socialite, Owen Dymond and his wife Pen Patel were exiting a car. Owen handed his keys to the valet before circling the Lexus to wrap an arm around his wife. The paparazzi were in hysterics for the couple. Shouting invasive questions while continuing to snap away.

"Vultures," Cain swore beneath his breath.

That they were as they swarmed around the carpet stealing moments from guests coming and going.

The valet attendant helped me out of my side of the car once we pulled up next. Cain was quick to come and tuck me close as he guided us toward the entrance.

"Mr. Carter, who's the new girl on your arm?" a man shouted Cain's way.

"Cain, are you happy for Kennedy?" one called next.

Kennedy?

The name didn't ring any bells.

Cain didn't engage with any of the cameramen. He walked us inside and the cool air from the AC was a reprieve from the warm night outside.

Up ahead of us at a glass podium a young woman stood poised to greet us with a kind smile.

Soft music played in the background. Just barely heard over the constant conversation going on in the dining areas. A peek into the room on our left saw that it was filled with patrons, and a glance into the room on our right saw that it was only Owen and Pen seated in the middle of the empty space.

A private dinner for two.

I returned my attention to Cain, reaching up and palming his smooth jaw. I shouldn't have, but I couldn't help but want a meal just for us, too.

"Party for Carter," Cain said to the hostess. Her name tag said her name was *Morgan*.

She read over the clipboard on the podium before her. "Ah, your table is right up on our enclosed rooftop deck." She lifted her head and offered Cain and me matching smiles. "Right this way."

Another hostess took her place as she led us away from the station. Morgan took us to the center of the first floor where two elevators were waiting. Together we boarded the lift and were transported to another world it felt like. The rooftop dining area was absolutely dazzling. Strings of light were draped overhead and wrapped around wooden beams all around, casting a glowing wonder. Heavy smells of beef and poultry soaked the air as Bill Withers played in the background. There was a balcony area outside of the enclosed bubble where people were either standing or seated stealing a smoke.

"I love this," I confessed as I took it all in. More famous people were on the roof, escaping from the vultures down below.

"The food is amazing," Cain told me just as Morgan guided us to our table where Cain's business party was waiting.

One look at who we were joining and I froze.

Seated at a round clothed table looking completely bored out of his mind, was Sinclair.

It wasn't that I couldn't forget a face, but Sinclair was too handsome to overlook. Sitting there, lounging back in the chair in a crisp deep purple suit and an unbuttoned white shirt, Sinclair was as remarkable as the first time I saw him.

To my surprise, Sinclair recognized me as well. His eyes lit up and he stood from the table in that way men used to do when a lady was coming or going.

"A member of our team will be right with you to take your

drink orders," Morgan said as she placed two more menus on the table.

No one was paying her any attention.

Sinclair was staring at me, and by the burn on the side of my face, Cain was as well.

To smother the awkwardness away, I forced out a small laugh. "Wow, it's good to see you again."

Sinclair came to greet me with a hug. "Pleasure's all mine." He planted a kiss to my cheek that had me blushing at the feel of his goatee on my skin.

We pulled apart and Cain's heat was too much to ignore. He was staring between Sinclair and me, just barely covering his annoyance. "You two know each other?"

Sinclair waited until I was seated before joining me at the table. "Something like that."

Cain narrowed his eyes as he sat across from me. "Elaborate."

He sat up straight, gaze boring into Sinclair, and the clipped manner in which he spoke should've frightened anyone. But Sinclair wasn't affected. He fiddled with the gold wrapped cigar that sat beside his cutlery. "We met at that janky little casino night Phil and Damon threw." He stole a look my way. "She was my good luck charm."

"Is that so?" Cain wanted to know.

"You were on fire that night," I chimed in, not wanting credit for Sinclair's lucky streak.

A smile tugged on his lips as he sat back in his chair. "It was nothing."

"I hear you cleared five-fifty," Cain responded.

"Almost five-seventy." Sinclair tossed me a wink and I hid a laugh into my hand. I hadn't done anything, but I was appreciative of the twenty grand he'd gifted me.

Cain rested his arms on the table, leaning over as he peered at the man across from him. "You took home over half a million dollars and you call it 'janky'?"

Sinclair shrugged indifferently. "I guess that's my problem. I'm not easily stimulated."

"Good evening, folks. My name's Andy. What can I start you off with to drink tonight?" A man appeared at our table suddenly, wading through the tension and saving me from continuing to ping-pong back and forth between Cain and Sinclair.

"A water," I spoke up, not interested in the sodas or juices The Sheridan offered.

Sinclair leaned over toward Andy, holding out a finger to him. "Bring me a bottle of D'ussé, please?"

Andy bobbed his head, scribbling down the order onto his notepad before facing Cain. "And for you, sir?"

"I'll take a glass of Chateau Le Pin Bordeaux Blend," Cain answered.

"Excellent." Andy closed his pad and gave us all a friendly smile. "Be right back."

Once he was gone the tension seeped back to our table like a hazy fog.

I swallowed thickly, wanting to know what was going on, but not knowing how to broach it. "H-How do you two know each other?"

Cain grimaced and Sinclair snorted.

"We happen to be cousins," Cain said to me. To Sinclair, he added, "Unfortunately."

Cain's discomfort seemed to amuse Sinclair as he smiled at the jab. "*Best* cousins."

Cain shook his head at what was obviously not true.

"So, wine guy, huh?" Sinclair remarked with a nod. "We should do a tour together. I've been meaning to define my palate."

It was a friendly offer, one that didn't appear to sway Cain either way.

"Maybe," was all he said in response.

Andy stopped by carrying our drinks from the nearby bar and was off to another table before I could pick his brain on what to order. Anything to have an extra party at our table.

"No tie?" Cain noted as he tipped his head to Sinclair's open collar.

A waitress breezed by with a shake in her hips. Sinclair tracked her movement and she tossed him a smirk as she kept on going. Sinclair turned back to Cain, shrugging his shoulders. "Couldn't find a suitable use for one."

The casualness in his response, the gravelly sound of his voice, and the indifferent look in his eye—he'd definitely tied women up before while in bed.

Something about this realization made me squirm and sit up straight.

Sinclair turned his attention to me, a twinkle in his eye. "So, Red." He studied my hair before coming back to my eyes. "Tell me, did you change it for him?" Sinclair's knowing smirk caused me to swiftly look Cain's way, finding him clutching his steak knife tightly.

"No," I said, but I couldn't hold his gaze.

His taunting chuckle echoed in my ears, rivaling the Alicia Keys song playing.

But thankfully, by the grace of God, Andy was back and ready for our orders. I chose the truffle fries as my appetizer, and went with the grilled turkey chops as my entrée.

"Um, excuse me." Once Andy was gone to turn in our orders downstairs, I stood from our table. I needed a moment to breathe. The testosterone alone was enough to strangle me right then and there. Sinclair was playing it cool and calm, but Cain's barely contained wrath couldn't be missed. Another second of it and I would cave and beg the both of them to settle their differences.

Cain and Sinclair stood as well, both looking at me curiously.

Easing a small smile on my face, I thumbed a finger over my shoulder. "Just...going to powder my nose."

They both remained standing as I backed off and made a getaway inside. In the women's restroom I blew out a long breath and braced the edge of the golden marble counter as I looked at my reflection. My hair was parted down the middle and hung in straight black locks past my cleavage. I was in a tiny expensive black dress and I looked like a million bucks. The men were upset, but I shouldn't let it ruin my night. I was in Hampton Hills, at a five-star restaurant. A month from now, I'd be lucky if I could catch Duane on an off day to have a meal in downtown Bedford Heights.

Gentle classical music played in the room, and a glimpse in the mirror saw that the rose-gold stalls behind me were all empty. No one was around to see me panic.

I practiced breathing calmly before washing my hands and stepping out of the restroom. Back up on the roof I was just entering the space when I spotted Sinclair passing by on his way out to the balcony. He saw me as I saw him. He tilted his head to the side, gesturing for me to follow. Something in my gut told me not to, but for some reason I did. A quick peek back at our table and I could see Cain was busy entertaining a man who'd stopped by.

I really should go back. Even while my conscience screamed at me to go to Cain, I felt my body disobey as I followed Sinclair out on to the balcony.

The night air had cooled down some as the sky had darkened. A steady chatter lit the area as groups and duos hung out to smoke and drink among themselves.

Sinclair grabbed a lone table and helped himself to sit. He showed a hand to the seat across from him, but I had just enough sense left to decline. Again, I amused him as he smirked and busied himself with unwrapping his cigar.

The Commodores could be heard from inside. "Zoom." A song that made me nod along and mouth some of the classic lyrics.

Sinclair's brows furrowed as he noticed me. "Whatchu know about this, Red?"

I pretended to roll my eyes. "Back home they play oldies and new music at this pizza place I hang out at. I always Shazam the ones I fall in love with."

Impressed, Sinclair went back to his cigar. "People my age go on and on about '90s R&B—and I will admit, it has its moments—but nothing's beating that soul the '70s and '80s embodied."

He had me, because even if it wasn't my generation, I was one of those who harped about '90s R&B. But even at nineteen, I could admit from what I'd heard of the '70s and '80s was pure gold. "We can call it a tie."

Sinclair pulled his cigar from the wrapper as he shook his head. "Can't be no tie. Not when a lot of hits from the '90s and even early '00s was sampling the '70s and '80s. You got Blackstreet sampling DeBarge's 'A Dream' with 'Don't Leave Me.' Even Tupac sampled that one with 'I Ain't Mad at Cha.' Ice Cube with The Isley Brothers's 'Footsteps in the Dark' on 'Good Day.' Back to DeBarge with Ashanti sampling 'Stay with Me' on 'Foolish.'" He absentmindedly pulled out a cigar cutter and clipped the end of his cigar as he spoke. "And can't forget The Notorious B.I.G. sampling The Isley Brothers's 'Between the Sheets' on 'Big Poppa.'" Sinclair flashed a smile as his dark eyes ran up my legs. "Think that one's my favorite."

He liked to be called *daddy*.

Sinclair was the kind of man that made your body react without your control. A flush swept through me, warming my blood and making me blush.

"So, you and my baby cousin," Sinclair brought up next.

It sounded like he was sonning Cain. Something I couldn't picture anyone doing, much less getting away with. "*Baby*?"

Sinclair shrugged. "I'm older." His tone was detached, showing he wasn't interested in the least to be talking, but was doing so to pass the time.

"How much older?" I found myself asking.

Sinclair flipped the lid of a Zippo lighter, once, twice, three times. "This year I'll be thirty, and he'll be twenty-nine."

My face deadpanned. "You're barely older."

For once, Sinclair appeared serious as the humor slipped from his face. "Doesn't matter. I was here first. That makes me the first begotten son of the kingdom."

Something clicked and I realized he was the son of the man who'd broken Cain's spirit Tuesday. Sinclair hadn't done anything wrong, but it felt *wrong* being with him just then. Knowing he was linked to the man who thought so lowly of Cain.

I peered at the magnificent view of Hampton Hills and LA beyond it. It was a beautiful night, among pretty people, but somehow I would've rather been home alone with Cain.

"You like my cousin?" Sinclair asked, bringing me back from my thoughts.

I wasn't supposed to, but I did. "Yeah, he's real sweet."

Sinclair made a face as if he doubted that. "Honestly, I barely know the guy. He just always seems to have something up his ass." Sinclair gave me a once-over, arching a brow. "Then again he sure knows how to pick 'em."

He was back to flipping the lid on the Zippo. From the moment we'd joined him at dinner he seemed to be antsy, itching to move somehow.

"Nervous?" I asked.

"Nah. I haven't been nervous in a minute." Sinclair licked his lips, a distracting habit he seemed to have. "ADHD." He flashed me a hopeless smile. "'Course I'm self-diagnosed." In a bold move, he reached out, touching the ends of my hair and marveling at it. Displeasure had him wrinkling his nose. He really preferred the red.

I wasn't sure the nature of the relationship he had with Cain, but something about Sinclair said he was harmless. Harmless enough so I could be honest.

"I...I wanted to fit in," I admitted as I shyly tucked a lock behind my ear.

Sinclair frowned. "Let me tell you something, darlin', fitting in is the worst thing you can do in a place like this."

Hampton Hills was always the dream for so many in Bedford Heights. It was just a city away. A goal within reach. An oasis away from our mundane lives where we worked day and night to live in a city that most of us would die in before ever leaving its limits.

"You make it sound awful," I joked.

Sinclair looked around us, his eyes dulling at the scenery and people. "I grew up here. Went to school with the best of 'em." He came back to me. "I've seen worse, and I've seen better."

This time when he flipped the Zippo, he finally lit his cigar and helped himself to a leisurely pull.

"You should come to my city." I offered a friendly smile as I leaned close and nudged him on the sly. "Unless you're scared?"

Sinclair perked a brow, not a hint of fear hung in his eyes. "If I come to your city, I'll be the *king* of your city."

Sinclair exuded a different kind of confidence. It was lazy, relaxed, and sophisticated. The type of cool money couldn't buy and schools didn't teach.

"Sure," I responded sarcastically.

A few women around us snuck peeks at Sinclair, who was otherwise oblivious. Or maybe he didn't care. He smoked on his cigar and flipped his lighter. I had to admit it was fascinating watching his hands move.

Sinclair blew out a thick stream of smoke and extended his cigar my way. "Want some? I only smoke the best."

I shook my head. I didn't really care to smoke or drink.

Sinclair wasn't giving up.

"Try it." He had the type of look that said women just did whatever he said. But as mystifying and handsome as Sinclair was —he wasn't Cain.

Playfully, I went closer. "I like my lungs pretty and pink, thank you very much."

A gleam sparked in Sinclair's eyes. "What *else* is pretty and pink?"

My eyes enlarged and my mouth clamped shut.

Oh my—

"I guess this is as good a time as any to announce that we'll be going."

Cain.

He was out on the balcony and clearly heard that last remark.

I opened my mouth, trying to smooth things over.

"Quiet." He kept his focus on Sinclair as he ordered me mute. "And by the way, you can go fuck yourself. As far as I'm concerned, we'll never do business together."

Sinclair had no grace. He didn't look the least bit apologetic or embarrassed. He was back smoking his cigar, staring at his cousin impassively.

"Inside, Eden. Now." It was an order, one Cain didn't allow me to even act on on my own. He had a hold of my arm and was bringing me back inside.

I didn't get to say goodbye to Sinclair. I didn't get to sit back at our table and enjoy our meal. In a blur, Cain had dragged me on to the elevator and down to the first floor where he released me harshly, almost causing me to trip as we were on our way to the exit.

"Cain!" I begged, wanting him to be anything but mad. I hadn't seen him like this. Hadn't experienced his anger. And I wasn't sure I could take it.

He halted, standing eerily still as he glared at me. "Let's get one thing clear: while we're working through our arrangement and you're in my care, you're mine. And no one can look at what's mine." He stepped closer until he was right up on me, his shoes brushing against my heels. "And no one can certainly touch what's fucking mine."

He was acting like he *owned* me.

"I—"

Cain took a step closer, causing me to take one back. "Make a scene. I dare you."

The darkness in his eyes chilled me to the bone. His face was empty, but his words were not. He was actually *threatening* me.

We were just outside the elevator. Not too far from the

hostess station. People were around, but they weren't paying attention. No one could save me.

For the first time, I didn't feel safe.

Tears welled in my eyes and I rushed past him, past the hostess, and out into the night.

Cain came and told the valet about his Mercedes. He didn't speak to me, and I couldn't look at him as tears rolled down my cheeks. The cameramen were mostly gone and no one was focused on us. When the car did come, I climbed into the back, something that had Cain paused at my door before he eventually went around and got in behind the wheel.

We didn't speak the whole way home.

23

Eden

Drip. Drip. Drip.

The steady sound of the faucet echoed throughout the bathroom as I sat in the tub. As tears slid down my cheeks, I was no longer sure what was causing the sound.

A brief mental checklist ran across my mind as I sat stewing in my decision. It was time.

A squeak let out and the dripping stopped. I felt him before I turned around and faced him.

Cain was taking a seat on the top step that led up to the tub. In just a white shirt and slacks, he was almost ready to go in for work.

Only, his interest was locked on me as he stared my way impassively.

A heavy silence engulfed us as neither of us budged to speak first. I had nothing to say and I wasn't sure he did either.

Except Cain tore through all the quiet and said the obvious.

"You packed your things." His voice was tired, yet velvet all the same. In that moment I hated him for having an effect on me despite the disaster the previous evening.

"Yes," I spoke up, going and resting my back against the opposite wall of the tub. It was useless really. With Cain's wingspan, it would take nothing for him to reach out and grab ahold of me. To drown me in this very tub.

The thought drove more tears to my eyes as I pulled my knees to my chest.

Cain studied me, his face vacant as his eyes searched mine. "Why?"

I ran my hands across my cheeks, trying and failing to rid them of tears. "Because I'm done."

"*Done*?" he questioned.

"Yes," I said with a vigorous nod. I threw a hand out in his direction. "I'm done with you and this bullshit. I've let you fuck me six ways from Sunday, and I'd say *you* owe me money at this rate. But I don't want it. I don't want anything to do with you. I am done."

Up. Down. Up. Down. Up. Down. I watched his index finger rapidly go up and down on his thigh as he continued to stare at me silently.

Still, I held on to my resolve, desperate to be strong and see this through.

"And why are you done?" Cain pressed for more.

His casualness and calm made me snap. Because we were not about to beat around the fucking bush. "Are you serious right now? You acted like an asshole last night! You treated me like I was your property!"

Cain took in my words and slowly bobbed his head. He looked away and appeared thoughtful. "Wanna know how *I* saw things?" He focused on undoing the plackets to his sleeves before pushing them up to his forearms. "I was regrettably out on the town having dinner with my dickhead of a cousin. It was suggested to bring *you* along for a buffer, and I decided that was a good idea because with you, I can rein it in pretty good.

"We get there and right away Sinclair's got his eyes on you. He's fucking *flirting* with you. And you, you're your usual bubbly self. Almost...oblivious in a sense to how he's working you. Tensions rise and you go off to powder your nose. Sinclair remarks how much he 'liked' the red.

"And at that point, I'm *still* managing to keep it together. By the grace of a higher being some business associate of Damon's comes and interrupts us and Sinclair excuses himself. Now this is where the story gets really interesting."

He didn't have to explain what happened next, because I knew what was coming.

"Time is ticking by and I look over across the room and spot Sinclair out on the balcony talking to some woman. But it wasn't just *some* woman, it was you. I'm not good with trust, I'll admit that's a flaw on my end, but I tried to think better of the situation. But then you were blushing and smiling for him and I couldn't." Cain snorted, shaking his head. "I go out to join you two and all I can hear is him asking how pretty and pink your pussy is. And somehow, *I'm* the bad guy for reacting."

I understood it looked bad—it was bold of Sinclair to say such a thing to me, but the way Cain reacted was terrifying.

"Because you don't own me!" I snapped.

Cain blinked and narrowed his eyes. "Let's get one thing clear. Every inch of you is *mine*. Your laugh, your smile, your ass—it *all* belongs to me. So, when I hear someone asking how good *my* pussy is, yes, I tend to get a little unhinged. And no, I'm not fucking sorry."

He was so blunt and crass. And yet, these words failed to disgust me. Failed to cause bile to rise to my throat. Instead, they sank deep beneath my skin, into my chest, clinging to a needy part of me that only wanted one thing in life.

I shook my head. Now *I* was losing it. I scoffed. "They got a word for people like you: possessive."

Cain gave a limp shrug, not at all apologetic for his actions or his words.

"You're insane," I let out. "I can't do this. I can't. I...I'm done."

More silence serenaded us as my words collided with his. A war of wits and stances. I had gotten up early this morning to gather all my belongings, what I brought over from home and what I'd bought here. I contemplated leaving all the items I'd gotten with Cain's money, but then I settled on taking it all. I'd earned it.

The water was warm but the air around us was cold and charged. This was the breaking point and there was no going back.

"Is this what you truly want, Tink?" Cain asked me when he finally spoke up.

The softness in his voice and the use of his nickname for me broke me deeper. I had walked away from far more toxic and volatile situations than this, but somehow, someway, this was undoing me more than those other times ever could.

"What are you going to do if I say yes?" I asked.

Cain sat up straight and scooted back, gesturing toward the doorway, emphasizing what he'd do. He'd let me go.

"You wanna leave me, Tink?" He was staring right at me, almost accusing me it seemed.

I sniffled, trying to swallow down a sob. "What do you want, Cain?"

He shook his head, not liking my counter question. "Whatever you want."

What *I* wanted.

I wiped away another blanket of tears and frowned at how pitiful I was. "I want you not to be so crazy."

A small snort sounded out of Cain as a smile tugged on his lips. "Can't help it over you."

"Do better."

He turned, facing me more. "I'll try, but I make no promises."

I looked away, down into the clear tub water at my reflection. "Do you have to go in to work?"

"Yes, but I'd like to resolve this."

And suddenly I was needy again and unable to help it as I

peered up at the man I could no longer deny I had fallen for. "I don't want you to go in. I want you to spend the day with me."

Cain seemed to think it over for all of a second before rising to his feet. Slowly, he reached for the top button of his shirt and undid it. In a steady quiet, I watched him shed all of his clothes before joining me in the tub. He went and rested back on the other end, stretching out his long legs. And because I was a wreck going to bed alone without him, I went to go lie against his chest.

I didn't make it an inch before his hands shot out and grabbed me, pulling me close against him and securing me there.

"I wasn't letting you go." He pressed the words into my ear as he held me tight.

I closed my eyes and more tears fell. "I thought you were going to hurt me."

His hold tightened around me. "Never. I was ten seconds away from shooting my cousin."

"I was so scared," I let out.

Cain reeled me back so that I could face him, see into his earnest eyes. "I would never hurt you, Eden. Can't say the same for any man who touches you."

"Cain—"

"You cooked me my first real meal. Sometimes, in the middle of the night, you reach out and hold me. You look at me like I'm your hero, when I've only ever been the villain. You could turn me in tomorrow and I'd gladly take any charge they threw at me before I ever lay a hand on you."

I believed him. Maybe I was desperate or naïve, but deep down, I knew in my heart he'd never hurt me.

"Okay." I rested back against him, not wanting to be free from his arms. "What happens now?"

"You said it yourself our deal is done. Now you're not here because you owe me, you're here because you *want* to be," Cain said. "Not much changes beyond that. You can have anything you want. What's mine is yours. You don't even have to stay here. You can go back to Duane."

I was free.

I gazed up at him, finding him already watching me. "I do like it here, but I should probably go back home. To visit Duane for a while and breathe."

"Okay," Cain responded.

"And no Malcolm. I can handle myself."

Cain frowned. "Humor me. Please?"

He wasn't demanding I take a bodyguard, but *asking*. God, I was so weak over this man. "He can take me there and hang out for one day." I held up a finger to signify this.

Cain only smiled before leaning down and stealing my next breath. His lips brushed mine and mine opened with little effort. Closing my eyes, I got lost in his familiar mouth and warmth. The taste of him made me hungry for more as I reveled being in his arms.

Cain's hand snaked around my throat as his other cupped me between my legs. "Who do you belong to?"

I tried to cling to my agency, but it was futile against my desperate heart. Against the raw sense of need I felt for Cain. He was alternating between stroking my clit and sinking his fingers in me, stirring me up. I was putty as I breathed out, "You."

That was all Cain needed to hear before his arms wrapped around me and he picked me up and carefully stepped out of the tub. He carried me back into my bedroom. With one swipe he'd pushed all of my bags and clothing from my bed to the floor before tossing the comforter over to lay me down on the sheets.

I knew what was coming and my heart beat hard against my rib cage anticipating it.

I watched as Cain nestled himself between my legs and stared down at my naked body as he brushed against my entrance. His body shook at the contact and my heart jumped in my chest.

God.

Cain peered down between our bodies and shook his head. "You're always making a mess on me."

I wasn't ashamed for how wet I already was. Not when we were seconds away from making up.

Slowly, Cain pushed inside me, drawing a sigh from my mouth as he groaned at the sensation.

"Don't take this away from me," he begged.

"You like my mess?" I asked.

Cain shook his head. "I like *you.*"

It was a confession, one that had him waiting on bated breath for my response.

"I like you, too," I told him.

That was all he needed to hear before he thrust deeper inside me.

Mouth to mouth. Skin to skin. Cry to groan. Cain made love to me for hours. Until I couldn't think or move. And when I was listless and numb, he climbed out of bed and went and made *me* a sandwich. Which I happily shared half of.

Work and obligations didn't exist as Cain gave me that whole day of just him. And I lay in his arms through it all, smiling, happy, and content.

24

Eden

"DO YOU HAVE TO TAKE *EVERYTHING*?"

Sunday morning Cain stood in the doorway to my bedroom watching me check my bags. His arms were neatly folded, his lips in a flat line, and the lack of joy was prominent across his features.

I paused in my activity. "Might as well."

Cain arched a brow. "Just how long will you be gone?"

I considered this. We lived an hour away from each other at most. It would be an adjustment at first going from seeing him every day to... I wasn't sure just then how long I intended to be gone.

"I'm not sure," I told Cain truthfully. "I mean, did all of your exes live here in Hampton Hills?"

Cain tilted his head to the side. "Some, but they didn't stay the night frequently."

"No?" This was surprising considering I practically moved in.

"No," Cain said with a simple shrug. "It's not often I allow people in my space for extended amounts of time. Besides you."

"Just me?" I repeated.

Cain nodded. "You've gotten closer to me than anyone else."

His words warmed me, enveloping me in a feeling I wanted to embrace for as long as my fingers could grip it.

"I'm sure it wasn't easy for you," I said, considering all that went with his life. His dealings in both the business and underworld must've kept him anxious and guarded, with good reason.

"For all intents and purposes, *this* is very new to me. I'm not sure what I'm doing," Cain seemed to confess as he gestured from me to himself. "I've been with other women, and it's never been like this. Beyond the surface."

I knew how he felt. I'd been with other men and it was *never* like this. I felt protected with Cain, looked after, and *safe*.

A paradox.

"So you'll miss me when I'm gone," I teased to lighten the mood.

Cain made a face, scrunching up his nose and shaking his head. "Maybe."

I rolled my eyes. He would.

Standing up, I took a final look around the room I'd barely called home for the last four weeks, making sure I'd grabbed everything essential. American Joe was curled up by the balcony doors, sleeping with his eyes closed tightly. The sun shined into the room, illuminating his gray fur. For my trip back home, I was bringing Joe with me. I'd made sure his things were all packed up as well.

There was hardly a trace of me left when I thought of all my bags I had ready down by the front door.

Cain was standing watching me. His face was blank, but a fondness hung in his dark eyes. A softness I only noticed when he was looking at me.

"You could just come out and say you'll miss me, you know," I said, planting my hands on my hips.

Cain appeared thoughtful, soon rocking on the heels of his shoes. "I'd rather show you."

I looked away to hide my blush. We both knew how carried away we'd get if I let that happen. We'd spent the entire day in bed Saturday having the best makeup sex.

I was forcing myself to leave more than anything. Staying would be all too easy. But I needed to go, to collect my bearings and rationalize things.

Because I would miss him too, I padded over to him. I wrapped my arms around him and rested my chin on his abdomen as I peered up at him with a goofy smile. "Hey."

"Hmm?" he hummed in response as he gazed down at me.

"What am I to you?" I asked.

Cain rolled his eyes, but there was no hiding those dimples of his from broadcasting his feelings across his face. "A pest."

I pouted, and he pouted right back. "I like you," I told him.

Serious, Cain reached out and caressed my cheek. "And I like you, Tink."

I wanted to kiss him but he stepped back before I could. He was soon reaching into his jacket pocket and procuring a thick white envelope and a sleek black card. "This is your earnings you made from the Monte Carlo night," he explained as he handed over the envelope before slipping me a black debit card that had my name emblazoned on it. *Eden Edwards* stared back at me from its matte black surface. Cain's finger tapped the edge of it as I held it in my hand. "And that's to get your nails done, your hair, clothes—pay a few bills if needed."

I looked from the card to Cain, feeling my forehead crease in confusion. "But..."

"It's no big deal. I can afford it," Cain said, brushing off my discomfort.

I closed my hand around the card. It was a big deal. Huge. Part of me wanted to give the card back—even though I knew he'd never accept it. "This isn't about—"

"I know," Cain cut me off. "I know how we got here, but I know my money doesn't move you. If I'm not around, I want to know you'll be able to get things done and have whatever you like. I want you secure."

Peering down at the card again I ran my thumb across my name. I had access to endless money now. A dream for many.

There just wasn't anything I wanted. No, what I wanted most couldn't be bought.

I closed the distance between us and leaned up on my toes so I could reach Cain's height and kiss him.

I knew it was a bad idea getting close with this man. Getting attached. It was downright dangerous. He *erased* people.

"Thank you," I said.

Cain pressed a torturous kiss to my neck, squeezing me close. "Don't mention it."

It was the wrong time, but I did care about him, so I broached a tricky subject. "Can I ask for a small favor?" I asked, holding up the amount with my index finger and thumb.

Cain arched a brow. "Anything."

"I...I know he crossed the line at dinner, but maybe while I'm away you could meet with Sinclair? He just doesn't seem as bad as your uncle. As cold and distant." At least from what I'd seen.

Quietly, Cain took a step back.

The space now wedged between us only signaled Cain's cold rejection.

"Or not," I said defeatedly.

Cain shook his head. "That's not a small favor." He gestured toward me. "You're leaving me dressed like that and then you ask me to meet with the man I've been trying my hardest *not* to kill? Not exactly a fair trade in the slightest."

Briefly I examined my spaghetti stringed dress and ran my hand down the mauve material. "Dressed like what?"

Cain took a step closer, going and looping his finger around a strap. "Like you always dress. Perfect. Adorable. *Mine.*"

I really needed some serious esteem because I was liking his claim on me more and more.

I *wanted* to be his.

I craved the heat that rushed over my body when he told me I was his.

I knew it was wrong, but I didn't want to be right.

"Please?" I begged. "Try. Just once, for me."

Cain released a breath through his nose, grimacing as he tugged on my strap. "Fine." And then he pulled me closer. His lips brushed against mine, once, twice, before he sealed my fate and kissed me deep. All too soon he broke away. "Hurry back. I already miss you."

His soft touch, his hungry gaze, and his presence were too much to walk away from, but I had to.

"You're, like, obsessed with me," I joked.

Cain cupped my chin, tilting my head back so I could look up at him. "Who else should I be obsessed with?"

I could've had it a lot worse. A very rich, attractive bachelor was solely into *me*.

"You'll be good while I'm away?" I asked.

Cain narrowed his dark eyes and said nothing.

He only wanted me.

It was hard not to smile at the thought of his fidelity. Powerful men with money could have any woman they wanted, and they often did. But Cain just wanted me.

What a feeling.

"Okay, that's everything," I said ten minutes later as we stood in the foyer with Malcolm after all my belongings were packed in the back of Cain's Bentley Bentayga.

Cain came over to me and handed me my phone I didn't know he had. "Call me if there're any problems." He faced Malcolm, lifting his chin. "Don't let there be any problems."

This whole time we hadn't exchanged numbers and now I finally had a means to contact Cain whenever I wanted. My phone felt heavy in my palm at the reality. Would I call him while I was away? After spending every day with him, it made sense to take the time to myself, but there was no denying that I would miss him. His voice. His face. His little moments where he'd be silly and fun.

I tucked my phone away, forcing myself to look over at Malcolm. "We have time to get back and maybe do a little shopping. Duane loves my roasts and that would be the perfect dinner to welcome me back."

The thought of dinner made me face Cain once more. "Will you be all right tonight?" There was plenty of leftovers in the fridge—because every other day I was cooking something new.

Cain lifted and dropped his shoulder. "I'll probably starve to death," he said, going as far as appearing nonchalant.

Malcolm rolled his eyes and went over to the front door, opening it for me. "You ready, Eden?"

Here it was, after almost five weeks, and I was finally going home.

"Yes," I said softly as I met with Malcolm at the front door. I clutched the strap of my purse as I took a deep breath, my heartbeat echoing in my ears, as I stepped out of the penthouse.

Malcolm went ahead of me and got in the elevator. I followed. Something thick lodged in my throat and I found it hard to swallow.

My hands felt clammy as I glimpsed over my shoulder back at the penthouse. Cain was in the doorway, not making an effort to follow us. He stood there, back straight, hands in his pockets, and his attention on me. His face was empty.

I was leaving and he was staying.

My heart throbbed and I couldn't wrap my head around the idea that this was *wrong*. Like I was walking in the wrong direction. I had everything with me to go, but looking back at Cain where he stood watching me impassively, I had never felt so empty handed.

I boarded the elevator and Cain remained standing in the doorway to his home.

Struggling to swallow and breathe, I lifted my hand in a wave goodbye.

Cain merely tipped his head at me in response.

The doors closed and I couldn't see him.

A strange ache settled deep in my chest.

Maybe...

"He'll be fine," Malcolm spoke up.

"Promise?" I begged.

Malcolm snorted. "He's used to people leaving. He'll survive. Although, this time is different."

Different. I couldn't explain it, but I wanted to be different to Cain. I wanted to matter more than the others before me. "Yeah?"

Malcolm silently swept his gaze over me. "Yes."

I couldn't hide the goofy smile that beamed across my face after that confirmation.

Malcolm and I got into the truck and started for home. *Home.* A place I wasn't sure I'd ever get to return to. Now here I was on my way back.

I almost didn't believe it. I kept sneaking peeks at the back window to measure the distance we were traveling from Cain's penthouse. To see if this were some prank.

But Cain wasn't cruel enough to do that to me.

Still, I hoped he'd miss me while I was away.

I waited until we were in Bedford Heights' city limits before breaking the silence.

"What if you don't report back?" I teased.

But Malcolm didn't find the humor in the situation. "If I don't call him, he'll drive all the way here. And you'll spend the rest of this trip back home on your back or on your knees— whichever position you prefer, and that'll be the end of it."

I didn't bother to gasp, because I knew deep down he was right. Cain wasn't a man to be tested or played with.

For the time being, Malcolm was my bodyguard whether I liked it or not. I didn't reflect on this fact for long because we were soon pulling up to my apartment building.

I let out the loudest squeal and practically jumped out of the truck before Malcolm was even able to park properly in front of the building.

"I'm home!" I hadn't let Duane know I was coming. I wanted it to be a surprise.

Quickly, I gathered American Joe's carrier from the back seat and was set to go inside.

I was just about to board the elevator when I realized I should stop and wait for Malcolm. He came over carrying two of my suitcases, shaking his head at my eagerness to get up to my apartment.

"It's been forever since I've been back," I told him as we climbed on to the elevator and I pressed the number 4 button.

Malcolm leaned against the back railing and eyed the numbers illustrating our ascent. "I suppose you should enjoy this."

While you can. He hadn't spoken these words, but they lingered in the air anyway.

Cain said I could stay home and not with him, but would he keep his word?

Or really, did I *want* to stay home now that I knew what life with him was like?

There was no forgetting the look his face when we parted. A stab of regret settled in the pit of my belly.

This was for the best. *Right?*

Ding.

The elevator arrived on my floor and I practically raced over to my apartment with Malcolm calmly walking behind me.

Rapidly I pounded on the front door, forgoing using my key to keep the surprise going.

On the other side of the door I could hear the chain lock being unlatched as the knob twisted before me.

"All right, all right. What's the—" Duane stopped midsentence as soon as he set eyes on me. His face lit up and in seconds I was engulfed in a crushing hug.

"Doll! You're back!" Duane set me down. The biggest grin was on his face as he took me in. And then it dwindled once he noticed Malcolm come and stop behind me. "With company."

I swatted at Duane's chest. "Stop. Malcolm has been ordered to look after me for a day while I'm here." I gaped back at him. "And then he's going back home."

The smirk on Malcolm's face let me know we had to iron out the agreement a bit more. I did not need a babysitter in my own city. I'd made do on my own for years, and with Duane's help, I would manage fine.

"And where is he stayin'?" Duane asked as he took my suitcases from Malcolm and brought them inside our apartment.

Malcolm merely stared at Duane. He was an easy six-three to Duane's six-four, but neither man seemed intimidated of the other. Quietly, Malcolm reached into his suit jacket and gathered a wad of money and went to hand it to Duane.

Duane snorted, waving the cash away. "You can keep your hush money."

"Di— Cain insists," Malcolm explained simply. "While Eden is back under this roof, he wants to make sure the amenities and rent is taken care of. And that things are clear with you."

Duane's face twisted in disgust.

Uh-oh.

"Hey." I went and got between them. "Why don't we go for a walk, D? Just you and me to catch up?" To Malcolm I held out my hand. "Just give us ten minutes to sort this out. Can you finish bringing up my things?"

Malcolm sighed. "I'm not supposed to let you out of my sight."

"Just ten minutes," I pleaded.

I could tell Malcolm didn't want to relent, but he did as he looked elsewhere while I steered Duane toward the door.

Duane usually wasn't this hostile, but being that this was a tricky situation I couldn't blame him for being protective.

"Eden, what the hell is going on?" he wanted to know the minute we were outside on the sidewalk prepared to head down the block.

I sighed. "Cain is very protective of me. He wants to make sure I'm safe while I'm not with him."

Duane narrowed his eyes, not buying it. "So you're still *with* him."

I peered down the street, looking at nothing in particular as the spring afternoon carried on before us. People were heading out of their buildings to get to work, or some were returning from their morning shifts to go in and take a nap. Life went on while mine was at a standstill.

Duane's question weighed heavy on my mind. It wasn't the most romantic way to start a relationship, what with Cain kidnapping me and all, but at the same time, unlike everyone outside of Duane, Cain was the only person who took care of me. Who saw my tears and *did* something. My whole life, no one had ever taken the interest or initiative to protect me, and Cain did so without a second thought.

"Because I know what it's like to still love the person who hurt you the most." My heart throbbed as I remembered his words. He also had a mother who hadn't loved him enough to care.

"Yes," I spoke up, gazing up at Duane. "He's my boyfriend."

Duane took a long look at me and soon shook his head. "Sis seen the red flags and said 'Ooh, I got shoes to match.'"

Somehow, I managed to laugh. "Red is a daring color."

Duane's arm came around me and brought me close as we continued on down the sidewalk. "I just... I don't know, E. Guns, suits, and blood? I don't get a good vibe from Cain at all."

Outside of the casino business he was a drug dealer and a murderer. He wasn't a good man by any means.

But I didn't *want* good. I wanted Cain.

"I'll be okay," I promised. "He's not perfect. Far from a saint, but I trust him. Just as much as I trust you."

Duane was silent and I didn't push. If he ever grew to like Cain or let up, it had to be on his timing.

Cain had the résumé of a monster, but I saw past all that. He was just as lonely and unloved as I was. Was it naïve of me to want him?

"I don't know what I'd do if I lost you." Duane's voice broke just a little as he tugged me closer. "God, I love you. And if he ever hurts you..."

He couldn't even finish the statement without shaking.

Cain had killed a man, and many others, but I knew instinctively, he would never hurt me.

Peering up at Duane, my heart softened and I clung close to my best friend. "I love you, Duane. For loving me. More than anyone else ever did."

He blinked back visible tears before squeezing me hard. We went on with our walk and never let each other go.

As much as I wanted to go out to the local supermarket and get some food to prepare a meal for us, Duane objected. He insisted I could cook the next night, that tonight was for takeout and relaxing. A couple hours after I had all my belongings unpacked and put away, and Malcolm and Duane had settled with Malcolm crashing on the sofa for the night, we sat around the coffee table, eating from our takeout boxes. It was nice to see a ceasefire.

"I can't wait to taste your cooking again," Duane said as he munched on a French fry. "It's been too long."

"I was thinking of making a roast," I let him know between bites of my burger.

Duane's mouth made an O shape at the idea. "Yes."

"So," I said as I sat up and grabbed my soft drink. Eyeing my roommate cleverly above the lid, I prepared to pry. "Seeing anyone new since I've been gone?"

Duane rolled his eyes. "Sure."

I pouted and took a sip of my Coke. "Oh come on, Duane."

He waved me off and scooted back from the table, not giving any more up about his lack of a love life.

Malcolm was quietly eating his chicken tender meal. Only listening and bouncing his attention from me to Duane.

"What about you, Malcolm?" I pressed. "Now that I'm back home, maybe you'll get some time off to find someone."

Now it was Malcolm's turn to make a face. "I'm committed to my work."

"I hear that," Duane agreed from across the table.

Ugh. "I'm just saying, it'd be nice to see either of you with someone."

Duane scoffed, turning to Malcolm. "Don't you hate it when your friend gets into a relationship, starts having some decent sex, and then all of a sudden turns into an expert? 'Oh, you should try it!' No, thanks."

Malcolm cracked a rare grin. "I may know someone like that."

Cain.

I thought about my cell phone and where it lay tossed aside on my bed. Would I call him or text? *Should I?*

To at least let him know I missed him already?

Nope. My subconscious kicked in and I realized I would take some time to reevaluate myself and my relationship with Cain and whether it was worth going back to, or if it was merely a case of Stockholm syndrome.

After dinner, I went down the hall to wash up for bed. I had just stepped into my bedroom when I overheard Duane and Malcolm talking in hushed voices out in the living room still.

"She's all I got," Duane said in an almost pleading tone. "When I was seventeen, I came out to my mom and she threw me out of the house. I've been taking care of myself ever since. Between a string of bad boyfriends and not finding love from my own family, that girl is the only person who's ever given a damn about me. She hasn't had it easy either. Her own mom chose men over her, and Eden's never been lucky in the man department either.

"*She's* my family, Malcolm. I'm not the strongest guy in the world, but I'll fight till my last breath if either of you so much as harms a hair on her head. I promise you that."

The threat hung in the air between them for a moment. A moment that had me waiting for any sign of life.

"When I was three my mother tried to sell me for drugs," Malcolm's voice surprised me by speaking up. "I guess thankfully, it was an undercover cop she was talking to. Unfortunately from there I was put in the system where there were no homes to be found. No hugs, no bedtime stories, no night-lights to keep the monsters away. Nothing.

"I was bullied for ten years until I met him. Until for the first time in my life someone stood up for me. He's *my* family, and I'll do what I have to, to keep him safe. He's all *I* have."

They were both quiet after that. My hand slid up my chest, clutching it as my heart beat hard. I hadn't known that about Malcolm. He'd had it just as bad as Cain, if not *worse*.

God, we were quite a bunch of damaged goods.

"I like Eden, I do," Malcolm said after a moment. "And I can tell without him even admitting it to himself, that Cain cares a great deal about her as well. Between the three of us, she's the safest person on the planet. He means her no harm, and even if he did, *I* wouldn't let him touch her. There aren't too many good ones out there, and Eden's special. She's safe with you, she's safe with D, and she's safe with me."

A beat went by with Duane weighing Malcolm's words.

Clapping sounded out next and I recognized it as the two of them shaking hands in agreement.

The dust was settled and I smiled as I slipped into my room for bed.

Home sweet home.

25

Eden

AFTER SO LONG IN HAMPTON HILLS, IT WAS DIFFERENT to wake up back home in my own bed. Almost *strange* even. My bed felt smaller. Colder. Emptier. And the room itself felt *off*.

I thought to Google how long it took Stockholm syndrome to wear off, but chickened out in the end.

American Joe was sitting against my windowsill, peering outside at the life happening below. I leaned over and ran my fingers through his thick fur, gazing out the window as well. Nothing had changed. People went up and down the block on a mission as cars passed by on the street. Everything went on as it always had in Bedford Heights.

"It's different here, but it's home," I said.

Joe purred in response.

I got out of bed and went over to the bathroom to freshen up. Upon pulling on a heavy T-shirt when I was done, I padded out to the kitchen, discovering Malcolm was still here and up reading the morning paper. The smell of fresh coffee lingered in the air and though I wasn't the biggest fan, a cup doused with sugar and Duane's sweet cream creamer seemed appealing.

"Morning," Malcolm greeted me as the rustle of paper sounded out as he turned a page.

I almost stumbled in my steps, but I caught myself and went on over to the fridge. On the stainless-steel door was a note from Duane listing his work schedule for the day. It was just me...and Malcolm. "Morning. Shouldn't you be trying to beat traffic?"

Malcolm snuck me a look from behind his paper, silently telling me to be serious.

I grimaced as I opened the fridge and grabbed the bottle of creamer.

Ordinarily, I didn't have an issue with Malcolm. And really, I didn't. But I needed to think and clear the air about my feelings post staying with Cain for a month. That couldn't be done with a constant reminder of him lingering around and watching me like a hawk. I knew he meant well and only wanted Malcolm to protect me, but I felt smothered. For the last few weeks every step I took was quickly shadowed by a bodyguard. I was shielded as if I were precious cargo, and while flattering, it was too much.

"I don't need you here," I came out and said.

Malcolm didn't flinch as he was back in his paper. "Regardless, I'm here to look out for you. To see that you don't run into any problems."

"I've been taking care of myself since I was fourteen," I said as I placed my hands on my hips, standing my ground. "If I need anyone, I have Duane. I'll be fine."

Malcolm sighed and put his paper away. He turned, facing me fully, and sat up. "Eden—"

"What are you going to do when we break up? I'm only temporary for Cain. You shouldn't get so invested." I wasn't the first, nor would I be the last, woman Cain dealt with, and I didn't see anyone rushing to guard *those* women.

Malcolm narrowed his eyes. "If you break up, I'll come work for you."

I paused, taken aback.

He *wanted* to be around me making sure I was safe. The thought touched me.

Pouting, I drew a circle on the marble countertop in front of me. "I can't afford your salary, Malcolm."

"I'd work for free." And then, without missing a beat, he added, "And a meal or two."

Against my will, my lips curled into a smile. I loved that he enjoyed my cooking.

"Please," I begged gently. "Just let me have some time to navigate and think. Things back in the Hills were...intense."

Malcolm considered this with a nod. "But you were happy?"

So happy. The happiest I'd ever been. And that scared me.

"Yes," I admitted, being brave and meeting Malcolm's gaze. "But that doesn't change the fact that I need time to adjust and really think about things."

For a moment Malcolm only stared at me as I peered at him. Though he wanted to be here, he was also here because he was told to be. Because his boss ordered him to look out for me. Cain had the final say, not me.

Malcolm eased out a sigh, his chest rising and falling. "Okay."

"Really?" I had to know.

Malcolm made a face. "This is your home. What you know. I'm sure you'll be fine on your own. If not, you have Duane. And I'm sure you know you only have to make a phone call and we'll be here in a flash."

A smile broke across my face as relief washed over me. He was compromising.

I went about grabbing a porcelain mug from the cabinet. The lavender *Golden Girls* mug I loved. There was just enough coffee left for me to have a cup.

"Thank you," I said as I peeked back at Malcolm.

He shrugged and went back to his paper. "I'll leave this afternoon. In the meantime, if you have any errands to run, I'll accompany you."

I poured the creamer into the coffee until it was caramel colored. I weighed my options and figured I could work with Malcolm being around for the day. I needed to go to the bank to deposit the money Cain had given me. But even more there was something else I wanted to do—*needed* to do.

An hour later after I'd drunk my coffee and eaten a blueberry muffin, I was dressed and ready to face the day. I stepped into the living room, bending down to adjust the straps of my heels to make sure they were fastened in place. Malcolm took one look at me and did a double take from where he sat on the sofa looking at something on ESPN.

He lifted a brow suspiciously. "What's on your agenda?"

In my pale pink corset, denim mini skirt, and pale pink strappy heels, I looked the part in where I was going. I modeled my 'fit for Malcolm and tossed him a dazzling smile. "Crazy Legs. I haven't been in a month and I need to stop in and see how the girls are doing."

Malcolm narrowed his eyes. "I don't think that's a good idea."

Of course he didn't. "Why not? Think I'll give them a run for their money and do one last dance for old times' sake?"

Malcolm wasn't amused by this idea. "Because your boyfriend would put a bullet in anyone's head who looks at you."

"He really needs to find better coping mechanisms to release his anger than violence," I quipped as I looped my purse over my arm and headed over toward the door. "I'm not asking. I'm going. If you want, you can come along."

The sofa squeaked as Malcolm sat up and soon stood. He sighed and came and joined me at the door. He took one more look at my outfit and shook his head.

The sight made me laugh. "Trust me, I'll be the one *over*dressed when we get there."

Crazy Legs didn't offer full-nudity, but it wasn't a shocker to walk the floor and catch girls stripped down to G-strings and their heels as they danced at tables or were up on stage. Breasts shimmering from body lava, legs shining from oils, and smiles pronounced from liquor and more—was the common atmosphere of the club. For a while, it was all I'd known, until the night David gave me an offer that changed everything.

I stepped out of the Bentley and did a double take. There was no missing it. The sleek pylon sign out front was brand-new. Previously, Crazy Legs had held a red-bulbed sign along the side of the brick building. As I looked up, shielding my eyes from the sunlight, I saw nothing but the faded imprint from where the sign used to be. My eyes went back to the sign at the curb. *Taste.*

He'd changed the name. This became clearer as Malcolm walked with me to the front entrance where on each glass door over the black silhouette of a nude woman against a pole was the same name. *Taste.*

"The name is different," I said out loud.

"It needed a remodel," Malcolm clarified.

Not only was the name different, there were two men standing at the entrance wearing dress shirts and slacks, guarding the door. Both men were large, as big as Malcolm, but less menacing, which was saying a lot because one look at either of them would make anyone nervous. Serious eyes, erect postures, and muscled bodies that told of their strength.

"Can I see some ID, miss?" The guard on the left—bald, with unblemished hazelnut skin and a hard look on his face—spoke to me first.

ID. Shit. Cain had confiscated all of my fake IDs, leaving me without an alias.

"She's fine," Malcolm said as he stepped up.

The two men exchanged looks before turning back to Malcolm, questioning him silently.

"She's a friend of Mr. Carter," Malcolm clarified, daring either man to hold us up any longer.

After hearing Cain's name, both guards loosened up, stood away from the doors, and allowed me to enter.

"That's new," I let out once we were inside.

Cain really had made good on his word of the club being twenty-one and over.

Not only that, one step inside the main room and I could see that wasn't the only thing he'd changed.

The room was dim as always, but that was the only thing that had stayed the same. This wasn't Crazy Legs. Fresh vinyl flooring was at my feet, new light fixtures hung from the ceiling, and two more stages were put up to rival the main stage. Mirrors replaced the walls of the club, reflecting all that was going on from every angle. The seating was new and the booths at the bar were as well. Everything was cleaner, shinier, and more opulent.

But the men were the same. I recognized several faces the more I stepped into the room as Future's "Lil Demon" played throughout the club.

"Sabrina!" a man shouted to me from where he sat in a chair by the main stage. "Where have you been, girl?"

Smiling, I offered him a wave as I kept on toward the bar. Some of the girls in the room were the same from Crazy Legs, but a couple new faces jumped out at me as well.

At least Cain hadn't switched bartenders. Behind the bar was the long-time bartender Kyana. She'd been working at Crazy Legs for as long as I had. She was one of the nicer girls and I was happy to see she was still around.

"Bri?" Kyana squinted her eyes upon seeing me. "Damn, where have you been?" She wasted no time leaning over the bar to pull me in for a hug. Waves of her fruity-smelling perfume washed over me as she hugged me close and tight. "It's been a minute."

"Yeah, it's been a while," I said as I settled back. I took in the room once more, unable to believe the turnaround Cain had achieved in so little time. "I feel like I'm in a whole new club."

"Might as well be." Kyana set a shot down in front of me along with a napkin that had the new club info on it. *Taste: A Gentleman's Club*. I didn't even get to shoot her down before Malcolm's hand hovered over the glass. One look at him found him shaking his head. Kyana sized him up before tossing back the shot herself.

"I don't really drink," I said by way of explanation.

Kyana meant well. She always offered girls shots to calm their nerves before a dance or private session.

Kyana shrugged. "Anyway, some big baller came through here a few weeks ago and bought the club from David." She scrunched up her face at the thought. "I don't know why. I don't even think he likes women."

Malcolm snorted and I did my best to suppress my smile. "What would make you think that?"

"He looked disgusted from the moment he walked in the door to when he left." She appeared thoughtful, looking off across the room at nothing in particular. "You should've seen him, girl. I'm talkin' en-ner-gy. He had on a nice-ass three-piece suit and was just cold. You should've seen the girls tryna get a dance out of 'im. He was fine as fuck too."

With anyone else, especially one of my old boyfriends, I would've been curious, nervous that he'd take another woman up on the seductive lure of a lap dance.

But not Cain.

"I can imagine," I responded. Whenever a big shot came to Crazy Legs, it was like flies on honey. Everyone rushed to be the girl that secured the bag for the night.

"He ain't been back here since, but they did a whole upgrade." Kyana gestured around the lavish room. "They cardin' heavy now, so be careful."

Cain meant well, but I hated to think about those girls who had no other choice but to dance so that they could eat for a night, rent a place to sleep—*survive*. In time, I'd talk to him about lowering the age back to eighteen. It wasn't pretty, but survival often never was.

Kyana leaned against the bar and tossed me a smile. "So, what's been up with you? Mercedes said you went ghost out there at that job David sent y'all on."

"I kinda met someone," I confessed. "He wants me to hang up my shoes."

Kyana chuckled. "Is that right? You got you a rich fish?" She studied me for a moment. "I can tell someone's treatin' you right. You look good, Bri."

"Thanks," I said. I stole a look around the room, coming up empty for a certain face. "Have you seen Mercedes?"

Kyana nodded. "Yeah, she in the back gettin' ready."

I'd never had any real friends outside of Duane. Something that became abundantly clear when Cain had given me my phone back after days of having it and I only found missed calls and texts from Duane.

I had vanished that night at the Monte Carlo event, and Jenesis hadn't even bothered to see if I was okay. I knew she was never good for me, but it was sobering to realize it in the moment. Still, I lifted my chin and made my way to the dressing room to talk to her.

"BRI!" Amber shouted as soon as I stepped into the dressing room area. In seconds I was stumbling back at the collision of her body against mine. She held me steady as she took a moment to hold me at arm's length and appraise me. "Damn, it's really you!"

The other girls in the room, Starr and Cali, hung back at their stations, paying my arrival no mind.

Jenesis was at her own vanity area fixing her hair and focusing on her reflection in the mirror.

I got back to Amber, giving her a hug and a smile. "I kinda retired."

Amber blinked. "For real?"

"Yeah."

Amber backed off, appearing impressed. "Shit, I ain't hatin'. Less competition around here." She nudged me on the sly. "But you good? I was worried a minute there. You *never* miss work."

It was nice to know she cared. "Yeah, I'm good. Dancing was just something to get by. I've always wanted to work in a bookstore or library anyway."

Amber snorted and rolled her eyes. She'd caught me back here in the dressing room more than a few times on my break reading a book. "Never change, Bri." She cupped my chin as she passed me by. "Take care of yourself. And don't be a stranger."

"I won't," I promised as she stepped out of the room.

Vibration from the latest club song floated into the room. The bass was pumping and the beat had Jenesis nodding along as she continued to focus in the mirror.

I made my way over to her, standing behind where she sat at her vanity.

"Well, if it isn't Cinderella," Jenesis drawled as she eyed me in the mirror. She turned, starting at my heels and ending at my eyes. Boredom hung in her gaze as she peered at me. "Heard you went and found Prince Charming."

There was so much I could say to her, but I was doing better about choosing people who genuinely cared about me and wanted me around.

I licked my lips and nodded. "Yeah, something like that."

Jenesis shook her head. "Figures you'd be the one to get the millionaire." She glanced at me once more in the mirror, her eyes settling on my middle. "You pregnant?"

I hadn't the energy anymore to be offended or shocked she'd suggest such a thing. The truth was the truth. She didn't know me. She'd never tried to. Why bother questioning her when she didn't care to begin with? This was no love loss.

I turned on my heel, prepared to go. "Have a good one, Jen."

Malcolm was waiting at the bar for me where I'd left him. A football game was on one of the TVs mounted in the corner of the room and he was stealing glimpses at it as his vision bounced around the room, making sure things were secure.

My purse vibrated against the crook of my arm. I reached inside and found my phone ringing. Cain was calling.

The sound of YG's raps was loud, but not loud enough where I couldn't hear myself think.

Pressing a finger to my other ear, I answered the call. "Hello?"

"You never dress that cute for me." Cain's velvet voice filled my ear and instantly calmed and relaxed me after my confrontation with Jenesis.

His words caught up to me, making me pause at a lone side of the bar. "Excuse me?"

"I think we both know you heard me."

I chanced a look around the room, coming up empty. It was weird, I'd already known he wasn't here. Sometimes, I could just *feel* when Cain was around. "How do you know what I'm wearing?"

He hummed melodically. "Because I'm looking right at you. What did I tell you about my club?"

A cool sense of awareness breezed over my skin as I looked up and suddenly noticed a camera staring right at me high up in the ceiling. There were cameras scattered all over the room I realized as I took the time to look.

My eyes shot toward Malcolm who was watching me now from across the bar. Of course he'd told Cain where I was.

"I had something to settle," I said as I got back to Cain. "Not that that's any of your concern."

"You *are* my concern," Cain said. "Now that you've settled whatever you came to settle, please leave my establishment."

He was miles away in Hampton Hills, and I felt playful. I felt bold. "And if I refuse?"

"Then I'll clear my schedule, take a trip to Bedford Heights, and do some very fun things with you and my belt."

Heat rushed between my thighs. I gnawed on my bottom lip, slowly swallowing. I knew he'd never hurt me, but the thought of being punished by him made me hot. Curious.

"Sure you're not just scoping out other women like some perv?"

"Eden." Cain's tone carried a lazy warning. As if he wasn't putting much thought into his words. "The only woman I ever see is you."

His words seized my heart in a vise grip. I was standing in a strip club, in a room full of barely covered women, and all he saw was *me*.

"What if I don't come back?"

"Well, I don't have fond memories in Bedford Heights, but I guess I'll be moving back if that's the case."

I felt giddy. "Obsession is a bad thing, you know."

"It's just real estate, Tink," he said simply, like it would be no big deal for him to pack up to move near me.

It was all fun and games to joke about the idea of him up and moving, but really, I was curious.

"Do you really think this'll last?" I asked, dropping my guard. "I mean, we can never tell people how we met. There's no romance."

Cain clicked his tongue. "Who wants that cliché fairy tale anyway?"

I did. It didn't have to be perfect, but I wanted a clean romantic ending. I didn't need to be saved, more so, maybe we'd just run away together and be happy.

"I'm not a good man," Cain went on, turning serious as vulnerability dipped into his voice. "I could never be the hero in your story."

I leaned against the bar, all the background noise and people faded away. In black and white, it wasn't neat or pretty. I was a thief. A former underage exotic dancer with barely a GED to my name. He was a drug dealer. A cold-hearted killer who moonlighted as a billionaire businessman. This was who we were. Cracked. Bruised. Imperfect.

And I wouldn't have it any other way.

Kyana swooped by, dropping off what looked like Sprite with a cherry in it. A virgin drink just for me.

"Maybe in this one, the villain gets the girl," I theorized as I fished out the cherry and toyed with its stem.

"If the villain gets the girl, he'd never let her go." It was a warning. Once I was in, I was all in.

A heaviness settled into my chest at the choice before me. Could I be all in? Or was it better to walk away while I still had the chance?

I looked around the room filled with greed. The men coveted the women dancing before them, and the women had dollar signs in their eyes. For a while, this was my normal. Until Cain stepped in and put his foot down. He wasn't *all* bad.

"Eden?" Cain pressed when I'd taken long to respond. "Take your time and think about it."

He wasn't rushing me, but giving me proper space to decide.

"Thank you," I breathed out, appreciating it more than he knew. I ran my finger along the condensation of my glass. "So, I guess I'll be going now."

His musical chuckle warmed me. "Take care, Eden."

I hung up and took a big gulp of my drink, letting the fizzy soda pour down my throat as I shook away a case of jitters. Crazy —*Taste* was still going on around me as I stepped away from the bar and made my way back over to where Malcolm was waiting. As I took a final glance around the room, knowing I wouldn't be back, I felt a bitter smile cross my face. I'd made it out alive and now it was time for something else.

Malcolm took me out to the Bentley and I mused over my conversation with Cain and the possibility of going back or staying away.

Duane saw red flags, and rightfully so. Trouble was, red was becoming my favorite color.

26

Cain

EVERYTHING WAS QUIET. STILL. COLD. *EMPTY.*

As I sat at home in my office, I reflected on how everything was different now that I was alone. Before, I wouldn't have noticed, but after Eden...it was easy to recognize the TV wasn't on in the living room. There wasn't anyone chasing behind after a cat —there wasn't one. There was no humming as a meal was being prepared. There were no gasps every moment or so as something happened in a book.

There was nothing but me.

The sterile scent of cleaner and disinfectant wafted into the room.

I wasn't alone. Vera was here cleaning and straightening things out. With my double life, I only scheduled her once a month and kept up after myself otherwise.

A daily or weekly housekeeper was too much of a risk. Vera inquired about the gun I kept under my pillow, the gun I kept in my desk, the gun I kept in my kitchen. "Why would such a successful man need a gun?" she'd wanted to know during her second shift with me.

"Envy is a deadly thing," I'd supplied as a reasonable explanation. It was true for both of the worlds I dabbled in.

Vera wasn't exactly nosy, but she was curious. Sometimes *too* curious for her own good.

Movement in the doorway found her entering the room with a rag in her hands. Behind her black frames, her eyes softened at the sight of me. A warm smile eased its way across her tan face as she neared closer.

"Would you like something for lunch, Mr. Carter?" she asked.

Lunchtime. I hadn't even noticed.

That was a lie. In the week that Eden had been gone, I found myself calling her around this time. Partially to check in, because I didn't like not having her in my sight and not knowing how things were, and partially because...

I *missed* her.

I wasn't sure how I'd managed so long without her. Even the healthy takeout didn't compare to a nice home-cooked meal, one made with love and attention.

With Eden gone, and all her leftovers finished off, I was back to ordering out or going out. The most expensive meals couldn't beat Eden's cooking and I realized it every time I was tasked with eating for the day.

Vera meant well in offering me food, and for that I obliged her.

"Sure, what do you have in mind?" I responded as I sat back in my chair and gave her my attention.

"I could put together that southwest wrap you like. With some pita chips?" Vera offered.

The effort wasn't missed, so I bobbed my head. "That'll be nice, thanks."

Vera pivoted to leave, but not without turning back around and pursing her lips, appearing concerned. "How are things, Mr. Carter?"

Some days I was irritable, others I was so busy I was distracted, but right then, I was grappling with the fact that I was lonely.

An odd feeling when I considered my childhood and

upbringing. There had only been my mother and me in our home, but it was still very much a *three*-person household. James Carter may have never lived there or spent the night, but his presence, or lack thereof, couldn't be missed. My mother kept herself single in waiting for the man to drop everything and be with her. When she took her life, it was then I realized just how alone I was. No one came and got me. I was left to the system, and what a cold and desolate place that was.

None of that compared to the absence of Eden. Of finally having someone around who *wanted* to be around. Someone affectionate. Caring. Nurturing. You can't give someone who'd never had a piece of TLC a sample and then just take it away. It was unfair.

But business was in full swing. The Residence at Cartier was moving along. Damon was actively listening to his wife and family about letting Phil and me take the reins more. And my Vegas property was thriving with a fresh residency contract.

I would have money until Hell froze over.

"Things are good," I told Vera, forcing a smile onto my face.

Vera accepted this with a nod. She peered around my office, finding it free of dust or clutter. She settled her brown eyes back on me. "I don't see that *guest* here anywhere."

Blinking, I suppressed the urge to chuckle. Eden had been right in Vera's not being fond of her.

In Vera's defense, she had been unsuccessfully trying to get me to go out with her daughter for a while now. As beautiful as Cecilia was, I only held a taste for Black women.

Particularly ones obsessed with books and romance movies.

"No, I'm afraid my guest has returned home," I said in the end.

Intrigue lit Vera's face at the opportunity my single status provided. Not that I was single—entirely. Eden had asked what she was to me before she left, her cheeky way of wanting to hear me call her my "girlfriend." But as I'd told her on the phone a week prior, to be official, would mean I'd never let her go. I didn't have the strength to. She'd gotten in and burrowed herself there. Ruining me for anyone else it seemed.

"You know," Vera began. "My Cecilia hasn't been lucky in the romance department either."

I hummed, humoring her. "I'm sure someone worthy will come along."

"I could...bring her by some time," Vera suggested with a casual shrug. "Who knows, you may hit it off. She's a very nice girl. Cultured and funny, too."

That got me to smile. "Gotta love a sense of humor."

"*Sí*. Yes, she's very silly when she wants to be," Vera went on, eager to paint the idea of her daughter as a suitable partner.

Before, I would've kindly told her I'd someday consider it. Now, I didn't have it in me to pacify her. "I'm sure Cecilia is a wonderful woman, but as you saw, I'm otherwise preoccupied."

Vera *tsk*ed, turning and preparing to go and make my lunch. "I supposed she's a lucky girl, Mr. Carter. You're young, successful, handsome, and have the world at your grasp. She'd be a fool to not come back."

She left me alone and I sat stewing in her words. Nice and kind, but far from the truth.

If Eden were to do the wise thing, she'd stay away.

I needed to be a better man and let Eden go. She was young, hopeful, and deserved better.

Trouble was, I'd always selfishly wanted what I couldn't have.

I was a man of my word. So, regrettably, I was at Nichols and Wagner Wednesday morning prepared for a meeting with Sinclair.

Beans and Vino were there to serve as buffers, Beans more than anything being the most levelheaded. Still, I would've rather had him back in the Heights; he was supposed to be with her.

"I've got far better things to do than this," I sighed as I sat awaiting Sinclair's arrival. Our meeting was at ten thirty a.m., and it was already ten twenty. He was as good as late as far as most businessmen would consider.

Vino sat comfortably on the sofa along the left side of the room with his leg propped up over the other. He didn't think I could get through this without harming Sinclair. I thought he was right.

"Vegas in a month, right?" he prompted.

I was due for an appearance at Cartier, as well as showing face at the next Jaguar Jones boxing match. Shaking hands, rubbing elbows, and all that. That wasn't the only thing on the agenda unfortunately.

"As well as the mayor's ball," I grumbled. A night of dinner, dancing, and a charity auction. I wasn't looking forward to it, especially since it required a date.

Vino snuck me a clever grin. "Why don't you drag Eden back? Take her to Vegas, put a ring on it, and then you're set. Can't make a wife testify against her husband if shit ever goes down."

For security purposes, it made sense. But in the long run, it wasn't right.

Peering down at my desktop, absentmindedly glancing at my calendar, I shook my head.

I couldn't tether myself to Eden for life. No matter how tempting the idea was. She wanted a happy ending. That wasn't in the cards for me.

Still, I would always look out for her. Even when she inevitably left me and started life on her own, or with someone else. My mood dipped and the urge to grab my gun consumed me. I couldn't stomach the thought of her with someone else. The others? It had been nothing to let them go. But Eden? The thought drove me mad.

Beans was watching me when I looked up, silently calling my bluff. "You wanted to force Kennedy to marry you and she didn't even like you. Eden does."

Didn't make it any less naïve on her end. I traced the scar on my bottom lip. "She's got her whole life ahead of her."

"Because we're so fucking old at twenty-seven and twenty-eight," Beans drawled sarcastically.

Vino chuckled. *He* was the oldest at thirty-two. He was always the anomaly among us. While we came from traumatic and dark backgrounds, Vino came from an illustrious stable upbringing. He did what he did simply because he enjoyed it. Got a kick out of fucking people up, by hand or by trigger. He was a wild card, unhinged, but loyal.

Vino gave me a lazy once-over, angling his head and studying me. "You're a little too invested for this to be a one-off, D."

Her head was phenomenal. She always got me right. But Eden's mind? What went on in that pretty little skull of hers? It was what obsessed me the most. The knowledge of romance and meals, the tender empathy I'd never been offered, the wise cracks that slipped out every now and then when I tried her nerve.

It could never be described so simply as a "one-off."

There was no denying the truth. "It's more than just pussy with Eden."

Beans smirked, the look of *duh* etched across his face. "So why fight it?"

I had gone so long without having a soft spot. A weakness. Something that an enemy could target and hold over me. And that's exactly what Eden was: soft. Too clean-cut for my world. Still, as much as I should've left well enough alone, my stomach knotted up at the thought of another person in my place. "When it comes to Eden, I'm not working with a full deck."

Vino rolled his eyes. "When were you ever?"

I resisted a smile. "This is different." I knew it before I even said anything.

"How so?" Beans challenged.

I lifted my gaze to his. "Because once I'm in, I'm *in*. I'm talking forever."

I *liked* Eden. I liked her so damn much it felt like a sickness that had crawled under my skin and altered my system.

Eden could do better. I couldn't. I could shower a thousand times a day and I'd never be clean enough to touch her. And even accepting and knowing this, I still felt the need to kill any man who stood in my way.

"Like I said," Beans began with a knowing smile. "You hung around too long and now you don't want to let her go. The sooner you accept your feelings *and* hers, the better off you'll be. That girl is a lot of things, and one of them is being very much into you."

Static filled the silence stretched between us as I stared at my closest friend.

The intercom on my desk was going off. LaShanti's voice spoke through next. "There is a Mr. Sinclair Carter here to see you, sir."

Closing my eyes, I tried, really tried, to hold my composure. "Tell me again why I'm not killing him?"

Beans rolled his eyes, as if bored already. "Because you agreed to meet with him for Eden."

I hit the Talk button, grimacing. "Send him in."

In another moment LaShanti opened my door. There was no missing the way she was blushing and smiling as she looked back out the doorway just as Sinclair slithered on through.

"Pleasure meeting you," he told her.

She ducked her head and saw herself out, shutting the door behind her.

His expensive cologne hit me as he strolled across the room, armed with a bottle of wine with a large bow on it.

He came and set it on my desk, extending his arms out as he grinned down at me. "I come bearing gifts. It's a Cabernet Sauvignon. You're a red guy, right?"

I nodded.

Sinclair sat down in the chair in front of my desk. Right away I noticed he was wearing a fitted gray suit, black dress shirt, and burgundy pocket square. Yet again he wasn't wearing a tie. He made the look effortless. The way he carried himself and showed he didn't have a genuine care in the world. I thought that was another reason I hated him. He walked around like the smoothest and coolest motherfucker.

"Well," I began, sitting back in my chair. "You wanted to talk."

Sinclair mimicked me, sitting back in his own chair and getting comfortable. He gathered a cigar from his jacket. Not even asking if it was okay—it wasn't.

He didn't light or unwrap it, though, just fiddled with it in his hands. He looked at me and gave a limp shrug. "My bad about Red." He placed his hand to his chest, shooting me an easy smile. "But in my defense, I saw her first."

Raising a brow, I inhaled and blinked. "Excuse me?"

Sinclair shrugged again. "She was my good luck charm at that casino charity. Helped me rack in a decent penny. Before you"— he pointed his cigar at me—"entered the room, she was beside me."

In the background, Beans scratched at his neck. "This isn't a good apology."

Sinclair only grinned. "I'm getting there." He returned to me, loosening up. "You were just engaged to someone else last year, and before that, there were others. Forgive me for not knowing Red meant something."

"Her name is Eden," I uttered through clenched teeth.

Sinclair squinted his eyes, appearing thoughtful. Behind him, Vino shot him with a finger gun. "I like Red." He held his hands up. "But I'll respect you and yours. It's nothing with Eden. I was out of line and I apologize."

It was a start. "Fine. Get on with why you're here."

Sinclair lit up, glad he didn't have to grovel. "Word on the street is you're interested in sports management. I want in."

I snorted. "Fuck out of here."

"Hear me out," Sinclair went on. "You and I, we're a lot alike. Our fathers built Vegas."

I tamed my temper as best as I could. "You and I are *nothing* alike. You're daddy's little trust fund baby. Even if I turn you down, you still have his cash to keep you afloat. You've never starved. You've never been hungry. You've never had to make it on your own."

Sinclair barked out a loud laugh, its echo bouncing around the room as he peered over at my men and back to me. "Do you hear this guy? Jesus, what are you, a fucking sociopath?" He waved me off. "Listen, playboy, spare me the evil orphan origin story and monologue. I get it."

He didn't. Especially if he thought we were anything alike. He was a fucking yuppie. "Do you?"

My idiot cousin was still amused as he shook with quiet laughter. "Cain, man, you gotta relax. All this tension, it's not good for the ticker."

One look over at Beans found him simply shaking his head. *Don't do it*, his eyes told me.

I'd killed for less.

Wasn't shit funny about me or our differences.

"Get on with your point," I snapped.

"My point is, no one believes in you." He thumbed a finger out my office door. "They don't believe you're fit for this position. To fill your father's shoes. Shit, my own pops is just like that. That's how we're alike. No one thinks we're good enough."

I wasn't moved. "If you're asking if I have daddy issues such as yourself, the answer is no. I suggest you see a therapist. I'm told they do wonders for the spirit."

A scowl marred Sinclair's face. "Not when you fuck them, they don't."

Of course this guy fucked his therapist.

"You're already set on the real estate front, so why bother?" I had to know. His father put him in a position to buy and sell properties for him. He was set.

Serious, Sinclair fiddled with the ring on his finger. "I want to be a boss."

"It's overrated," I confessed with a limp shrug.

"I'm serious," Sinclair pressed, all traces of humor gone. "People talk around this city. When you showed up, people were pissed. No one thinks you deserve Cartier. You said it yourself; you think I'm a nepo baby. No one wants to take me on because outside of Sandford Carter, they don't think I'm good enough or have earned a seat at the table."

"And?" I challenged.

"I wanna own that fucking table," Sinclair stated. "Shit, Pops will probably leave me nothing, or put some clause in my inheritance that I gotta have a wife and kid first." Disgust covered Sinclair's face. "You wanna make something on your own, and I respect that. I want in on that. I know two things in this life." He held out two fingers to illustrate. "Women and sports."

Despite my disdain for him, I understood where he came from. Both of our fathers were pieces of shit, even if Sandford was doing better by him than mine ever had for me.

I didn't care for the Carters. I didn't care for Sinclair. He wasn't serious about anything. Even if he sat looking back at me with his cards on the table.

A glimpse at Beans and Vino found them genuinely curious on where I would take this.

Eden wanted me to hear him out, and I had. My part was done.

I gave Sinclair a once-over. "You're too easily enticed and distracted by pussy. That is a weakness I cannot have on my team," I let out.

Sinclair accepted this criticism. "I'll clean up my act. I'll try to keep things on the low so the blogs won't hear about anything."

I had to see it to believe it. The sports management idea wasn't set in stone, but a part of me did want to do something with my own name versus James's. Sinclair had me there.

I threw him a bone. "You wanna be an intern?"

Sinclair's face twisted up. "And start at the bottom?"

I shrugged. "You gotta start somewhere."

Sinclair's nostrils flared. "I'm not a bottom feeder."

Maybe this would be fun. To fuck with him. I peered up at my ceiling, thinking the idea through. "You can...collect mail for everyone."

Sinclair scoffed. "A mail carrier? Do people still do that?"

I wasn't even sure myself. "You're on probation with me if I take you on."

Sinclair clasped his hands together. "All I need is one shot."

"Start with wearing a tie," I ordered.

My cousin rolled his eyes. "Fine."

I held up my finger. "One rule: do not fuck anyone in this building."

Sinclair made a face. "I won't. *Again.*"

Of course he had already fucked someone at Nichols and Wagner. Of course.

I wasn't thrilled or too sure about getting involved with Sinclair, but at least it would piss Sandford off and keep me distracted. Keep my mind off wanting what I shouldn't have.

27

Eden

TWO WEEKS. THAT WAS ALL MY SANITY COULD TAKE. For two weeks I stayed home in Bedford Heights catching up with the life I'd left behind. I went for walks, stopped by the bistro to visit Duane during his shifts, and lounged around our apartment with American Joe reading books or rewatching my favorite movies.

It was relaxing, freeing, but if I were being honest, it was all a distraction.

There was no denying Bedford Heights was home, but I couldn't fight the longing I felt for the Hills.

I missed Cain.

"You sure about this, Doll?" Duane asked as we stood out on the front sidewalk. I was waiting for Malcolm to come and get me that Sunday evening.

Duane was only concerned about me, hence his hovering. I couldn't ever fault him for that. I would've been just as worried if he were in my shoes. Of course, then only he would know what it would be like being wrapped up in a man so tightly he didn't care about the risks. That he couldn't put into words what his heart knew was a safe decision.

For that, all I could respond to his question was with, "Yes."

Duane sighed, shaking his head. "I'm not sure I'll ever trust this guy."

Cain's presence and reality were intimidating. I could only hope someday Duane and he would reach common ground.

Malcolm was soon pulling up in front of the curb.

Duane grimaced. "Call me if anything goes wrong?"

Nothing wrong would happen. That I knew for certain when it came to being with Cain. "I'll call you even when things are going great."

Duane shot me a pointed look and I countered it with a goofy grin.

"Hey, love you like a brother," I told him softly.

Duane loosened up, going and tugging me close and resting his head on top of mine. "Love you like a sister."

We separated just in time for Malcolm to get out of the all-black Range Rover. He came over and collected my luggage first as I stood holding on to Joe's carrier.

Duane gathered a bag and helped Malcolm stow it in the back of the truck while I set Joe into the back seat. With one last tight squeeze, Duane let me go and we were off to Hampton Hills.

"You didn't say anything, did you?" I asked once we were on the highway.

Malcolm snorted beside me and shook his head. "I can keep a secret, Eden. D has no idea you're coming back."

Cain wouldn't admit it, but he was used to being left and counted out. I knew he didn't expect me to come back, and it was just another driving force in why I was.

But I wasn't going to make it easy for him. We seriously needed to talk before we continued seeing each other.

"He's in his own way when it comes to you," Malcolm spoke up after we made it back into the city. We were at Cain's place. Just off the elevator by his door. American Joe was anxious to get out of his carrier, he kept sticking his nose through the gate on the door.

"Whether the underworld or business world, our whole time

in this life, there's been other women, but none of them were you," Malcolm continued.

I tried not to feed into his words or the kernel of hope growing inside me. I was sure Cain had his demands, I just hoped he was willing to listen to mine.

Surveying my belongings as they surrounded our feet, I took a deep breath and let it out. "Maybe you should wait right here if this doesn't go well."

Malcolm smirked, trying to play it off by looking elsewhere.

"I'm serious," I insisted.

Malcolm gathered his key to Cain's front door and calmly shook his head. "Like he'll let you go that easily."

He went and opened the door and gestured inside. "I'll humor you and wait five minutes."

I wanted to pout about it, but instead I squared my shoulders and slipped inside.

Five minutes.

It was seven in the evening. The lights were dim in the penthouse as I descended the hall. Music was playing. Cain's beloved jazz. Something smell good, and that's when I laid eyes on him.

Sitting in the dining room at the end of his long black lacquer table was Cain.

He was clad in a dress shirt and pants, probably just home from work. He was eating what looked like pasta with one hand as he scoured something on his phone in the other. *Lonely.* That's how he looked sitting there by himself with no one to share his life with.

He hadn't noticed me. There was still time to turn around and leave. Still time to make what was probably a smarter decision.

But I went with my heart instead.

"That looks good," I spoke up from where I stood at the edge of the room watching him.

Cain froze, immediately halting eating and watching whatever he'd been looking at down on his phone. His head snapped to my direction and within a blink of an eye, he was holding a gun and aiming it at *me*.

A lump lodged itself to my throat and I had the grace not to wet myself at the sight of the sleek black weapon.

Upon recognizing me, Cain lowered his gun and let out a breath. We were frozen in place. Him at his feet at the table and me glued to the floor unable to move.

All Cain could do was stare at me for a moment as he visibly relaxed. His dark gaze started at my rose-gold six-inch heels before roaming up my bare legs, lingering on where my pale pink mini dress clung to my body, before continuing up to my eyes and staring into my soul. His face was unreadable and I almost lost all my confidence in what I wanted to say. As if him nearly shooting me wasn't terrifying enough.

"Do you always shoot first and ask questions later?" I managed to get out.

Cain let loose a grin as he tucked his gun away and came from the table, thumbing at his bottom lip. "Remind me to do exactly that to Beans." He pulled me close, placing a kiss on my forehead and inhaling my scent it seemed as he held me tight. "Missed you."

Heart, calm down.

Cain turned, eyeing his place at the table. "Hungry?"

I hadn't eaten before I left the Heights, too consumed with nerves to stomach a bite. "What is it?"

"Lobster carbonara. Not nearly as good like you would've made it." He went over to the kitchen island where a steaming aluminum pan was, before preparing to make *me* a plate.

"I'm happy to hear you like my cooking," I responded as I watched him give me a portion of the pasta.

He glanced my way, serious as ever. "I love your cooking."

Easy. I willed the butterflies in my belly to calm down as I hugged my middle. I needed to be strong. To voice what I wanted. To be heard.

Cain gathered my plate and a utensil before stopping by the table and noticing where I remained. "Join me?"

I smoothed my hands down my dress and approached the table. "Sure, we'll make this a business dinner."

Cain arched a brow, studying me. "I don't like games, Eden."

Choosing the chair closest to him, I snuck him a smile. "Oh, come on, play along. We have things to talk about before I decide if I want to come back or not."

Cain set my plate and fork down. "*If?*"

I took my place at the table and nodded. "Yes, we need to talk."

Cain made a face, but took his seat across from me. "You didn't answer my call today," he pointed out.

He'd been calling me every day around noon since I left. It had become the highlight of my day back in Bedford. Hearing from him made not seeing him easier, but it didn't make me miss him any less.

"Yes, I'm surprised you didn't rush over to get me," I said.

"I'm trying this new thing called patience." Cain appeared thoughtful before shaking his head. "Not a fan of it."

A smile arrested my face as I dug into the pasta. Lobster carbonara. I had to try making it myself. It was delicious and rich. I could've gotten lost in the meal if I wasn't distracted by the impending conversation I needed to have with Cain.

Cain was back into his own plate, but his phone lay abandoned on the table. I had his complete attention as he kept stealing glances my way almost to see if I were real.

"So..." He dabbed at his mouth with a napkin. "...you wanted to talk?"

I sat up straight and came out with it. "If we're going to be together, I want it to be serious. Boyfriend. Girlfriend."

Cain bobbed his head, accepting this. "Okay."

That wasn't *all* I wanted. "I want love."

Cain wrinkled his nose in distaste. He sat back in his chair, scratching at his neck. "'Love'?" He questioned it as if it were a foreign concept.

"Yes," I said. "I want to be *in* love."

I wasn't asking for the moon and the stars. Or anything of material value, because nothing truly measured up to what I wanted most.

"You've killed for me. You've crossed the line and done the unthinkable to make sure I'm safe. But that's not enough. I could name a price and you'd pay it. But that's not enough," I went on. "Action without meaning is nothing."

Cain's finger tapped rapidly against the tabletop. He didn't look moved or swayed by my words. "I'm not a go-to-the-movies-and-eat-popcorn kind of guy."

Coming from where he was from, that was understandable, but there was always room to change. "Too bad. I've never had *normal*. Before you brought me here, I was barely getting to *stable*," I responded. "I want dinner and a movie, because it's cheesy and simple. I want candy and flowers, because they're nice. I want to be loved, because I deserve it."

Cain regarded me with what looked like pity in his dark eyes. "You're a romantic and there isn't room for romance in my world."

He wasn't willing to try. My gaze fell upon my plate. It was too bad really. The pasta was immaculate, but I wasn't about to sit there and enjoy it. I wasn't going to *beg* this man to love me. All the money in the world, gifts included, couldn't make up for what I'd never had with my previous boyfriends.

I stood from my seat, steeling my spine and standing firm in my beliefs. "Then I'll find a man who can do both. Love me *and* fuck me."

Cain closed his eyes, taking in a silent breath that spoke volumes.

I didn't stay to watch him recover from my declaration. No, I turned on my heel and headed for the door, hoping Malcolm was—

Cain had a hold of my arm. He whirled me around to look at him. The annoyance covering his face was hard to miss.

"I told you, I don't like games," he said, his grip tight.

I tried and failed to free my arm. "I'm not playing any."

Cain narrowed his eyes, not loosening his hold. "If you have anyone else in mind, why don't you call them up so I can get rid of them now?"

Because he couldn't stand the thought of me with another man.

I turned my face. "It hurts your ego so much at the thought of another man touching me. Yet you feel *nothing* at the thought of one loving me."

Gently, Cain massaged my cheek with his thumb. "Not true," he insisted as he turned my head, making me look him in the eye. "Forgive me for not wanting you to make a choice you'll regret. You want white picket fences and rose petals. Sunshine and rainbows. *Love.* I'm not a good man, Eden, but you want to love me."

My heart was in his hands and he had no idea. "You may not be a good man to the world, but you're a good man to me."

Pain coasted across Cain's features as his brows furrowed. "A better man would let you go. You're younger and have more ahead of you."

It was only nine years. That wasn't enough to stand between us.

"I'm an old soul. I get excited about buying new appliances," I said limply.

Slowly, Cain softened, a ghost of a smile on his lips. "I don't like people touching what belongs to me."

"Oh, baby," I cooed, cupping his jaw. "That sounds psychotic."

He didn't see the humor. "If we do this, you're mine."

There was no missing the finality in his tone. "You let the others go."

"I didn't *like* them."

I meant more to him than the women before me. I wanted love and Cain wanted forever. Surely we could meet in the middle.

"Told you not to be so crazy about me," I teased.

"Can't help it with you."

He'd said these words before and they made me melt just as hard.

Curious, I asked, "How would we tell people we met?"

Cain smirked. "You stole my heart."

Blushing, I held back a laugh. Of course he knew just what to say.

"I'm not ashamed of what I did to take care of myself," I said with my head held high.

"I like that about you."

"Do you? What'll you feel if someone asks me what I did before we met and I tell them?"

"I'll kill anyone who judges you, Eden. Don't test me on that," Cain said vehemently. "Before I killed my father, I was selling drugs to make it. It's not something I brag about. Some people can't handle the truth—the harsh reality outside of their gated homes. I don't care what anyone thinks of you, but I don't want you ever feeling small, either."

Protected. That was something I'd always feel around Cain.

I went closer and wrapped my arms around him, burrowing my face into him. "Okay."

Cain's arms came around me, his hands seizing my waist possessively. "Tink in pink," he mused at the sight of me in my fitted pale pink Shallow dress.

I took a step back and modeled my dress for him. "You like?"

Cain reached up, loosening his tie. His gaze flickered to the living room behind us and back to me. Gesturing his head, he said, "Come sit in the living room with me."

I took his hand and followed his lead over to the living room where I sat down on the sofa. He didn't join me. Instead, he stood in front of me and guided me to lay back. His soft hand traveled from caressing my shoulder, down the curves of my body, until it rested on my bare thigh. Underneath his touch I became alive and ached for more. It had been too long.

He was so close, I was positive he felt the heat emanating from me.

"You're not wearing any panties," he observed, his eyes ablaze with lust and want as he peered down at the apex of my thighs.

"I knew I was coming home to you," I admitted shamelessly.

Cain regarded me, his touch turning into a grip. "'Home to me'?"

I nodded, feeling on fire the longer he looked at me, touched me. "I missed you."

His hand traveled higher up my thigh, but not to where I needed it. Instead, it came to my waist, going and fisting the material of my dress in a tight fist where he pulled it up and exposed my nudity to him.

Stepping back, Cain flicked his attention toward me. "Show me how much you missed me."

A deep throb set in between my legs and I felt my arousal take over me at the command Cain had just ordered.

With his eyes on me and mine on his, I ran my hand down my stomach and between my legs. A moan escaped my lips at the feel of my fingers touching myself. Cain watched with intrigue as I kept rubbing my clit, sending my heart drumming against my rib cage.

He blinked, coming back to me, frowning. "I thought you missed me?"

He wasn't impressed. He wanted more.

Sending my hand lower, I slipped two fingers into myself. I was so wet there was no missing the erotic sounds my hand was making as I slid my fingers in and out of me. I had done this before but there was nothing like doing it with Cain right there, watching hungrily. His face was expressionless, but the look in his eyes was prominent. And it was just for me.

My thighs clenched around my hand as I felt my orgasm coming. I worked my fingers faster, chasing it, needing it.

Oh fuck.

I couldn't take my eyes off Cain's as a wave of pleasure washed over me, drowning me in a sensation that left me numb as I rode it out on my fingers.

I was just winding down from my high when Cain snatched my fingers out of me and drove them into his mouth. Labored breaths slipped past my lips as I watched him suck my juices from my fingers. There was something so *hot* about it, I couldn't speak. He looked like a man starved. I should've known then what I was in for. What beast I'd just awakened.

My gaze traveled to his pants, at the thick bulge that was straining to break free. My mouth watered, wanting to please him more than anything.

Cain took a step back, dropping my wrist. "Dinner's getting cold."

The only thing I wanted in my mouth at the moment was him. Reaching out, I massaged his member through his pants. "Thank God you own two microwaves."

Cain angled his head, looking down at me. He stroked himself. "You want this?"

I nodded, too turned on to be ashamed.

His nostrils flared. "You have ten seconds to get up to my bed."

I hopped up so fast I almost collided with him. I hadn't made it an inch by him when he took hold of my arm and pressed into my ear, "I'm more than a little crazy about you. Don't test that ever again."

He released me and I knew then that there was no making it out of this unscathed.

I was too far gone for this man. Head over heels and fumbling toward a four-letter word that would probably be the end of me.

But I was a slave to my lust. Too caught up in my carnal needs to argue or protest. Up in Cain's room I stripped down and got on his bed and waited for him, wanting nothing more than for him to ease the ache between my thighs.

Cain appeared in the room and I sat up on my knees, anticipating. He came over to the bed, eyes hooded, still riled up, still appearing ravenous. He went for the buttons on his shirt and I for the zipper on his pants. He watched me pull him out and put him into my mouth, going slow as he peeled his shirt off.

I savored the taste of him, trailing my tongue down the length of his shaft before taking him back into my mouth. My eyes watered as I took him in deep, but I kept going, needing to feed the hungry part of me that wanted every bit of him. Cain smoothed my hair back out of my face as he watched me. His tender touch caused tears to spill out of the corners of my eyes.

In lightning like movement, Cain jerked back, holding himself and offering me a sheepish smile. "Fuck. You're too good at that. I wanna finish inside you."

A shiver passed through me at the thought. Suddenly I felt *empty*.

Cain stepped out of his remaining clothing and I lay back as he joined me on the bed. He planted kisses on my skin as he crawled up my body, searing me deeply.

"You're wrong, you know," Cain said as he lifted his head and stared at me. "It isn't just the sex. I *like* coming home to you. Not even just for the hot meals. Just the fact that you're here, living, breathing, *existing* in my space. You've created a monster because I can't get enough of you."

I started to respond, to tell him how much I liked being here with him, taking care of him as much as he took care of me, but he simply shook his head, silencing me.

Chest to chest, I felt him brushing against my entrance, sending my mouth falling open.

Oh God.

Cain came down and crushed his lips to mine, stealing any chance at a last breath as he entered me in one strong thrust.

He groaned so deeply and stilled, I thought he was in pain.

"You shouldn't have given me this." He thrust more into me, his face contorting. "Because I'm *never* letting you go."

Gone was his patience as he took me like he owned me, aggressive and possessive as he gripped my thighs up and apart while he pounded into me. I was a mess of pleas and moans all while he watched from above me. This was more than just sex. He was sending a message. I belonged to him. I was *his*. And there was no going back.

28

Eden

SOMETHING SMELLED GOOD. LIKE BACON, HOT, FRESH, and greasy. Eggs, and fluffy, sweet pancakes. A feast that had my mouth watering at the thought.

I was otherwise facedown, naked, tangled up in Cain's sheets as I recovered from the night before. As good as the aroma was, as well as the idea of food, I wasn't planning on getting out of bed any time soon. On walking or moving ever again.

"You alive?" His voice. His deep, musical voice. How he held the power to sound heaven-sent after the devilish things he'd done to me, I wasn't sure.

"Barely," I grumbled out as I peeked one eye open.

One peek was all it took to send both my eyes flying open.

I now knew where the decadent smell was coming from. Cain was at my bedside, holding a large wooden tray of food—breakfast.

He took in my utter state of shock and grinned. "Morning."

I struggled to sit up, using the comforter to cover my breasts when I finally did. "What's this?"

"Breakfast," Cain offered as he set the tray down on my lap. On it was a plate of croissants, another of bacon, eggs, pancakes, a bowl of what looked like oatmeal with berries, and a plate of French toast sticks.

It was quite a surprise. One that had me blinking rapidly as I sat there taking it in.

"You hate it?" Cain questioned when I'd been too quiet.

"No!" I rushed to say. "I just... I can't think of the last time I've had breakfast in bed. I'm speechless." My hand brushed along my collarbone as I drew my attention from the single red rose in the glass of water at the corner of the tray up to the man beside me. "Thank you."

Cain accepted this with a simple shrug. "It just came to me."

He said it like it was no big deal. But it was.

"I can't believe you did all this." I grabbed a croissant and tore a piece off. It was flaky, buttery goodness. *Mmm.*

"Well, I wouldn't say *I* put it together. The caterer did. I mean, the French toast was my only touch," Cain said. "I put it all on the tray if that counts."

I tossed him a pointed look. Catering or not, it was still a thoughtful gesture.

I went back to the tray. Back to the French toast sticks. I could tell he'd used the frozen kind, which meant he must've air-fried them or baked them. *Cain,* using an appliance. What a thought.

It was just after nine in the morning, meaning Cain must've gotten up extra early to pull this off. It wasn't too bizarre considering his routine of working out before he went in to the office.

Early or not, he was running behind since he was still here.

He was standing there in low-slung black running shorts, a black towel draped around his neck, and nothing else. I considered him in this state, sculpted middle and toned arms. I liked that Cain was muscular but still on the slim side. He was already intimidating in presence and manner, his height doing nothing to tone it down, but his size was just enough without being too much.

Still, I couldn't believe he could get up, work out, and put together a breakfast order while I was still finding my bearings from last night. My thighs still ached from his firm grip. Cain's stamina was insane.

"Want some? It's way too much for me," I offered as I started to scoot over for him to sit beside me.

Cain's lips twisted into a half smile as he shook his head. "Maybe after my shower."

"Aren't you running behind?" It was Monday, and from what little I knew about his work here in Hampton Hills, they always held office meetings on Mondays to go over figures and what had gone on during the previous week.

That half smile broadened a smidge. "I'm taking the day off."

The last time he'd taken the day off... "Why?"

Now he was full on smiling as he peered over at me. "Because we've got a very busy schedule, Miss Edwards. Might wanna eat up now and get dressed. We've got somewhere to be."

He started to walk away and that's when I noticed.

Rose petals.

Scattered along the rich, dark wooden floor leading from my bedside to the bathroom were red rose petals.

My mouth fell open. "Rose petals?"

Cain paused at the bathroom door, giving me a limp shrug. "Seems kinda messy, but they say it's romantic."

It was. It *so* was. "I love it."

He grinned. "*Love*, huh? Guess we're on the right track."

He was about to get ready to shower and I still couldn't grasp what he was up to. "Wait. What's going on?"

He poked his head back into the room, that devilish smile sending my heart beating wildly in my chest. "Romance. Spontaneity. Now eat."

Cain said no more before disappearing into the bathroom where he showered for the day.

Another day. He was devoting another day to us. For me.

I concentrated on the food and ate as much as I could, but truly, it was too much for a single person. Reluctantly, I climbed out of bed and carried the remains down to the kitchen and put the rest away. I could eat it later.

There was no missing that in the doorway Malcolm had placed my bags I'd brought with me and he'd even let American Joe out of his carrier. He'd probably done so as soon as I slipped inside. Last night was a whirlwind of defining what I wanted with Cain. I wouldn't have noticed anyone else if I tried.

Still, in disbelief over the turn of events, I found my cell phone and shot Duane a text.

> ME
>
> It's official!

Over on Duane's end, a series of three ellipses bubbled up as he prepared to respond right away.

> DUANE
>
> Oh? You laid down the law?

> ME
>
> I told him what I wanted and was about to leave when he wasn't willing to try.

> DUANE
>
> Atta girl

> ME
>
> He stopped me from leaving and we came to an understanding. Now this morning he wakes me up with breakfast in bed and says we've got plans today

> DUANE
>
>

> DUANE
>
> Well okay, Cinderella! Think you girls call this the "soft girl era"?

A laugh erupted out of me at that last text.

If only it could be so easy. That I'd really secured my own fairy tale ending.

Back upstairs I got ready in my own bathroom. In all the fun and heat of the moment the previous evening had provided, beyond feeling a little sore, I was left with one small regret. I'd gone to bed without taking care of my hair. It was wild as I stood dressed for the day in a red strapless top and a denim skirt. I'd just gotten my extensions put in and ordinarily I knew better when it came to maintenance, but one thing had led to another and here we were.

I managed to fix my leave-out and pull my hair up in a ponytail for the day in just under twenty minutes. By the time I was ready and back downstairs, Cain was dressed to go.

While he wasn't wearing a suit, he was still almost business casual in his fitted T-shirt that clung to his middle and black trousers. His look gave no tell on what he was up to, and neither did he as he led me out of the penthouse and took us down to the parking deck.

There was no Vino or Malcolm today as Cain took the wheel of his Bentley and drove us some place. Music played on the radio, wind slipped in through the crack of the window, and the sun was shining bright in the clear June sky. The smell of his cologne washed over me as I sat beside him, cocooning me in a comfort I couldn't put in words. The fact that he was willing to try, to go out of his way to give me romance, stole my breath away.

It didn't matter where we were going. I was up for anything, just as long as I was with him.

Not too long into our drive Cain came to a stop at a valet lane. We got out as the valet came and took Cain's car. One look at the building we'd arrived at and I got a clear idea of what Cain had in mind. The stenciled sign on one of the front glass doors told me this was a spa and massage parlor.

Cain led us inside where no one else but staff was around the clean white space of the lobby area. The calming sound of trickling water could be heard as we approached the front desk.

The receptionist perked up immediately at the sight of Cain. She stood from her plush black chair and rushed to the counter to greet him with a smile that lingered too long to be friendly. I watched as her gaze drank in all of him before she met his eyes and seemed to blush.

I rolled my eyes. Of course he had this effect on women.

"Mr. Carter, we're all ready for you, sir," the woman, whose name tag read *Gloria*, said. She reached out, placing her hand on his where it rested on the countertop. "We've arranged everything just as you requested."

Cain stepped back, leaving her hand to fall away, as he made room for me to be in her direct line of vision. "Good. I'm sure she'll like that."

"H-hello." Gloria swallowed, gathering herself together to focus on me. "Right this way."

Gloria came around the counter and led us down the glossy white hallway to an empty room with only a chair and a bench in it. "Please, get undressed and we can start your day."

Another staff member came up and handed Gloria a bright, white fluffy robe. Right away I noticed my initials monogrammed on the right side.

"Oh wow." I accepted the robe and Gloria disappeared to offer me privacy to change. I fingered the velvet material of the robe as I looked over at Cain. "A spa day?"

He bore a crooked smile. "Figured you'd be sore from last night." He flicked a finger at the robe's tie. "This is just our first stop."

There was more?

Because I was sore, I wasted no time getting undressed and slipping on the robe. Cain didn't join me. Instead, he hung back as the staff members went to work on getting me in a chair and began fussing with my nails. I chose lavender for my fingers and pale pink for my toes as a member of staff placed a clay mask on my face along with cucumbers over my eyes.

"You've got such good skin," she observed as she finished

covering my face. "But there's nothing wrong with keeping a routine just in case."

I allowed myself to be pampered for the first time as I lay back while a woman worked on my feet and another on my hands. Throughout the spa, on the speakers, Cain's beloved sound of blues and jazz could be heard. A sound that I could only recognize as *home*.

When my nails were done and dry, I padded down to another room for a massage. The sudden sound of Cain's cell phone ringing interrupted the otherwise easy flow of the morning as we all settled into the room that offered a magnificent view of Hampton Hills' downtown area.

I couldn't be upset that Cain was getting caught up with work or whatever. He was a successful businessman, so of course he couldn't completely take the day off. While I laid on the massage table and got comfortable, Cain stood by the floor-to-ceiling windows, a hand in his pocket, his ankles crossed, as he listened to whatever the caller was saying.

Etta James was playing in the background as my masseuse worked the tension out of my sore body. I melted into the table as her fingers kneaded into my skin. The mix of Etta's singing and Cain's quiet timbre across the room were comforting to say the least.

A contented sigh escaped my lips as I looked over and caught Cain's attention. He was speaking business, but his gaze was locked on me.

Molten. Magnetic. Mine.

There was something about him that left me greedy. I loved having his undivided attention. It made me realize I'd been starved my whole life and now I could finally feast.

Etta was singing about a Sunday kind of love when Cain said something, soon ending his call and putting his cell phone away. He came from the window and approached me where I lay on the table.

"Let me finish her?" he asked the masseuse.

"Yes, Mr. Carter." My masseuse put up no fight before leaving me to Cain.

He rounded the table and soon those soft hands of his were on the skin of my back, soothing me far deeper than just touch alone.

Oh.

"That okay?" he asked, working his way up to my shoulder blades.

"Yes," I let out in a breathy moan.

He snorted and went on. "How was Bedford Heights?"

I thought of my time back home and smiled in the freedom of being with Duane and having no obligations. "It was nice. Different than before, but better. For the first time, I felt free."

Cain hummed, continuing to work magic on my back as he massaged my aches away.

"I like what you did to the club, intrusive or not," I admitted of Crazy Legs' turn around and rebrand into *Taste*.

I hoped his changes also included better benefits for the girls. David had been cheap and selfish with us. He didn't provide retirement, paid time off, or costumes, but would complain if you asked for a day off.

"In all your time there, no one tried to help you? Outside of Duane?" Cain wanted to know.

It was sad when I thought about it.

"Not really," I admitted. But then I knew that wasn't entirely true. "Well, there was someone. He was older with a quietness about him that just made me curious." I rested my chin on my hands as I thought of Keith. "I first met him at this pizza place in town. He was ordering food for this community center he volunteered at. When he first approached me, I was reading and I thought he was going to hit on me. But that wasn't the case.

"He told me if I knew anyone in need of help, that I should bring them by to the center. He asked about the book I was reading and that was it. I ran into him once more and he actually had gotten a copy and we talked about it. Still, he was distant. He knew I was young and he kept a boundary. The last time I saw him, I was in trouble."

Adele was singing now. A newer voice among the legends from the past.

"What kind of trouble?" Cain prompted when I didn't go on.

"My friend—*coworker*, and I was at this gas station. She likes to do things, for the thrill of it. I stole some candy and of course we got caught. She ran and I just couldn't." I was too soft, because I knew I was in the wrong and I couldn't run when called out for it. "That guy was there. He stuck up for me. Gave me a lecture, too, but he was there for me. Outside of Duane, he was the first man who didn't want anything from me, but just to help."

For a beat, Cain was quiet as he worked on my back and focused.

"Sounds like a good guy," Cain decided to say when he spoke up.

Keith was. A rare breed of man, that I could tell from the little I knew of him.

"What about you?" I wondered next.

"Outside of staying with one nice family for that one night? No, not really," Cain said. "Meeting Beans was the only beacon I had. When I was leaving again, we exchanged e-mails and we talked that way at first before I sold enough dime bags to get me a phone."

My heart thudded for the little boy who'd had to do what he did to survive. For the little boy who hadn't a hand to hold to make it through the system.

I turned and leaned back on my arms. Cain looked at me as I looked at him. No judgment. Just pure respect and understanding.

My hand found his where it lay on my lap. "Perhaps, maybe, we were always meant to find each other?"

He didn't respond. Instead, he came closer, tipped my head back, and brushed his lips along mine. Chaste. Soft. Simple. It was all that I needed.

I felt rejuvenated as we stepped out of the spa. My skin was glowing and I couldn't contain the smile splitting my face. Professional or not, I loved having Cain take over and massage me. He was so attentive and thorough, his soft hands making me dissolve into mush.

"I didn't know how much I needed that." I moaned as we climbed back into the Bentley. I felt incredibly loose and capable of anything now.

Cain grinned as he buckled in. "I'm glad you liked it."

"I *loved* it," I clarified.

His free hand captured mine and he brought it to his lips to kiss. Tingles spread through my body as goose bumps covered my flesh.

Cain drove over to Townsend Boulevard. From my first shopping trip with Malcolm, I knew this was where all the high-end stores were located. We'd gone into a few boutiques and a salon before I felt ready enough to face all the who's who of Hampton Hills at that art show Cain had me meet him at.

Cain pulled next to a meter that was in front of a jewelry store.

Jewelry.

Up and down the sidewalk locals were coming to and from. Some holding bags from shopping, or others on cell phones probably discussing business. My eyes took in the jewelry store with its name in chrome letters above the front door. *King Jewelers.*

Cain came around my side of the car and helped me out. He fed the meter before ushering me inside the storefront. Once inside we were hit with a fresh blast of AC. Along the vinyl flooring were case upon case of jewelry, from watches, to necklaces, and to rings. Rings. Right away I noticed the couple on the left side of the room at a counter with a worker admiring a set of rings. The woman was trying them on, giddy, as the man watched with pride.

The sight made me smile.

"They say diamonds are a girl's best friend," Cain mused as we stepped more into the store.

"Mr. Carter." Right away a man materialized in front of us, extra happy to see Cain. The pin on his shirt said he went by *J.L.* "We've been expecting you."

Cain's arm came around me as he tugged me close. "Whatever she wants."

J.L. lit up as he appraised me. "I'm assuming money is no object then?"

"No," Cain told him as he let J.L. take my hand.

This inspired J.L. more as he quickly breezed through the room showing a hand at cases. "What do you have your eye on? Anything in particular? Watch? Earrings? *Rings*?" The emphasis on rings had me peeking back at Cain. He held my gaze, saying nothing, but there was no missing the amusement on his face. I looked away first, feeling dizzy.

Rings.

"We just restocked our tennis bracelets. Of course, Van Cleef is all the rage right now," J.L. went on.

Running my hand down my arm, I looked around us uncertainly. Outside of my belly button ring, I wasn't really into jewelry. Even with the money I made at the club, I'd never thought about splurging on any.

J.L. wasn't lying, though. Van Cleef bracelets were trending when I thought about the few glimpses I'd seen in the club on clients or the girls.

"Tennis bracelets?" I wondered as I got back to J.L.

J.L. clasped his hands together and rushed over to a case in the back corner of the room. Once there my breath got caught in my throat at the price tags of a few. The cheapest bracelet was forty thousand dollars, while the highest Cartier piece was well over a hundred.

I stepped back. Even if Cain could afford it, I wasn't so sure.

"Only the best," J.L. encouraged as he gestured toward the case.

"We'll take it." Cain had joined us. Not even bothering to look at the price. "Give us all of them." He peered over at me, his eyes lingering on my neck. "And a matching necklace, too."

My hand rushed to my throat at the thought.

Talk about icing me out.

J.L. was all too delighted to rack up the bracelets from the case and quickly grab the priciest necklace in the case next to them.

"Be right back," he practically sang on his way to the register once it was determined I didn't need custom sizing.

The heat of his gaze warmed my face. I tore my eyes away from J.L. to find Cain watching me. His eyes narrowed and his expression was empty.

I should've been ecstatic. And really, I was appreciative of the gesture. The bracelets and the necklace were beautiful.

"Thank you," I told him. "I'm almost afraid to touch them, they're so pretty."

Cain said nothing. He looked around us, taking in J.L. at the register, a new couple who had entered the shop, and the now empty case of tennis bracelets, before settling his attention back on me. He shook his head. "This isn't you."

It wasn't, but I couldn't ignore the amount of money he'd just spent on me. "Stop, I like—"

Cain silenced me by holding up one finger. J.L. was back with a King Jewelers bag and a receipt wrapped around Cain's matte Black Card. He must've worked on commission, because there were nearly tears in his eyes, he was beaming so hard.

"Anything else, sir, don't hesitate to call," he said with a firm shake of Cain's hand.

Cain tipped his head toward him. "Sure thing."

He had my hand and was whisking me for the door in a quick stride. I had just enough time to turn and wave before we were out the door.

We didn't get back in the car. No, Cain walked with purpose down the street and it wasn't until we came to a stop that I knew why.

Bueller Books.

A large bookstore stood in front us.

On one side of the large front window was a display of fantasy books. In the other was sci-fi.

The biggest smile arrested my face and I couldn't stop myself from jumping with joy. No matter how never-ending my to-be-read pile was at home or at Cain's, there was always room for more books.

"This is more your speed, Tink." Cain's whispered words in my ear brought me back down to earth.

As if he hadn't just spent well over six figures on me not even ten minutes before, I stood on my tiptoes and kissed him. It was meant to be a quick peck, but Cain's free arm came around me and pulled me in and soon it was more. His tongue dipped into my mouth, my eyes slipped closed, and my chest tightened. Right there on the sidewalk, in the middle of the day, I hoped he never let me go.

I pulled back and got lost in his dark eyes. Eyes that only seemed to soften when they were looking at me. When it was just us. And he wasn't a CEO or king pin. When he was just mine.

"Thank you," I breathed out, feeling too much just then.

A smile lifted the corner of his lips as he peered back down at me. He shrugged as if it were nothing. "I'll be right back." He lifted the bag from King Jewelers. "I'll meet you inside."

If he could find me.

I almost laughed at the idea. Back home, I owned a few recipe books, some biographies, but nothing could distract from the fact that my true favorite genre was romance.

Bueller Books had a whole section dedicated to Black romance and I quickly got lost scavenging for my newest fix.

"Ooh." On an end cap was the week's newest releases, and I caught a favorite author of mine who had just put out a new book. I grabbed the dark blue paperback with the title in faded script writing. *Scenes From a Movie.* I quickly turned the book over to see what Robyn Whitney had come up with next. It looked to be a heart-wrenching romance featuring survivor's remorse, a family who had lost their way, and a female and male lead from opposite sides of the track.

Right up my alley.

I flipped to the prologue and was delighted to see the book was written in dual narrative.

"Must be good."

The book landed on the floor in a *smack* as I nearly jumped out of my skin.

I had been so caught up in reading I hadn't noticed someone approaching me.

Cain.

He was holding back a laugh at my startled expression.

So, I swatted him. "Don't do that!"

Cain chuckled as he came closer and examined my book. "Just one?"

Considering the books I had scattered all over the penthouse bookmarked in various stages of my reading, one was enough.

But it was a shopping spree, so in the spirit of letting Cain spoil me, I grabbed a few more books on our way to the register. I wrapped my arm around Cain's and leaned into him as he went and paid for my paperbacks. I didn't say anything, but I loved how well he knew me after so little time together. That I didn't have to voice it, but he'd already known that buying jewelry or clothing wasn't my thing. That I would much rather get lost in a bookstore.

Outside, I noticed Cain had gone on a shopping trip of his own as he was holding a bag from Burberry. It wasn't until our next destination that I knew what he'd bought. A large wool blanket.

He parked in a parking lot next to a huge lot of land belonging to a park named Bishop Hill. A big gathering of people had come as well. Cain said nothing before grabbing the blanket and wrapping an arm around me and leading me toward the path that led up to the highest peak of the park. The sun wasn't on us and a comfortable breeze passed as we made our way up the hill.

Up ahead near a large tree a man was standing looking down at his phone in one hand, as the other held a sizeable picnic basket. Cain led us right up to the man and shook hands with him.

"Afternoon," Cain greeted the man. He dug into his pocket and pulled out his wallet. He fished out a few bills before passing them over. "Appreciate you."

The man handed the basket over and accepted the money with a wide-eyed look. "Thank you. Thank you so much, Mr. Carter." He tipped his head generously at Cain before taking off down the hill with a spring in his step.

"What's all this?" I asked as I gestured to the basket and how we seemed to be the only ones up on the hill. A glance down below saw a massive screen propped up and I almost thought we were about to witness a concert. Except there was no stage. The buttery smells of popcorn wafted up to us and I looked farther and spotted vendors down below as well. Some selling popcorn, others hot dogs, as well as beverages and desserts.

Coming back to Cain, I was curious.

He nodded off toward the screen below us. "Movie in the park. I saw it in the paper this morning and thought maybe it'd be *romantic* for us to attend."

All at once I got excited. This was some surprise, one that I loved already. It didn't even matter what movie we were about to see, although I wondered. "What's the movie?"

Cain looked rather proud of himself suddenly. "*Casablanca*." He set down the picnic basket and went about spreading out the Burberry blanket for us to sit on. I stepped out of my shoes and walked on to the blanket, making myself useful and grabbing the picnic basket. Inside, was a lunch of berries, grapes, cheeses, a bottle of wine, and bottles of water. There was fresh bread that smelled delicious, as well as deli meats and what looked like chicken salad. There were wooden plates and a tray to set everything on and I quickly went about setting things up for us, all too giddy at the gesture.

I'd never gone on a picnic, much less a *romantic* one. I stole a peek at Cain, watching him fuss with his bottle of wine and feeling that tightness in my chest again. I could ask for the moon and the stars and I knew he'd do whatever he could to get them for me. He could afford anything my mind could think of, but he went with the simple things, a picnic and a movie, because that's what I wanted.

Healthy green grass surrounded us as Cain settled down across from me. With the food spread out, the moment was picturesque. I couldn't stop myself from taking my phone out and angling my head back to snap a quick photo, for photographic proof of this day. Cain didn't smile big and cheesy, but small and shy it seemed. I liked this side of him, where he was unsure of himself, where he wasn't afraid to show his vulnerability and that he wasn't perfect.

Running my thumb across his image in my phone, I found it crazy how much I'd grown to like *him*.

The movie hadn't started yet, which gave us a little time to focus on our food first.

"This is so thoughtful," I gushed as I munched on a few red grapes. "And I've never seen *Casablanca* before, so this'll be a first for the both of us."

"I saw that it was old and figured maybe you'd seen it or would like it," Cain admitted with a small shrug. He was preparing himself a chicken salad sandwich. I dug into the basket and pulled out the yellow bag of plain potato chips for him. His hand brushed against mine as he took them from me. A quiet shake of his head was all I needed to see to discern he didn't want me doing it all.

I settled back and grabbed some cheddar cheese cubes to eat next.

A comfortable silence bestowed us and I reveled in the sensation of being happy and content. Before long, I was nestled up beside Cain, resting into him for warmth and just to be close.

I'd asked before and he hadn't given me a direct answer, so I asked again, "What makes *you* happy?"

Cain took a sip of his wine, smiling to himself. "You."

I pretended to roll my eyes. "Oh come on, there's gotta be something else that makes you happy."

"Some might say I'm a simple man," he mused.

He made me happy too.

"What's your favorite movie?" I'd never asked before and now I really wanted to know. We could have a movie night at the house, just us and Joe.

"*Scarface.*"

I kinked up my nose, knowing the film by poster and subject. "Does it have a happy ending?"

Cain reached out and tapped my nose. "It does for her."

He was a man; of course he wasn't concerned with happy endings or whether the boy gets the girl.

"Maybe I'll watch it someday," I said.

Cain wrapped an arm around me and pulled me closer. "I don't think you'd like it."

Probably not, but I wanted to watch it and see it through his eyes. "We'll see."

Cain snorted, shaking his head at me. "If *this* were a movie... perhaps it'd be something like a romantic tragedy."

I glowered at him and he laughed. Why did he have to be so negative?

The movie started down on the screen and no matter our distance, the speakers carried the sound all the way up to us. I rested against Cain and was soon lost in the classic film starring Humphrey Bogart and Ingrid Bergman. I already had high hopes for it, seeing as how Humphrey was also in *Sabrina*.

It wasn't a love story, exactly, but definitely a tale about two lovers. Rick, a saloon owner, and Ilsa, a woman on the run with her husband to escape Nazis as they all meet in Casablanca,

Morocco. A period piece, it could only end in tragedy, I almost thought, considering the stakes.

I hung on to every line and every scene, holding out hope for all characters, especially Rick and Ilsa, whose love story still felt very much tangible every time they were in a room together.

But in the end, no amount of hope could change the ending. No, it wasn't tragic, but so much more as Rick made the ultimate sacrifice for love. My eyes watered and I let out a breath as the credits began to roll.

Hooting and hollering sounded down below as fellow movie viewers cheered for the film's ending.

In all the commotion, I could feel him watching me. Blinking back my tears, I looked up and found Cain staring down at me intently. A sober expression covered his face and I wondered if he'd enjoyed the movie.

"What?" I asked.

His hand came up and caught my tears, wiping them as they rolled down my cheeks. "Nothing."

"No 'nothing.' Tell me what's wrong."

Cain caressed my face, running his thumb along my skin. "That's the thing. Nothing's wrong."

"No?" I questioned.

He shook his head. "No." He appeared thoughtful, gently rubbing circles along my cheek the more he stared down at me. "I just... I never thought I'd know what it feels like to have the whole world in my hands."

Time froze. My heart stopped. And I couldn't breathe.

All I could do was stare at Cain as he gazed down at me. One minute he was there, and the next he was blurry as my eyes watered once more.

The whole world. In his hands. Me.

Suddenly I was crying and I couldn't stop it. I never thought I'd get so lucky to be so valued. To be treasured. Adored. And admired.

He really was a simple man. He could have any rich heiress or socialite on his level, multiple if he wanted, but he didn't. He was happy with me.

Reaching out, I cupped his jaw in my hand and could only nod. I wanted him to know I felt the same. I didn't have to say it; he could read it on me. He came down and I leaned up and we met in a kiss. A kiss that broke any walls I had left. A kiss that told me what I'd already known. I'd fallen for this man and there was no stopping from tumbling all the way down to *love*.

Cain packed up our picnic and we were off once more. This time, he took us to a restaurant where we had a small dinner. Steak and a potato for him, and pasta and a salad for me. With so much having gone on that day, I could barely keep my eyes open. I didn't remember dessert. Or Cain paying for the check. Or the ride home. No, the last thing I remembered was being carried in Cain's arms up the stairs for bed, listening to his steady heartbeat all while he hummed the melody of "As Time Goes By."

29

Eden

SO SERIOUS AND METICULOUS. THAT WAS THE VIBE I got as I sat on the bathroom counter with my back to the mirror watching Cain get ready to leave. For once *I* was done first.

It had been a week. All my belongings were gone from the room I'd occupied my first night here, and now stored in Cain's bedroom. I didn't have much, so my clothing barely filled a quarter of the *hers* side of his walk-in dual closet.

"Move in with me," he'd whispered one night after sex.

I was so high and caught up in my postcoital bliss, I'd almost agreed. Living full time with Cain would mean completely uprooting my life out of Bedford Heights. There was nothing there for me anyway, outside of Duane. Who I absolutely could not abandon.

Cain wanted all in and everything from me. Sometimes, when I considered how happy I was, I wanted nothing more than to just give in. I was living the dream. Rich billionaire who was loyal, caring, and incredible in bed? I woke up every morning pinching myself.

Dimples embedded his cheeks from all my staring. Unable to stop myself, I reached out and stuck my finger in one.

"Eden." It was a soft threat. I giggled at the implication. "If you think for one moment I'd rather be going out than staying in making love to you, you're mistaken."

Making love. I loved how tender he was with me. From the moment I was born, life wasn't easy on me. It often was ugly and brutal. And now, after holding out hope, it was finally beautiful.

"We could always cut out early," I suggested with a lazy shrug.

Cain bore a lopsided frown as he shook his head. "We really shouldn't. Part of tonight's ball has something to do with a close friend of mine. We'll stay as long as he's in attendance."

Cain didn't have many friends, and by the somber expression on his face, I could tell this one meant a lot to him.

I cupped his jaw. "Okay."

Cain began fussing with his bow tie, unable to get it how he wanted. I scooted closer and fixed it myself, following the steps I knew by heart all the while he watched in silence.

"My grandfather taught me when I was little," I offered because I knew he was curious. "Some things you never forget."

Cain examined himself in the mirror when I was finished. When his look was to his approval, he came back to me with a thumbs-up.

"You know, I've been thinking," I started, a little nervous when it came to a brewing idea I'd been sitting on for a while. "What if you started a foundation—a shelter or village, for kids who age out of the system and have nowhere to go and no idea where to start. For queer kids who get kicked out when their families don't accept them. For runaways who feel safer on the street than in their own homes. A place with free counseling for those with bruises, the physical and mental. A sanctuary."

When I thought of Duane, Malcolm, Cain, and me, we were very fortunate to be where we were. To have made it despite the odds. Everyone else didn't get so lucky.

"Why not put some of those billions to use?" I teased with a small shrug. "Instead of spoiling me so much."

For a moment, Cain only stared at me, searching my face silently and thoroughly.

I had no right telling him what to do with his money. And there was no telling how expensive this idea could be, but if there was a shot at helping the next *stray*, I had to take it.

Soon, Cain came and planted his hands on the counter on either side of me, caging me in as he leaned down to my level. Serious again, he peered into my eyes, a grim expression on his face. "And what would we call this sanctuary?"

I couldn't contain the blush that overtook me. "I was thinking Home. That's what every stray truly wants at the end of the day, a *home*."

"Castaway," Cain said softly. "That's what we are. You wanna build a village of shelters for those who were cast out of their homes. Exiled to the streets. Left to survive on their own."

That was the perfect word for it. "Yes."

Again, Cain took a moment to just look at me.

"What?" I asked when he didn't speak up.

He shook his head, his nostrils flaring. "I don't deserve someone as pure as you."

Reaching out, I placed my hand on his chest, above his heart. "Give yourself some credit. You're an incredible man."

Cain didn't seem convinced, and I hated that he wasn't so sure of himself. "I'll do it. My hands are tied with this casino out in LA, but I'm going to get with the right people and sit down and get the ball rolling for this. Bedford Heights, Lindenwood—the whole country if that's what it takes to do my part."

The whole country. I hadn't even thought of that. To have Homes in every state, to possibly save millions of youths? My vision was getting blurry and I did not want to ruin my makeup.

I waved my hands in my face, fanning myself to calm down. "Thank you so much." It was all I could get out. I was too overwhelmed. I could already see Duane and myself there volunteering, helping in any way we could.

Cain came close, giving me a rush of him before coming and kissing me. Deep, where I felt it in my bones.

"What are my two rules?" he demanded, running his thumb along the column of my throat.

"Always come back, and never tell anyone your business," I recited.

Darkness passed behind Cain's eyes, a look that said he was fond of me, and I'd hate to be the person who got in his way of having me.

"Let's go." He helped me down from the counter and let me go by him. I wasn't an inch away before he was in my ear. "You look beautiful, Tink."

I was covered in Saint Laurent from head to toe. The dress I was wearing was a black velvet skater style dress that was backless. My heels were black as well. Because my dress was long sleeved, my only accessory was the diamond tennis bracelet I wore around my ankle.

I looked and felt expensive.

"Thank you," I said.

Taking the lead, I went down to the first floor. Sharp whistling pierced my ear before I reached the last step.

Vino was leaning casually against the front door, his hand tucked into his tux's pocket as his eyes were fixed on me. "If there's one thing you do well, it's clean up."

Malcolm entered the room from the living room and tossed Vino a smug look. "She does a *lot* of things well." To me, he tipped his head in my direction. "You look amazing as always, Eden."

Together we went down to the parking deck and climbed into Cain's Range Rover. Vino took the wheel and we were off.

The whole way over to the mayor's ball I was buzzing with anxiety. This wasn't my first event with Cain, but it was my first as his *girlfriend*. Something about this detail made things feel different.

Would I be enough? Would they accept me? Would his friend like me for him? Was I going to make a fool of myself?

Without looking at me, Cain reached out and placed his hand

on my thigh, giving me a gentle squeeze. And slowly, just like that, those worries dissolved.

This event had a red carpet. While Vino and Malcolm parked the truck, I was on Cain's arm as we descended the carpet among all the flashing lights and frenzy of questions from reporters.

Up ahead of us bigger faces could be seen. I nearly drooled at the sight of Judah Barrett in person.

The Second Coming, as his fans opined.

I knew him from Duane's incessant chatter about the Long Beach Sharks. That and I couldn't forget a face *that* gorgeous.

He was wearing a navy suit, no tie, and black loafers. His freshly twisted locs were pulled back, leaving his handsome sculpted brown face on display.

"Want me to introduce you?" Cain cut into my line of vision, a hint of humor gleaming in his eye.

I blushed. We'd had plenty of high-profile men come through Crazy Legs—up-and-coming rappers, rising athletes, and the occasional businessman—but this was Judah Barrett. "Oh, no, I couldn't."

Cain studied me and where I was visibly nervous the closer we got to Judah. "Easy. You're going to make me regret getting into sports."

"I mean, talk about competition," I teased, reaching out and tickling Cain.

He took one look at me, pausing and ignoring the fleet of questions floating his way, and kissed me. Right on the mouth as the cameras flashed.

After that there were no more thoughts of Judah.

Cain held me close and ushered me inside the hall. Right away I noticed up on stage was a live band, and on either end of the stage were speakers set up. The band wasn't playing as we entered the space, but instead we were being serenaded by a Stevie Wonder song. I thought it was called "Visions."

At the opening of the floor we were emersed upon the upper echelon of Hampton Hills. So many notable Black faces jumped out at once. Cain of course wasn't fazed after being used to being among them for so long, but I was still a little nervous.

"You're with me and I got you," Cain whispered in my ear.

I squared my shoulders and walked with my head up as he guided us through the room. I thought back to the night I met Cain, where I wasn't so timid and had floated around the space confidently doing my job as model and waitress. I could do that here, be my charming self and nonchalantly hide under Cain's shadow when things got to be too much.

Men walked up to Cain, eager to shake his hand and talk business. Women came by, openly eyeing him like a juicy steak and then frowning in disappointment when they noticed me.

But my most favorite part?

"This is Eden, my girlfriend," Cain would say when introducing me to whoever had walked over.

Cain's arm was around me as we moved through the room. The gold wooden floor was clear for socializing or dancing, while on each side of the space were the tables. It was June—outside the heat was unrelenting, inside the air was on, but a few people were seen fanning themselves with paddles.

"There's going to be an auction," Cain clued me in.

"You buying anything?" I asked.

He squeezed my hip. "I have everything I want."

It didn't take any thought at all to know that he meant *me*.

"Well," I began, feeling playful. "I'm going to bid for you."

Cain kissed the crook of my neck, sending my breath halting as my heart stilled as well. "Whatever you want. I have it."

A big smile spread across my face that felt like it would never end with Cain near.

He brought us to a table closest to the stage, where a man in a motorized wheelchair was seated. He seemed larger than life with the way everyone gravitated toward him. A woman who must've been his wife was at his side, smiling and greeting whoever approached them next. She was in a glittery gold dress that made her look stunning as it complemented her brown skin, long dark hair, and subtle makeup.

The place card at their table read *Nichols*. Each table seated ten people, beyond Mr. and Mrs. Nichols, there was another older couple on the other side of the table busy talking with other guests. Cain pointed out that they were Phil Wagner and his wife Harriett. Phil being half owner of the company Cain was partnering with.

"And who is this pretty little lady?" The path had cleared and Mr. Nichols was looking right at me.

Cain steered us closer, actually appearing bashful as he grinned, showing his dimples. "This is Eden, my girlfriend." Cain gestured from me to Mr. Nichols. "Eden, this is Damon Nichols, a business partner and a good friend of mine."

I extended my hand toward Damon, offering a smile. "Hi, I'm Eden."

Damon's hand wrapped around mine in a firm grip. "Wow." It was one word, but it was packed with some hidden meaning. I could tell as his eyes floated over to Cain and he gave a small nod of approval.

"This explains a lot." Mrs. Nichols came closer and gave me a friendly smile as she glanced at Cain in an almost motherly way. Warm. Fondly. With pride. All the ways my mother never looked at me. She leaned over and planted a kiss on each of Cain's cheeks. "All these dinners you missed makes sense now."

"Angela, this is my girlfriend, Eden. Eden, this is Damon's wife, Angela." Cain showed a hand from Mrs. Nichols to me.

Angela held her hand out and we shook. "It's nice to meet you, Eden."

"She's been cooking for me," Cain explained as he wrapped an arm around me. "I don't like to miss a meal."

Angela's eyes doubled and she blinked as she examined me again. "She cooks."

I blushed, burrowing further under Cain's arm. "I cook."

"That certainly beats catering," Angela seemed to joke, causing the men to laugh.

"We'll have to have you two over sometime," Cain suggested before looking my way. "If you don't mind."

"Of course not," I agreed. "It'd be nice to have them."

It almost felt like it was *our* home we were inviting them to. The thought made me giddy.

Cain looked around and seemed to come up empty when he didn't find what he was searching for. "Is Kennedy here?"

Kennedy. I'd heard that name before.

Damon made a face, rolling his eyes playfully it seemed by his smirk. "They're running behind."

I watched the same smirk cross Cain's face as Damon's. I wondered who Kennedy was.

"Well, we'll grab our table. I'm sure I'll run into them before this night is over." Cain steered me away, going and leading me through the room once more until we found the table reserved for his party. Vino and Malcolm were already there.

Cain pulled my chair out for me and then joined me once I was seated.

The mayor's ball was a formal black-tie event featuring dinner, dancing, and an auction from what the programs at our table said. The dinner menu offered red meat, seafood, and vegetarian options. I went with the eggplant rollatini and pasta while the men chose steaks.

"And to drink, miss?" a server asked once our meals were sent to the chef. We'd been given water to start off with and now it was time to choose a drink. "We have a wonderful wine selection available."

"No wine for her," Cain cut in.

I wouldn't have ordered any, but I couldn't help but frown as I went with lemonade instead.

In a few weeks, I would be twenty years old. Not exactly legal drinking age, but still.

So I waited. I kept quiet until our server was back with a tray of our drinks. Cain was unsuspecting as he accepted his glass of red wine.

And then, to defy him, to do what I *wanted*, I grabbed his wineglass and helped myself to a big gulp before he could snatch it away.

Only, I hadn't anticipated the awful flavor of the wine. Tart. Bitter. Rancid. Very uncouth or not, I quickly let the wine drain from my mouth back into his glass. In the background I could hear Vino chuckling at my epic failure.

Smirking, Cain took a sip of his wine and shook his head. I wasn't sure if I found the act to be disgusting or a turn-on. I leaned toward the latter.

I smacked my lips in distaste. "I can still taste it. Am I going to be drunk?"

Cain came close, grinning, before placing his lips to mine in a chaste kiss. "Not at all."

It was official: I liked wine when it was on Cain's lips.

After dinner they began the first portion of the auction. I relaxed comfortably into Cain as the announcer took the stage and began listing the items up for bid.

There were a variety of things for grabs. Season tickets for the Los Angeles Lakers, as well as the Long Beach Sharks. VIP tickets to a Galen Dymond concert. And probably the cutest, a chance to have Samuel L. Jackson walk your dog. It was no surprise to see that lot skyrocket up to fifty thousand before a winner was declared. The charities ranged from childhood leukemia, to supporting community centers across southern California from Compton, to Crenshaw, to Bedford Heights and more, as well as research for St. Jude's.

It was all new and exciting. I almost felt too shy to speak up and bid.

"The proceeds from this next lot will go to the Nichols ALS Foundation," the auctioneer started off. "Founded by Damon Nichols, the Nichols ALS Foundation aids people battling with amyotrophic lateral sclerosis through support, awareness, and advocacy. The group strives to empower those dealing with this disease all while researching effective treatments and someday finding a cure."

The room exploded with applause as all eyes landed on Damon. He simply nodded at the man on stage, clearly not wanting his persona to overshadow the cause.

"All right, this lot is a seven-night stay in a private villa in beautiful Costa Rica," the auctioneer explained. "This villa includes seven luxury suites, making this a perfect getaway for ten guests. Included is seven days of breakfast and dinner from an on-site personal chef, as well as housekeeping and concierge services. Who wants to start the bidding?"

"Three thousand!" a man's voice called out.

"Thirty-five hundred!" another shouted.

More and more bids came through. It was enough to make my head spin as I looked back and forth between guests trying to get the lot.

Seven nights in a tropical villa sounded heavenly. Before the next person could bid, I raised my paddle and waved it vigorously.

"Going bid is eleven thousand," the auctioneer stated as he glanced around the room. "Do I hear eleven thousand and one hundred?"

"Fifteen thousand!" I shouted as I continued to wave my paddle, hoping fifteen was enough to scare off the competition.

The auctioneer peered in my direction. "I think I hear shouting coming from over here."

The room was abuzz with chatter and numbers being shouted over one another. But I wasn't that small to not be heard.

I waved my paddle some more. "Fifteen thousand!"

The auctioneer squinted, soon angling his head and placing his hand by his ear. "Do I hear a bid?"

Before I could process what was going on, arms wrapped around me and I was airborne momentarily before being settled onto Cain's lap. He sat up, giving me leverage to be seen more.

"Fifteen thousand!" I shouted breathlessly.

The whole room rattled with laughter as they took in Cain's move to help me win. My cheeks burned from blushing and smiling so hard as I now without a doubt had the auctioneer's attention.

He was laughing with the others as he bobbed his head. "We now have fifteen thousand." He looked out at the sea of guests. "Do I hear fifteen and one hundred?"

No one spoke up, too busy laughing to try to outbid me.

The auctioneer banged his gavel. "Fifteen thousand to the eager young woman right over there."

Vino and Malcolm were laughing as well and I couldn't help but join in.

Soon, Cain's lips were in the shell of my ear, only for me. "What am I going to do with you for seven days in Costa Rica?"

My heart pounded hard as goose bumps littered my skin at the proximity of Cain. One glimpse back at him found pure amusement covering his face.

The auction had moved onto the next lot and no one was paying us too much attention. Boldly, I wined my hips back into Cain's, feeling a thrill dance down my spine at the feel of his hardening length.

"Oh, I'm sure we can think of something," I responded.

Cain's arms tightened around me and never let me go as the auction went on.

After the first half of bidding was finished, an intermission came and the dance floor opened. Music streamed through the room and guests were up and moving. The infectious sound of Frankie Beverly and Maze had me up and tugging Cain along with me. I found a spot on the dance floor and began moving along with the melody.

Cain stood back, bobbing his head and shyly looking around us at the people dancing.

"Come on!" I encouraged as I kept moving.

Cain ducked his head, his dimples popping out. "Not really my thing."

Vino was quick to send an elbow into Cain's side as he came over to us. "D can't dance, girl."

This appeared to be the case as Cain didn't deny or try to prove him wrong.

"Aw, baby," I cooed as I reached up and cupped his face in my hands, putting on a soothing tone. "It's okay!"

Vino pulled on my wrist to take me away. "Let me show 'im how it's done."

Cain rolled his eyes, but said nothing as Vino began dancing with me. Instead, he stepped back and joined Malcolm at the edge of the dance floor, keeping his eyes on me. The heat in his gaze sent warmth below my belly and a caress across my heart.

"Don't be so mean," I said as I got back to Vino.

"He can't just have you to himself if he can't dance," Vino said with a cool smile. "That's the problem with only children, they never learn to share their toys."

I scoffed and swatted at Vino's chest. "I'm not a toy."

A smile eased across his face. "Of course not."

We fell into the groove of the song and I kept thinking of his words. "So, you have siblings?"

Vino bobbed his head, keeping up with the beat with ease unlike Cain. "I'm the baby. Got four older sisters."

It was hard to think of Vino as "a baby." His stature and aura were too strong and intimidating to ever downplay any part of who he was. "They call you Vino, too?"

He shook his head. "Chip." By the confusion on my face he knew I didn't get it. Humor sparked in his eyes as he stared at me, daring to get close. "Short for chipmunk. Which is based on an old cartoon where I share a name with the main character: *Alvin*." He stepped back, a warning in his eye. "You'll forget I told you that."

In the world he was in, it was best to never get too personal with anyone in case the law was around and watching. The less people knew about you, the better. Still, I respected him for telling me his name.

I played along and kept dancing. "Of course, Terrence."

Vino laughed a hearty sound. "I hope he puts a ring on you. You're much too fun to have around."

A ring.

My gaze floated over to Cain and collided with his. A girl could only dream.

When my feet got tired Cain came and whisked me away, taking me outside the venue for some fresh air. Other people were lingering around the doorway and valet, stealing a cigarette or having a conversation.

Cain found us a private place to wind down out front by the sidewalk. He helped me sit up on the wall as he remained standing. Even more, he removed my heels and went about massaging my foot, chasing the ache away.

God, this man.

For a moment he admired my toes. "Tink in pink," he mused. I was beginning to love being in pink as much as he appeared to like me in it.

"What's your middle name?" I decided to ask, taking a chance at getting to know more of him.

Cain bore a soft small smile. "James."

Somehow, I just knew. "After your father?"

He nodded, a pinch of pain across his face. He kept rubbing my foot, allowing the moment to pass and not settle over us. In a minute, he looked over and studied me. "What's yours?"

"Rose," I answered.

Softness touched Cain. "Really?"

"Yeah," I breathed out.

He blinked and looked away. I shivered as the late evening breeze passed by. I knew why he was silent now. Rose was his mother's name.

His grip on my foot was firm when he looked at me again. "Are you happy, Eden?"

I hated that he had to ask. "I'm always happy when I'm with you."

He paused his massage, peering into my eyes. "Always?"

"Always."

I couldn't think of anywhere else I would've rather been than with Cain. Whether we were out on the town rubbing elbows with his business associates, or at his penthouse snuggled up watching a movie. It didn't take much for me to look at him and feel peace and happiness.

"Cain?"

We were no longer alone.

Just like that, the spell that had fallen over us burst as another couple stood down the sidewalk not too far from us.

I recognized the sound of his name but not the woman who had spoken it until I looked over and saw her. It was her. The beauty from the night I'd met Cain, and...*Keith.*

Of all people I could've run into at this gala, I was shocked to see Keith. He was standing next to the woman in a black tuxedo, and like always, he didn't look the happiest.

Beauty was standing there in a gorgeous black and white toned strapless gown. The plunging neckline called attention to the pearls around her neck, the black bodice accentuated her svelte curves, and the sweeping white train made her appear like a queen. I was surprised there wasn't a tiara or crown nestled on top of her long black wavy hair.

Cain fastened my heels back on my feet before helping me down from the wall.

I still couldn't believe my eyes at the sight of Keith. I hardly knew him after our brief encounters in Bedford Heights last year, but that didn't stop me from going over to him.

"Oh my God, Keith!" I gushed, taking him in from head to toe. He really did clean up nice. He was in an all-black tux with gold accents to complete his look. Gold glasses, gold watch, and a gold chain around his neck. Like Judah, he wasn't wearing a tie, but it worked for him. Made him appear rugged and dashing at the same time.

Keith pulled me in for a small hug and stepped back next to the woman at his side. He tipped his head my way before showing a hand to the woman. "Eden, what a surprise to see you." He looked from me to the woman and back. "This is my fiancée, Kennedy. Kenny, this is Eden...she's from Bedford."

Kennedy. So this was her. She was beautiful in that way you had to stop and stare. Elegant and nice looking that you couldn't help but smile at her in awe.

Kennedy offered me a warm smile as she held her hand out. "Kennedy."

I shook her hand and got lost staring at the diamond on her finger. A princess-cut ring with a stone that wasn't too big or too small, but just right as it sat on a diamond-encrusted white gold band.

Fiancée. I stole a peek at Keith as my eyes enlarged. *Way to go!* "Eden. It's nice to meet you. And congratulations on the engagement."

Kennedy nuzzled against Keith and patted his chest. "Thank you. And..." Her words trailed to a stop as she peered over at Cain curiously.

He came up beside me, wrapping an arm around me. "Kennedy is Damon's daughter. She's like a *sister* to me."

Kennedy blinked and Keith seemed to be glowering at Cain for that remark.

I had a feeling the sentiment wasn't mutual.

Kennedy cleared her throat, looking from me to Cain and back. "And you two are...?"

"Dating," I spoke up. "I'm his girlfriend."

"*Girlfriend?*" Keith looked put off as he repeated my status back to me.

I nodded. "Yes."

Keith said no more but the distaste on his face couldn't be missed. He always was the strong silent type, but something about his energy felt off. Charged. Alert. While Kennedy was being polite and all smiles, Keith had yet to shake Cain's hand or so much as acknowledge him in a friendly way.

"That's right," Cain said, meeting Keith's gaze.

The tension was thick enough I doubted a knife could cut through. The animosity between these two men couldn't be ignored.

Kennedy took Keith's hand in hers, squeezing gently as she looked up at him. "Well, I think we should get back inside. Don't you?"

Keith tore his attention away from Cain and examined his fiancée. All at once he seemed to relax. Still, he regarded me solemnly. "It was good seeing you, Eden. We'll have to catch up next time we're back home."

Cain squeezed my hip, but stayed silent as Kennedy and Keith pivoted around and headed back inside.

When they were gone his gaze landed on me.

Something was off between him and Keith. Hell, even him and Kennedy as well. But I didn't want to get into it just then. Tonight was about fun.

Still, I felt obligated to explain who Keith was even if I only knew him in a small capacity. "That's the guy I was telling you about before. The one who tried to help me back home."

Cain looked off in the direction Keith had gone. "Interesting." He got back to me. "Such a small world we live in."

It really was when I thought of the chances of running into Keith. I was happy for him, though. It seemed like he had a chip on his shoulder before when I thought about our run-ins back home. Now, I didn't see any of that tonight as he stood with Kennedy.

Kennedy.

"So, who's Kennedy to you?" I wondered. "Beyond Damon's daughter."

Now Cain was stepping away from me, going and rubbing at the back of his neck as he glanced down at the sidewalk.

Intuition told me it was more than just casual between them. Especially with all the uneasiness not even five minutes ago.

"Last year..." Cain seemed to struggle to say. "...we were engaged."

I blinked. Unsure I'd heard him. Had he just said...*engaged*? "Excuse me?"

Cain met my gaze sheepishly, frowning at the reveal. "I'd asked her out twice before and she turned me down each time. When her father came to me with a business proposition, I got a little arrogant and demanded Kennedy be a part of the deal. If I could have her hand in marriage, I'd partner with him and Phil."

Speechless, I couldn't think of a word to say. So, I reached out and slapped his arm for good measure. "Are you kidding me?"

Cain ducked back, holding out a hand. "Trust me, I'm more than aware how fucked up it was. Shit got twisted and long story short, she met Keith and fell for him." He scratched at his temple, shaking his head. "It was one thing that she didn't want to try with me, but it was another having her *love* another man. So, I let her go."

Rolling my eyes, I scoffed. As if she needed to meet another man just for him to realize how sick and twisted it was to wring her arm into a marriage all because he couldn't take no for an answer.

"I'm not proud of what I did," Cain admitted earnestly. "But I like to think some good came out of it because she's happy."

There was no denying how happy Kennedy *and* Keith looked as a couple. The tangible chemistry between them. Or the way they looked at each other.

Something beautiful had come out of something so ugly.

It was funny how life turned out.

Sighing, I leaned into Cain, deciding that it wasn't the time or place to scold him over his *poor* choices. "Let's get back inside, okay?"

Cain let it go and we went back inside. We took group photos in the black and white photo booth with Malcolm and Vino, as well as a few other young couples. The energy from outside evaporated as the night went on and we fell into our own little haze.

As Cain loosened up, I goaded him back out onto the dance floor. A slower song was playing. Luther Vandross and Cheryl Lynn's "If This World Were Mine."

The mood bled over into something less playful as Cain stared down at me and I looked up at him. It was heavy. Powerful. Potent. Pulling us under where everyone else faded away. As if there was a spotlight shining down on us alone.

A sober look captured Cain's face as he stared at me. "You take care of me. So I want to take care of you."

In one way, I felt insignificant on my side of "taking care of him," but in another, I felt important knowing he valued me in my meals, my company, and my wanting to be more together.

"We take care of each other," I said in agreement.

Resting my cheek on his chest, I felt his heart beating strong and steady. A rhythm that was all his own.

I liked to think that when we were together, just us, we were in our own little bubble. And I never wanted it to pop.

Sneaking a peek back at him, I reached up and ran my hand from his jaw to the back of his head and cupped it as I stared up at him. My heart was beating softly, comfortably, *safely* because I was with him.

"Could this ever be enough for you?" I wanted to know.

He reached out, a gleam in his eye, and felt my cheek. "Don't ask big questions you're not ready for."

It wasn't a yes, but it wasn't a no either.

We danced on and I had never felt more content.

The night went on and I almost didn't want it to end, but after so much dancing and laughter, I was ready to go home and rest. Vino and Malcolm must've been tired and worn out as well, because they didn't follow us up to the penthouse to recap the evening. Instead, they let us out at the parking deck before going and getting into their separate vehicles to go on to their own homes. I wished them both a good night before following Cain up to the penthouse.

He had been quiet the whole way home and as he opened the door I knew why. We weren't inside a full minute before he spun me around, had my back pressed against the door, my panties ripped off, and him inside me as he stole my breath away in a searing kiss that left no room for confusion on where he saw things between us.

We went at it against the door, our bodies swearing oaths and promises our lips didn't have to.

Some would call it passion. I was beginning to call it *love*.

30

Cain

"You should keep her." It was the first thing Damon said to me when he called me Monday morning. "That's the one for you."

I wiped at a smile on my face as I humored him. He hadn't even been this excited when I was supposed to marry his daughter. "Is that so?"

"Yes!" Damon didn't hesitate to double down. "She makes you young. You *are* young, but—"

"I know what you mean," I cut in. I'd grown up far before my time. In many ways, so had Eden. Anger seized me every time I thought of her dancing underage just to eat and have a roof over her head.

"I've never seen you like you were when you were with her. That's the woman for you. Lock that down now."

I could only respond with a chuckle. The thought of marrying Eden both fed into my possessiveness over her and made me feel guilty.

She's too young. With much more going for her.

But the thought of letting her go?

Something pierced me deep in my chest just at the idea of life without Eden.

Fuck, I was a selfish bastard.

My stomach knotted up at the thought of someone else taking care of her. Seeing her smile. *Having* her.

It was a frustrating dilemma that left me responding to Damon with, "I'll keep that in mind. Perhaps we'll have a double wedding with Kennedy and Keith."

Damon's laugh was hearty and rich, a pleasant sound coming from him. "So you noticed the ring?"

It was hard not to. It wasn't as big as the one I'd given her, but there was no missing the way Kennedy would absentmindedly fiddle with it, or be gazing down at it lovingly. She was *proud* to be his.

"I may have gotten a good peek at it," I said.

Damon sighed, and all at once the light humor dissipated. "They got engaged and he didn't even ask me. He said he didn't need my permission to marry her, only hers."

I snorted, rolling my eyes. *Fucking Keith.*

"I feel stable, but the thing is, this disease, what I have, isn't predictable. Tomorrow isn't promised. I get it now, that family matters more than anything. I just hope she lets me see her walk down the aisle, even if I can't be beside her."

From the moment I'd met him, Damon Nichols had exuded one thing: power. Even with his battle with ALS, I didn't see him as weak or any less powerful. This conversation, this moment where he was being vulnerable and candid, let me know his one true weakness was his family.

He wasn't without fault, but it was because of me he was in a position that his future son-in-law didn't approach him in the traditional way of asking for his daughter's hand in marriage.

"I'm sorry, Damon," I said, and I was. What started off as business, turned into something like a friendship when it came to Damon. "Things are a little touchy right now, but I can assure you, you won't miss your daughter's wedding."

"You sound certain," Damon replied.

Pulling out those old familiar red dice from my jacket pocket,

I shook them in my palm. "I'm not much of a gambling man, but I'd bet on it."

Damon chuckled. "Let's hope so. I'll let you get back to work."

We hung up and I sat back in my chair, my eyes immediately floating over to where Beans sat across the room. Vino was out taking a call from Frank, securing a connect for our trip to Vegas.

"Damon approves of Eden," I let it be known.

Beans only smirked. If I voiced my feelings, he'd only call bullshit and tell me to keep her.

A buzz went off and a minute later I heard LaShanti's voice coming through the intercom. "Mr. Carter, there's a guest out here to see you. He says it's important." In a low voice she added, "He doesn't have an appointment and he seems *very* upset."

A smirk arrested my features. I already knew *who* was here.

I pressed the Talk button. "Let him in."

Beans raised a curious brow and I quietly shook my head. "This oughta be fun."

A moment later the door was opening and LaShanti was showing Keith into the room. She was quick to keep her distance from him and scurry away immediately after introducing him.

In his jeans, white tee, and blue LA baseball cap, he wasn't that intimidating. It was when you got to his face that you were taken aback. Anger covered every inch of Keith's face and it was aimed at me.

Huh.

I gave him a chance and went for nice as I greeted him with a smile. "Keith! Come to personally invite me to the wedding?"

There was no missing Kennedy's engagement ring, but surprisingly last night, I'd noticed a band on Keith's finger as well. They could've eloped, but my gut told me they hadn't.

Keith narrowed his eyes and his nostrils flared. "Stay the hell away from her."

One more chance.

"Kennedy and I've been cordial. She's like a sister to me now," I responded.

Keith gritted his teeth, his fists clenching up at his sides at the mention of Kennedy. "Eden."

At once the shutters went down over my eyes, blanketing my vision in a mean red.

"Beans, step outside," I ordered.

"No."

My gaze peeled from Keith and landed on Beans. "Your disloyalty was forgiven last time. I won't extend that courtesy again."

Even if he meant well, he answered to me.

Beans grimaced, conceding despite his want to stay. With one fierce look my way, he said, "Remember where you are."

I gave that response a deadpan expression and he quietly walked by Keith and left.

Beans was always, *annoyingly*, right. But even I knew I couldn't kill Keith in my office at Nichols & Wagner. It would stain the marble.

Keith remained standing by the door, glaring my way.

Showing a hand toward the two chairs in front of my desk, I said, "Have a seat."

"I'm not here to talk. Stay away from Eden," he barked out.

I thumbed at my bottom lip, at my scar, musing over my plight. I'd let him live when I discovered the affair Kennedy was having with him. And *this* was the thanks I got?

Still, I didn't let my ego show on my face. I wouldn't react to his demands over Eden. So help me. I had to play this smart.

"Kennedy know you're here worried about another woman?" I asked.

That got him to move. One minute he was in the doorway, the next he'd crossed the floor and was looming over my desk. Hands planted as he leaned into my space.

"This has nothing to do with Kennedy," Keith snapped.

I reclined in my seat, lacing my fingers together. "Worry about yours, because *mine* is none of your concern."

Keith continued to glower at me. Not letting up.

I angled my head, getting a good look at him. "Eden would never lie to me, but somehow I'm having a hard time believing you're *this* pressed about a random woman you met in a pizza parlor."

There.

For the briefest of seconds, his eye twitched. A tell.

Keith was an open book. He wore his anger on his sleeve while I tucked mine away.

In front of me, he was all charged up. I could feel his energy from across my desk. Radiating off of him in thick waves. You'd need a machete to cut the tension between us. He did not fear me. And fuck, if it didn't make me like him a smidge because of it.

We were from the same neighborhood, but we weren't cut from the same cloth. His version of hell was a holiday for me. I respected him, though. He was one of very few from our neighborhood who didn't fear me. Even with a gun in his face.

Didn't mean I relished seeing him with Kennedy. For a year I watched them, making appearances at galas and events, stopping by the Nicholses' estate—happily in love.

At least another fuckup got the girl, I supposed.

"We met officially at Italo's," Keith came out and confessed.

"And unofficially?"

"I saw her dancing at Crazy Legs."

My fingers twitched to curl into fists. Eden had never danced completely naked, but she'd been close enough.

Kennedy came to mind and I figured perhaps we were even. I'd seen all of her in her desperate attempt to make our engagement work.

But I didn't care for fair.

"Keith... If you've fucked Eden I'll kill you." I looked him straight in his eye and let it be known. "It was different with

Kennedy because I've never had her. She was never *mine*. Eden is a different story."

Pure revulsion covered Keith's face. "She's a little young for me, don't you think?"

His genuine abhorrence showed that he was protective above all things regarding Eden rather than an ex-lover. And that in itself annoyed me. Keith was so disgustingly good, of course he wouldn't touch her.

"Funny enough, the last time I saw her, was the night we had our run-in, and I can't forget how she looked." His eyes met mine accusingly. "She had a mark on her cheek. Like she'd been hit. And then you showed up."

Just the reminder of what Bobby had done to Eden darkened my mood even more. I really hadn't killed him slow enough.

Keith wasn't backing down. It was admirable he was sticking his neck out for Eden, but it wasn't needed. Eden was mine and I took care of what belonged to me.

I released a breath through my nose, calming down, taming my temper. "I don't hit women, Keith."

His response was narrowing his eyes, doubting me.

I rolled mine. "Ask Kennedy. I'm sure despite the situation, she'd vouch that I never touched her." Steepling my fingers together, I felt the need to say, "But I'm aware of Eden's predicament. Of *who* was putting their hands on her." I looked Keith in his eyes, stone-cold serious. "And I took care of it."

He was smart enough to read between the lines, and to my surprise, he seemed to shrug it off. Like the fucker was indeed better off dead than alive among us. My type of thinker.

Keith nodded and he managed to sit down finally. "Good."

Slowly, I smiled. "Eden is in good hands."

Still, Keith didn't seem so sure. "Eden is a good kid," he started.

"She's a good *woman*," I corrected. She was younger than me, but she wasn't *that* young.

Keith snorted. "You like her."

I couldn't keep the sneer from masking my face. *Like* was such a minuscule word when it came to my feelings for Eden. I'd "dated" and fucked other women before, but none of them were Eden. None of that was anything like *this*. Then, I'd gone with the flow, my feelings only surface level at most. Now, I couldn't explain it. Couldn't put it into words.

It was a feeling I couldn't shake. It rocked me to my core. Made me delirious. I just knew if anyone even looked at her wrong, I'd rip them apart limb from limb with my bare hands.

My heart was out of my chest with Eden. Exposed. Raw. Vulnerable.

She'd asked me if what we'd done last night could ever be enough for me, this life of public appearances and charity events, and she had no idea I could've done it forever with her. She'd made my condo a home and I never wanted her to leave. Never wanted to come back to an empty space with no one waiting up for me or around to talk about their day. I even liked the cat at this point.

"If that's how you want to put it," I decided to say.

Keith deadpanned. "Dice."

"She's happy. I may not be the best prospect for her, but she's happy. She *wants* to be with me," I said.

He gave my words some thought, taking a moment to ease back in his chair and really think. "How old is she?"

It was none of his concern, but I threw him a bone. "She'll be twenty in a few weeks."

Keith blinked and my phone rang.

"Not my favorite thing about her," I offered as I gathered my cell. Kennedy was calling. While I had no grievances toward Keith, it did amuse me that his fiancée was calling me. So, I answered, holding up a finger for Keith to wait. "Carter."

"You sound so serious and formal." I could hear the eye roll in Kennedy's joking voice. "Are you busy?"

"I can always move things around for you."

Again, another eye roll. "Don't I feel special? Can you stop by Petal and we can grab brunch?"

In the year since our parting of ways, it wasn't that she'd avoided me, but more so, kept her safe distance outside of a cordial greeting or nod of acknowledgment. I was too curious to turn her down.

"Of course," I responded.

"So, it's...eleven now. Do you want to meet at noon?" Kennedy asked.

"Works for me."

"Okay, see you then."

We hung up and I returned to Keith, feeling like I had one up on him. Call it petty or a grudge, but I couldn't keep the smirk from my face.

And then my eyes traveled to his left hand. To that ring.

"Was it your idea to wear a ring as well, or was it hers?" I had to know.

At once Keith examined his left hand. "Mine." He lifted his gaze to me. "Approaching her about marriage wasn't easy. As you can imagine after her last engagement, I was sure she was apprehensive about marriage. I just wanted to let her know I'm all in. That I'm not shackling her down against her will."

I could've had a toothache that was so sweet.

Still, because I did like Damon, I swallowed my pride. "I need a favor."

Keith arched a brow. Here was his chance to have an ounce of power over me and say something slick.

He didn't.

"What is it?"

My eyes went to his ring again. "You have every right to feel the way you do regarding what happened last year. You and Kennedy both. But..." I paused, wincing at the situation at hand. "If you marry her without Damon present, it'll kill him."

Keith's face was unreadable, giving me no tell where he was leaning.

He sighed, though, in the end, scratching his neck and soon folding his arms. "I wouldn't do that to *Kennedy*. She'd never forgive herself."

At least he wasn't vindictive.

"You ever been to Greece?" Keith suddenly asked me.

I shook my head.

"Eden's a good woman. You, you've been hard at work with Damon for the last year. It wouldn't hurt to take some time off. Go on a vacation. See something new. It's something to consider. I never thought I'd need a passport, but sometimes when you meet that one, everything becomes possible," Keith said. "Kenny wanted to go to Greece and I've known for a while I wanted to marry her. Being out there, seeing those sights, watching her in that setting...that moment was special. It was only ours."

I tried picturing myself overseas, but my mind couldn't configure Greece, but France.

"Eden believes in the fairy tale. She deserves to have it. I gave up my vices for Kennedy; make sure you drop yours for Eden." After one long and serious look, Keith stood from his chair and saw himself out.

Petal was a pet project for Kennedy. The floral shop was on the corner of Townsend Boulevard and Smith Lane. When I first laid eyes on Kennedy, I thought she was just another socialite with a few influencer gigs on the side. Seeing her step out and create a space for beautiful floral arrangements where she actually got her hands dirty was a pleasant sight.

According to Damon, she personally worked at the shop twice a week and was strongly considering opening a location in Bedford Heights.

I wonder why.

One step inside, though, and I couldn't fight the smile that was crossing my face.

It was a world of black marble floors, white wooden tables

and shelving, and tulle draped here and there. On either side of the wall of vases for sale were decorative willow trees with strings of lights. Some trees were weeping and the others were cherry.

Petal was fairly steady for a Monday afternoon. Another thing that had my smile broadening. I was *proud* of Kennedy.

When I didn't see her, I helped myself over to the section for roses. With so many color options, it was a wonder what I would get for Eden. I loved her in pink.

Pausing, I mused over my thoughts. I *liked* a lot of things about her. Yet it felt too simple a way to describe it. *Love*? It fit just right.

My stomach dipped and my palms suddenly felt sweaty. A sensation I wasn't familiar with.

What was—

"Red roses symbolize love." Kennedy materialized out of nowhere beside me. Like the rest of her staff, she had on a khaki-colored apron over her white thermal and shorts. *Petal* was embroidered on the top left side of her apron while her name badge said she was the shop's owner.

I peered at the roses, studying them. "Love, huh?"

"Yep."

I got back to Kennedy. "What about pink?"

Kennedy eyed the pink roses, which ranged from light to dark. "Light means admiration, grace, joy, and gentleness. Pink represents appreciation, perfect happiness, 'thank you.' And dark stands for appreciation as well as gratitude."

She was knowledgeable. She wasn't some nepo baby trying to look good. She actually was into floristry.

I appraised Kennedy, like I always had to do whenever I was around her. She was beautiful. Every time we crossed paths, I had to reach out and tug on her cheek, just to see if she was real. She was. Just not for me.

I examined the roses once more, even if I admired the pink, my attention kept coming back to the red and their meaning. *Love.*

Another fit. Huh.

Kennedy undid her apron and grabbed her purse before taking a lunch with me. Together we walked down a few shops to The Cabana Lounge, a cozy café snuggled among all the shopping on Townsend Boulevard.

It was the last of June. Not too hot, but just right. So we sat out on the patio opposite each other at a small round table. She ordered the house juice blend and I kept cool with an ice water.

We hadn't been alone since we split, and I was all too curious to see what she wanted. For a year I watched them, Kennedy and Keith, and she was every bit of happy as she looked in the photos the private investigator I'd hired had taken of her.

Sitting across from her, watching as she read over the menu, I felt nothing. I was fond of her, from the little I'd gotten to know of her during our brief engagement, but I no longer wanted her.

Not since Eden.

The mere thought of her invoked thunderstorms in my chest. A tightness that lingered. A feeling that stole my breath.

I was happy too.

"So," I began once our server left us to finalize our meal selections.

Kennedy looked over at me, a smile tugging on her lips. "Nineteen is a little young, don't you think?"

Closing my eyes, I found myself chuckling. *Of course.*

"You didn't really think I'd come have brunch with you without running it by Keith, did you?" Kennedy challenged. "Especially with the way he was so riled up when he saw you with Eden."

"Nice to know he keeps you on a short leash," I quipped.

Kennedy shot me a pointed look.

"I try not to get too caught up on her age. If I were a better man, I'd let her go."

Kennedy settled back in her chair, pursing her lips, appearing thoughtful. "I have to know, is it the same like us?" Worry stretched across her delicate features. I couldn't be mad she and

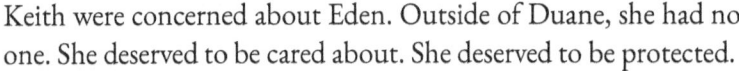

Keith were concerned about Eden. Outside of Duane, she had no one. She deserved to be cared about. She deserved to be protected.

Another squeeze to my chest.

I cared about Eden.

I wanted to be her protector—I *was*.

Clearing my throat, I got back to Kennedy. I wasn't a fan of lying, but my situation with Eden didn't exactly start out so sweet. "We met at the casino night event. She stole my heart."

It wasn't a lie, I realized as soon as I spoke up. The thought was sobering.

Our server came for our order, and I wanted a spinach and mushroom omelet while Kennedy chose waffles and a bowl of berries on the side.

Once we were alone again, Kennedy studied me. Her gaze searching mine it seemed. "I like her for you."

I wasn't expecting that. I could see her joking about being glad she was off my mind, but she actually looked sincere.

"For as long as I've seen you around town, or even known you, I've never seen you as happy as you are now. I love the way you look at her," Kennedy confessed. "The way she looks at you, too. It's just nice seeing this side of you. I'm happy you found love."

There it was again. *Love.*

Kennedy was quick to hold up her hand as if to stop me from speaking. "Do yourself a favor and don't deny it. You may have a questionable past, but that doesn't mean you deserve a horrible future."

I let her words soak in. For once allowing them to resonate.

Eden wanted to save the next group of castaways, and beyond. She'd climbed out of the gutter and wasn't above turning back and holding out her hand for the next person to make it out too. This was just who she was. Shit, she even saw the good in *me*. What wasn't to love?

"Between you and Beans, I'm starting to believe it," I said, cracking a smile.

"Good," Kennedy said as she raised her glass and eyed me over the rim. With one fierce look she was telling me not to fuck this up.

And just then it was settled: I wouldn't.

"Maybe sometime you could get together with her and show her around," I suggested. While Eden insisted she was fine being at the penthouse cooking or reading, I still wanted to present her with an option to get out more on her own. "She could use a friend in the city. Maybe you guys could do a video on cooking or books."

Kennedy sat back and considered this, soon appearing thoughtful. "And what if I tell her to run?"

I could barely suppress my smirk. "I'd be offended if you didn't."

Kennedy let out a laugh that I soon joined in on. This actually felt nice. To be here with no bad blood between us.

"She also mentioned that I should invest in building shelters or communities for foster kids who age out of the system. Runaways with nowhere to go too," I said, unable to hide how proud I was when it came to Eden's heart.

Kennedy blinked, taken by surprise. "You two talk."

Talking to Kennedy had never been hard, but talking with Eden came with a different level of understanding. "We talk."

The smile that arrested Kennedy's face at my admission filled my chest with pride. "That's an amazing idea. I'm sure whenever you're ready Keith would love to help out as well."

He was already well invested in the community center in Bedford Heights, I didn't doubt for a second he wouldn't be down to help out at a Home if I reached out.

"He treating you good?" I knew I didn't have to ask, but I did anyway just to check in.

All at once Kennedy was glowing and soft as she fixated on her ring, smiling to herself. "And then some."

I nodded. "Good."

"The only thing is he hates going to events and schmoozing."

Kennedy frowned and gave a what-can-you-do shrug. "But you know how that goes."

Networking came with this life we lived, whether we liked it or not.

"Speaking of which, will you be attending the Dymond Dinner this weekend?" Kennedy asked.

The Dymond Dinner was a coveted Black event. Host by the legendary hip-hop star Willie Dymond and his famous sons who were in the music industry as well. All the who's who of Black Hollywood wanted an invite to their annual summer cook-out. *That* wasn't as tedious as other events. Good food, good music, and good people. Not much I could complain about.

I'd gone a total of three times. Each with a different date. Last year, Remy Dymond had pulled me aside and joked I was making him look bad with all the models I pulled and kept in rotation.

It would've been humorous to show up *this* year with Eden on my arm, but I had other plans.

"Can't," I told Kennedy. "I'm headed to Vegas in the morning."

Kennedy pretended to roll her eyes. "Oh joy, another Jaguar Jones fight. How barbaric."

Of course white-clothing-loving Kennedy wouldn't want to sit ringside at a boxing match.

Something told me Eden would probably deem it "barbaric" as well, but I'd cross that bridge when I got to it.

For the time being, I sat and enjoyed brunch with Kennedy, reveling in the fact that we could do this. Be friends and get along after everything.

It was nice to have a friend.

Instead of going back to the office after brunch, I cut my day short and headed on home. Eden was at the island when I came in. Bare faced with a bonnet on, I caught her eating a cup of Kraft mac and cheese and looking at something on her phone. Joe was at her feet, eager to eat anything she dropped.

"Oh! You're home." Eden sat up on her stool. Her eyes doubled in size at the sight of the large vase of red roses I'd purchased from Petal. "For me?"

I set the vase down on the island, trying to make it a centerpiece. "I haven't gotten you flowers in a while," I offered simply.

Eden grinned as she examined the vase and the three dozen roses jutting out of it. Soon, she looked around, almost appearing guilty. "I haven't started on dinner yet."

I waved her off, going and helping myself to a fork full of her macaroni before sitting beside her.

"I'm feeding my inner kid," she said by way of explanation.

Nothing beat homemade mac and cheese, but Kraft wasn't bad either.

I took in the scene, Eden at ease as she ate and watched some video on her phone. The curtains were drawn, letting sunlight seep into the living room. The skyline was a sight to see, eliciting peace. A feeling I often took for granted. These days, with Eden, all I felt was at peace. Happy. Content. It was never this way with any of the others.

No matter what, I wouldn't fuck this up. I *couldn't* fuck this up, because I didn't want to lose her. Not many could handle the ugly, the bad maybe, but never the ugly. She accepted me, and deep down, I knew that was where the peace came from.

"Do you have a passport?" I wondered, thinking of Keith's words from earlier. I wanted to fuck her on five different continents if time would let me.

Eden paused her video, giving me a small smile. "I've never even been on a plane before."

"We'll have to fix that."

She looked at me quizzically, arching a fine shaped brow. "Why?"

I leaned into her face, suppressing my smile. "Because we're going to Vegas."

31

Eden

I HAD NEVER BEEN ON A PLANE BEFORE, AND NOW HERE I was, sitting on a private jet.

I ran my fingers through Joe's fur as he sat in his carrier bag in the chair beside me while I stole glances out the window, peering at the clouds.

On the table before me housed a variety of options: a glass of champagne poured as a welcome on-board gift from the flight attendant, a bottle of water covered in condensation to show just how chilled it was, as well as a tray of sliced sandwiches and another filled with fruit. I nibbled on green grapes and an Italian wrap during my sightseeing.

"Look at us, Joe. Who would've thought?" I said. We'd come a long way from Bedford Heights.

Vino was in the chair across from me, shaking his head and holding back a smile behind his fist. He thought I was adorable.

"Don't judge," I said.

Vino sat up and grinned, helping himself to a cucumber sandwich before looking from me to Cain where he sat three rows up going through paperwork at his table. "I don't know why you let him convince you to come. You not leavin' Vegas unmarried, girl."

He was only teasing, but I still chanced a glance in Cain's direction, our gazes instantly colliding. His dark eyes perused me, taking their time to reach back up to mine. His face was expressionless, giving no tell on what he thought of Vino's joke.

Malcolm was lost in something on the TV as he sat on the sofa paying us all no mind.

I sank into the buttery soft leather chair I was in as I went back to looking out the window. The world was truly magnificent from way up here. The clear blue sky above all the fluff of the white clouds was breathtaking. I had never seen the sky so blue. A part of me wanted to take my phone out and record, but I knew better.

Vino would never let me live it down.

Our flight was only an hour. We touched down in Las Vegas in no time. There were two large black Range Rovers waiting for us as we climbed off the jet. Both drivers were out of the vehicles and heading our way to grab our luggage before we left the steps.

"Ever been on a yacht before?" Cain was in my ear. I could hear the smile in his voice before I turned to see it.

I shook my head.

The grin increased and I knew I had it *real* bad the way my stomach jumped and my heart beat wildly. Everything was visceral with him. I didn't just feel things for Cain, I felt them completely with every part of my body and soul. My heart had been all-in since he took up for me against David and Bobby, and it was only my mind that was just now catching up.

Over an hour later I was in an orange bikini looking out at Lake Las Vegas. Beyond the beautiful water, the scenery was to die for. Lavish lakefront resorts, large water sport attractions, and the skyline was the cherry on top.

Who knew life could be like this?

Nestled on top of my head was a white sailor's hat with the words *First Mate* embroidered on it. Cain refused to wear the one that said *Captain*, but I'd taken it for him just in case. I wanted a selfie of the two of us wearing our hats. Cheesy or not.

I adjusted my cap and raised my phone out before me, blowing a kiss as I snapped a photo to send to Duane.

ME

I'm on a boat!

DUANE

I know that's right. Happiness looks STUNNING on you, Doll 😘

It was only Cain and me on the boat. Vino and Malcolm were back in Vegas at the suite Cain had booked.

We were in the middle of the reservoir when Cain dropped anchor. He came and joined me where I lay out on the daybed on the deck. While he hadn't yet adorned his captain's hat, he was rightfully dressed down in trunks and a black T-shirt.

He lay back beside me and I wasted no time going and crawling on his lap. Grabbing my phone, I held it out above us and turned the camera to face us for a selfie. Cain was all things private and discreet; I wasn't sure if he'd even be up for a photo. But he surprised me, going and lifting his black shades and tossing the camera a devilish smile. No teeth, but the sight of his dimples made me melt. He was so classically handsome it hurt. *Nineties fine*, as some of the girls from back at the club would say.

I smiled and snapped our photo.

Cain pulled me close, pressing a kiss to my bare shoulder. I nuzzled back against him.

"You smell good," I reflected on his scent. A heavy potion of masculinity, spice, and something that was just *him*.

Cain squeezed me gently. "You *feel* good."

We lay like that, taking in the day and looking out at the water and the sights beyond us.

This was what safe felt like. What home felt like. What content meant. And dare I say it, *love* too.

The violent sound of his phone ringing cut through our moment of peace.

I groaned as I sat up so he could see who was calling.

He eased back and lifted the device from his pocket. His husky chuckle erased my scowl as he reached out to run his fingers up and down my arm while he checked the screen on his phone with his free hand.

"My plug must've come through," he commented as he read the name of the caller.

Drugs. We weren't just here to check in on Cartier and attend a boxing match. He had underworld dealings too.

I frowned, watching as he answered his call. "Couldn't you just give it up?"

Cain regarded me thoughtfully as he listened to whatever the person on the line was saying. He cupped my jaw, smiling as he did so. Holding the phone away, he said, "And do what with all my free time?"

He stared at me as I stared at him, the exchange burning over to something hazy. I could feel it in the air as a throbbing set in between my thighs.

I couldn't explain it. Couldn't put into words how much I felt for him. He had saved me from a life of dancing. Gave me access to an endless stream of money. Made sure I wanted for nothing, and he didn't ask for anything in return outside of loyalty.

I wanted to save him too. From being lonely. From a life of all work and no personal happiness. From feeling like a burden. Unwanted. And unloved.

I slid down until I was beside him. With my eyes on his, I reached out and pulled down his trunks, freeing him.

Cain took in a sharp breath through his nose, anticipating my next move as I looked up at him beneath my lashes. "And you're sure about this guy? A lot of people talk a big game about flipping houses, until you give 'em a few bricks and they can't even build a shed... This is on you if I don't like him."

I stroked him in my hand, his smooth skin silky and hot under my touch. I watched as Cain's face started to twist in pleasure at the contact.

Leaning down, I slowly licked him from base to tip, laving him up.

And then I went in for the kill, taking him into my mouth until I felt him hit the back of my throat and my eyes watered. In seconds Cain's hand was lodged in my hair, guiding me as he sank back in his seat.

He didn't let the phone go or end his call, but his eyes were screwed shut and his teeth were bared as he gnawed on his bottom lip. He was in heaven.

As horny as I was, as wet as I felt, I let this be about him. Because I loved pleasing him. Just like I loved cooking for him. Loved when he pulled me to the shower to clean me up and then dried me off and rubbed lotion on me. Loved going to bed and being in his arms. Loved being with *him*.

I didn't just have it bad, I realized. I was in love.

32

Eden

Sports weren't really my thing. Especially boxing. It was too brutal and violent, well, not as bad as MMA, but enough to make me squeamish at the thought of watching heavy-handed men pounding into each other's faces.

As I lay across the bed in the master bedroom, dressed in a white mini Celine dress, I wished Duane had come on our trip. This was more his speed than mine.

"Duane would love this," I said.

Cain was finishing getting dressed as he came out of the bathroom. Cartier had a luxurious four-bedroom presidential suite, complete with a grand living room space with cozy couches and a well-stocked bar. There was definitely room to accommodate Duane.

"Maybe next time," Cain said. "We've got a business meeting set up after the fight. The less people around to ask questions, the better."

I frowned. I hated he was insistent on dealing. There was too much at risk.

Peeking at him, I measured the way he carried himself with the confidence of knowing he held a gun, that he had men guarding his steps. "Can you fight?"

Cain fastened his cuff links, quirking a brow. "Hand-to-hand combat?"

"Yeah," I said. "Or you know, just a regular fist-fight."

He shrugged. "I can do all right, but I'm better with the trigger."

Cain didn't give off "tough guy," but at the same time he definitely read of someone you didn't fuck with either. Perhaps with the combined duo of Vino and Malcolm things would work out.

Cain came and tugged on the bow to my high-heeled ballet shoe, before running his soft hand up my leg. When he got to my thigh, he squeezed it. "You ready, Tink?"

I wasn't sure what I expected, but the boxing match was no different than any other high-end event I'd gone to with Cain. Only here was a much bigger spectacle filled with many legendary faces. A-list actors, major football and basketball stars, as well as people from the music industry from rapping to singing. Camera crews were all about, filming the crowd and stage setup.

As I clung close to Cain in our front-row seats, I tried not to fangirl.

The match hadn't started yet, and I was already anxious about being so close to the stage.

Maybe white was a bad idea.

I imagined a fresh splatter of blood spraying onto my dress and frowned. *Definitely a bad idea.*

Someone was using a microphone in the middle of the empty ring. People started murmuring and rushing to their seats around the arena. It was time for the introductions.

People were standing up and camera flashes ensued as they began taking pictures and filming. This was a headlining event. Jaguar Jones versus Ángel Noriega, with Jones being highly favored to come out as victor.

Noriega came out first and his fans screamed in the hopes he would win.

I didn't know a thing about either man, but listening in on Cain's chatter with Vino and Malcolm, it wasn't looking good for Noriega when it came to Jaguar's 28 and 0 record.

I was reaching up to cover my ears when a flash of red appeared beside me as someone claimed the empty seat next to mine. Covering my ears, I looked over and up. At once taking a step back against Cain.

Standing there in a tailored red suit, sporting a dimpled smile that only promised sin, was Sinclair.

He leaned close, stopping by my ear. "Pleasure seeing you again, *Eden*."

The emphasis on my name and not "Red" felt dirty for some reason. Intimate even.

Sinclair's decadent cologne rushed over me with its warm, spicy, cedar scent.

It was easy to discern how any woman could get caught up in Sinclair. His handsome looks and hypnotizing dark eyes were a devilish pair.

He regarded me once more before going and tapping Cain's arm.

Cain turned and eyed me and then his cousin, narrowing his eyes.

Sinclair merely grinned, as if he enjoyed getting under Cain's skin. "Couldn't miss the big fight."

Cain nodded, looking down at me. "Let's hope it's a good one."

Sinclair settled back to await Jaguar's arrival.

A familiar hip-hop beat came on through the arena and soon at the south entrance Jaguar Jones was emerging with his team in tow. He also was being accompanied by West Coast rapper Furious Stylez who was on a mic boasting about Jaguar's title and achievements.

The arena went wild at the sight of Jaguar. And who wouldn't with his record and status?

It *really* wasn't looking good for Noriega.

Still, as Jaguar approached and stepped into the ring, Noriega stood tall, head up, unafraid as if his mind were clear and he was focused.

Soon the two men were standing toe to toe and facing off and I already couldn't take it. Neither man was Herculean, but broad and muscular enough to know that every punch that landed would surely leave behind some extensive damage. And the crowd was anticipating it, hungrily peering on at the battle about to take place.

"Oh God," I let out as I looked on.

Cain chuckled, coming close to be heard. "Relax, it shouldn't get messy or gory."

I reeled back to gape at him. "You like this stuff?"

Cain shrugged, going and eyeing the stage. "I like Justice—*Jaguar*. He's not a flashy, cocky guy. He started fighting to feed his family and take care of himself, and that's all he fights for now. He comes from the bottom and I relate to that. I want to see him win because he's humble, real, and deserves it."

Those words resonated with me as I found them to be true for Cain as well. He may not have known it, but he deserved to win too.

The first two rounds of the match were unbearable, but by round three when neither man was backing down or pulling punches, I was wincing.

Noriega threw what looked like a vicious punch, only for Jaguar to gracefully pivot back and dodge it.

When it looked like Jaguar was going to retaliate, my vision was suddenly obscured by a hand coming from my right.

Sinclair.

He blocked my view with a teasing grin. Really, I was grateful. *My* jaw was beginning to ache as if *I* was the one in the ring getting pounded on.

Sinclair came behind me to get to Cain and tap his arm for his attention. "Hey, how about I step out with her? Get some air? She's getting woozy over here."

Cain appraised his cousin, studying him to see if he was up to something.

Sinclair didn't back down. "*You* can't leave the fight. You're too important to be seen leaving. Let me do something."

Given the last time we were alone together, I didn't blame Cain for being apprehensive. I would've suggested stepping out with Malcolm, but one glance over and I found him enjoying the fight as he gestured to the ring while talking to Vino.

In the end, Cain relented, allowing Sinclair to guide me away from our seats, up the aisle, and out of the arena. One step out into the lobby amid the cool refreshing air and near quiet was a reprieve. Finally, we were away from the violence.

"Thank you," I said as I stood back against the wall by the doors leading into the arena and just breathed.

Sinclair gave an indifferent shrug, going as far as to dig into his jacket and gather a cigar. Security was around, guarding the front doors and the entrances to the arena, as well as building staff, but no one bothered to approach Sinclair as he lit up. He did it so effortlessly, no hesitating like he owned the universe and dared anyone to disturb him. Sinclair was exactly who he thought he was.

"Don't mention it," he said.

He was just trying to get in Cain's good graces, but it meant a lot he offered to get me out of there, especially since he still seemed eager to watch.

"Fundraisers and dinners I can handle and don't mind attending with Cain, but this..." I gestured toward the screen that hung up on the wall opposite us. The screen illustrating the match still going. Noriega appeared to be breathing hard, his only tell of becoming tired, and Jaguar was relaxed and seemed like he could go all night if needed. "...isn't my thing."

"It's all a part of the dance," Sinclair said before taking a pull from his cigar.

"*Dance*?" I repeated.

"It's good for business," he offered. "Too many men in a room?" He shook his head at the thought. "It's bound to get testy. Having a feminine presence softens 'em up a bit, takes the edge off, and lessens the tension."

I could see that, especially considering Cain brought me along when he had dinner with Sinclair.

"Sorta like that time he grabbed drinks with your father." There'd been no buffer and that hadn't ended too well.

Sinclair faced me, giving a small smile. "Sorta like that time we all grabbed dinner together."

Yeah.

Sinclair was back into the match as he went on. "I'm more than aware C only tolerates me at best. Luckily for me he hates my dad more than me so..."

The lesser of two evils.

"Your family doesn't like him," I said more as a statement than a general question.

"In their defense, it's a faux pas to embrace the bastard born of a love affair. Thirty-something years of marriage just to knock-up some showgirl?" Sinclair frowned, clicking his tongue at the picture. "That, and my dad will always have a grudge because Uncle Jimmy signed Cartier over to Cain. He wants it in the family."

"And Cain's not family?"

Sinclair shook his head. "He's not from around here. Didn't grow up in this world. He doesn't belong. He may bear the last name, but he'll never have a seat at the table." He was lost in the fight, speaking absentmindedly almost. "And he doesn't give a single fuck about it. I envy that. I *respect* that a lot about C."

It was clear that unlike the rest of the Carters, Sinclair was the only one trying to meet Cain halfway, that he wasn't blaming Cain for the actions of his parents, who perhaps saw Cain for the innocent party in it that he was. Hopefully in time Cain could see that Sinclair wasn't his enemy.

Because I was curious, I found myself asking, "Where's your mom?"

Sinclair shrugged. "Somewhere wanting grandchildren."

"Oh?"

A frown marred his face as he came back to me. "I enjoy fucking too much to settle down and deal with one woman and screaming rugrats."

The perpetual bachelor. I couldn't picture him dealing with a crying baby either. He was too put together, polished, curated—neat. There was no room for imperfection in his life.

"What about you?" Sinclair suddenly asked me.

In the background a bell rang and soon they were announcing another round.

I shook my head. "Cain doesn't want children."

Sinclair took a pull from his cigar, confusion masking his face as he let smoke stream out of his nose. He looked my way, arching a brow. "You just do what he wants?"

Even before Cain I'd never imagined myself as a mother. With everything I wanted the Cinderella story, but I wasn't fixated on babies. "I mean, I was never in a position to take care of someone else. I took care of Joe because he was a stray cat, and he's more independent than a child would be. Plus, I don't think every couple needs a baby to complete them. Sometimes you just have a love built for two."

Sinclair paused, narrowing his eyes, studying me. "You *love* him?"

I hadn't said it out loud and I wondered how it would sound to confess the truth. "I do."

Sinclair angled his head, blinking. As if love was a concept he hadn't ever pondered. "I believe you."

"You do?"

He nodded. "It's the way you look at him. Like there's

nobody that comes close. Like he could lose it all and you'd still be there. It's real."

Real. That's how everything felt with Cain. Real close. Real intense. Real emotions. Real love.

He wasn't a knight in shining armor. Some perfect prince you grew up dreaming about, but a man with scars and a heart that matched the beat of my own.

I loved him. I really did.

"Shit!" Sinclair gritted his teeth and visibly shuddered. "That'll do it."

I didn't have time to ask what was going on. The crowd was screaming in praise with small echoes of a few boos. The bell was ringing and chants of *Jaguar* could be heard next.

"Ladies and gentleman, the winner by technical knockout, the reigning champ, Justice 'Jaguar' Jones!" the announcer was shouting through his microphone.

The crowd's cheers and hollering sounded out into the lobby. On screen the referee was in the middle of the ring lifting Jaguar's arm to declare him the rightful winner. Every one of Cain's words resonated as I watched Jaguar take his win with humility. What more, he left the referee's side to seek out Noriega to pound his glove against his. Both men were smiling, and it was too loud to make out what Jaguar was saying as he pulled Noriega close for a brief hug before letting him go.

It was an amazing display of showmanship and I couldn't help but clap along as I watched.

Sinclair placed his cigar into his mouth, baring a grin. "You ready, Eden?"

The worst was over so I didn't mind going back into the arena and finding Cain and the others.

"Hey." Sinclair was looking back at me as he led the way inside the arena. "Don't let him lose you. I like you for him. The guy actually smiles now that you're around. Don't let it go."

Inside, people were celebrating. Some bragging about the money they'd won on bets, while others were gloomy in Noriega's defeat. I held on to Sinclair's arm as he led the way down the steps to our seats. Everyone was in a frenzy as the lights came on, but one look over and I saw Cain. Butterflies erupted in my belly the closer we got to him. They all but took over once I was standing in front of him.

"You see that we won," he said as he wrapped an arm around me and held me close.

Everyone was ecstatic and talking about the match, and all I could do was grin as I nuzzled closer to Cain, loving the sound of that word. *We.*

33

Eden

Tension filled the car ride back to Cartier. The first few minutes in the ride had been playful, filled with banter as Malcolm and Vino went back and forth over the match.

Now, something else took over as a grim mood sank in.

The drug deal, or at least, a drug-related meeting, was about to take place.

Cain had been doing this for years, but still I felt uneasy about it. Like he was making a mistake.

I wanted to believe I was different, that I meant more to him than the others before me, that I could convince him to give it all up. It was just about figuring out *how*.

The car came to a stop. We were back. Only, neither Vino nor Malcolm budged to move. When the valet came to take the truck, Malcolm shook his head, making things clear.

They were dropping me off.

I looked to Cain, warring with myself to find the words to say.

He looked at me as if he knew me. As though he could read my mind.

Cain sat up. "I'll walk her up."

Malcolm was behind the wheel. He eyed us through the rearview mirror. "Don't be long."

The bellhop came and opened the door for Cain. He climbed out first and held his hand out for me to join him. My feet were beginning to ache and I relished the fact that we were back so I could take my heels off.

Using Cain for stability, I leaned down and untied one heel before doing the same to the other. Heaving a sigh of relief, I came down to my five-three height and relaxed as I wiggled my toes.

We were still in the lobby, something that caused Cain to chuckle as he collected my heels.

"I cannot believe you just did that," he said on the way toward the elevators.

It was late into the evening and yet the lobby, front desk, waiting area, and bar were still bustling with people.

"What?" I asked innocently. "My feet hurt."

"Well, we can't have that."

Very quickly Cain came and swept me off of my feet, deciding to carry me the rest of the way. Leaving me caught up in a fit of giggles. I was appropriately dressed in white and Cain wore a fine bespoke black suit. We fit the image of a groom carrying his bride over the threshold effortlessly.

When we got to the room, I waved the card over the censor and pushed the door open to let us in.

"Home sweet home, huh?" Cain teased as he looked down at me. There was a twinkle in his eye and it was all mine.

"Don't go." I cupped his cheek, admiring the feel of his smooth skin. "Stay with me." Peering into his dark eyes, I pleaded with him.

Everything stopped and it was only us. Cain stared at me as I stared at him. My chest grew heavy and a lump lodged in my throat.

Never in my life had I imagined feeling so much for a person.

I opened my mouth to say something. To utter those three words that had been sitting in my belly for too long.

But Cain set me down and everything came back into place. He was leaving.

"It's not like that, I promise. It's just another business meeting. I'll be back before you know it." He came close and stole a kiss that left me breathless. Soon, like it wasn't enough, he was picking me up again and carrying me down the hall to the living room. He set me on the couch, and more, he sank to his knees before me.

All I could feel was this moment as I waited on bated breath for his next move.

Keeping his eyes on me, Cain's hands slid up my thighs, warming my skin until they disappeared beneath my dress where he found purchase. Timing was terrible. His men were waiting on him. He knew it, and so did I.

A gasp escaped my lips at the feel of him ripping my panties and tearing them down my legs.

I watched as he stuffed the remains into his pocket. An act that turned me on until I could only see through a lust-colored haze.

I *needed* him.

"Something to remember me by?" I teased.

Cain's grip on my thighs tightened as he yanked me to the edge of the couch. "As if I could forget."

"Please," I begged, already desperate for what was coming.

His hand came up and he caressed my cheek gently before guiding me to lay back.

"I have to go, but I need you to know you're *always* on my mind," Cain said before placing a tortuous kiss on my inner thigh. He looked at me, as if to sear the message into me. "I'd give you the world if you asked. Burn it down too."

My breathing became laborious the higher his kisses got. "Why?"

"Because *my* world ends and begins with you."

The declaration washed over me as his lips brushed against me. The feel of his tongue sweeping over me drove my eyes to slide shut. My fingers clawed at the sofa cushions. My lips parted, but I couldn't make a sound as he devoured me so sweetly I couldn't think or move.

Two fingers entered me and I let out a strangled groan at the intrusion.

Oh God.

The curve of his fingers. The pressure of his tongue. The perfect coordination. It was too heavenly for words. And I hoped he never stopped.

It was building. With every slow and deliberate stroke of Cain's tongue I felt myself drift closer to the edge.

And then it hit me. Taking me by storm as I rocked my hips into Cain's face, riding out the orgasm I could feel all the way in my toes.

By the time he pulled back, going and standing to his full height, I was a puddle of mush that could only look at him through half-lidded eyes.

Cain gazed down at me, a hint of vulnerability across his face. Like he felt what I felt for him but hadn't yet said.

He opened his mouth, but nothing came out.

Yeah.

Smoothing a hand down his jacket, making sure nothing was out of place, he looked at me one final time before turning and heading for the front door.

I was too high to recognize the pain of him going. Instead, I rolled over and drifted off to sleep.

34

Eden

I WASN'T SUPPOSED TO, BUT I LEFT THE HOTEL WHEN I woke up alone an hour or so after my encounter with Cain.

The suite provided a lovely kitchenette, and being that I had nothing better to do, I got myself together and Ubered to the closest supermarket. I couldn't tell Duane. He'd ask too many questions, and I wasn't in a position to break the one thing Cain asked of me.

Instead, I collected all that I needed to try an attempt at homemade honeybuns. I needed the distraction as I played music from my phone and rolled the dough for my second batch.

American Joe was asleep in the living room. Passed out after feasting on the shredded salmon I'd picked up for him.

I eyed my first batch of honeybuns where they were cooling off on the rack farther down the counter. I was hoping they were ready to be iced. I wanted to make sure they were good before the men came back.

A glimpse at the clock on the wall in the next room said they'd been gone for almost three hours. I wasn't sure how long these things lasted, but the longer it took, the more—

Murmuring sounded out above my music causing me to reach over and pause it with my knuckle. I stood still, listening for another sign of life. There was loud wrestling with a doorknob out in the hall.

Pivoting, I wondered if—

"Fuck!" someone yelped.

Other voices came into focus now. I could just make out Cain's.

It didn't matter that I couldn't understand what was being said. One step out into the hall and horror washed over me at the scene I was stepping into.

Cain was ushering Vino down the hall as Vino slouched into him for strength. Their jackets were open and their white dress shirts were no longer clean and white, but red. *Red*. Red meant trouble.

Vino had his arm slung over Cain's shoulders as he moaned in apparent pain. "Fuck, this shit burns."

My hand flew to my mouth as they passed by me and headed for the living room. Frightened, Joe scurried out of the room, taking off down the hall past Malcolm who was coming into the room with a phone pressed to his ear. Despite the situation, he was calm and collected as he joined Vino and Cain in the next room.

"He'll be here in ten minutes," Malcolm said as he stood over where Cain was attending to Vino.

Cain was calm as well, going and removing his jacket and tugging on his tie. "You with me, V?"

I should've stayed away, but I stupidly crept closer. And that's when I saw it. Vino's shirt was open and there was no missing the hole in his body that was seeping blood. There, on his bottom right side, he'd been shot.

"Oh God!" I thought I was going to be sick as bile rushed to my throat and my vision blurred.

At once all three men faced me, as if remembering my existence.

Even with being wounded, Vino managed to toss me a

crooked smile. "Hey!" He soon coughed, blood lining his otherwise perfect white teeth. "This is nothing. Just a scratch."

Cain grimaced, going and shooting Vino a pointed look. "Shut it." He came back to me and frowned some more. "Go to the room. You don't need to see this."

My feet were rooted in place. I choked as I shook my head. "He...he's been shot!"

Cain blew out a breath through his nose. "You're awfully observant, Tink."

I struggled to swallow the mass that had appeared in my throat. It was too much. Vino was probably dying and yet this was their normal. They weren't even fazed.

"Eden." Cain's tone and features said he was practicing patience he didn't have. His tired eyes raked over me, letting me know he wasn't asking me to leave the room, but rather, he was *telling* me to.

Vino was bleeding as his face twisted in more pain. Malcolm and Cain were in one piece, but it could've been them. It could've easily been much worse with Vino shot and one or both of them *dead*.

I hadn't always made the best decisions being on my own, but I'd always drawn a line in the sand. I never got mixed in with any of the dealers who would come through Crazy Legs hitting on me. I never wanted any trouble.

And that was exactly what this was. Trouble. Cain *was* trouble.

Deep in my chest I felt a fierce pain as my heart tore in two.

One minute I was looking at Vino as he laid back on the sofa, and the next two soft hands, hands I'd grown to love, were taking my face and turning my vision toward where Cain was now in front of me.

He stared at me intently, searching my eyes thoroughly as he leaned down to my level.

"Go to the room. I'll be up there in a minute, I promise," he swore.

It would've been the easy thing to do. To just go up to the bedroom and wait for the worst of it to be over. But I couldn't do that. I couldn't go with this.

So I stepped back, out of Cain's grasp and shook my head. "I...I can't."

Cain pinched the bridge of his nose, like he was dealing with a defiant child. "You don't want to see him like this."

My eyes drifted back over to Vino. I didn't want to see him like this. On any other day he was a tall, strong, intimidating man, and now he lay there suffering.

Catching my attention, Vino held up a blood-soaked hand, offering a thumbs-up. "It's just a flesh wound."

This time, I thought bitterly. Even if a doctor cleared him and patched him up, there was no telling how he'd fare the next time they went out to do a "business" deal.

I couldn't do this. I *wouldn't* do this. It wasn't right. Lives were at risk.

I got back to Cain, feeling myself begin to shake. "I can't."

He squinted, confused. "You can't what?"

I didn't want to say it. Didn't want to let the words spill from my lips. But I had to set them free. "Be with you."

Those three words lingered in the air between us, silencing the entire room.

Cain looked at me and it was only us then. Vino wasn't hurt on the sofa and Malcolm wasn't awkwardly standing by with his phone clutched in his hand. There was only Cain and me taking in the aftermath of the words I'd spoken.

"What are you saying?" he asked, his voice clipped of emotion.

I squeezed my eyes shut, forcing myself to be brave and strong. When I opened them, Cain remained standing there, waiting for me to go on. Neither anger nor hurt overtook his face as a blank mask stared back at me.

There was still time to take it back. To change my mind. But I couldn't. "I can't do this. I can't be with a man who could be here today, and gone tomorrow. You're a very successful business owner and yet you still choose to gamble with your life dealing drugs. Out of habit, greed, or selfishness. I don't want any part of it. People in that world, they hurt the ones attached to you. And I don't want to be a casualty."

Cain snorted, thumbing at his bottom lip. "You've seen far too many movies."

It was like he called me silly for what I'd said.

I didn't have much of a life before him, but it was mine, and I had every right to live it safely and sound.

"I may be the one who's nineteen, but you're the one who needs to grow up," I said as I stood tall and squared my shoulders, refusing to back down or feel small in this moment that was tearing me apart internally.

"This is my world. I've been doing this for—"

I held my hand up, not wanting to hear any more. "I'm not asking you to choose me because nobody ever does." Looking up at the ceiling, I refused to cry. To break down and reveal how much this was hurting me. "I'd just like to go now and be done with this...and you."

My words were final and they cut like a knife to say.

I felt him take a step back. His energy suddenly cold and distant. "If that's what you want."

Don't cry. Don't cry. Don't cry.

I lowered my attention to Cain one final time, seeing a hardened man in front of me. There was no light in his eyes. Only darkness.

"Are you going to kill me if I walk away?" I asked.

His gazed went to the ground, until he turned his back on me and examined Vino. My question going unanswered.

Swallowing what was left of my pride, I turned and went in search for Joe.

The suite was quiet as I collected my purse from the bedroom and found Joe under a chair curled into a loaf. My luggage was unpacked and neatly put away in the dresser the master bedroom provided, but I made no effort to grab anything. I didn't want it.

I picked Joe up and placed him into the green, black, and mesh cat carrier bag I'd brought him in. With the bag on my shoulder, and my purse strap on the other, I made my way from the room and went back down to the main floor. Malcolm and Cain were by the front door. Malcolm looked on at me, while Cain's focus was on the floor. His sleeves were rolled up, his shirt splattered with blood, and his shoulders were low.

Tipping my chin up, I went over to the door, prepared to leave.

But my wretched heart couldn't let me go in peace.

Whirling around, with tears in my eyes, and anger festering in my veins, I glared at Cain, unable to believe he really didn't answer me. "Why was it so hard to say no!" I hated myself for the crack that broke through. For the pain laced in every word. For showing weakness in this moment.

"Why was it so easy to even ask!" Cain snapped back, glaring at me just as hard, like the betrayal went both ways.

Sniffling, I shook my head.

Without another word, I turned and opened the door, stepping out into the hall, feeling cold and lonely, as I shut the door behind me.

Each step toward the elevator felt heavier than the last. I was fighting with all that I had to keep it together and not turn back. My hand shook in front of me as I reached over and pressed the call button for the elevator to come up to the penthouse.

A soft *click* alerted me to the door opening and shutting behind me once more in the distance.

Quietly, Malcolm came and stood with me as I waited for the elevator to arrive. Of course he would.

The elevator reached us in a *ding* and soon the doors were opening to take me away.

This was it. I was leaving.

The empty lift sat there waiting for me to board and I couldn't move.

Suddenly my body was being steered in another direction and I had just enough time to process what was happening as Malcolm brought me in for a hug.

I lost it.

And what really hurt the most? I still loved him. With everything I had. And for that I cried and screamed into Malcolm's chest, hoping he wouldn't let go.

35

Cain

His blood-caked hand clutched mine as he writhed in pain. Six stitches was all it'd taken to patch him up. He'd gotten lucky. One shot had hit him and that was it.

The rattling of a transparent orange pill bottle caught our attention as the good doctor dug them from his medical bag and held them out before Vino.

"Oxy for the pain." He soon grabbed two more bottles. "Anti-inflammatories. Don't mix them with alcohol." With a steely look he stood from his crouching position and tipped his head at Vino.

He pushed his glasses higher up his septum as he faced me next. I stood as well and handed him the stack of money promised for his immediate services.

It paid to have people in high places when shit hit the fan. And shit had truly hit.

I *hated* Las Vegas.

Too much of this city reeked of James Carter. From Cartier to the streets, the touch of my father was stained everywhere. It was the very reason I didn't reside in the presidential suite reserved for me at the Cartier full time. James had lived in an immaculate mansion on the outskirts of the city, but when he was in town, this suite was something like a bachelor pad for him. Even with my hiring a team to remodel and redecorate, there was no escaping what was. I didn't stay here for that exact reason. Shit, I was probably *conceived* here. Everything about Vegas felt tainted with the reminder of the past.

It was why I made my trips short and was in and out as fast I could be. I'd never had a true home in California, but any place was better than this.

Dr. Bryant Miller accepted the money without any questions. His aged and weathered tan face was impassive as he stuffed the stack into his plaid pajama bottoms. Even with a late-night call he'd arrived promptly and taken care of Vino with precision.

He looked at me with eyes that were immune to trauma and grief. "Pleasure doing business with you, Mr. Carter. Let's hope there isn't a next time?"

His words weren't lost on me. Talk about a fucking wake-up call.

"Let's hope," I agreed before quietly seeing him out of the suite.

When the door closed, I pressed my back to it, lolling my head back and taking a moment to not fold. It had been a long night, with the promise of so much more when it had started. How quickly had it gone up in flames.

I really fucking hated Vegas.

I closed my eyes and heard *her* humming and I was transported to a better moment in time. It was some innocent tune she'd made up as she was in my office one day. Laying on her stomach, feet up in the air, flipping through a cooking magazine. She was wearing one of my dress shirts and a pair of socks. As if she could feel my stare, she'd peeked my way, a soft smile on her face. Just for me.

When I opened my eyes, I didn't see her. The entryway to my suite stretched before me empty and quiet.

My eyes drifted toward the ceiling, a frown soon covering my face as I knew she wasn't up there on the second floor in the master bedroom.

She was gone.

My shoulders sagged with the reality and heaviness of what was lost. She'd *begged* me to stay and stupidly I'd gone. Walked into a mess that ended in gunfire with one of my men wounded and a body that needed to be disposed of from the other side. Frank's connect had wanted to be partners in a heroin operation they were starting. I wasn't interested. It had never been my thing.

Ego or pride took over Frank's guy and he opened fire. Vino did what I'd paid him to do: step in and take a bullet for me. Once he'd been hit, I acted on instinct and taken care of the problem. Now here we were.

Vino would live, but the consequences of this night lingered.

Eden was gone.

Running my hand down my face, I did my best to remain calm, despite the dullness in my chest.

Heavy footsteps could be heard coming down the hall on the other side of the door. I moved away just in time as the *click* sounded and the knob turned. Beans was coming back. He was alone.

He closed the door behind him and I hung my head, trying and failing to accept she'd really left.

It was for the better, I tried to convince myself, but that didn't mean it didn't hurt any less.

One look up and Beans was glaring at me. His nostrils flared and I'd never seen him so worked up. So pissed off.

"You're a fucking idiot," he let out, low and accusatory.

With anyone else there'd be a bullet lodged in their skull for uttering such an offense to me, but with Beans, I respected him too much. I expected him to give it to me straight every time. Even when I didn't want to hear it.

"I was never going to be the doting type," I tried to say, as if this were inevitable and I was meant to be alone.

"No." Beans shook his head, narrowing his eyes at me. "You just refused to allow yourself to be seen as more. To *be* more."

There was truth in his words and I wasn't ready to face it. "Between the two of us—"

"I've buried your bodies the same way you've buried mine. Don't make me a saint when my hands are as red as yours," Beans said. "You're all I've got. If you weren't here tomorrow, I don't know what I'd do. Tonight could've tested that. And now what? You just lost the best thing that ever happened to you."

Beans didn't wait for me to respond before taking off for the living room to check on Vino.

I hung back in the foyer, soaking in his words, trying to collect myself.

There'd once been a time where this life was all I knew. I'd been younger, ruthless, colder, and satiated by it. Why aim for Forbes when I was already in the cocaine hall of fame? I was who drug dealers aspired to be. I *owned* the West.

At twenty-eight, it didn't hit the same anymore. Especially not after her.

With Eden I'd truly known and felt peace. Before and after her was only chaos.

It was easy with her, more than it had ever been with anyone else outside of Beans and Vino. My guard was lowered—there wasn't one. I could be my truest self and she accepted me wholly, still looked at me fondly, still wanted me despite my flaws and scars.

Of all the women I'd been with, Eden was the first to simply want *me*.

I wiped my hand down my face, feeling sick at the thought of her leaving.

"Nobody ever does." My heart shattered and fell out of my chest hearing that.

Fuck.

Dried blood covered my hands and I quickly headed down the hall over to the kitchen to wash them in the sink. Beans and Vino were speaking in the next room and I paid them no mind as I lathered my hands and scrubbed the rust-colored blood from them. When I didn't see a roll of paper towels or a towel, I turned and searched the island, and that's when I saw it. The sweet smell of cinnamon hit me hard in the chest as my eyes focused on what was before me.

She'd been baking while we were out. She'd been in the middle of it when we returned. There, on a cooling rack, was a tray of something that would've been miniscule to someone else, but meant a lot to *me*.

Eden had gone out of her way to make homemade honeybuns, not just because she loved cooking and baking, because I'd told her they were my *favorite* dessert.

One minute the tray and mixing bowls were on the countertop, and the next they were crashing down to the ground with one clean sweep of my arms.

Neither of the men in the next room were fazed by the banging and commotion. Beans in fact sank back in his seat with a smirk on his face.

All of me felt like a livewire. I was practically bouncing on my feet as my heart raced. I had duties and obligations—but all of me wanted to be out on the street, looking for her.

"You got that out of your system?" Vino raised a finger in the air as he questioned me.

There still was too much energy in me to stand still. I crossed over to him, taking him in as he reclined across the sofa. The pain meds must've kicked in as he was forming sentences that weren't the one-word utterance of "fuck."

His all-knowing dark eyes looked up at me, a smug smile on his face. "Beanie Baby isn't wrong."

Keeping my cool, I humored him. "No?"

Vino gestured to himself and where he lay coolly on the sofa. "I do this because it's a rush. I enjoy the hustle, the money, taking care of anyone who steps in my way." He soon shook his head, eyeing me with what could be described as *pity*. "But sometimes you get too old for the game. *You're* too old for the game. You've aged out."

Lifting a brow, I asked, "Have I now?"

Vino nodded. "You're still trying to survive, but you're not that skinny little kid anymore. You made it, D. You don't *have* to do this. You got in through the back door and now you own the fucking building."

In this life of ours, there were rarely any happy endings. Hardly anyone crossed over and excelled in a different avenue. "Not many make it out unscathed."

"Exactly. If the shit ever hits the fan you still know how to cook, how to get to it," Vino reasoned. "For now, all you gotta worry about is stocks and mergers and how that casino in LA is going."

It could all be so simple. Why make it hard?

This life didn't make me happy. Instead, it was nothing but stress and bullshit.

"So, this is it? Sure you can handle life on the other side?" I challenged, looking on at Vino.

He eased back against the throw pillow behind him and closed his eyes, giving a shrug. "I'll manage. Maybe I'll give golf a try."

For the first time in hours, I cracked a smile.

Years after building my empire, brick by brick, contact by contact, and deal by deal, I was done.

A weight lifted from my shoulders. An unnecessary door was now closed.

Still, darkness hung over me and I didn't feel any better.

We were going to pack up and go home. Vino would take it easy and heal. And business would resume as usual come Monday morning. Back to the status quo. *That* I could handle.

Going back to my penthouse to emptiness I couldn't.

It had never been a *home* before, but rather a place to stay. After she'd come along, brightening up every room, adding her touches here and there, it had become a dwelling, a sanctuary—a place I looked forward to returning to after a long day at the office. The smells of her cooking, the sounds of her up and around living in my space, and the sight of her precious smiles provided a sense of comfort and normal I'd never had before.

My life before Eden had been mechanical and I forced myself to get used to it. I'd written myself off of relationships after things fell through with Kennedy last year. I was the black sheep of a family that didn't want me. And outside of Beans and Vino, I didn't see myself drawing close to anyone, much less letting them *in*.

And then Eden stole from me.

I snorted, shaking my head, and thumbing at my bottom lip. She'd truly stolen my heart.

I didn't just *like* her, it was too small a word to ever begin to describe the depth of my feelings and appreciation for her.

There was only one word to paint the picture. And I couldn't run from it any longer.

I looked at her and finally understood what the movies were going on about. That feeling everyone chased and some never acquired. *Love.*

I loved her. I was *in* love with Eden.

Feeling the burn of Beans's stare on me, I ignored it and focused on Vino. "You going to be okay?"

A crooked smile crossed his face. "Whatcha need, D?"

It was back to business. "Rest up, but when you're good to go, call up Frank and Curtis and let them know we're out. And then I want you to call up Daytona and have him clean up any loose ends should he find any."

That smile broadened lazily. "I've been wondering if Day still has it."

The hit squad. They were as anonymous in identity as they were in the presence of their kills. They went by code names, specifically after random cities. Daytona, Houston, Harlem, and Canton. They were all skilled in various fields, but Daytona was often our go-to when things went off the rails.

If tonight didn't end with Frank's connect being put down,

Daytona would find out and take care of it for us. It was always good to have him and his crew in my back pocket.

With that squared away I was faced with one last task. Reluctantly.

I released a sigh from deep within the depths of my soul as I faced Beans finally, finding him already watching me. Shaking my head at what I was about to do, I couldn't help but smirk as I looked on at my oldest friend. "Do me a favor and call Sinclair."

36

Eden

FLASHING LIGHTS, A STEADY BUZZ OF TRAFFIC, THE constant steps echoing in the air as people roved up and down the street, and bold solicitation on every corner. All of it was hollow. Bleak. Emotionless. Sin City was unforgiving. It didn't sleep. It didn't love. It didn't give a single fuck.

No one paid me any attention where I sat alone on the bench with only American Joe beside me to keep me company. I stuck my hand inside the top flap of the carrier and ran my fingers through his thick fur absentmindedly.

The Eiffel Tower stood across the street, stretching high up into the sky majestically. It was nowhere near as grand and large as the real one in Paris, but something told me this was as close as I'd ever get so I stopped my Uber when we were passing by and found myself seated across the street getting lost in the view. The Paris Hotel & Casino was such a dazzling attraction and distraction from the nightmare I had fallen into.

I was in no rush to get back. Not that there was much to get back to.

Truth be told, I still had a large sum of money in my bank account. I could go anywhere I wanted. Just not home—to him.

I tried and failed miserably to get over the prickle of loneliness and rejection at the thought of our last encounter being *final*. I'd managed for nineteen years just fine, and now I wasn't sure how I'd ever go on without him. It would've been better if he had ended my life instead of sequestering my heart so selfishly.

Peering down at Joe through the mesh siding of the bag, I sighed and soldiered on. I wasn't the first woman to get her heart broken, and I wouldn't be the last. I would be okay.

Perhaps I'd go to the beach. I'd never seen the ocean. Maybe I'd take Duane and we could—

"Of all the tourist traps in all the cities in all the world you walked over to this one?"

Casablanca.

A shiver of awareness coasted over me at the sound of his rich voice and I struggled for warmth just then.

When I walked away, I was prepared to never see him again. Turning and seeing him now in the middle of the night disarmed me. He was undone in just his slacks and a clean dress shirt. His tie was gone and the first few buttons were open with the sleeves rolled up. One look up into his dark eyes and he appeared tired and grim. Like there was no more fight left in him.

Cars honked in the street. People cursed as they walked by. The warm night wind blew bringing the smells of alcohol from the local bar and fried food from a vendor parked down the sidewalk. Life went on and I was stuck on standby at the sight of Cain.

"You found me," I let out, at a loss for words.

A muscle in Cain's jaw ticked as he stared down at me. "They got a word for people like you: *mine.*"

My treacherous heart throbbed at the idea.

I knew everything about him. I knew the good, the bad, and the ugly. I had no trouble at all accepting him wholly if only his underworld dealings were in the past.

When I didn't respond, Cain took the liberty to sit down with Joe's carrier between us. He sat back, nodding off toward the glowing Eiffel Tower before us. "If it were anyone else, I would've considered rushing to the airport or the bus station." He turned, regarding me, a soft and shy smile crossing his lips. "When Sabrina got her heart broken, she went to Paris and found herself. You don't have a passport, so why not stop and admire the next best thing?"

Tears lined my vision. No way was he referencing my favorite movie.

He knew me so well.

I looked away and wiped my eyes, shaking my head. "Cain."

"You deserve Paris, love, light—all the happiness you can stand," Cain said. "And I want to give it to you."

It could all be so simple, but he had to make it hard with his reckless choices and association.

I stood up and walked off, hugging myself tightly. "I can't be a part of your lifestyle. I told you when we met that my life may not have been much, but it's mine, and I deserve to live it how I please. *Not* in fear."

"I hear you." He was up off the bench. Behind me. His proximity burning my back and warring with the wall I had up. "I wanna be whoever and whatever you need me to be."

I turned around, finding him standing there like his cards were all out on the table.

"I give up. I'm done with it, I promise," he pleaded.

After all the years and all the effort he would just walk away so easily?

"Just like that?" I asked.

"Nobody ever chooses me either." Cain shook his head, his nostrils flaring, as if he were pissed at himself as he released a breath. He looked up and stared right at me, vulnerable and helpless it seemed. "Except you. I was so used to being left and used, I wasn't aware of what I had until you walked away.

"There isn't a woman more right for me than you. You're my soul mate, Tink. My one true equal. You've seen the darkness that life has to offer the same as me, but more, you strive to see the light as well. You *are* the light. You're everything I never thought to ask for, and everything I could ever want. You're the light I've been searching for my whole life. The thought of you ruins me, and I wouldn't have it any other way."

Speechless, I could only look at him with blurred vision as my lips trembled. My heart swelled and had never felt so full.

Was this really happening?

"Cain..." I didn't know what to say. Had never been told in so many words how much I meant to someone. "I was so scared."

"I know, and I'm sorry for putting you through that." He came close, going and taking me into his arms and wiping at my tears. His soft hand cradled my face as he leaned down to see me at eye level, a crooked smile arresting his handsome features. "Please, give me one last chance to make this right. To rewrite the ending."

He was speaking my language. Soothing me right where it ached the most. And even after everything, I couldn't close the book on us.

I let out a sob, unable to hold it together. "Yes."

Satisfied, Cain focused on cleaning up my face some more. "I was thinking we'd fly back to Hampton Hills and apply for a passport for you. And in the interim, I'd train Sinclair to step up and prepare to be my partner."

I blinked. Had he just said...? "*Sinclair?*"

Cain smirked, dabbing at my eyes some more. "I killed my father and took over his kingdom and it didn't bring me joy. Didn't fulfill me or make up for the past." Cain ducked his head, trying and failing to hide a smile. "Giving half the company to Sinclair would not only piss off Sandford, it would free up my time so I can spend it with you. We've got some Homes to build. But first, I think it's time I took a vacation. How's Paris sound?"

"Paris?" The name left my lips breathlessly.

He was no longer hiding his handsome grin now as he nodded along. "Someone told me it's the city of love. Figured I'd try my luck in taking the woman I love there to see it."

I couldn't breathe. Had he just said...?

Stone-cold serious, Cain bobbed his head, peering down into

my eyes. "I love you, Eden. For loving me as I am, even when I don't deserve it."

Sniffling, I shook my head. "I love you because you *do* deserve it. Because—"

The words never made it out as he came forward and pressed his lips to mine, tilting my head back and giving me all that he had. Closing my eyes, I wrapped my arms around him and got lost in the truest bliss I'd ever known.

All too soon he pulled back, leaving me looking up at him with half-lidded eyes. "So how about Paris first? And maybe Italy next?"

Exploring the world hand in hand with him sounded too good to be true. I couldn't wait.

"And then after that?" I asked.

Cain gave a small shrug. "Maybe forever if you've got the time."

Forever. I loved the sound of that.

Standing on my toes I met him halfway in a kiss that promised forever.

He swore he wasn't the hero of my story, but really, he was so much more.

Cinderella got her prince by leaving a shoe at the ball. And I got my dark knight by stealing his heart.

We weren't exactly a storybook or a whimsical fairy tale. We were flawed. Raw. Real. And I wouldn't have it any other way. Our story was ours and I could already picture the ending before the credits rolled.

And they loved, and loved.

the end

ACKNOWLEDGMENTS

To all my readers who read book one and rooted for Cain (you weren't alone) and wanted this redemption arc. I so hope it was worth it!

Cass, thank you so much for following up with another stellar cover!

Yenthe, for the GORGEOUS character art. You nailed Cain and Eden perfectly.

Erica, for once again being incredibly kind, patient, and helpful with my prose. For being there when I added that extended scene last minute. For loving these two characters as much as I do. P.S., it's so time to watch *Breakfast at Tiffany's*!

To everyone who's enjoyed these this duet.

Until my next release,

Britney July

ABOUT THE AUTHOR

Britney July is a dreamer from the Midwest who grew up camped out in her local library gorging on books. Now as an author, she endeavors to write fun and steamy edge-of-your-seat romances that leave you devouring page after page and emotionally undone.

When she's not writing, Britney can be found watching films, as her second love is cinema.

.